Pietro slammed open the door and yelled, *"Andi-amo!"* He left the door open behind him.

"Um, that means—" Bianca started to say.

"I know what it means," Katharina interrupted. She blinked up at Pietro. "I'll come out when I'm good and ready, Fonzi. And as you can see, Fonzi, I am not good and ready, so you will just have to wait."

Pietro waited, his arms crossed, cold air filling the room.

Katharina stayed in her chair, her arms crossed, feeling the cold air flowing into the room and sneaking up her leggings. "You mind shutting the door, Fonzi?" she asked.

"Is Alessandro."

Katharina smiled. "Whatever, Fonzi."

They locked eyes.

I am more warmly dressed, Pietro thought. *She will crack first.*

I am closer to the fire, Katharina thought. *He will crack first. I will not back down.*

Pietro returned Katharina's stare. *She has . . . beautiful eyes. I like how oval, how sexy—But she is evil! I will not back down.*

"Miss Minola," Bianca pleaded, "the draft is making the fire burn faster, and we're almost out of dry wood, so maybe we should, um, go."

Katharina stood slowly. "I am now ready."

Books by J. J. Murray

RENEE AND JAY

SOMETHING REAL

ORIGINAL LOVE

I'M YOUR GIRL

CAN'T GET ENOUGH OF YOUR LOVE

TOO MUCH OF A GOOD THING

THE REAL THING

SHE'S THE ONE

I'LL BE YOUR EVERYTHING

A GOOD MAN

YOU GIVE GOOD LOVE

Published by Kensington Publishing Corporation

she's the one

J. J. Murray

KENSINGTON PUBLISHING CORP.
http://www.kensingtonbooks.com

KENSINGTON BOOKS are published by

Kensington Publishing Corp.
119 West 40th Street
New York, NY 10018

All Kensington Titles, Imprints, and Distributed Lines are
available at special quantity discounts for bulk purchases for
sales promotion, premiums, fund-raising, and educational or
institutional use. Special book excerpts or customized print-
ings can also be created to fit specific needs. For details, write
or phone the office of the Kensington special sales manager:
Kensington Publishing Corp., 119 West 40th Street, New York,
NY 10018, attn: Special Sales Department. Phone: 1-800-221-
2647.

Kensington and the K logo Reg. U.S. Pat. & TM Off.

ISBN-13: 978-0-7582-5896-0
ISBN-10: 0-7582-5896-8
First Kensington Trade Edition: March 2011
First Kensington Mass Market Edition: February 2013

eISBN-13: 978-0-7582-8899-8
eISBN-10: 0-7582-8899-9
First Kensington Electronic Edition: March 2011

10 9 8 7 6 5 4 3 2 1

Printed in the United States of America

A woman moved is like a fountain troubled.
—William Shakespeare, *The Taming of the Shrew*

Shrews are sharp-snouted mice covered with short, dark hair. Ferocious tiny warriors, whose hearts can beat as fast as fifteen hundred times a minute, shrews must feast constantly to stay alive, their bite sometimes lethal to their prey. Shrews' rank, garlicky scent shields them against rivals, and some shrews have large brains, immense eyes, and claws on their fingers and toes.

A shrew is not dangerous to humanity—

Unless the shrew is human and an out-of-work actress who has not made a hit movie in fifteen years . . .

Chapter 1

Vincenzo Lucentio, the CEO of Lucentio Pictures, stared in awe at the thick file his staff had compiled on actress Katharina Minola.

Geez, he thought. *And I think this woman will be a match for my younger brother, Pietro? I must be crazy. This might never work.*

Unless we have some nasty weather, the muddier and snowier the better, and just a little bit of luck.

He weighed the file in his hand, a good pound of newspaper and magazine clippings, glossy and grainy photographs. He even had a list of links to Web sites that still carried some of Katharina's infamous interviews and stories of her notorious exploits.

He sighed often as he read the cover sheet written by Penelope Bishop, his senior production assistant and executive secretary, the real power behind Lucentio Pictures since his grandfather's time. Vincenzo frowned here and there, but mainly he cringed at Penelope's acidic and far-too-accurate prose.

"A scold," "a fury," "a spitfire"—the press has had a field day with Katharina "Kate the Cursed" Minola (born Dena Hinson in Roanoke, Virginia), 36, a DIVA (Dismissive, Insensitive, Villainous, Audacious) fully immersed in her "divatude" since winning an Academy Award for best actress (*My Honey Love*, Lucentio Pictures) in her first major role when she was only 21.

Katharina has yet to repeat what *TIME* called "a breakthrough performance for women of color," cranking out eighteen consecutive mediocre movies (three for Lucentio Pictures) and one so infamously bad (*Miss Thang*) that she won a Golden Raspberry Award (the dreaded "Razzie") for *worst* actress. *Miss Thang* currently ranks sixth on the ten worst movies ever made, behind *Plan 9 From Outer Space, Glen or Glenda, Santa Claus Conquers the Martians, Gigli,* and *Catwoman.*

Katharina did not show up to claim her Razzie.

(Note: Oscar-winner Halle Berry *did* show up to claim her Razzie for *Catwoman*, saying, "I never in my life thought that I would be here, winning a Razzie. It's not like I ever aspired to be here, but thank you. . . . When I was a kid, my mother told me that if you could not be a good loser, then there's no way you could be a good winner." Berry also said, "First of all, I want to thank Warner Brothers. Thank you for putting me in a piece of shit, God-awful movie. . . . It was just what my career needed.")

At least Halle Berry had the class to show up and make it work for her, Vincenzo thought. *Berry did* Their Eyes Were Watching God *right after* Catwoman *to considerable acclaim, has never been out of work since then, as far as I know, and now she's doing some producing and enjoying her greatest role as a mother. If we can't laugh at ourselves and our mistakes, especially in this business, what good are we?*

What followed was a list of Katharina's rumored, alleged, and factual divalike behavior since her success with *My Honey Love*:

- During the only Macy's Thanksgiving Day Parade she was asked to cohost, Katharina yelled at a musician for "playing *way* too close to my face" (*New York Post*).

- Only days after getting engaged to Ward Booker, an up-and-coming black actor, Katharina ran off to Paris with Booker's best friend, David Stanley, a bodybuilder, for "a restful holiday and shopping trip away from the stress of daily life" (*People*).

- Upon her return from Paris, Katharina watched "in utter horror" (*Los Angeles Times*) as Booker and Stanley had a fistfight at Spago, both men arrested for "fighting over little ol' me" (*Us*).

- Katharina has consistently made "worst dressed lists" for ten of the past fourteen years but says the compilers of those lists are "all incredibly, horribly wrong, beyond stupid, and very, very blind" (*Vogue*). Her favorite "worst" outfit is tiger-striped from head to toe including headband, sunglasses, blouse, pants, handbag, and stiletto-heeled shoes.

- During the filming of *Miss Thang*, Katharina refused to leave her deluxe motor home and trailer (complete with hot tub) until the script improved. "I spent a *lot* of time in my trailer with that awful picture"

(*Premiere*). Three directors quit the production, two citing mental breakdowns. The director listed in the credits is "Alan Smithee"—that notorious and obvious nom de plume used by dissatisfied directors since 1969's *Death of a Gunfighter* starring Lena Horne and Richard Widmark. One of the directors retired from filmmaking entirely, now sells shoes at a local mall, and at last report, seems quite happy.

Katharina never should have left her trailer, Vincenzo thought. *No one should have ever made that ghastly farce of a picture, which earned her that "Kate the Cursed" nickname, a nickname she just can't seem to shake.*

- Until four years ago, her entourage (which the media still calls her "porta-posse") included:

  o a makeup artist
  o a personal hairstylist
  o a wardrobe designer
  o a "dresser" ("I wouldn't dream of getting dressed and leaving without her"—*Woman's Day*)
  o an official photographer and videographer (recently fired)
  o her yoga instructor, Rajiv (recently deceased)
  o a masseur named Mikhail (recently deported)
  o a dog walker (hit by a car, still in rehab) for her Scottish terrier, Scottie

- o a director of photography for interviews (see below)
- o one or more gophers / assistants (see below)

- Katharina has fired numerous assistants for the following "infractions":

  - o not bringing her daily *Los Angeles Times*, *Variety*, and *New York Times* to her before 8 AM
  - o not putting a straw in her drink, "and it must be one of the crinkly kind" (*Elle*)
  - o not cutting the crusts off her sandwiches (she prefers chunky chicken salad on plain white bread)
  - o not bringing enough shoes or bringing the wrong shoes to a shoot
  - o She fired her last assistant for baking a birthday cake for her thirty-sixth birthday. Her most recent assistant, Bianca Baptista, has been on the job for six weeks, four days longer than the average employment of Katharina's other assistants.

- Blessed with a peculiar sense of smell, Katharina claims to sense odors that seemingly do not exist. She wears only her own perfume (¡Katharina!, sold only at Kmart now).

- All but a handful of airlines have banned Katharina for life for cabin crew abuse. Here is the list of airlines that still tolerate her: Air Vanuatu, Croatia Airlines, Air

Kazakhstan, Phuket Air, and Virgin Atlantic.

- After filming the romantic comedy *Filet of Dish* (a box office flop that earned a special Razzie for worst *title* ever), Katharina disparaged the city of Boston: "It smells like the ocean" (*Boston Herald*). She also took potshots at the people of the State of Massachusetts: "I'll bet ninety percent of these people cannot even spell their state's name" (*New York Times*). After a public outcry in Boston, Katharina issued an apology through her publicist (long since fired and rehired—*twice*), adding, "I hope the Yankees win the pennant." Boston won it all that year.

- At meet and greet sessions to autograph pictures of herself during the height of her fame, Katharina routinely asked that fans not hug, kiss, or look directly at her at *any* time.

- On *The Today Show* five years ago, Katie Couric asked her, "So, do you see yourself as a mother in the future?" Katharina's reply: "Oh, I just *adore* children. I want to have a little girl just like me."

Vincenzo shuddered. *Just like she is now or the nice person she used to be? No matter what, that girl would be a beautiful child. She and Pietro could have a gorgeous daughter, and I would pray every day that she took after her father in the attitude department . . . unless Katharina changes back to the wonderful woman I met fifteen years ago.*

- For extended hotel stays and shoots, Katharina demands all-black furniture, a vase full of long-stemmed red roses, a humidifier, 400-count cotton sheets, and blackout drapes on all windows. She once rented a suite at New York's Plaza Hotel (at $4,500 a night) but walked out on a two-week reservation because the staff forgot to make the bed with the 400-count sheets.

- Addicted to Prozac after the fallout from *Miss Thang*, Katharina has kicked the habit (*without* going into rehab) through regular exercise, meditation on the Bible, and yoga. "I don't know why more people don't use yoga and meditation to cleanse themselves. . . . It works, and I'm the proof" (*Shape*).

"Good for her," Vincenzo said aloud. *That will be one fewer demon for us to deal with.* He shook his head. *We're going to have enough demons to deal with as it is.*

- Katharina permits no one on the set to have her "signature" blue-green eyes. During the filming of *Shoots and Letters,* a child actor and a dog lost their jobs because they had such eyes. A production assistant had to remove a doll with similar eyes from the background of one shot in *When Mama's Mad, Everybody's Mad.* "Call me superstitious" (*HollywoodSleaze.com*). (Note: This isn't superstition. This is the grossest form of vanity—Penelope.)

- Weeping when given her star on the Hollywood Walk of Fame two years ago, Katha-

rina gave her "best acting performance
since *My Honey Love*" (*Hollywood Insider*).
Only two photographers and one network
showed up for the nonevent. The network
promptly posted Katharina's three-minute
sob session online, and it's been a running
joke on YouTube ever since.

- Considering herself a singer after her
  memorable humming scene in *My Honey
  Love,* Katharina cut *Lovin' My Honey,* a CD
  that contained ten instantly forgettable
  love songs. Sony pressed 50,000 CDs; 813
  sold. The remainder has been "selling" for
  $0.01 on eBay at two per year.

And I'm one of the idiots who bought it, Vincenzo
thought. *My cat liked it. Katharina's a good hummer. Lyrics,
however, gave her (and anyone listening) the blues.*

- Her self-styled director of photography
  (Sven, since fired) had so angered the
  technical staffs on *Oprah, Ellen,* and *The
  Tyra Banks Show* that producers for those
  shows no longer considered Katharina for
  guest spots. Since then, she manages the
  lighting herself on whatever talk show will
  have her, reportedly asking that there be
  no "shine" on her face and that the cameras capture her only from the waist up.

Why is she hiding her lower body? Vincenzo thought. *She
is in outstanding shape and has the nicest legs!*

- For her pre-Oscar party fifteen years ago,
  Katharina tried to get *Vogue* to foot the bill,
  but *Vogue* wouldn't ante up for her dress,
  makeup, fifty dozen roses, and, reportedly,
  $100,000 for champagne. A caterer from
  Glendale did the event at last notice. Several
  stars showed up for a few minutes and left
  soon after. She hasn't thrown a party since.

The wings were good, Vincenzo thought. *Even the pigs in
a blanket weren't half bad.*

- At the height of her "powers," Katharina
  could phone Il Pastaio in Beverly Hills and
  close it down just for herself and (at that
  time) a number of men reputed to be her
  bodyguards. According to an unidentified
  Il Pastaio worker, even though no other
  diners were in the restaurant, her
  bodyguards still surrounded her so the
  wait staff couldn't see her eat. "She said we
  couldn't speak to her or even look her in
  the eye," the worker posted on Hollywood-
  Gossip.com. "And then she had the nerve
  to order wonton soup! The bitch ordered
  Chinese food in an Italian restaurant! On
  top of that, she didn't even leave a tip! I'll
  bet she even expected her meal to be
  comped! It's the same with all these divas!
  They expect the world to lick their shit and
  ask for seconds!"

- In one of her most infamous acts five years
  ago, Katharina refused to walk the red car-

pet at the Kodak Theatre for the Academy
Awards ceremony (on *live* television) until
the carpet was *completely* empty. Though
not nominated since *My Honey Love,* she
stayed in her purple limousine for a half
hour, delaying the arrivals of many other
stars, several of whom were actually up for
awards. Reed Richards, the eventual best
director winner, had to go through a side
entrance. She then ordered her limousine
driver to "stay put until I finish this phone
call and I'm inside the theater." (Note: Although I have not confirmed this, *E! Online*
claims her "thirty-nine-minute sashay up
the red carpet" is by far the all-time record.
The delay allowed photographers to get
cigarette breaks and pushed the entire ceremony back thirty minutes—Penelope.)

- The O'Gara Coach Company of Beverly
  Hills has taken Katharina to court over
  nonpayment of a gray-violet Bentley Azure
  convertible. According to court
  documents, Katharina placed her order,
  signed all the necessary papers at noon,
  and demanded that the Bentley appear in
  her driveway no later than 8 PM. O'Gara
  told her that one was available in San Francisco and would have to be shipped south
  to her. "She wanted no mileage at all on
  the odometer," O'Gara Coach Company
  owner Wilson O'Gara said. "She wanted
  zeroes all the way across." O'Gara was able
  to deliver the Bentley on time, but O'Gara
  says that Katharina balked when she saw a

"1" on the odometer. O'Gara refused to take the car back, and the Bentley still sits in her driveway. The court case is ongoing, and "birds have reduced the convertible top to a chunky, ashen blob of goo" (*Los Angeles Times*).

- Katharina allegedly calls ahead to department stores and boutiques so that they can clear their stores before her arrival. (Note: She obviously prefers to shop alone and unmolested, another gross form of vanity—Penelope.)

- In her most recent interview, a quarter-page blurb (no picture) *four* years ago, Katharina said, "I guess I am allergic to marriage. I do *not* want *any* man to see how I really look in the morning" (*Jet*).

Vincenzo looked glumly at Katharina's financial information. After *My Honey Love*, she commanded five million for each of her next three Lucentio pictures, none of which rated more than three stars but did well at the box office. After that, she consistently demanded to be paid as much as "the white heifers in Hollywood" (*Variety*). She left Lucentio Pictures entirely after that when she was offered fifteen million for *Miss Thang*.

She made a *total* of ten million for her next *thirteen* pictures, hadn't worked in over four years, had fired, re-hired, and fired her agent, and had to reduce her porta-posse from twelve to four. She retained her makeup artist, dresser, hairstylist, and one assistant, Bianca, who presumably took care of Scottie.

Why am I about to do this? Vincenzo thought. *Oh yeah.*

I fell in love with Katharina in My Honey Love. *We all did. The entire world did. It was Lucentio Pictures' first hit movie and opened the doors for many more. I was there when they filmed it, I've seen it a hundred times, and I still tear up at the end.*

Vincenzo had served as an assistant to the director, and Pietro had had a bit part as a taxi driver in the unforgettable humming scene with Katharina. She handed him a card with an address, she got in the backseat, he drove, she hummed her guts out with tears streaming down her face, and she threw her fare money at him.

All in only fifteen *takes. Pietro did nothing wrong, but Katharina blamed him for her miscues. The shots of Pietro eyeing her through the rearview mirror never made the picture, but the look in his eye said: "She's the one for me."*

Either that or his eyes said, "I hope she dies a slow, horrible, painful death."

Vincenzo was never quite sure what his brother's eyes were saying.

But that was fifteen years ago, when Pietro and Vincenzo were just starting out, learning "the business" from the ground up until they could one day take over Lucentio Pictures from their ailing father, Antonio, son of Frankie Lucentio, the legendary and flamboyant founder of the independent film company. Now that their father had passed away and Pietro had taken his part of the inheritance north of the border to Ontario, Canada, Vincenzo was in complete control of a *thriving* independent film company, consistently nominated for (though never winning) awards at Sundance and Cannes, and usually doing well at the AFI Dallas, Palm Springs, and Santa Barbara international film festivals.

Vincenzo buzzed Penelope—ancient but stable, able, and the only person his father and grandfather ever trusted. "I'm ready, Penelope. Send 'em in."

Let's get this charade started.

Chapter 2

"We cannot afford to pay her that much!" Jim Block, the director of accounting, shouted as he paced the room. "We'll be the laughingstock of Hollywood!"

Vincenzo shrugged because Jim was always saying "We can't afford" this and "We'll be the laughingstock" of some place or other. He winked at Penelope, who wore her usual navy blue power suit with a white ruffled blouse. She sat taking notes while seated demurely on his grandfather's old black leather sofa.

Penelope rolled her eyes. "Calm down, Jim."

"It's *only* three," Vincenzo said.

"*Million,*" Jim said, his chubby jowls flaring red and contrasting terribly with his maroon suit, crème shirt, and aquamarine tie. "Katharina Minola is not worth one-*hundredth* of that amount. We'll be throwing away our money!"

Vincenzo leaned back in his grandfather's old chair, swiveling with a squeak to look at the smog perched like an arthritic cat over West Hollywood. "You're right, Jim. We're not going to pay her three million."

"Thank you." Jim sighed. "I thought you'd lost your—"

"We're going to pay her *five* million, the same amount we paid her for *My Honey Love.*" Vincenzo swiveled back to look at Jim's jowls bouncing off the floor. "Let's look at this logically, Jim."

"Five, five . . ." Jim stammered. "Your father and grandfather—"

"I know, I know," Vincenzo interrupted. "They'll be rolling in their graves." *But if I know Grandfather,* he thought, *he's probably lighting another cigar, nodding, and saying, "Is a good risk."* Vincenzo smiled. "Lighten up, Jim. It's only money."

"It's only—" Jim started to say. "That's almost forty percent of the entire budget for this film!"

Vincenzo smiled, amazed that Jim's head had yet to explode after serving three generations of stubborn Lucentio men. "That's why I said we need to look at this logically. *Calma, calma,* Jim."

"I am calm, Vincenzo," Jim whispered. "You pay me to worry about these things, remember?"

"Jim, we have deep pockets now, and our ultimate goal will hopefully pay off tenfold." *I trust and pray.* "The stage is set. The location is a go. We don't need to build anything. There's no need for set designers, painters, carpenters, electricians, or gophers, or the massive amount of food and drink to keep them all happy. We won't even have much of an electric bill. We can do an entire movie without a caterer, or drivers, or stunt performers, or even grips and boom operators. Costuming will also be at a minimum."

"Katharina will probably bring *all* her clothes," Penelope said.

Vincenzo tapped Katharina's file. "If this is correct, she'll also try to bring an army of shoes with her."

"Such a waste," Penelope said, and then she laughed. "But then again, where we're sending her, she won't be able to use most if any of her clothing and shoes."

"And they won't even get there," Vincenzo said. "Her luggage will be traveling to Costa Rica."

Vincenzo turned to John "Fish" Fisher, one of the few black directors of photography on earth, who stood at the window in a Cubs jersey and jeans. Fish, a Chicago native and rabid baseball fan, was also Lucentio Pictures' resident computer authority, who loved making his own gadgets. "Are the cameras and mikes all set, Fish?"

Fish nodded, turning and leaning his shoulders on the window. "I've got thirty full acres of mountains, hills, bogs, streams, and fields covered from just about every conceivable angle. As long as Katharina stays within that grid, anything she does and anything she says will be recorded. She burps, we'll see and hear it."

Jim picked up his jowls. "You haven't put cameras in her bathroom, have you?"

Fish rolled his eyes. "Just one in the mirror to film her from the neck up."

"But if she walks away, um, in the nude . . ." Jim said. "You know Katharina has never done nude scenes, and Lucentio Pictures does not do soft-core porn."

Fish sighed. "Like I told you before, Jim, everything is motion activated. As soon as she's in range, the camera and sound turn on. As soon as she leaves, it turns off and another camera picks her up. It's like a chain of daisies. As she moves, at least one camera picks her up and hands her off to the next, and all the images will transmit via relays back to a bank of monitors and servers at Pietro's house and the monitor Vincenzo will have with him. It's like . . . it's like walking away from an automatic urinal in a men's room, only another camera will pick you up zipping up and washing your hands. Besides, it will be far too cold for her to walk around au naturel."

"Won't she see, um . . . ?" Jim asked.

Fish waved his hands dismissively. "These cameras are tiny, Jim, some no bigger than a pencil point. She won't hear a thing or see a thing. They all blend into the scenery beautifully, and I have Vincenzo's brother to thank for that. Pietro is amazing at hiding and disguising things."

But without a wife to amaze, Vincenzo thought. *Pietro has had six straight broken engagements to the most erotic and exotic women.* Vincenzo looked at the ceiling. *Except for the last one, the Amazon woman. She was scary. Very big teeth. Wide jaw. She made me think "Horse Woman" the first time I saw her.* "How is Pietro?"

Fish shrugged. "Same as always. Quiet. Staring. Brooding. A workaholic. Hairy." He laughed. "He dug a thousand-foot trench to bring electricity and a phone line for the fax from his house to Cabin 3, laid all the conduit and lines, and covered it over. You can't even tell he dug the ditch at all, and the soil up there is practically permafrost."

And he did it completely by hand, Vincenzo thought. *Pietro was always the brawny one in the family.*

Vincenzo looked at Walter Yearling, who sat at the other end of the sofa with a notepad. Walter had made a name for himself as a screenwriter with an Oscar nomination for *My Honey Love* and had gone on to a lucrative career, most of it away from Lucentio Pictures. Vincenzo had asked him back for this project, and Walter had wholeheartedly accepted.

"How's that script coming, Walt?" Vincenzo asked.

Walter smiled. "It isn't."

Vincenzo smiled. "As planned."

"But I do have a title," Walter said, "*A Woman Alone.*"

"Fitting," Vincenzo said. "I like it."

"Look," Jim said, spreading to his full five-foot width in front of a bookcase. "*No* actress worth her salt is going to sign on to a picture without a script. She'd have to be out of her mind."

"That's why we're going to give Katharina full script approval," Vincenzo said lightly. "If she doesn't like it, it won't get filmed." *Not to her knowledge, anyway.* "If the producers of *Miss Thang* had done that, we might not be here today trying to reclaim her natural talent. Katharina Minola is a smart woman. We'll give her full script approval, and I know that she will come through."

"Vincenzo, please, no one gets full—" Jim started to say.

"*Calma, calma,* Jim," Vincenzo interrupted. "She'll have full approval for a script that doesn't exist. Yet. We'll just dangle the money, the entitlement, and the control she craves, and see what happens." He turned to Walter. "Are you sure you can do this, Walt? I'm asking a lot of you."

"No, you aren't," Walter said.

"Well, I'm basically asking you to write a shaky script that Katharina will *want* to change," Vincenzo said.

Walter nodded. "I'll have to be at my, um, *least* creative, but sure. It'll be fun."

Jim sat and shook his head. "I don't like this one bit, not one little bit. Writing a script for a movie *as* it happens and sometimes *after* it happens is absurd."

"It will be real, though," Walter said. "How she reacts to, well, everything that happens to her will determine the direction the script will take. And since she's going to fiddle with it, anyway, we'll practically be giving her ideas for *her* script. It's foolproof. We could even give her a screen credit as cowriter, or as the only writer, when it's over."

"We could," Vincenzo said. "Good idea, Walter. Glad you're back with us."

"It's good to be back," Walter said.

"You and Fish can go," Vincenzo said. "See you up north. Dress warmly."

"But Walter and I will be at Pietro's drinking hot chocolate by the fire," Fish said. "I don't plan to go outside for sixty days."

"Lucky you," Vincenzo said.

Walter stood. "Vincenzo, I just want you to know that this is a revolutionary idea, and I'm glad to be a part of it."

"Even if you don't get a screen credit?" Vincenzo asked.

"It will be worth it to see Katharina acting like the Katharina of old," Walter said. "I have missed her so much. I want to see that old magic."

After Fish and Walter left, Jim whined, " 'This is a revolutionary idea.' " He grimaced and rolled his eyes. "This revolutionary idea of yours could one day put us out of business. They let *her* back into the movies. Just when we thought we were rid of her, here she is again! The shame!"

Vincenzo smiled. "It won't put us out of business, Jim." *I hope.*

"What if Katharina catches on?" Jim asked. "What if someone in her porta-posse catches on?"

"They won't, Jim," Vincenzo said. "Remember: Three of them are going to Costa Rica for the duration of the shoot, and I'm sure they'll be happy to get a paid vacation from Katharina for two months. Even Scottie ought to have a good time on the beach. Only Katharina and her current assistant, Bianca—"

"If she hasn't been fired by then," Penelope interrupted.

"True," Vincenzo said. *We'll just have to cross that bridge if it comes to that.* "We're hoping that those two will make it up there." He shrugged. "And what if Katharina or Bianca catches on? It's not as if they can leave quickly or walk away." *Or even call anyone—except Pietro and me— for help.* "Besides, Katharina's an actress, a real, true artiste. A trooper, as my grandfather used to say."

"So you say," Jim spat.

"She is a trooper," Vincenzo said. "She's just . . . off her game, that's all."

"For the last fifteen years?" Jim asked.

Hmm, Vincenzo thought. *That is a long time to be off your game.* "The three pictures she did for us after *My Honey Love* were good, Jim, don't forget that. It was that . . . that stupid movie."

"Miss Thang forgot to leave the role at the studio," Penelope said.

"She is *still* playing that role!" Jim shouted. "Lucentio Pictures has never had a diva like her."

Penelope raised her eyebrows. "What about me, Jim? Or are you forgetting *my* old acting days."

Jim waved a hand dismissively. "It was a different time, Penelope. You played the femme fatale. You were expected to vamp." Jim took a breath. "I want it on the record that I am scared to death about this. Lucentio Pictures makes family-friendly movies, and Katharina Minola is not nor will ever be family-friendly again." He sat down in a huff on the sofa.

Vincenzo sighed. "Look, fame just went to her head, Jim. You and I have seen it time and time again. One hit, one award, one monster paycheck, and . . . poof, a monster is born, and rehab clinics and *Entertainment Tonight* get calls at three in the morning from police stations. America sees mug shots of their favorite stars on the evening news. Unauthorized videos and photo sessions surface on the Internet. So far, Katharina has stayed relatively clean compared to all of the other fallen stars. She has never been arrested. She has never struck a photographer."

"What about her drug problems?" Jim asked.

"Katharina had her problems with Prozac, but that's all in the past," Vincenzo said. "She hasn't made any sex tapes, hasn't lowered herself to taking parts where she had to take all or part of it all off, and occasionally she's had wonderful scenes in otherwise atrocious movies. She still turns down all stereotypical roles. She has never played a 'mammy,' the 'tragic mulatto,' a criminal, a whore, a drug dealer's or kingpin's girlfriend, a 'kept woman,' a welfare mother, a battered wife, an entertainer, or, since *Miss Thang*, a true, hateful diva. She has played, well, normal, educated, cultured people who find themselves in unusual circumstances. Her characters hardly ever even cuss."

"Because she curses like a sailor off camera," Jim said.

"So do a lot of actors, Jim. So do you." Vincenzo sighed. "Look, Katharina really needs our help, Jim. It's up to us to bring out the real Katharina Minola, the one who blew the world away in *My Honey Love*, the one who has been hiding for fifteen years."

Jim shook his jowls. "Only now *we're* doing the hiding."

"The ends justify the means," Vincenzo said. "We may have to be cruel to be ultimately kind."

"This is too much like *Candid Camera* for my tastes, or—what's that show?" Jim asked, looking at Penelope. "*Punk'd?*"

Chapter 3

Katharina Minola—her skin as brown as hazelnuts, her palate sated by a crustless chunky chicken salad sandwich almost like the kind her grandma Pearl used to make for her—was at a total loss. She could not believe what her signature blue-green eyes were reading as she soaked up the shade in her purple gazebo overlooking her "endless" inground pool and the Pacific Ocean somewhere in the distance beyond the smog.

She even had a little trouble breathing, though her fifteen-room mansion wasn't that high up in the Santa Monica Mountains. She shivered in spite of the dry September heat, pulled her tiger-striped bathrobe closely around her neck, and noticed several more frayed spots on her cuffs and hem. She adjusted her tiger-fur headband tightly around her ears and squirmed her toes more deeply into her tiger-fur slippers to hide the fact that she hadn't had a pedicure in months.

"Bianca!" she yelled. The sound used to echo through the mountains but not anymore. Katharina's roar now was nearly as nonexistent as her fame.

Bianca, barely out of UCLA, and shaking like a wind-blown Bobblehead doll, took a single step forward, her well-worn Chaco sandals barely making a sound, her cutoff jean shorts and plain white T-shirt hanging limply on her waiflike body. "Yes, Miss Minola?" she asked, keeping her gray-blue eyes firmly focused on the ground.

"You said this package came by courier?" Katharina asked.

"Yes, Miss Minola."

"Did you have to sign for it?"

"Yes, Miss Minola."

"What was the name of the courier service?"

"The Entertainment Delivery Group of West Hollywood, Miss Minola."

This could be the real deal, Katharina thought. *Thank God!*

She waved Bianca away, and Bianca dutifully took one small step backward to her "post."

I used to get tons of these every month, Katharina thought with an audible sigh. *But now the phone does not ring, my cell phone does not buzz, and typing my name on Google pulls up files four and five years old. And I'm now the true victim of an anonymous life because David Letterman and Jay Leno no longer include me in their monologues. Such is fame, so fleeting, so fickle, and so . . . painful.*

"Bianca!"

Bianca shuffled forward. "Yes, Miss Minola?"

"Did you have to pay anything for this?"

"No, Miss Minola. I only had to sign for it."

A careless wave later, Bianca vanished farther into the shade, and Katharina read the letter again, slowly this time, trying to wrap her mind around the incredible offer on the page.

September 21

Vincenzo Lucentio
CEO, Lucentio Pictures
Hollywood, CA

Have I ever heard of Vincenzo Lucentio? Katharina thought. *He must be one of Antonio's sons. Lucentio Pictures gave me my first big role and has been dying to have me back ever since. But why is the CEO of a film company and not a producer writing to me? Is Lucentio Pictures footing the bill alone? They must be.*

Re: A WOMAN ALONE—Offer for Ms. Katharina Minola

Dear Ms. Katharina Minola:

I represent Lucentio Pictures concerning the upcoming production of A WOMAN ALONE. Lucentio Pictures would like to employ you for the title role of "Jane Doe," shooting for two months from on or about September 30 to on or about November 30 of this year.

Knowing your desire for privacy, we will shoot this picture in a secret location far from the prying eyes of paparazzi. To keep this project a secret and to protect the integrity of the shoot, we will provide you with a script only when you are on location.

The title suits me. Except for Bianca, it is me. The name of my character, though, is almost as anonymous as I've become. Maybe I'll get to name her. That would be fun. I've always wanted to play someone named Roxanne. Or Z. Hmm. Rox-

anne, Roxie, Rox . . . or Z. Rox-Z? Different. Let's see . . . Two months to shoot? Not terrible. Sixty days, roughly four hours a day, two hundred and forty hours of work. Secret location— ah, yes. These people know all about me. I do not want to be seen anymore. I like that. No script until I get there? Intriguing. Trade secrets must be kept. Maybe Lucentio Pictures is breaking new ground again, and I'm the groundbreaker.

You will receive five million on a pay or play basis.

That's . . . that's . . . She sat up straighter. *That's more money than I've made on my last . . . six movies. But isn't that what I'm worth? Have I ever been worth even a million? I mean, it's nice that somebody finally noticed my talent again, but . . . What's the word? Ambivalent. I am ambivalent about this. There has to be a catch.*

Further, upon condition that you shall appear recognizably in A WOMAN ALONE as released, Lucentio Pictures shall accord you credit in connection with A WOMAN ALONE as follows:

(a) On-Screen—On-screen on a separate card, in the main titles, just after the title of A WOMAN ALONE, in first and sole position in a size of type no smaller than eighty-five percent (85%) of the size of type used to display the title and in a size of type larger than the size of type used to accord an individual "directed by" credit to the director;

Katharina was completely speechless for one of the rare times in her life. *The title and then little ol' me? All by myself? Just my name on the screen? A larger type than the director gets? I wonder who it is. Probably some first-timer. Oh, it doesn't matter. Five . . . million. I might just be able to get out of debt again and pay for that stupid car with cash.*

(b) Paid Advertising—In all paid advertising for A WOMAN ALONE issued by or under the control of Lucentio Pictures (subject to the customary exclusions of each distributor and/or broadcaster of A WOMAN ALONE), above the title of the picture alone, in a size of type no less than seventy-five percent (75%) of the size of type used to display the title and in a size of type larger than the size used to accord an individual "directed by" credit to the director. Notwithstanding the foregoing, you shall receive such credit in all excluded advertising issued by or under the control of Lucentio Pictures in which any other cast member is accorded credit, other than award, nomination, congratulatory, institutional or film market or festival advertising.

I may finally get a poster that actually looks like me. The others? Man, I was airbrushed to death and given much larger breasts than God gave me. I'm concerned how they're downplaying the director, though. What, is this person just out of UCLA film school? Maybe Bianca knows him—or her. Hmm. I hope it's not a female director. But what if there is a female director? I've never had a female director before. "There can be only one diva on the set," I used to say. What are they telling me without telling me? It's simple, really. They expect me to carry this picture. Katharina shuddered. *That's . . . delightful and terrifying at the same time.*

The parties will enter into a more formal agreement, which agreement shall incorporate the foregoing terms as well as other customary terms and conditions contained in comparable agreements, including customary representations and warranties, mutual indemnification, your waiver of injunctive and other equitable relief, full depiction release including merchandising rights, Lucentio Pictures' right to assign rights, extensions for force majeure including any period in which a member of the principal cast and / or a director is unavailable, and application of arbitration in California and international law.

Blah, blah, blah—ooh. International law? I'll be leaving the country? Very nice. I haven't been out of the United States in ages. Wait. I haven't been out of California in ages. Wait. I haven't been out of L.A. in ages. Wait. I haven't been out of this house in ages. Wait. I haven't been out from under this umbrella in ages.

Lucentio Pictures will pay all travel, lodging, and meal expenses for up to four people—and your dog, Scottie—for the duration of the shoot. You will be provided with a dedicated dressing room (a four-room suite with bathroom and cooking facilities) and have full script approval. We would also like to offer you back end point participation of no less than ten percent (10%).

Ten . . . t-t-ten percent. Minimum. They can pay me five million, so they obviously expect to make much more. Dare I say . . . fifty million? That's another five million minimum. For little ol' me.

Katharina rubbed her signature blue-green eyes.

Julia Roberts never makes this kind of dough! But full script approval from the very beginning? I wonder if Julia gets that. This is almost too good to be true! Lucentio Pictures is a wise company. I never should have left them.

If you are willing to accept this offer, please contact me by September 25. If I do not hear from you by that date, this offer will lapse. If you accept this offer, unless and until such more formal agreement is executed, this letter agreement, supplemented by the aforementioned customary terms and conditions, shall constitute the parties' agreement.

Thank you and I look forward to hearing from you.

Sincerely,

Vincenzo Lucentio

Vincenzo Lucentio
Lucentio Pictures

If I'm willing to accept? Are they kidding? I'd have to be a fool not to accept this offer right away! I'd be crazy not to jump at another chance, a chance to redeem myself, a chance to prove to the world that I am not a one-hit wonder.

"Bianca!"

"Yes, Miss Minola?"

Wait a minute. I'm forgetting who I am. Deep breaths.

Katharina waved Bianca away.

Okay, I'm forgetting who I was. I'm no diva. I have never been a diva. Yes, I did some divalike things and didn't mind if the media portrayed me as a diva, but that was just for my image.

Katharina closed her eyes. *What image? I used to be so . . . nice. I was friendly. I was even . . . caring. I was the honey in* My Honey Love, *sweet, golden, and pure. Why did I allow my agent, Cecil, to convince me that being nice, friendly, caring, sweet, golden, and pure was a waste of time if I wanted to succeed in Hollywood? Money. And why did Cecil want me to make more money? So he could make more money. And where is most of my money? In his pocket. And where is Cecil? Gone and hopefully biodegrading somewhere. And why won't I raise a fuss over finding him and my money? Because then I'd have to admit to the world that I was naïve and stupid, that I was just ignorant Dena Hinson from Roanoke, Virginia, the one-hit wonder who got lucky once and let it all slip through her fingers.*

Katharina opened an eye and examined the fingernails of her right hand. *Through my seriously jagged fingers. I'll have to have Bianca work on them later.*

She looked at her house. *Ah, the house of my dreams that I just can't leave for some reason. And why is it the house of my dreams? Oh yeah. It's the only thing that's entirely paid for, unlike that stupid car sitting in the driveway. What was I thinking? No one on earth needs a car like that, especially one that gets only eleven miles to the gallon. I'm not even sure I have a valid driver's license anymore. The media says that I had trouble with the odometer reading because O'Gara said I did. Hearsay becomes truth in Hollywood in a hot minute. It wasn't the stupid odometer reading. One mile on a car? I'm not that petty. It was the freaking seven thousand-a-month payment! And I just . . . I just didn't have the money. I thought I did when I went in there, but thanks to Cecil I didn't, and I was too stubborn to admit it, and there it sits gathering bird shit.*

She opened her other eye. *I should never have become a diva. Cecil said playing the diva role would add to my al-*

Penelope nodded. "There *are* some similarities, Vincenzo."

"Only this is real," Jim continued. "We'll be filming her every little quirk and habit for two months. We're like voyeurs, like permanent paparazzi, like—"

"Permanent paparazzi," Vincenzo interrupted. "I like that."

"What if she cracks up?" Jim asked. "What if she goes completely over the edge? What if while you're breaking her down, she breaks down? What then?"

Vincenzo smiled to himself. *Then Pietro will just have to save her.* "I think she has already cracked up, Jim. She has already fragmented. She has fractured into a person I'm sure even she doesn't recognize or like very much. We're going to break her down, sort out the good pieces, and help her put *herself* back together."

And then, hopefully, we're going to give her the role of a lifetime.

But with no script approval of any kind.

Pietro just wouldn't let that happen in his—dare I think it?—marriage.

lure—and to my bank account—to be such a bitch. "Always keep your name in the press," he told me. "Negative press is just as good as positive press, and in this country, it's sometimes the best kind of press. It's all free advertising, anyway, right?" *It seemed to be working, I mean, I was getting roles, wasn't I? Thirteen pictures in ten years. I was the female Gene Hackman. You couldn't go to the cineplex without seeing me in something or other. And while I was working, Cecil was reworking my contracts in* his *favor using my forged signature. I should have read all that fine print. And I should have included a damn lawyer in my so-called "porta-posse."*

She looked at her slippers. *I look ridiculous. Tiger stripes? I look terrible in stripes of any kind.* "It's your signature look," Cecil said. "It's a look that says, 'Katharina Minola, queen of the jungle.'" *And for a while, I* was *the queen. No one could out-diva me. I was ferocious. And then . . . I became a little cub. And now, I just can't afford the newest, latest clothes anymore. I haven't gone shopping in years, not since that* one *time I had Nina Ricci stay open after-hours so I could try on a few outfits.* One *time, and the media says I did it* all *the time. I haven't made a worst-dressed list in four years, and I don't intend to start. When you stay home all the time and don't get your picture taken, they can't put you on those hateful lists.*

I'm filling with hate right now thinking about it. Deep breath. Exhale. That feels better.

No, it doesn't. I'm too full of hatefulness. Is that a word? Well, it should be, and I'm full of it.

I know I've done and said some foolish things, but the whack media has distorted everything I've done and said all out of whack. Yes, I overdid Prozac and under-did a CD that can't even be given away to cure insomnia. But I kicked Prozac to the curb all by myself, didn't I? I didn't need any clinic or spa or hideaway. I kicked it in plain sight. But where's the story on that? Yes, I skipped out on the Razzies when I could *have and should have gone. Nearly all actors and actresses have appeared or starred in a bomb at least once in their lives. I should have taken my lumps then so I wouldn't have so many lumps now. Yes, I'm picky about wearing my own perfume. Just about every other perfume I try breaks me out, makes me sneeze, or gives me a headache. Yes, I walked out of the Plaza, but it wasn't because of the sheet count. The sheets were filthy dirty, and the blackout drapes had nasty white stains on them. I get the worst migraines sometimes, and any amount of light tears into my eyes like little daggers. No one pays $4,500 a night to sleep on slept-on sheets and stare at drapes covered with dried male bodily fluids. And yes, I spent a lot of time in my trailer during the filming of* Miss Thang, *but that was because I had the worst case of diarrhea. That's not information studios release to the media, which would most likely gleefully announce: "The movie already stinks because the star has the shits!" And yes, I* suggested *that one kid actor and a dog be fired, but not because they had my color eyes! The kid peed himself in nearly every scene, and the dog, who missed seven out of every eight cues, peed* itself *and several costars in nearly every scene. As for the doll, it was a white girl's doll in a black girl's room in the seventies. Duh. I suggested they find an Ideal Tressy doll or a Shindana Tamu doll, and the properties people had all sorts of little cows. "A what?" You know, I told them, Tressy, the doll with the hair that grows 'n' grows. They didn't know. I had to have Grandma overnight ship Tressy and my Tamu doll to the set. Tamu was so cool. She had this nice, soft 'fro and said things like: "Cool it, baby," and "Can you dig it?" and "I'm proud, like you." The director decided Tressy and Tamu were* too *ethnic, and they changed the script to remove* any *doll from my movie-daughter's life. They couldn't possibly let realism ruin a movie based—loosely—on real events.*

That trumpeter I fussed at in New York? I had an ear infection. That shit hurt! I had a right to yell. It was already freaking cold and windy that day, and they wouldn't let me wear earmuffs. They even made me take out the cotton balls in my ears.

The fight between Ward, who I was never engaged to, and David, who I was never romantically entangled with, was never a fight over me. It was a lovers' spat between them. Ward thought David had cheated on him in Paris with me! I should have busted them out, but I promised I wouldn't, and Ward is still making those action-adventure movies, and David is still winning bodybuilding contests. Only now do I realize that no one keeps promises in this town . . . except little ol' me, evidently.

Katharina sighed.

Bianca sighed. *She's depressing herself again,* Bianca thought, *and it's only ten thirty.* Bianca shifted her weight from her left foot to her right foot and imagined herself surfing. She then slid her right foot back and rode that wave, the sunlight dancing off the water, her hair free and whipping wildly in the wind . . .

And don't get me started, Katharina thought, *about how the media ruined me over the truly wonderful city of Boston. I loved that city! Yeah,* Filet of Dish *was shit on a shingle, but the city of Boston wasn't to blame. Boston was so beautiful, and the cinematography proved it. But that myopic reporter misquoted me all to hell. I even got a copy of the actual notes that reporter took:*

KM: I love the smell of the ocean, and I love Massachusetts. Wish I could spell it! We're about 90% done with shooting. I'm not that into baseball. I only root for VA Tech football.

When I still had a Web site, I posted those actual notes online after they tried to crucify me, and none of the media cared. They were more content with the mixed-up quotes that turned me into a Bean-town pariah overnight. The truth just isn't hot enough news in Hollywood.

The truth about Il Pastaio got someone fired, and that someone—my server—ran to the Times *and spilled a bunch of lies. I didn't call ahead and close the place down—I just got there a little before closing time when it was practically empty. My so-called "bodyguards" were the wait staff waiting for me to finish eating. I chew my food very carefully, thanks to my grandma counting for me back in the day. The meat was undercooked, so I sent it back three times. "Well done," I said three times, and it came back bloody each time. I don't eat bloody meat. My server gave me attitude, I gave it right back, and they fired her on the spot. Wonton soup? What was she thinking? I mean, I like wonton soup, but I much prefer Grandma Pearl's chicken noodle.*

Katharina sighed again. *I don't want to think about Grandma today, but I can't help it. She was so much a part of everything I ever did, the reason I even tried to do any kind of acting. "Little Miss Thang," she used to call me whenever I'd overdress for school or church. And even when I became Miss Thang for that abysmal movie, Grandma Pearl still loved me. She raised the hell out of me and turned me into an angel. Okay, I was one of those diva angels like the ones who parade around in wings for Victoria's Secret, but I was still an angel.*

That night on the red carpet . . . "What was she thinking?" they said. The fact is, I wasn't thinking at all, but I had the best reason. While I was in that limo, Great-Auntie Nancy had just called to tell me that Grandma Pearl had just had a stroke and had been admitted to the ICU back in Virginia. I told the driver to get me to the airport, but the limo in front of us wouldn't move. That limo was blocking my way out! As for that thirty-nine-minute walk of mine—which I swear was only ten minutes at the most—I don't remember a bit of it. Auntie Nancy said it was only a mild stroke, not to worry, she's in the hands of Almighty God. All I know is that I was wandering back and forth in near hysteria thinking about my grandma . . . who pulled through, only to die six months later in her sleep.

Katharina felt tears bubbling behind her eyes. *And Grandma Pearl's why I blubbered like a fountain on the Walk of Fame. I was missing her so much. I knew she was looking down on me from Heaven, but I just wished she was there to . . . I don't know, tell me that everything I went through would work out in the end, make me some of her chunky chicken salad sandwiches, make me some of her homemade chicken noodle soup, tell me to hold my head up proud—anything. I was* really *weeping, and the world thought it was fake. That was no "performance." That was the real me missing my grandma.*

Bianca saw a tear slide down Katharina's cheek. *It's going to be one of* those *days.* In Bianca's mind, she hopped off the surfboard and began climbing El Capitan, Yosemite's coolest and most dangerous rock formation—barefoot. *Yeah,* Bianca thought. *No one's ever done this three-thousand-foot rock barefooted. I am going to get the nicest tan!*

If I only knew then what I know now, Katharina thought, *I wouldn't be in this mess. I would have kept my mouth shut. There would have been no quotes to misquote, no Prozac to inhale, and no CD to exhale. I would have kept my money in my possession so I'd have some now. But no, I had to live the role and spend money as if it were an endless supply. I would have kept a closer eye on Cecil, and when I caught his ass, I would have taken him to court instead of hiding my shame. If anyone knew that I was living royalty paycheck to royalty paycheck now, almost like the rest of the world, I'd probably be on one of those "Where Are They Now?" segments on* Entertainment Tonight.

And now, delivered straight from Heaven, are five million reasons to leave this house and start over. She let a tear drop to her robe. *Grandma Pearl, your little Miss Thang is about to shine again.*

Katharina nodded once.

Bianca shook and almost fell off El Capitan in her mind. *She's made a decision? No way. I thought it was her job not to think. This could actually be an interesting day for once.*

Katharina nodded again. *I have four days to make my decision. If I call Lucentio Pictures today, they'll think I've lost my edge and attitude—which I have, but I don't want them to know that. I will wait three days, then. No, all four. Yes. I need to sweat them a little. And they have to expect me to play this little game, right? It's all part of this business. You give me an offer, I act uninterested, you sweeten the offer, I act less uninterested, and then you give me an ultimatum that I grudgingly (and now joyfully!) accept.*

What a business. And the real acting hasn't even begun.

Now, if shooting begins on September 30, and if it takes a day's travel to get there, that leaves me . . . eight days.

Hmm.

Eight days to pack is cutting it kind of close, but sacrifices will just have to be made. Oh, the weary, troublesome life I lead . . . for five million dollars! Yes! Thank You, Jesus!

"Bianca!" Katharina yelled, and she distinctly heard an echo this time. *I've missed that echo. The world is going to hear that echo again, and soon.*

Bianca slipped, fell off El Capitan, and actually made a whistling sound as she plummeted back to earth. She stepped forward. "Yes, Miss Minola?"

"Find my passport."

We're leaving the country? Yes! Bianca tried not to smile. "Yes, Miss Minola."

"You have one, don't you?" Katharina asked.

You bet! "Yes, Miss Minola."

"I need you to start packing," Katharina said. "Today, Bianca. Not tomorrow. Today."

Damn. Bianca nervously twisted a yellow rubber bracelet on her wrist. "What do I pack, Miss Minola?"

I need to make a grand reentrance to the filmmaking world, an entrance no one will ever be able to forget. And since I don't know where I'm going . . . "Pack it *all*, Bianca. Everything."

Bianca swallowed. "Everything, Miss Minola?" *Even the truly trashy stuff that even mannequins would be ashamed to wear?*

Katharina smiled. "Everything." *My entire, mostly out-of-fashion arsenal of once-fabulous if-only-to-me clothes.* "And if you need to purchase more luggage, do so."

Bianca swayed a little. *I may not get paid again* this *week,* she thought. *The bags Miss "Katha-diva Bologna" buys cost one thousand dollars each!* "Um, maybe we should just call U-Haul, Miss Minola. Or Allied Van Lines. They could box it all up in no time."

She's right, of course, but a U-Haul? For clothes, maybe, but never for shoes. Katharina turned sharply to Bianca. "What are you trying to say, Bianca?"

Bianca looked at her Chacos. "I'm just saying that you have a lot of clothes, Miss Minola. The shoes alone will probably fill fifty large suitcases, unless I take them out of their boxes first. Then it might only take twenty suitcases."

"They *must* be boxed." Katharina sighed and frowned.

Yes, Bianca has a point, and yes, Bianca is lasting longer than some of my other worthless assistants, but I am her employer. "Prove your worth, Bianca."

"I'll do my best, Miss Minola."

"You have . . . *six* days to pack."

A tremble flashed up Bianca's body. "Yes, Miss Minola. Six days." *Witch! Whore! Heifer!* Bianca thought, turning to go.

"And don't forget Scottie's clothes, too!" Katharina yelled.

Scottie, the dog that has more clothes than I do. "Yes, Miss Minola."

"Make sure his clothes are cleaned and pressed."

Scottie, the dog that has a twenty-dollar-a-week dry-cleaning bill. "Yes, Miss Minola."

Katharina waved Bianca away.

I may be a woman alone, Katharina thought, *but I will be dressed for each and every occasion, whatever and wherever it may be.*

It is about time the movie gods . . . Katharina frowned. *It is about time the movie gods did what? Oh. Yes. It is about time the movie gods remembered their goddess!*

Geez, Katharina thought, *I had forgotten how much* work *it took not only to be a diva but to* think *like a diva.* She smiled. *I'll just practice in front of the mirror and on Bianca for a few days. That should do the trick.*

Katharina Minola smiled at the smog. "I'm back," she whispered. "Miss me?"

Chapter 4

Pietro Lucentio smiled at his new mule, Curtis, as they wound their way through a cold and muddy peat bog near the Quebec border in northern Ontario, Canada. Curtis looked back occasionally with his striking blue-green eyes.

It had taken Pietro several weeks of searching to find Curtis, who was grazing with some cows and horses near Fincastle, Virginia, a small town twenty miles northwest of Roanoke.

"Why's it so durn important the mule has this color eyes?" the cattleman had asked, looking at a splotch of color on a postcard.

Pietro had no earthly idea why his brother Vincenzo had asked him to find such a rare mule, but he had answered, "Very important," and he had handed the cattleman one thousand dollars in cash to prove it.

"Curtis is just a mule," the cattleman had said. "I couldn't ask you for no more than . . . four hundred. At the most. And I'm still practically stealing from you."

Pietro had stared hard at the wiry old man. "Keep the change—and keep your silence."

The cattleman had nodded. "Who'd believe me, anyway?"

Pietro and Curtis paused on a rise above "the set," as his brother Vincenzo called an undeveloped part of Pietro's land, some thirty acres of mountain, peat bog, and mostly pine forest 725 kilometers (450 miles) dead north of Toronto near the Abitibi River and 140 kilometers (87 miles) from Rouyn-Noranda, Quebec, the closest substantial town. Lucentio Pictures couldn't have picked a more inaccessible, brutal spot on the planet for its experiment. Today the temperature was a balmy 9 degrees Celsius (48 degrees F). By the end of the week, it would drop to –2 degrees Celsius (29 degrees F) and usher in the season's first significant snow.

Pietro had already placed dozens of cameras throughout the set with the help of John Fisher, and he had already stocked Cabins 1 and 2 with enough food and wood to last four months. He had measured off an acre next to a cascading stream midway between Cabin 1 and Cabin 2, but Vincenzo had told him not to clear it. "Leave it wild," Vincenzo had told him, "and don't walk around on it at all. No footprints. It must appear pristine, the ultimate unspoiled wilderness." Pietro hadn't asked why, trusting his brother to know his stuff.

Vincenzo had instructed Pietro to leave Cabin 3 completely alone, except for adding a fax machine, a ream of plain white paper, and several *dozen* more cameras, and again Pietro didn't ask why. Cabin 3 was about one thousand meters east and five hundred meters up a steep slope from the other cabins, facing the teeth of the wind. Cabin 3 was where—Vincenzo had told him— "a spoiled actress is going to live, complain, whine, moan, go off, and scream . . . and eventually make film history."

Pietro never asked who this particular spoiled actress

would be. They were all the same to him since his first brush with that rude actress—Katharina Minola—fifteen years ago. She was one of the prime reasons he left show business for the untouched wilderness of Canada. He decided that he couldn't put up with such ridiculous behavior from a woman he was paying millions to be someone other than herself for a few months. He also preferred the pure solitude of Ontario to the smoggy bustle of Southern California.

Pietro Lucentio wanted to *see* his breath—not hold it.

Vincenzo had instructed Pietro to pick up this actress and her assistant at Val-d'Or Airport over in Quebec on September 29 and drive them 275 kilometers (170 miles) to the set.

"Try to drive over the worst, most spine-jarring roads possible, cart paths and dry creek beds preferred," Vincenzo had said.

Pietro was also told to blindfold both of them for the entire journey before taking off their blindfolds at the beginning of the S-turn–filled, rough-cut path to the "set." He was to provide Curtis for the actress to ride on that rugged path.

"And after that, who knows?" Vincenzo had said. "Just make sure you deposit them at Cabin 3 in time for dinner."

For a dinner that won't be there, Pietro thought. *Hollow wood. I'll never understand that place as long as I live.*

Nor did Pietro understand women.

At all.

His six *dis*-engagements proved it. He didn't even remember their names anymore—just the dates they returned the rings. He had marked six spaces on his calendar to "celebrate" his solitude, his freedom, and his manhood.

And ultimately, his loneliness, but it was a contented loneliness.

November 27. She was the tall one. Athletic, ripped, a beach volleyball player from São Paulo, Brazil. So many curves in all the right places except for her stomach, which had to be the flattest on earth. Her bathing suit barely contained her, and volleyball action shots of her "shaved area" and bubble butt showed up all over the Internet at porn sites. Her derrière was briefly the number one computer wallpaper on the planet. He had proposed to her after she and her equally hot volleyball partner won a tournament at Venice Beach, and she had accepted. The marathon sex they had was steamy, powerful, and gritty. "Yes!" and "More!" were her favorite English words. He introduced her to his estate during the depths of a bitter ice storm in November. She acted like a caged leopard for her entire visit, stalking back and forth in front of the big picture window and cursing the snow and ice in Portuguese. "No!" she said once the roads cleared. "I no marry you! No tan here! Beach, not snow!"

Pietro decided his next girlfriend and lover would speak English as a *first* language.

December 24. She was the shy one. Stocky shoulders, powerful legs, a champion triathlete with triceps cuts, from Stockton, California. Second-generation Californian by way of Italy. Spoke some Italian, too. Strongest legs he had ever had wrapped around him. Looked very good in Spandex shorts and top, especially on a cold day. He had proposed to her after she had won a triathlon in the Rocky Mountains of Colorado. She had accepted with a shrug, a smile, and an "Okay." The sex was shy, tentative, slow, and peaceful. He brought her to Ontario on Christmas Eve. He told her they could be snowed in for months but that he had plenty of wood to keep her warm. That's when he found out that she was acutely and, as it turned out, *violently* claustrophobic. She broke the main picture window in his great room with two pounding fists, shouting, "I can't breathe! I need to feel the air on my face!" He had to break out two of his snowmobiles to get her to the airport and away from his life.

He decided he would make sure his next girlfriend and lover wasn't psychotic in any way.

May 29. She was the curviest one. As much front as back, and more than his hands could contain. A heart surgeon born in Nairobi, Kenya, whom he had met, strangely, at a Toronto Maple Leafs hockey game. She spoke better English than he did and looked hot (and bothered *him*) in whatever she wore. The softest lips he had ever kissed. He had proposed to her while giving her a massage. "Yes, oh yes!" she had whispered. "Work me lower all night long!" The sex was miraculous, sweaty, loud, and spiritual. He waited to bring her to his estate in late May . . . when the horseflies, mosquitoes, and sweat bees feasted on her tender, dark African flesh. She broke it off when he told her she'd "never have to work again." She had scratched at her bites and said, "I did *not* leave Africa *not* to work! And the bugs here are worse than the ones in Kenya!"

He decided his next girlfriend and lover wouldn't have a career she couldn't easily leave for him.

July 21. She was the sultry one. Eyes as big as saucers, brown thighs as smooth as oleo. A waitress whose parents immigrated to Toronto from India and had opened a restaurant. Again, she spoke English better than he did. Traditional, brightly dressed, mysterious—and chaste, at least in front of her parents. When they were alone, however, she had the softest hands, moistest lips, and strongest tongue he had ever had roam his body. He had proposed after a late-night meal of tandoori chicken, and she had accepted. He waited until the bugs weren't as bad in July to bring her to his estate. He also had to bring her entire extended family. Her father was not impressed. *He,* and not July 21, returned the ring, calling it "a trifle."

He decided that his next girlfriend and lover would not respect her parents' wishes as much and have a mind of her own.

August 18. She was the wild one. A Chinese-Canadian artist with the sexiest stomach tattooed with little yin-yang symbols. They had met at a charity art auction, mostly of her work, in Montreal. She was always looking for the next rush, and she could say the nastiest things in bed in three languages. The sex was crazy, involved, and acrobatic—and as it turned out, *crowded.* The fastest, hungriest, most educated tongue he had ever known. He had proposed midstroke, she had accepted, and the tattooed couple in the bed next to them had applauded. He never got her up to his estate, because in the morning, she was intertwined (in a position the *Kama Sutra* never imagined) with the tattooed couple. She paused long enough to hand him the ring, then said, "Oh well," and turned into a human pretzel again.

He decided his next girlfriend and lover would not be a sexual freak of nature.

December 12. All Pietro could say was she was the most recent one. A local Abitibi woman of the Abitibi 70 Indian Reserve. Very long hair. At six-one, nearly as tall as he. Hardy, healthy, strong, and proud. Vincenzo feared her, and with good reason. She could chop a cord of wood between breakfast and lunch, and skin a bear in minutes. An elementary schoolteacher. The sex was nonexistent because of her six long-haired, chaperone brothers, though she kissed him with fervor and gusto and promised him lots of children. He had proposed to her while the two had shopped at The Soap Lady in Béarn, Quebec, her brothers in the beat-up truck outside. She smiled and nodded. They were going to have the strongest, most weather-resistant children ever born, a new breed of Canadians who could survive comfortably even in the Himalayan Mountains. She *loved* his estate . . . until she consulted some long-lost treaty that said his land really belonged to her tribe. She had hurled the ring into the night and vowed to sue.

He had never found the ring.

She had never sued.

He was alone.

Curtis stamped his front feet.

"I know, I know," Pietro said. "It's too cold to take a walk down memory lane today."

I just hope that actress brings some sensible shoes.

Curtis paused to excrete a particularly nasty blob of poop.

And shoes she doesn't mind throwing away.

Chapter 5

As she carefully dusted, boxed, and packed Katharina's shoes for the third straight wearisome day, Bianca fought the urge to slip on a pair of Katharina's unworn six-hundred-dollar Alexander McQueen sandals. They were a half size too small, but they looked so comfortable and so black.

It will only take a few seconds, just to see how I look . . .

She looked around. Katharina had told her that cameras covered and recorded every room, nook, and shadow in the entire mansion, but Bianca had never actually seen a single lens. *It's because she thinks I'm a Latina,* Bianca thought at the time, which was partially true. She was actually a "Latalian"—half Caracas, Venezuela, and half Ravenna, Italy—her parents having met at USC.

She slipped out of her Chacos and into the McQueens, her feet feeling . . .

What? Bianca thought. *Rich? Buttery? Creamy? Like double-churned butter pecan ice cream? Like Godiva chocolate crisscrossed by licorice?*

My feet still feel like feet.

She looked down at her toes.

My toes are not rejoicing.

She replaced the sandals with her two-year-old Chacos.

My toes rejoice!

Bianca Baptista was an earth woman working for a sky queen.

And it still made no sense to her.

Bianca, an English major, was an assistant to a woman who occasionally spoke pleasant English and possessed Bianca's alter ego. Bianca didn't get her eyebrows plucked twice a day. She actually liked her thick black eyebrows, though Katharina often told her to "trim those bushes." Bianca didn't get her nails done—ever. She simply trimmed and filed them smooth with an emery board. Bianca didn't get facials, preferring to wash her face and apply some damn lotion, thank you very much. Bianca didn't get her feet scraped and sanded. She actually liked the feel of her rough feet on carpet, and the sand at the beach kept them smooth enough—and for free. Bianca never wore makeup, desiring the world to see what she *really* looked like at all times. Bianca rarely dressed up, choosing to dress comfortably and economically, shopping primarily at clothing outlets and Walmart.

And Bianca ate her entire sandwich, crusts and all.

Bianca wasn't even supposed to be Katharina's assistant anymore. Katharina should have already fired her by now. *Like all the others.* And then Bianca would be hard at work writing a tell-all book that she'd probably never send to an agent or publisher, mainly because there wasn't a whole lot to tell. Katharina Minola was actually quite boring. *Now, if she had only fired me just after she won her Oscar, I'd be set,* Bianca often thought. *But what was I, seven at the time?*

Bianca, who spoke Spanish and Italian fluently, knew she should be teaching at a bilingual elementary or middle school somewhere in L.A., knew she should be working with special needs children, knew she should have been saying more than "Yes, Miss Minola" while mind-surfing, mind-climbing, and thinking "Die, Katha-diva, die!" all day long.

I need a vacation from all this opulence, these bad vibes, and Scottie's noxious gas.

Bianca was supposed to be driving her ancient sky blue Jeep Cherokee to Yosemite to go mountain biking and mountain climbing with her camera, snapping away in black and white and in vivid color. She was supposed to have sand-encrusted toes while exploring tide pools in Carmel or San Clemente. She was supposed to be biking up Highway 1 to San Francisco on her Moots Vamoots Compact Dreamride Edition Distance Racer (a wonderful graduation gift from her father) at least once a year. She was supposed to be playing her trumpet in a jazz combo down in Newport Beach. She was supposed to be going to an Eagles reunion concert. She was supposed to be anywhere but matching boxes and packing one freaking *thousand* pairs of shoes, most of them unworn, while wearing Chacos almost as old as the puking, farting, neurotic dog she bathed, dressed, fed, and walked every morning, noon, and night.

Katha-diva is holding me back! Bianca reasoned. *I have to get fired. Getting fired by Katharina Minola is a mark of distinction in this city. All I have to do is slip and call her "Dena Hinson" or "Katha-diva Bologna" just once, and I'll—*

"Bianca!"

Bianca walked to the nearest purple intercom. "Yes, Miss Minola?"

"Have you finished packing yet?"

Bianca closed her eyes. "Not yet, Miss Minola. I

should have your shoes done by midnight. I will start on your, um, lingerie in the morning."

Bianca waited for the commands. She didn't have to wait long.

"Make sure you fold everything neatly!"

Bianca sighed. "Yes, Miss Minola."

"But before you do another thing, I need you to run over to Lucentio Pictures to deliver a letter to Vincenzo Lucentio."

Hopefully it's the announcement of your permanent retirement from show business, Bianca thought. *Wait. She asked if I had a passport. I want to go somewhere! I'm wearing little feet into the concrete under that stupid purple umbrella by the pool.* "Yes, Miss Minola."

"And take Scottie," Katharina added. "He needs a little fresh air."

And you're sending him and me into the city? "Yes, Miss Minola."

This day can't possibly get any better.

Chapter 6

Penelope buzzed Vincenzo a little before noon. "A Miss Baptista is here with a dog and a letter from Katharina Minola."

Vincenzo relaxed for the first time since he sent the offer. Katharina had kept him waiting for only three days. He had fully expected her to wait until the last possible moment to accept his offer. *I'm glad she's feeling desperate,* he thought. *Desperate actresses often turn in outstanding performances.* "Send Miss Baptista in."

When Bianca entered his office, Vincenzo relaxed even more as he marveled at Miss Baptista's natural beauty and skill at holding a snarling, drooling Scottish terrier under one arm and a large purple envelope under the other.

"Bianca, right?" he asked, standing and offering his hand.

Bianca nodded and put Scottie on the floor. "Sorry about the dog. His name is Scottie." She sighed. "Katharina said he needed some fresh air." She shook Vincenzo's hand firmly.

Nice eyes. I'll bet there's a nice smile under those pouting lips, too. What is she, Latina? Such nice skin tone. "Katharina doesn't get into the city much these days, does she?"

Bianca wrinkled up her lips and shook her head. "Nope." She handed the envelope to Vincenzo and stuck both hands in the back pockets of her faded cut-off jeans. "She hasn't been out of her house since I've been working for her."

"Please, sit," Vincenzo said.

"I need to stretch first," Bianca said. "I hate sitting in traffic." She glided to the window, Scottie sniffing along behind her. "Isn't there an ocean out there somewhere?"

Vincenzo stood beside her and pointed. "If you look very carefully, you can see Catalina Island right . . . there."

"I don't see it," Bianca said.

Vincenzo laughed. "Neither do I most days, but I know it's out there."

He returned to his desk and opened the envelope, removing an elegantly handwritten (in purple) letter. He waded through a full page of Katharina's usual demands—a *certified* dog walker on the set, all-black furniture, blackout drapes, humidifier, roses—until he found a single sentence:

I hereby accept your offer.

Vincenzo buzzed Penelope. "It's a go. Deposit the money."

He found a pair of blue-gray eyes looking at him. "Well, um . . ."

"Please don't send me back already," Bianca said. "It's so nice not to hear my name echoing through the mountains for a little while."

Poor kid. "Has Katharina told you what all this is about?" Vincenzo asked.

Bianca shook her head and drifted to the only book-case in the room, pulling out an ancient copy of Washington Irving's *The Sketch Book.* She flipped through a few pages and looked up. "Is this a first edition?"

Vincenzo shook his head. "I don't think so. I've had that one since college. UCLA."

"What was your major?" she asked.

"Art," Vincenzo said, "with a minor in film. Didn't you graduate UCLA, too?"

She nodded, returned the book to the shelf, and gazed at several Ansel Adams prints on the wall. "Do you go to Yosemite often?"

Vincenzo moved out from behind his desk and leaned on a chair. "I used to. Before my father died and I had fewer responsibilities."

Bianca smiled. *What is Vincenzo, forty?* Bianca thought. *He wears it well. Kind of Richard Gere-ish without the squint. Quite handsome. Dark eyes, seems fit. Wearing a T-shirt, blue jeans, and hiking boots! Very cool for an executive.* "You should go back. The air tastes like jasmine this time of year."

Vincenzo smiled. "After this picture is over, I think I will."

Bianca squinted. "What picture?"

How much can I tell her? Vincenzo thought. *If Katharina fires her in the next twenty-four hours, Bianca could run immediately to the media and ruin everything.* "You seem like a nice, honest person."

Bianca continued to squint.

"That was a dumb thing to say," Vincenzo said, returning to the safety of his chair behind his desk. "What I should have said was . . ." He sighed. "I'm so used to dealing with, um . . ."

"Head cases? Egomaniacs? Two-faced people? The

terminally self-serving? The continuously stuck-up? The functionally dysfunctional?"

"Yes." Vincenzo hesitated. *And so cynical for one so young. A captivating combination.* "*Them.* You seem normal, Bianca, and that's a wonderful compliment around here."

Bianca laughed. "Thank you. I like being normal."

And I like your normal attitude, too, Vincenzo thought. *And you have dimples when you laugh.* "Bianca, what I'm about to tell you cannot leave this room."

Scottie chose this moment to fart.

"Um, does he have to go outside?" Vincenzo asked.

"No. That was an airy fart." Bianca frowned. "It's the wet ones you have to worry about."

How do I respond to that? Vincenzo wondered. *I guess I don't.* "Well, um, you see . . ." He sighed again and listened a moment for a wet fart from Scottie. Hearing none, he said, "We're paying Katharina five million dollars to make a movie."

Bianca's eyes betrayed no surprise. "Why?"

She's sharp and unshakeable, this Miss Baptista, Vincenzo thought. "We're trying to sort of, um, rehabilitate her."

"You're doing an intervention," Bianca said evenly.

Vincenzo smiled. "That's it! Yes. An intervention. That's exactly what we're doing. Why didn't I think of that?"

Bianca finally flopped onto the overstuffed black leather couch, a favorite of his father's. "Is this the casting couch?" she asked, raising a single eyebrow.

Vincenzo blushed. "Um, no. I'm not . . . I don't . . . We don't do that sort of thing at Lucentio Pictures. We make family films, um, wholesome, uh, for the family."

He's so cute! Bianca stared at his desk. "I don't see any pictures of *family* on your desk. I just thought that maybe . . ."

Is she flirting with me? He blinked away the thought. He was almost twice her age. "Um, no. I haven't found the right woman yet." He cleared his throat. "Getting back to our intervention, we, um—"

"Why not?" Bianca interrupted.

"Hmm?" Vincenzo asked.

"Why haven't you found the right woman?" she asked.

Vincenzo stared into space, trying not to make eye contact. "I, um, I haven't really been looking, Bianca. This is . . . this is a busy job."

"Oh," Bianca said. "Just wondering."

Vincenzo blinked. *Bianca is an interesting person.* "Um, where was I? Oh. The intervention. We've already gone to great lengths and made some serious investments of time, talent, and energy to make this work, and if we're successful, Katharina will be back to the actress the world fell in love with fifteen years ago. We want to help her get back on top."

Bianca leaned forward and clasped her hands together. "And what do you need me to do?"

"Um, we don't need, um, we really hadn't planned to . . ." *Bianca's eyes are dancing. Why are her eyes dancing?* "What, um, what *could* you do for us?"

She put her hands behind her head and leaned back. "Hmm. There are *so* many things I'd like to do to her. Some of them are illegal." She shook her head. "Nope. Most of them are illegal. What exactly are *you* going to do to her?"

Now she's suddenly coy, Vincenzo thought. *Bianca has range.* "Please keep all this in strictest confidence, Bianca. If Katharina found out, we'd be out five million dollars and most likely have no picture to show for it."

Bianca sat up. "Found out about what?"

Vincenzo took a deep breath. "We're taking her to

the middle of the middle of nowhere, to the heart of the cold, dark, snowy Canadian wilderness, and she'll be there for sixty days with just her wits and mainly the clothes on her back."

"That doesn't sound so—"

"*And,*" Vincenzo interrupted, "we'll be filming her every word and deed without her knowing it the entire time."

Bianca's face remained blank. "What else?"

What else? Vincenzo thought. *What does she mean by "What else?" What else could—*"What else do *you* think we could do?"

Bianca laughed softly. "You're going to strip her to her essence in an attempt to banish her current evil diva self from planet earth, and all you're doing is taking away her clothes?"

"Um, no," Vincenzo said. "We're taking away her shoes, too."

Bianca groaned. "I have been packing them for three days and I'm almost finished." She sighed. "What else are you going to do?"

"Well, we're going to keep all but you and Katharina from entering Canada," Vincenzo said. "Two jets will take off, but only one will arrive in Canada. The other jet, containing the rest of her porta-posse and Scottie, will go to Costa Rica with all her luggage."

Bianca nodded. "Sounds like an okay plan. Makes me wish I was her hairstylist, though." She smiled. "Poor Katharina. She'll have to do her own makeup and hair because I have no skills that way." She fluffed her dark, naturally wavy hair. "As you can see."

"You have nice, normal hair, Bianca."

"Thank you." She suddenly frowned. "Oh. I may have to dress her."

"In what?" Vincenzo asked.

"Oh yeah." Bianca smiled. "Cool."

"I mean, other than the costume we provide for her, she'll have nothing really to be dressed in."

"It won't be purple or tiger-striped, will it?" Bianca asked.

"No."

"Some days I think I work at the children's zoo," Bianca said. "Only no one's doing any petting."

I will leave that one entirely alone. "Katharina will be staying in a rough-hewn cabin with the barest of necessities and none"—he picked up Katharina's letter— "and *none* of her usual demands. There's no phone, no television, no Internet, and no cell phone service. There isn't any electricity, either. There isn't even any food in the cabin, and the only running water is ice cold. No hot baths, unless she figures out how to do it. She'll have to cross a mountain stream that has no bridge each day to get to and from the set." *In for a penny, in for a pound.* "And we'll be writing the script as *she* happens."

Bianca smiled broadly. "How positively existential. But, what if Katharina decides *not* to happen? She is the moodiest, most stubborn person I have ever met. She can sit under a pool umbrella from sunup to sundown. If she doesn't leave her cabin, I'll be stuck with her. Does Canada have the death penalty for capital murder?"

Vincenzo blinked rapidly. *I hope that was a rhetorical question.* "Bianca, she'll have to leave her cabin. It will be in the script."

"But doesn't she trash scripts?" Bianca asked.

Vincenzo sighed. "Yes. All the time. But essentially *she'll* be writing the script, right?"

"Oh yeah," Bianca said. "Pretty shrewd. How, um, how remote is this place? I mean, can she escape?"

Vincenzo shrugged. "I doubt it. It is about ninety miles to the nearest town in Quebec, over a hundred miles to the nearest airport."

Bianca wrinkled her lips again. "This is beginning to sound like a kidnapping, and that could make me an accomplice."

Again, I hadn't thought of this. "But we're paying Katharina a ransom *before* she gets there," Vincenzo said. "It's being deposited to the old account she had with us even as we speak."

Bianca nodded. "So the contract you sent was basically bogus."

"No, it's a genuine contract that we will honor to the letter." He paused. "With or without a movie. We would much rather have one or even two movies for our efforts."

Bianca closed her eyes. "Let me get this straight. You're filming her for sixty days, sunup to sundown, which is roughly . . . sixteen hours a day."

"Something like that."

"So you'll have about . . . a thousand hours of footage," Bianca said, opening her eyes.

Vincenzo nodded. *A very sharp girl.*

"And you plan to condense it all down to two hours?" Bianca asked. "What about what's left over?"

Vincenzo shrugged. "We're not sure what we'll do with it. We may do nothing with it, and we may release parts as extras for the DVD. Keep in mind that we will be in Canada to film a real movie. And, um, I'm the director slash cinematographer." *Sort of. Fish will get the cinematography credit.*

Bianca laughed. "*You* are going to direct Katharina Minola?"

Vincenzo nodded.

"But you're not a director, are you?"

"No, and I've never wanted to be one," Vincenzo said. "I assisted Katharina's director for *My Honey Love*. She wasn't the diva she's become back then, but she sure could spit the venom. I have seen hundreds of directors at work since then, so I know how to overreact, scold, scowl, berate, throw tantrums, throw up my hands, praise, flatter, walk away, and criticize with the best of them."

Bianca blinked. "She might not leave her, um, cabin if you scold her. She might not leave her cabin just because you *want* her to leave the cabin. She might not leave her cabin if she has a hangnail or sneezes just once or doesn't get her precious chunky chicken salad sandwiches with the crusts cut off."

Vincenzo nodded and smiled.

"But you have cameras hidden *inside* her cabin," Bianca said with a sigh. "I get it. You have her on 'the set' no matter where she is. It's pretty slick."

And so are you, Bianca Baptista, Vincenzo thought. *And this gives me a great idea.* He buzzed Penelope. "Penelope, please bring in a Form Fifteen."

Bianca's eyes darted from Vincenzo to the door and back to Vincenzo. "Mr. Lucentio, trust me, I won't say a word about any of this to anyone. You don't have to have me sign a confidentiality agreement. I mean, I'm going to have a front-row seat to the death of Katha-diva Bologna. I'll be the first person on earth to see that wench go." *And then,* Bianca thought happily, *I'll be free!*

Vincenzo chuckled and wrote down "Katha-diva Bologna" on a notepad as Penelope swept into the room and laid a file folder on Vincenzo's desk. "Bianca," he said, "this is a standard *acting* contract. You're going to appear often on those thousand hours of video, whether we use them or not, so you should be compensated accordingly."

"Will there be . . ." Bianca's eyes widened. "You're not filming in the bathroom, are you?"

Here we go again, Vincenzo thought. "You'll only be filmed from the neck up and at the mirror only." He had an idea. "You could even communicate to us that way if you ever had to, you know, while Katharina's sleeping."

"Mirror, mirror, on the wall . . ." Bianca whispered. "I guess I could. I'll probably crack myself up."

Vincenzo filled in the basics on the contract, then looked up at Penelope. "Any suggestions, Penelope?"

"Don't tell Jim," Penelope whispered.

"I don't intend to," Vincenzo said. "I meant, how much . . ."

"And pay her SAG dues," Penelope said, whispering, "She's very cute."

Bianca was now sitting up on the couch. "You're going to pay me?"

Vincenzo glared at Penelope. "If Penelope will just tell me how much."

Penelope smiled at Bianca. "Have you ever acted before, dear?"

"Well," Bianca said, "I've been acting like a complete moron for the last six weeks working for Katharina Minola. Does that count?"

Penelope nodded to Vincenzo. "She's experienced. I'd go ten, maybe fifteen, minimum."

Bianca's eyes widened. "Ten . . . thousand?"

Penelope nodded. "At *least*, Vincenzo. She has presence." She squeezed Vincenzo's shoulder, then stood in front of Bianca. "Stand up, young lady."

Bianca stood while Penelope peered at her face, humming and squinting.

"Good jawline, a softened Maria Shriver," Penelope said.

Really? Bianca thought. *I didn't know I had a jawline.*

"Serious eyebrows like that Jennifer Connelly," Penelope continued. "Incredible gray-blue eyes. Girl next door quality. Healthy skin tone. Innocent. Could be a cover girl with a touch of makeup."

"Oh, I never wear makeup," Bianca said.

"Don't," Penelope said. "You don't need it, which is why I hate you. Hair needs work, but what woman's doesn't? Has a fresh, lively voice. Has to be brave to work for Katharina."

And has to be a moron, Bianca thought.

"Fifteen," Penelope said.

"Um, hey," Bianca said, "that's really generous, but I'm no actress."

Penelope hushed her. "And humble, too. Twenty." She narrowed her eyes. *"A week."*

Bianca fell back onto the couch. "Twenty . . . thousand . . . a week?" *Katharina barely pays me two thousand a month!* Bianca thought. *They have to be kidding!*

Vincenzo wrote down the figures. "That's roughly . . . one hundred and seventy thousand dollars for sixty days' work." He stood and brought a pen and the contract to Bianca. "Unless you want more."

Bianca looked from Penelope to Vincenzo to the contract in front of her. It looked legitimate. It had all the right amount of legalese, and it had the right number of zeroes. She exhaled slowly. "You two are crazy." She looked up. "Aren't you?"

Penelope winked. "I've been crazy since the fifties, dear. Vincenzo has only recently become infected."

Bianca took the paper with shaking hands. "This is real?"

"Yes, Bianca," Vincenzo said softly. "We'll take care of your Screen Actors Guild dues and fees for a year as well."

I can't feel my hands, Bianca thought. *Why can't I feel my hands?* "But, I'm not an actress," she said again, flitting her eyes from Penelope to Vincenzo. "I was never even a tree or a squirrel or a dog in a school play."

Penelope sat beside Bianca. "All you have to do is be *you*. Be Bianca Baptista."

Bianca sighed. "I have to kiss a *lot* of ass. Oh, I'm sorry. I curse sometimes. Is that all right?"

Penelope put her arm around Bianca. "You are so precious! You can do and say whatever you like, Bianca, and when the time is right, and if I'm reading you right, you can—how do they say it? You can 'break bad' on your employer and quit."

Vincenzo knelt in front of Bianca, Scottie sniffing at his legs. "And you can quit in perhaps the most memorable confrontation in film history. The lowly, long-suffering assistant gets to stick it to her stuck-up employer. You do have a lot to say to Miss Katha-diva Bologna, don't you?"

Bianca dropped her eyes. "You heard me say that, huh?"

"Yes," Vincenzo said.

Bianca couldn't keep her toes still. "I have a great deal to say to Katha-diva. The film may need an intermission. Could we do it in 3-D? There are some shoes and some bread crusts I'd like to throw at her. You may have to do a sequel."

Penelope hugged Bianca to her. "I wish I was going to be there to see it. I'm a tough old bird, but northern Ontario is not the place for me this time of year. I'll be in Costa Rica working on my tan and keeping the rest of the porta-posse happy and quiet." She stood and patted Scottie *and* Vincenzo on the head. "Good dogs." She winked once at Bianca, and she left the office.

Vincenzo stood. "If you think you should get an even two hundred," he said, "just say so."

Bianca looked up, her eyes shining. "I don't think I should get even five thousand." Her mouth dropped open. "Oh no! What if Katharina fires me today, or tomorrow, or only a few days into the shoot?"

"Relax, Bianca. We expect her to *try* to fire you, and whenever she does, you have to beat her to the punch and quit. Then you will become a technical advisor for the film." He sat beside her, letting Scottie lick his hand.

"Scottie was licking his penis on the ride in," Bianca said.

Vincenzo removed his hand quickly, wiping it on his jeans. "How nice. Um, once you quit, you'll walk off into the wild, hopefully during a blizzard. It's only about a mile or so to my brother Pietro's very nice, very warm house where you'll have a four-room suite all to yourself. We're filming *A Woman Alone* on his land."

"Is that your title?"

Vincenzo nodded.

"Fitting."

And, he thought, *she thinks like me, even says the same things. I am officially intrigued.* "Um, once you're at Pietro's, you could give suggestions to Walter Yearling, our screenwriter, as you watch Katharina's further disintegration. He can then fax new script pages to Katharina with your ideas."

"I don't know," Bianca said. "Katharina has a way of changing things, of getting her way, of messing things up. You have this nice plan, but she's not of this world, okay?"

"We'll figure it all out." He bumped her knee with his. "Just don't quit for at least a week, maybe two."

"I'll try not to." She signed the contract and handed it to Vincenzo. "Does this mean you own me or something?"

Vincenzo stood and placed the contract on his desk. "Of course not." He smiled at his shoes. "Not for a few days, anyway." He looked up. "Sixty days is all we're asking, whether you're with Katharina as her assistant or with us as a technical advisor. Do you have any questions?"

"This is going to sound petty, but if Katharina's luggage is going to Central America, does that mean that my luggage is going there, too?"

"No. Yours will go to a holding area at Val-d'Or Airport in Quebec to be shipped to Pietro's after you and Katharina leave the airport."

Bianca shrugged. "I don't have much, I was just wondering." She giggled a little. "Could you maybe send my Chacos with Penelope? They've never been to Costa Rica. They like the sand."

Vincenzo smiled. "Sure."

And I'm starting to like you, Bianca, Vincenzo thought. *I really, really am.*

Chapter 7

Whom should I call first?

Katharina sat on a purple velvet throne chair in her mirrored bathroom at her vanity, at twenty feet long most likely the world's largest *purple* vanity, a purple intercom within shouting distance. She wore only a dark purple bathrobe, a matching head wrap, and matching fluffy slippers.

Shoot! I can't call anyone to gloat. I can't tell anyone that I'm making another movie.

This isn't any fun.

It's only for two months. I can handle that.

Hmm. Whom would I call? Ah. It would be a long-ass list.

She picked up one of the brushes her hairstylist had just used on her and pantomimed dialing a number. "Hello, Cecil? Hi. Katharina. Yes, *the* Katharina, the Katharina who made you a filthy-rich man. How *is* the agent thing going for you since you stole my money? I'm sure you're fatter and sloppier now. Still wearing those tents you called suits? I hope your cholesterol level is pushing three hundred. You see, you sniveling, bloated toad, you just lost out on . . ." She did the math.

"Seven hundred and fifty thousand dollars in commissions. Yes, you are so right. You *are* a turd-eating, gorilla-butt-sniffing piece of overripe roadkill. I hope you've spent all my money by now and are as broke as the federal government. Enjoy your poverty! Get that cardboard sign and squirt bottle ready! I hear you can get maps of the stars' houses real cheap these days. *Adios!*"

Who's next? Oh yes. That wench from that useless TV show, Enter-Slander-Me Tonight.

"Cathleen, hi, this is Katharina Minola. How are you? Yes, it *has* been a long time. Your show is still on the air? It is? Why? Oh, I just wondered why a dishonest show that treats hearsay, rumor, gossip, and unconfirmed reports as the gospel truth would still be on the air. Didn't I read that it's still dead last in the Nielsen ratings? You poor, miserable dear. Oh, I *know.* Seven o'clock is *such* a dreadful timeslot when most of America is filling its face or going out for fast food or simply doing something more interesting than your show. Speaking of eating, and I'm sorry if I offend you, but you have gained *quite* a bit of weight, haven't you? It's more like tonnage, actually. Are you expecting quintuplets? No? Are you taking steroids? I hear they bloat your ass. No? Stuck on your time of the month? Terminal bloating? No? You mean, you're just a freaking fat-ass blimp? Well, I just wanted you to know that I'm making another movie, and that I had to buy a widescreen TV to take you all in, you bovine, porcine, monolithic *cow!*"

What was that reviewer's name . . . She frowned. *There were a lot of evil reviewers. Hmm. I'll just invent one.*

"Hello, Roger Leonard *Dick?* Yes, it's Katharina Minola, Mr. *Dick.* You remember me, don't you, Mr. *Dick?* I just wanted to thank you for all the *kind* words you have said about my abilities over the years, especially that phrase you kept repeating over and over one night on your show—what was it? Oh yes. 'Community theater.' Um, how many acting credits do *you* have, Mr. *Dick?* None? Then what makes you such an expert on acting, Mr. *Dick?* Oh, you've *watched* a lot of movies. My goodness. I guess that makes you the world's biggest couch potato. You like to eat, don't you, Mr. *Dick?* I hope you do, because I am doing another movie, it will be fantastic, and you are going to eat every one of your lies doused in rancid camel snot and goat piss for the rest of your pathetic, limp-dicked, no balls–having life! *Ciao,* Mr. *Dick!*"

She slammed down the brush.

She heard a door close. "Ah. Bee-donk-a-donk is back." She faced the intercom and used her refined voice. "Bianca, darling?"

Was that a giggle? Katharina thought. *I don't pay people to giggle.*

"Yes, Miss Minola?"

Was that another giggle? "Bianca, have you been drinking?"

"No, Miss Minola. You know I don't drink."

True. The child has no life at all. It's a good thing she's working for me or she'd have no excitement in her life whatsoever. "Did you deliver my letter?"

"Yes, Miss Minola."

She is so mousy, Katharina thought. *If I had a cat, she'd be dead and excreted already.* "How did Mr. Lucentio receive my letter?"

"He seemed content and relieved, Miss Minola. He also gave me your itinerary."

Yes! "Has the money been deposited, or do you even know?"

"The money has been deposited to your old Lucentio Pictures account, Miss Minola."

Really? Wow. Lucentio Pictures is certainly efficient. I'm surprised Cecil didn't raid that account. "How's Scottie?"

"He's taking a nap, Miss Minola."

"Carry on, Bianca."

Katharina picked up her brush. "I'd like to thank the Academy for finally recognizing the talents of someone who isn't a bleached blonde or foreign or insane or made mostly of plastic and silicone. I'd like to thank the Academy for giving the award to an actress who doesn't play a nun, a serial killer prostitute, a dying boxer, a pregnant cop, or the Queen of England. I accept my Academy Award for my miraculous work in *A Woman Alone* . . ."

I just wish I had a script to redline and rewrite. Maybe I can get Vincenzo to provide one for the plane ride.

She faced the intercom again. "Bianca!"

"Yes, Miss Minola."

More giggles? What's with this girl?

"Bianca, where does the itinerary say we're going?"

"Um, let's see, um"—a rustling of papers—"leaving at ten on the twenty-ninth from Bob Hope Airport, private charter, a Learjet."

Katharina waited a few seconds. "And what else?"

"That's all it says, Miss Minola."

"That's it?" *That can't be it!*

"That's all it says, Miss Minola."

Katharina scowled. "Did you even ask how we should dress for our destination?"

"No, Miss Minola."

Katharina sighed and whispered, "All this secrecy shit is driving me crazy."

Katharina then distinctly heard Bianca laugh. *That was no giggle. That was an outright guffaw!*

"What is so funny, Bianca?"

"Um, Scottie was just licking my toes, Miss Minola."

Katharina squinted at herself. "I thought you said he was asleep."

"He, uh, he just woke up, Miss Minola."

Bianca might finally be cracking up, Katharina thought. *And at the worst possible time. She hasn't even started packing my draws yet.* "Make sure you wash out Scottie's mouth with Scope before his bedtime."

"Yes, Miss Minola."

"And get back to work on my shoes, Bianca. Then start on my draws."

"Yes, Miss Minola. Right away. Thongs and then thongs. Right away, Miss Minola."

Katharina shook her head and batted her eyes. "'Thongs and then thongs.' The child has definitely lost it."

Still, she thought, *Bianca has lasted a long time, and she makes a mean chunky chicken salad sandwich. I just wish that she had a personality.*

Katharina raised her eyebrows.

With all this new money, I could probably afford two assistants again. Hmm. It's about time I had at least one man for an assistant, anyway. Maybe two men, neither of whom speaks English. Yeah. Muscular men, men with long legs and really long . . .

She cleared her throat.

Fingers.

She "dialed" one more number on her brush. "Hello, Julia? Katharina. How are you, *darling?* Guess what I'm about to do? Oh, you are so perceptive. You knew they wouldn't forget about me, didn't you? You know what they're paying me? Nope . . . nope . . . not even close . . . You're just going to giggle like a little schoolgirl when I tell you, and there's even something called 'full script approval' this time. . . ."

Chapter 8

Bianca had to rent the largest truck U-Haul had available to carry more than one hundred pieces of Katharina's luggage to Bob Hope Airport. They arrived an hour late because Katharina had fallen asleep in the bathtub, woke up "ashier than the moon," and needed nearly a full bottle of Vaseline Intensive Care Lotion to bring her skin "back from the brink of destruction!" Bianca followed behind Katharina, in her favorite tiger outfit, as she entered the jet.

"Where is everybody?" Katharina asked. "Where's the cabin crew?"

There would be no flight crew, as Vincenzo could not pay enough to *any* off-duty crew of flight attendants to serve and pamper Katharina Minola. The pilot and copilot locked themselves into the cockpit twenty minutes prior to her arrival and would not be opening the door for the entire flight.

While Katharina settled herself in a comfortable leather seat on the right side of the cabin, Bianca looked for two seats on the left side. She needed to peel off some of her clothes before she died of heat exhaustion. She was wearing long johns, two pairs of boxers, and two pairs of heavy wool socks under her jeans. Her thermal, waterproof boots barely fit over the socks. And she was wearing a sports bra, a long-sleeved flannel shirt, and a long-sleeved T-shirt under a heavy black oversized fisherman's sweater. She laid her 3-in-1 winter jacket, a hat and mittens stuffed inside a sleeve, on the seat next to her.

"Bianca, you are going to roast," Katharina said.

"I'm always cold, Miss Minola," Bianca said. *But not as cold as you're going to be when we get there,* she thought. *Can evil freeze solid? I'd like to see that.*

"I wonder where the crew is," Katharina said. "Probably out getting drunk." *I wish I drank. I'm getting motion sickness already.* She turned to the window and tried to pull down the shade. *Why won't this budge? If I look outside while this plane is moving, I will throw up! Why didn't I bring some Dramamine? This is why I freaked out on so many other flights! When the shades are up, my blood pressure shoots up and anything I eat won't stay down!*

Bianca stood, the button on her jeans threatening to ping off. "I don't think there's going to be a cabin crew, Miss Minola."

"Why not?"

They saw a tiger coming and ran away. "We really don't need them, do we? I can serve you just as well as they could." *And for nearly three thousand dollars a day, too!*

"Get me a cranberry and 7UP."

Bianca found the necessary ingredients in the tiny galley, made the mixture, contemplated sneezing into the glass, felt guilty and didn't sneeze, and brought the drink to Katharina.

"There they go," Katharina said, pointing out the

window and waving at Scottie, his tail wagging in a window of the plane next to theirs. *At least I think that's Scottie.* She squinted. "Is that an old lady with them?"

Who's that? Bianca thought. *Oh yeah. Penelope.* "Um, I think that's the certified dog walker, Miss Minola," Bianca said.

"She's too old to walk Scottie," Katharina said. "He'll run her to death."

"I hear she has fifty years' experience dealing with dogs," Bianca said. *Vincenzo is such a cute puppy. But if he's forty, how many years is that in dog years?*

"Hmm." Katharina tipped up her sunglasses. "Why do *they* get the bigger jet, anyway?"

"For all your luggage, Miss Minola." *And my Chacos! I wish I could be* in *them when they hit the beach.*

"Oh." Katharina turned her attention to her drink. "Straw, Bianca."

"Oh, sorry." Bianca found a straw, but it was long and skinny. "Um, it's not a crinkly straw like you like."

"It'll do."

Bianca put the straw in Katharina's drink and waited. Katharina took a sip. "It'll do."

Bianca sighed and sat. *That was a first.*

Katharina set her drink on a tray. "Scottie loves to ride in planes. I should have sent Scottie on his own plane."

Bianca fumed. The fact that people could afford to do that, and that a certain nameless musical diva actually did it, nauseated her to no end.

Blackout shades descended all around them automatically as the plane moved away from the terminal.

"Now that's classy," Katharina said, her heart rate slowing. "Lucentio Pictures knows how to treat a lady." *A lady who spazzes out on flights. I hope I can sleep.*

Bianca switched on some lights.

"Turn 'em off, Bianca," Katharina said, putting on her tiger-striped sleeping mask. "You weren't planning to read something, were you?"

Bianca glanced a moment at her backpack, the latest J. J. Murray novel she had been dying to read tucked inside. "Um, no, Miss Minola."

"Well, turn 'em off, then," Katharina said. "I need my rest."

Bianca switched them off.

"How long until we land?" Katharina asked.

We haven't even taken off yet, you wench! "About five hours, I think, Miss Minola."

"Do not disturb me until we get there, Bianca," Katharina said.

Sweet! "Yes, Miss Minola."

Bianca sat and loosened the button on her jeans. *Whew. Sorry, stomach. You'll thank me later.*

In twenty minutes the plane took off, and Bianca started to relax.

And think.

Do I feel bad about my role in Katharina's reawakening?

No.

Do I feel bad about making all this money and possibly harming my employer?

No.

Would I rather be anywhere else in the world at this moment?

Other than Yosemite or the beach, no.

Three for three. She shrugged. *I'm good.*

She looked over at her snoring employer. *She even sounds like a tiger. But wasting so much money on new luggage! With that kind of money, I could have fed and clothed three thousand children in Venezuela for a year!*

Do I feel guilty about what I've already done and what I am about to do?

No.
I am doing the right thing.
She loosened her boots and slipped them off.
Sorry about that, toes. You'll thank me later, too.

Fish, Vincenzo, and Walter had watched the entire plane scene from Pietro's estate in Ontario. Fish and Pietro had set up a wall of twenty-four monitors to the right and left of Pietro's huge stone fireplace, a 50-inch monitor over the mantel now capturing Katharina's sleeping form. Fish's "command center" consisted of a line of computers and servers covering several oak library tables, and Fish used a rolling chair to push himself from computer screen to computer screen while the others lounged on antique leather sofas.

"I didn't know you did that, Fish," Vincenzo said. "I didn't know you *could* do that."

Fish sipped a Coke and turned down the volume on Katharina's growling snores. "Technology is amazing, isn't it? I just thought it might be interesting to see before-and-after shots. Today the tiger, tomorrow, hopefully, the pussycat."

Walter approached the largest monitor, putting his hand on Katharina's forehead. "Did He who made the lamb make *she?*" He turned to the others. "I can't believe this is even her. I haven't seen her in so long. She looks . . . used up."

Fish shook his head. "She's still fine, and I can't believe Katharina didn't notice all of Bianca's obvious cold-weather gear. That girl looks like Frosty the Snow Woman."

Vincenzo stared only at Bianca. "I don't think Katharina even sees Bianca, and not just because of the sleeping mask she's wearing. Bianca is just an appliance to

Katharina. She's like tonsils or an appendix. She's there, but Katharina really doesn't need her."

Fish tapped a key, and the picture of Katharina grew. "Zooming in on the tiger." He looked carefully at her face. "You know, we could title the 'making of' segment 'The Tiger Comes to Canada.' "

Vincenzo smiled. "We could."

Walter sighed. "I haven't seen her in the flesh in years. She has changed so much. I hardly recognize her. She has always been a real piece of work, but this . . . She's almost not human. All that makeup."

Fish finished his Coke and crushed the can. "Too bad Pietro couldn't see this to warm him up, you know, get his anger going."

Vincenzo shook his head. "Pietro will warm up all right. He might even steam. I never told him the name of the actress he's picking up."

"Oh shit," Fish said. "I wish I had put a camera in his Suburban. We'll see him when he gets on the plane, though. That should be fun."

Walter turned to Fish. "You know they have a history."

Fish blinked. "And not a good kind of history, huh?"

Walter shook his head.

Fish smiled broadly. "Oh, the horror . . . the horror . . ."

Chapter 9

The Learjet touched down smoothly at Val-d'Or Airport in Quebec, and Bianca had to whisper Katharina awake. Bianca couldn't shake or touch her—that was one of Katharina's most important rules—so she had to make a fool of herself in front of the customs agent, who had graciously come onto the plane to check their passports.

"Miss Minola, Miss Minola, wake up, Miss Minola," Bianca whispered. *Wake up, you snoring cow!* "Miss Minola, Miss Minola, wake up, Miss Minola, we're here, Miss Minola."

Bianca turned to the customs agent. "She's, um, she's a heavy sleeper." *Because she was up all night before we left, fussing at me!* Bianca retrieved their passports from her backpack and handed them to the agent.

"She looks familiar," the agent said with only a trace of a French accent. He looked at Katharina's passport photo. "I must see her face."

But you'll turn to stone, Bianca thought. *I can't have an international incident like that!*

"Miss Minola, Miss Minola, please wake up, Miss Minola."

Katharina stirred, sliding off her mask.

The customs agent took a closer look at Katharina, stamped the passports, and left the plane.

"What was that about?" Katharina asked.

"Oh, that was just a customs agent, Miss Minola. He took care of us."

A moment later, Pietro strode into the cabin holding two black blindfolds. He froze when he saw Katharina. *Her! Of all the people on this planet, it has to be her! I left the United States because of her! I gave up any ideas of acting because of her! I left the business because of her! Thanks a lot, Vincenzo.*

Bianca blinked at the huge man dressed completely in black, each of his broad shoulders bigger than her head. *Definitely another Lucentio, definitely Italian, and definitely European, his mouth open for the flies. Why do some European men do that? Vincenzo did it a couple times . . . when I was trying to embarrass him. Looks as if this Lucentio has all his teeth. Why does he look so pissed off? What's he got to be angry about? He didn't just fly five hours in the company of Katharina Minola. Dag, I'd hate for him to be mad at me! Does he have only one eyebrow? No. There's a millimeter gap. Is his face dirty? No. That's just his stubble. Dark, penetrating eyes. A jaw that could cut wood. I'm glad Vincenzo has softer features. My hands would probably bleed if I touched his face.*

Katharina sat up. "Are you our security?" *He's huge!* Katharina thought. *I should hire him as a bodyguard when this is over. Probably dumb as bat shit, but okay looking. Should be in some Mafia movie. I bet he'd be mean enough to keep the paparazzi away once I'm famous again. I'll have to get his name.*

Pietro held his breath. He didn't even want to breathe Katharina's air.

"Well?" Katharina asked. "Are you or are you not our security?"

"This reminds me of an old Clint Eastwood movie," Fish said. "What was it called?"

"The Good, the Bad and the Ugly," Walt said.

"That's the one. It has that stare-down scene." Fish pointed at Bianca on the screen. "She's good." He pointed at Katharina. "She's bad, and I mean that in a good way." He tapped Pietro's head. "And he's seriously ugly. No offense, Vincenzo, but your brother is a brute."

Pietro took a step forward. *"Parli italiano?"*

Bianca smiled. *"Sì."*

Pietro nodded at Bianca. *"Come stai?"*

"Bene, grazie," Bianca said.

"I didn't know we'd need subtitles," Fish said. "What are they saying, Vincenzo?"

Vincenzo laughed. "I didn't know Bianca spoke Italian."

"What are they saying?" Walt asked.

"Just 'How ya doin'?' 'I'm fine,'" Vincenzo said. "What . . . What an amazing turn of events."

Katharina stood and put on her sunglasses. "Hello? Yo! Over here."

Pietro glowered at Katharina.

"Answer my question," Katharina demanded.

Bianca looked from Katharina to Pietro. "I'll, um, I'll ask him. I don't think he understands English very well."

Pietro nodded slightly.

Katharina stretched her back. "And ask him if those are blindfolds."

Bianca shrugged at Pietro. "My Italian is a little rusty," she said in Italian.

Pietro nodded. "Sounds fine to me," he said, also in Italian. "How was your flight?"

Bianca bit her lip. "What do you think?" she asked in Italian. "I had diva duty the entire time. Luckily, she slept for most of the flight."

"Bianca," Katharina said, "I'm not asking you again. Is he my security, and are those blindfolds?"

"Yes, Miss Minola," Bianca said. "But he's mostly our driver." She turned to Pietro. *"Come ti chiami?"*

"Mi chiamo . . . Alessandro," Pietro said.

Bianca turned to Katharina. "His name is Alessandro. We're to put the blindfolds on for our journey to the set."

Katharina marched up to Pietro. "What for?"

Pietro turned to Bianca. "Tell her Vincenzo's orders," he said in Italian.

"What about Vincenzo?" Katharina asked.

"Oh," Bianca said. "It's Vincenzo's idea, mainly for your benefit. Vincenzo feels that the less you know about the location, the better."

Katharina snatched a blindfold from Pietro's hand. "Whatever." She tied on the blindfold loosely. "There. Happy, Fonzi?"

"His name is Alessandro, Miss Minola," Bianca said.

"I don't care," Katharina whined. *Just get me off this plane!*

Pietro stepped forward and readjusted Katharina's blindfold tightly.

"Hey, Bianca!" Katharina yelled. "Not so damn tight!"

Bianca smiled. "Um, sorry, Miss Minola."

"Did you see that?" Fish asked. "The way Katharina's head got smaller! I didn't think that was possible."

Pietro and Bianca were talking rapidly in Italian on the screen.

Vincenzo laughed. "Oh, this is better than I ever could have planned."

"What are they saying?" Walt asked.

Vincenzo couldn't stop smiling. "Pietro says for Bianca to put on her blindfold. Bianca says, 'You can walk me into a wall if you like, put me out of my misery. I can take a hit.' And Pietro says, 'I should walk *her* into a wall. She hasn't had a hit in years!' "

"Man," Fish said, "that's cold."

Walt looked at his watch. "When are they arriving at the set?"

"After dark," Vincenzo said. "I better get going."

"Man, I wish you could stay," Fish said. "If those two spew Italian at each other all the way to the cabin, we won't know what they're saying."

Vincenzo put on his coat. "You'll just have to wait for the translation." He sighed deeply. "Well, gentlemen. Our experiment is really about to begin. Are all systems go?"

Fish let his fingers roam speedily over the computer keyboard. "All cameras are up and running, zooms operative . . . Sound is a go." He paused and listened to the wind whipping through the trees. "Yeah, we're ready."

Vincenzo shook their hands. "I don't know when we'll get to be in the same room together like this, hopefully not too long. Use the transmitter if you need to. Just remember that only I have a walkie-talkie."

"We'll only squawk you in an emergency," Fish said. "We got everything under control."

Every little thing *is under control,* Vincenzo thought. *Just not every*one *yet.* "Then, gentlemen, it's showtime."

Pietro led Bianca and Katharina to his black Chevrolet Suburban parked on the tarmac. He removed Bianca's blindfold so Bianca could help Katharina into the backseat and shut the door behind her. He pulled Bianca to him in front of the SUV.

"You can't see out the windows," Pietro whispered, "and there's a divider between me and you two, so you can tell her to take off her blindfold if you want to."

Bianca frowned. "I really don't want her to see me. I like to make faces at her."

Pietro smiled. "Then have her keep her blindfold on."

They got in, shut their doors, and Pietro roared away.

"Can I take off my blindfold now?" Katharina asked.

"Um, no, Miss Minola," Bianca said. "Alessandro said not to. The windows aren't tinted. He says it's illegal to tint windows in this country."

"What about the others?" Katharina asked. "Have they landed yet?"

"Um, Alessandro said their plane had engine trouble and had to turn back," Bianca said.

"*Sì,*" Pietro said.

"He says it should be here tomorrow or the day after," Bianca added.

"I'm glad we weren't on *that* plane," Katharina said.

"I'd be raising holy hell if I were them." *Can you be banned from a charter flight?* "Did you pack a separate bag with my necessities?"

Bianca smiled. "Oh no! I didn't! I am *so* sorry, Miss Minola. I just assumed both planes would make it here."

Katharina shook her head. "Ain't that some shit."

Bianca had to rub it in more. "I wish you had asked me to pack that bag, Miss Minola."

"Do I have to think of every damn thing?" Katharina yelled. "What the hell do I pay you for?"

Bianca stifled a giggle. *Um, technically, wench, you aren't paying me at all for the next sixty days.* "I'm sorry, Miss Minola. Perhaps they'll have clothes and toiletries for you there at your suite."

"They had *better*," Katharina said.

Bianca and Pietro arrived at the same thought simultaneously: *Not.*

Thankfully, the first part of the journey was quiet. They traveled on decent roads for several hours, driving into the sunset. After taking Highway 11 north for another smooth half hour, Pietro backtracked on Highway 101 east for a bit before turning onto a series of butt-cracking, vertebrae-breaking, spine-smacking, unnamed gravel, dirt, and rock roads.

As Katharina held on, she yelled, "Is Fonzi wearing a blindfold, too, or what? Tell him to keep us on the damn road!" *And I'll try to keep from puking! Think still thoughts, think still thoughts . . .*

"I think this *is* the road, Miss Minola," Bianca said, gripping the door handle tightly.

Pietro spewed several Italian curses.

"Why is he fussing?" Katharina asked. "Shit! We're

the ones getting our bones broken! Ask him how much farther."

Bianca asked in Italian. Pietro told her it would be about a half hour.

"Only a few more *minutes,* Miss Minola," Bianca said. *I am having too much fun!*

A few minutes later, Katharina said, "A few minutes is up. Why aren't we there?"

"I'll ask, Miss Minola." She tapped on the divider and said in Italian, "I haven't had this much fun in years!"

"I should have brought a muzzle," Pietro said in Italian.

Bianca bit her tongue. "Um, I misunderstood Alessandro, Miss Minola. He actually said about half an hour."

"Mother—"

A huge bump ripped the rest of Katharina's curse from her mouth.

"This is some serious bullshit here," Katharina muttered. "I am not going to take much more of this!"

The road calmed down somewhat for the next half hour, and Pietro brought the Suburban to a halt a few feet from Curtis the mule, who was tied to a fence at the beginning of the path to the "set."

"Finally," Katharina said, removing her blindfold. *Hey . . . these windows are tinted. What gives? Not that I would have looked outside, anyway, but . . . Oh. Maybe they're just dirty.*

Bianca got out and shut her door. She immediately put on her hat and mittens while Pietro stretched his back.

"She's not getting out?" Pietro whispered.

"She expects someone to open her door," Bianca whispered.

"That isn't going to happen," Pietro said, going to Curtis and patting him on the back. "Sorry, old buddy.

You're gonna have a passenger in a minute. And if you feel like bucking her off, you go right ahead."

"Bianca!" Katharina yelled. "Open the damn door!"

Bianca stepped around a juicy cold puddle and opened the door.

"About time," Katharina hissed, stepping out into the icy mud, her right tiger stiletto stuck fast in the muck, her bare foot poised in the air. "Mother . . . Jesus, would you look at that!"

"I'll get it, Miss Minola." Bianca pulled the stiletto out of the muck and examined it. "It's not too bad." *It's just slightly ruined and forever useless.*

Katharina held out her foot. "Well, put it back on."

Bianca slid on the stiletto, mud dripping.

Katharina took another step—and lost her left stiletto the same way.

"Motherf—!"

"I'll get it," Bianca interrupted, and she replaced the second stiletto.

Katharina hobbled around to Pietro. "You got a lot of damn nerve parking in the mud like that! I'll get you fired! No, I'll do better than that. I'll get you killed. I know people, oh yes. One phone call, and Fonzi is gone!"

Pietro only smiled.

Katharina finally noticed the mule. "What the hell is that?"

Chapter 10

Pietro patted Curtis. "Is *mulo*, Curtis."

Katharina hobbled backward, nearly falling into Bianca's arms. "I know what a mule is, Fonzi. And what a stupid name for a mule! Curtis isn't even an Italian name!"

"Italian name!" echoed through the night.

"Jesus, where the hell are we?" Katharina asked. "The Alps?"

Bianca rolled her eyes. "I don't think so, Miss Minola."

In Italian, Pietro said, " 'Curtis' is the only name he responds to."

"He says," Bianca said, "that Curtis is an American mule."

Katharina sighed, and even her sigh echoed. "Whatever. What's it doing here?" *Wherever* here *is. Are we in Iceland? No, we'd still be in the air. I'll bet we're in Alaska.*

"*Mulo* is your ride," Pietro said.

Katharina took off her sunglasses and waved them at Pietro. "The hell it is. I'll wait for a golf cart."

Pietro smiled. "No."

"No?" Katharina turned to Bianca. "Is he saying 'no' to me?"

"Yes," Bianca said. "How much farther?" she asked quickly in Italian.

In Italian, Pietro said, "Sorry to say about an hour through the woods, but only if she rides the mule. It could take two hours or more if she walks on those stupid heels."

I cannot last another two hours! Bianca thought. "Only a few minutes, Miss Minola, but he suggests strongly that you ride the mule to keep your feet dry."

Katharina put on her sunglasses. "Really? It's too late for that!" She shivered. "It's freaking cold, Bianca!" She stepped closer to Curtis and looked at Curtis's eyes. "What's up with the mule's eyes?" *Blue-green? What's this bull—*

Pietro chose this moment to grab Katharina from behind and lift her high into the air and onto Curtis's back.

"Bianca!" Katharina yelled.

Several wolves howled in reply.

"Bianca, did you see that? Did you see him touch me?"

Bianca didn't answer. *Pietro has to be strong as an ox to lift that much evil off the ground. I hope he didn't get a hernia.*

Katharina pointed her long, curved nails at Pietro. "You tell him that no one touches me, and I mean no one." She looked around her. "And also tell him that I do not ride mules!"

"Mulo rapido," Pietro said, and he began pulling Curtis toward the path.

"He says the mule is fast, Miss Minola," Bianca said, trailing behind.

"What the—" Katharina put her hands on Curtis's back. "I have a brain, Bianca. I know what *'rapido'* means. Doesn't Fonzi have a golf cart, a four-wheeler, something else?"

Pietro smiled, and in Italian said, "We have to get moving. The temperature is dropping, and I can only take so much of this witch."

"He says he doesn't, Miss Minola," Bianca said. "This, um, this is the best way to travel here."

"Where are we, Russia? Shit, it's cold! Give me your boots, Bianca."

She's high! "They're far too big for your feet, Miss Minola."

"So they'll fit me just fine," Katharina whined. "And give me your mittens and your hat, too."

Bianca removed her boots, caught up to Curtis, and took off one of Katharina's stilettos.

"Hurry!" Katharina screamed.

Bianca gritted her teeth. "You want some nice wool socks, too, Miss Minola?"

"Yes," Katharina said.

I should have asked for two hundred thousand dollars. Thirty more thousand for pain and suffering. Bianca took off one pair of her socks, put them on Katharina's feet, slid on the boots, and handed her mittens and hat to Katharina.

"And your coat," Katharina said.

Bianca gave Katharina her coat. *Yeah, this is going well. I may die before I get a chance to quit.*

"It's about time you earned your keep, Bianca," Katharina said. "Why are you so far behind? Keep up, Bianca!"

Fish zoomed in on Bianca's face. He and Walt had been watching the scene using the infrared. "I hope I don't say this a lot," Fish said, "but Katharina is a witch!"

He zoomed out and saw Bianca swinging Katharina's stilettos back and forth. "Go on, girl. Let 'em fly."

Bianca tossed the stilettos into the darkness and wiped her hands on her pants.

"Thata girl," Fish said. "Some squirrel will have a nice tiger-fur-lined nest this winter."

"Bianca certainly is a trooper, huh?" Walt said. "She's only wearing that sweater, some socks, and a smile."

"She ain't smiling," Fish said. "Her teeth are chattering. Pietro should have worn a coat to give to her. Bianca's shivering her ass off."

"And that's not acting, either," Walt said. "It's *that* cold."

Fish hit a few buttons on the computer and sat back. "I've programmed it so we can just look at the big screen while we follow their progress."

Walt joined Fish at the command center. He pointed at two metal switches mounted under the table. "What are these two switches for? The ones with tape on them."

"Oh," Fish said, "those are just backups."

"In case what happens?"

Fish sighed. "In case something crazy happens."

"Oh," Walt said. "Can you turn up the volume?"

Fish clicked and dragged his mouse. "Increasing volume . . ."

"This jackass smells like thousand-year-old shit!" Katharina was saying.

Bianca and Pietro remained silent.

"My pants are ruined! Zip me all the way up, Bianca. My ears are cold. Doesn't this thing have a hood? It does? Then put it on for me. Why are we going so slow? If I don't get warm soon, I'm going to lose my mind . . ."

* * *

"Decreasing volume," Fish said.

Walt stopped Fish's hand. "No. Leave it up. It will make me appreciate my wife more."

"You're a masochist, Walt," Fish said.

"That I am," Walt said.

The trio and Curtis passed Cabin 2, and Katharina looked back with her mouth wide open. "That's not my whatever that is?"

"*Il mio cabina,*" Pietro said.

Bianca's teeth chattered audibly now. "It's his c-c-cabin, M-Miss Minola."

Katharina finally took off her sunglasses, holding them out for Bianca to take.

Bianca took the sunglasses, made sure Katharina wasn't watching, and tossed them into the woods.

"What's wrong with your voice, Bianca?" Katharina asked. "You can't be cold. Look at Fonzi. He's only wearing a damn sweater just like you."

"I'm f-f-fine, M-Miss Minola," Bianca said, hoping a bear would tear out of the woods and attack the tiger-lady so she could get her coat back. "Really I am."

Twenty minutes later, they reached Cabin 3. Pietro tried to lift Katharina off Curtis, but Katharina slid quickly to the other side, rubbing her butt while Bianca shivered uncontrollably beside her.

"What, Bianca?" Katharina spat. "You didn't have to ride on a jackass led by a jackass."

Pietro opened the cabin door. "*Fa freddo.*"

Bianca's heart sank. "He says it's c-c-cold in there."

Katharina took the steps to the porch. "Tell him 'no shit.' "

"Can I quit now?" Bianca asked Pietro in Italian.

J. J. Murray

Pietro shook his head. "You signed a contract," he said in Italian.

"Um," Bianca said, staring hard at Pietro, "Alessandro says he's going to build you a nice, hot fire."

Pietro nodded.

"Chop chop, then, Fonzi." Katharina walked past Pietro to the doorway of the dark cabin, searching for a light switch with her left hand. "Where's the damn light switch?"

Pietro disappeared into the cabin and returned with a kerosene lamp, lighting it in front of Katharina with a wooden match struck against the door.

Katharina stared into the cabin. She saw only a simple wooden table and two chairs in front of a stone fireplace, three shut doors along the far wall. A fax machine sat on the floor in a corner.

"There must be some mistake," she whispered. "I was promised a four-room suite."

Pietro smiled. "Yes, sweet *cabina*."

Chapter 11

While Katharina stood mainly in place cursing Lucentio Pictures in general and Vincenzo in specific, Pietro started a small fire in the fireplace, Bianca as close to the mesh screen as her socks would allow.

"There has been a *major* screwup here, Fonzi!" Katharina yelled in a more lucid moment. "No electricity? Are you kidding, Fonzi? What Third World country is this?"

Pietro stood, towering over Katharina. "Is Canada. I am Alessandro."

"Where's the four-room suite, Fonzi?" Katharina asked.

"Is four," Pietro said. He counted the doors and then pointed to the floor. "Four." He touched his chest. "Alessandro, not Fonzi."

Katharina laughed. "Where's the bathroom, *Fonzi?*"

Pietro's eyes narrowed. *"Che?"*

Katharina stepped closer. "The shitter. The toilet. The ladies' room. The freaking place where I can freaking drop off the kids."

Pietro's eyes narrowed even more. *"Che?"*

Katharina pecked Pietro's chest with a sharp nail. "The room de *bath*, Fonzi."

Bianca walked over and opened the middle door. "It's in here, Miss Minola."

Katharina wheeled around and went into the bathroom, where Bianca had found a little box of matches and lit another kerosene lamp. A large white tub took up most of the room; an ancient toilet rested next to a tiny sink. "It's a . . . it's a bathtub," Katharina muttered. "I must be getting punked." She turned to Bianca. "Where are the cameras?"

Everywhere, Miss Minola, Bianca wanted to say.

Katharina turned the knob marked HOT.

Nothing happened.

Katharina laughed, but it was not a nice-sounding laugh. It was the laugh of a maniacal, deranged serial killer about to go on a little killing spree. "No hot water, huh?"

Pietro stood in the doorway. "No."

"Uh-huh," Katharina said. "Very funny." She strode out of the bathroom and over to the fire. "Okay, where are the cameras?"

"She's looking right at one!" Fish said. "She's on to us already?"

Walt shrugged and gripped the table in front of him. "She can't be. Can she?"

"I'm on one of those shows, aren't I?" Katharina asked. *Serves me right for being so gullible! Right, they're going to give me five million bucks.* "Aren't I?"

Bianca kept a straight face, her eyes averted to the

pine plank floor. Pietro, however, stared hard into Katharina's eyes.

"Bianca, tell me I'm on one of those shows," Katharina said.

Bianca looked up briefly. "I think we're on the set, Miss Minola. I think this *is* your cabin."

"No," Katharina said with determination and tight lips. "It cannot be. No one treats me like this. I wanted a nice, smooth ride here, but what do I get? A roller coaster that gave me another crack in my ass. I wanted a nice, quiet golf cart to take me to my cabin, but what do I get? A mule that has never bathed and farts every other step. I wanted a four-room suite with everything I asked for in my letter, but what do I get? Abraham Lincoln's first house! I also wanted a hot shower after my horrific trip, but no, there's a tub the size of Connecticut in here that can only be filled up with cold-ass water!" She stalked toward Pietro. "I want to speak to Vincenzo. *Now.*"

Pietro didn't move. "Vincenzo, no. Alessandro."

Katharina looked around. "Where's the phone?"

"No *telefono*," Pietro said.

Katharina held out her hand. "Bianca, my cell."

Bianca fumbled with her backpack and came out with Katharina's purple cell phone.

Katharina snatched the phone and flipped it open. "No signal. Are we on planet earth anymore? Where the hell *isn't* there a cell phone signal?"

Pietro shrugged and left the cabin, leaving the door wide open behind him.

"Where does he think he's going?" Katharina snarled.

Bianca sat in the chair closest to the dying fire. "I hope to get some more wood for our fire."

*   *   *

"Are Bianca's lips turning blue?" Walt asked.

"Zooming," Fish said. "Yeah. That's not good." He pressed the squawk button on the transmitter. "Vincenzo? This is Fish."

A moment later, Vincenzo answered. "Is there something wrong already?"

"Vinnie," Fish said, "they're safely in their cabin, but they have to have more wood in there. Pietro's doing the best he can, but Bianca's lips are turning blue."

"I'm already on my way there," Vincenzo said. "And don't squawk me any time I'm around Katharina unless it's an extreme emergency, okay? I want her to feel more isolated."

"She can't get much more isolated than this, Vinnie," Fish said.

"Don't forget the wig," Walt said.

"The wig is on," Vincenzo said. "And I hate it."

Fish laughed. "Did I ever tell you how much you look like Andy Warhol in that wig?"

"Yes, Fish."

"But your eyebrows are black," Fish said. "Maybe you should bleach them bushes."

"Go play with your buttons," Vincenzo said.

Katharina still hadn't sat. "I don't know whose idea of a joke this is, but I am *not* staying here tonight!"

She is a broken record! "Where else can we go, Miss Minola?" Bianca asked. "Like you said, we're in the middle of nowhere, it's dark outside, and the only way out of here is by mule."

Katharina adjusted Bianca's hat. "Someone is going to get fired for this. You watch."

Pietro returned with more wood, adding it to the fire. He still left the door open.

"Yo, Fonzi," Katharina said.

Pietro stood. "Alessandro. You say."

"I will not *say*," Katharina sneered. "And why don't you close the door? Were you born in a stinking barn?"

Pietro took a giant step toward Katharina. "Yes. I was. So was Jesus."

Yes, He was, but it wasn't this freaking cold in Bethlehem! Katharina looked away for a moment, then stared up at him. "I don't like anyone grittin' on me, Fonzi. Didn't anyone teach you that it was rude to stare?" She poked him in the chest for good measure, but it was a half-hearted attempt. "No one looks me in the eye."

Pietro took Katharina's finger from his chest, and in Italian, said, "I'd really not like to look into your evil eyes of doom, but I have no choice. You are the Devil incarnate, and I do not wish you to take me to Hell."

Bianca bit her tongue so hard she almost drew blood.

"What the hell was that all about?" Katharina asked Bianca.

Bianca raised her eyebrows. "He says he will bring no more wood tonight if you do not show him more respect."

Katharina slapped her hand on the table. "Show *him* respect? Is he kidding? He's the freaking help! Screw him!"

Pietro threw up his hands and talked with them in Italian. "You tell her she cannot have my other wood, either."

Bianca drew blood from her tongue that time.

Katharina tapped the table with her nails. "Well?"

If I say exactly what he said, I will never stop laughing. "Um, he says that he is paid to keep the cabin warm, to keep you fed, and to keep you safe. He says he is not paid to sleep with you."

Bianca watched Katharina's mouth fall a few inches.

Priceless, she thought. *That look is worth the pain of this whole trip so far. I hope I don't have frostbite. Do I still have all my toes? I do. Whew.*

Katharina couldn't find her voice at first. "What the—?" She threw up her own hands. "Well, you tell Fonzi that it would be his *privilege* just to smell my feet. Tell him there are millions of men out there who would give their left *nut* to be in the same area code with me. You tell him that."

Bianca smiled. "It really is cold in here," she said in Italian. "We're from L.A., remember? She has my boots, my mittens, my hat, and my coat. My toes are numb."

Pietro laughed heartily, shaking his head at Katharina. In Italian he said, "The fire will warm up the cabin in no time. I left the door open to create a draft so it would fire up more quickly because some of the wood is wet. There are thick down comforters on the beds. But it is not very cold at all tonight. Tomorrow, it will be colder. Later this week, it will be much colder with snow in the forecast."

Katharina blinked at Bianca. "Well?"

Pietro nodded.

"He says," Bianca said, searching for the right words, "he says that he has a girlfriend a thousand times sexier and bolder than you are."

Pietro blinked several times and eventually smiled. *"Bene."*

Katharina rolled her neck. "Tell him his mule doesn't count."

That made no sense, Pietro thought.

"That made no sense," Bianca said in Italian.

Pietro nodded.

"You know," Bianca said in Italian, "you can say just about whatever you want, and I can embroider it a little. I was an English major, after all."

"Just don't get too carried away," Pietro said in Italian. "It can't look as if I'm surprised at the translation."

"What the hell, Bianca?" Katharina asked. "What is Fonzi saying?"

Bianca winced and turned to Katharina. "He says his mule is a boy mule and that even his boy mule is a thousand times sexier than you are."

Katharina Minola, diva, didn't say a single word, pivoted, stormed to the bathroom, and slammed the door.

We're winning, Pietro thought. *But it's oh-so-early in the game.*

Chapter 12

"Amazing," Pietro whispered.

"Fun," Bianca whispered.

Pietro motioned to the door, and the two of them left the porch and walked several feet into the darkness.

"Maybe we should close the door now," Bianca whispered.

"That wood is really wet," Pietro said. "If I don't leave the door open, you'll get smoked out."

"Just put lots of extra wood by the fireplace, okay?"

Pietro nodded. "You'll get used to the cold in no time."

Bianca looked back at the cabin. "Yeah, I've had a lot of practice working for her." She smiled at Pietro. "What's next, Alessandro?"

Pietro smiled. "Tell her she arrived too late for dinner and that it had to be thrown out."

Bianca pouted. "I'm hungry, too. My stomach is speaking in tongues here."

"We have you covered," Pietro said. "She will take the biggest bedroom, yes?"

Bianca nodded.

"In the smaller bedroom, the door on the far left, between the mattress and box spring are some raisins and granola bars. Vincenzo's idea. You made an impression on him." *And me, too,* Pietro thought. *I hope they're paying Bianca well.* "Chew quietly, though."

"What reason do I give her for the food getting thrown out?" Bianca asked.

"I've had trouble with black bears up here," Pietro said. "Really. If they smell any kind of food, they'll come clawing. They can be very mischievous and destructive."

Bianca grabbed Pietro's arm. "Can they smell what's under my mattress?"

Pietro shook his head. "The raisins are in a big plastic bag, and wrappers cover all the granola bars. Just make sure you seal the big bag tightly."

Bianca sighed and patted Pietro's arm. "I better get back inside."

"You're doing wonderfully," Pietro whispered.

"Grazie," Bianca said with a bow.

Katharina was still in the bathroom when Bianca shut the door to the cabin. Bianca added another branch to the fire and warmed her hands. Smoke curled almost immediately around the branch she had just added.

"Where's my dinner?" Katharina yelled from the bathroom.

Bianca slid over to the bathroom door. "Alessandro said we're too late for dinner and that he had to throw it out."

"What? What the hell for?"

Bianca did a little victory dance outside the door. "He says there are bears up here, huge grizzly bears, some weighing a thousand pounds and standing over nine feet tall. If they smell even the slightest scent of food at this hour, they might break in and attack us."

"Grizzlies? How far north in Canada are we?"

I have no idea, but . . . "Alessandro told me we're only a hundred miles from the Arctic Circle."

"I'm *sitting* on the Arctic Circle, Bianca," Katharina said. "Well, you tell Fonzi that I want food, I want it hot, I want a lot, and I want it *now*. Also tell him that he must stay out on the porch tonight to keep us safe from the grizzlies."

Pietro banged into the cabin, and Bianca jumped. He dumped another load of wood by the fireplace. "This gives me an idea for breakfast," he whispered.

"You heard her?" Bianca whispered.

"All of northern Ontario and half of Quebec heard her," Pietro whispered.

Bianca smiled. "We're having bear stew, aren't we?"

Pietro nodded.

The toilet flushed.

"Vincenzo said you were sharp," Pietro said louder, and in Italian.

Katharina opened the bathroom door, shutting it quickly behind her. "What did he say about Vincenzo?"

"Um," Bianca said, turning away from Katharina, "only that Vincenzo didn't put it in Alessandro's contract to guard us from the porch. Alessandro is only one cabin away."

"A half mile away at least!" Katharina shouted. "What good can he do for us there?"

In Italian, Pietro said, "I've had just about enough of her tonight. I pity you, I really do. You'll be in my prayers. Will you be up early?"

Bianca nodded.

"Don't be surprised," Pietro continued in Italian, "if you hear a shotgun blast at dawn."

A rapid knocking sound on the door made Katharina and Bianca jump.

"Who the *hell* would be out here on a night like this?" Katharina asked. *Besides gullible me.*

Pietro opened the door to Vincenzo, dressed completely in black except for a curly blond wig sticking out from under his knit cap. "Hello! I am *direttore.*"

I will have nightmares, Bianca thought. *Though the wig does make him look younger.*

I will have nightmares, Katharina thought. *Another freaking Italian!*

Vincenzo bounced into the room and shook Bianca's hand. "Oh, but your hand is so cold!" He turned to Pietro. "Make the fire hotter!"

Pietro ducked his head and nodded. "I try, but wood wet."

"You try? Get dry wood!" Vincenzo grabbed Pietro's arm, cursed him in Italian, and dragged him from the cabin. He shut the door behind them.

"Thanks a lot," Pietro whispered as they walked down the path. "Why her? Why Katharina Minola? Why do you want to save that parody of a human being in there?"

Vincenzo grabbed and hugged his brother. "It's good to see you, Pietro."

Pietro stepped back. "Yeah, whatever. Why her, Vinnie? Of all the women on this earth, why does it have to be her?"

"I think she's worth saving, brother." He squeezed Pietro's arm. "There is much more to her than meets the eye."

Pietro frowned. "That is the scariest thing you have ever said to me. And by the way, you look ridiculous."

"*Grazie,*" Vincenzo said. "Go get some dry wood from your place and bring it back. I better go inside and get better acquainted with my star."

"Good luck," Pietro said, and he turned and walked away slowly. "Oh, by the way, I've taken the name Alessandro."

"I've been watching," Vincenzo said. "Um, how slowly are you going to walk, brother?"

Pietro stopped and turned. "Dude, I need a break from that . . . from *that*. I'll be gone at least ten minutes, maybe more."

Vincenzo reentered the cabin and stopped in front of Katharina. "I am so sorry about that. My cousin, Alessandro, he is, how you say, not a people person."

"His mule is nicer," Katharina said.

One of the reasons we got the mule. "It is so good to see the great Katharina Minola," Vincenzo said. "I trust your journey was pleasant?"

Katharina only blinked and shook her head. "It was the worst journey I've ever had. Who and what are you, anyway?"

"I am Luigi Gremio, the *direttore*," Vincenzo said. "But my friends call me Sly."

"I don't believe this shit," Katharina said, finally slumping into a chair. "Let me guess. This is your first picture, isn't it, Sly?"

Vincenzo smiled broadly at Bianca. "Oh no. I direct many, many movies in Italy. Um, my first was *Un tavolo per due*."

Ha! Bianca thought. "A Table for Two." *Funny!*

"You have not heard of it?" Vincenzo asked.

Katharina only sighed.

"It won two awards for best set design and cinematography. My next movie, which was a *big* hit in my country," Vincenzo said, "was *Desidero farsi tagliare i capelli*."

"I Want a Haircut!" Bianca thought, *I hope he stops*

doing that. I am glad that he hates that wig, though. It might look good on me . . .

Vincenzo looked at Katharina. "You have not heard of it, either?"

Katharina shook her head.

"It was *comico*. Funny. Ha-ha! Won awards for best costuming." He smiled again at Bianca. "I have just finished what I think is my best film. It is called *Gabinetto freddo*."

Bianca burst out laughing. *His best film was* Cold Toilet! *I am in a comedy, all right!*

Vincenzo nodded at Bianca. "You have seen it!"

Bianca nodded. *And Katharina just sat on it. I'll bet it's even colder now because of her.*

Vincenzo moved closer to Bianca. "And what was your favorite part?"

Bianca widened her eyes. "The bathroom scene with the huge, hungry wildebeest inside trying to, um, trying to take a bath. That was hysterical."

Vincenzo turned to Katharina. "Is also *comico*. I am so honored to be working—"

"Enough of this chitchat, um, Sly," Katharina interrupted. "Where's the damn script?"

"It is not here?" Vincenzo asked. He trotted over to the fax machine. "It is supposed to be here!" He pressed several buttons, with each press a tiny beep cutting into the air. "It seems to be on. What is today?"

"The twenty-ninth," Bianca said.

Vincenzo smacked his forehead with his hand. "Ah. So. The script will be here tomorrow. I have lost a day from the time change. I only fly in from Ravenna, Italy, today."

Hey, that's my daddy's hometown, Bianca thought. *Has Vincenzo been researching me? I'm flattered. A little. Maybe*

*he's stalking me and wearing a blond wig to disguise his in-
tentions. Would I mind him stalking me on a dark night
like—*

Katharina groaned so loudly that Bianca jerked in
her seat. "I am *not* happy, Sly."

"Oh no," Vincenzo said. "Why not, Miss Katharina?"

Katharina stood. "Actually, Sly, I'm pretty damn
pissed." She placed each hand on the table, palms
down. "Where is the humidifier? I have very dry skin.
Oh, right. There's no electricity. Where are the flowers?
Oh, right. They'd already be dead in this freezer of a
cabin. Where is the all-black furniture? Oh, right. We're
in the Dark Ages up here where everything is made of
sticks, stones, and branches. Where are the blackout
drapes? Oh, right. There's no need. It's black as shit
outside. But where . . . is my *freaking* . . . dinner? How
hard could *that* be to have ready for me?"

Vincenzo blinked and looked directly at Bianca. "I
was not told this. Vincenzo did not tell me all this."

Bianca looked away. *This is too funny!*

"We must fix this at once!" *I should have been an actor,*
Vincenzo thought, shooting his right index finger high
into the air.

Fish pantomimed making a phone call. "Overacting
Anonymous? Yes. I have a pickup in Cabin 3. Bring a
straightjacket. Yeah, you got it. He's a blond Italian."

"But Katharina's buying it," Walt said.

"Only because she recognizes the diva in *him*."

Katharina bent down and bounced her forehead off
the table. "Well, shit, Sly, send somebody *out* to get dinner, then."

"Oh no, Miss Minola," Bianca said. "No food after dark. The grizzly bears, remember? They're very vicious."

Vincenzo nodded. *Grizzly bears? There are no grizzlies here . . . are there?*

Katharina turned her head and laid her cheek on the table. "Just one little . . . sandwich?"

"Bears have a great sense of smell, Miss Minola," Bianca said. "I'm sure they'll be able to smell the bread—"

Katharina raised a hand. "Well, can't you send out for something *else*—wrapped up in plastic or something?" She raised her head and looked at Vincenzo. "All I want is a simple sandwich. I'll even settle for bologna. A grilled cheese. Anything."

"The closest store is ninety miles away," Vincenzo said.

Pietro burst in with another armload of wood, slamming it on the floor and making Katharina shoot up off the table.

Katharina pointed at Pietro. "Does he have to be so loud? I have a major headache. I get headaches whenever I travel and especially when I'm starving. Can't you at least *try* to get me something to eat?"

"Oh, but by the time we get there," Vincenzo continued, "they will be closed if they are not closed already."

"Fonzi here should have stopped and picked up something, then," Katharina said with more acid than usual. "Am I right?"

Vincenzo walked over and pushed Pietro. "Why you not stop? Huh? Can you not see she is hungry? *Idiota!*"

Pietro backed away. "I sorry." He narrowed his eyes at Katharina. "I go." He went to the door. *"Ciao, bella,"* he spat, and then he left.

"Oh no, I am not having that . . . that sarcasm in here!" Katharina fumed. "What did he call me?"

"He said 'good-bye, beautiful,' Miss Minola," Bianca said.

"Well, he didn't mean it," Katharina said. "Sarcastic jackass. I want you to fire him, Sly."

Vincenzo shook his head. "Oh no, Miss Katharina. I do not have the power to do that. Only Vincenzo does."

This is quickly becoming the theater of the absurd, Bianca thought.

"Well," Vincenzo said, "I must go, too. We have a busy day tomorrow. We will begin bright and early in the morning, Miss Katharina. Let us hope tomorrow will be a better day. We will fix everything. I cannot wait to begin working with you."

Katharina ran to and blocked the door. "You ain't leavin' just yet, Sly."

Vincenzo stopped moving. "There is something more?"

"Is there something . . ." Katharina's voice trailed to a whisper. "Can you at least tell me what this film's about?"

"Ah. Yes. You are a runaway American slave from Virginia who has escaped to Canada and is trying to make it on her own in the wilderness. *'A Woman Alone,'* yes?"

Katharina forced a smile. "Okay. An action-adventure. Good. It's about time I did one of those. Who else is in this picture?"

Vincenzo smiled broadly. "Just you, Miss Katharina. *Just you.*"

Katharina blinked. "No, really. Who else is in this picture?"

Vincenzo winked. "Just you." He turned to Bianca. *"Ciao, bella,"* he said, and then he slipped by Katharina and left, shutting the door behind him.

Bianca's heart fluttered a little. *Vincenzo meant that. That was nice. I don't look or feel beautiful, though. Vincenzo is . . . sweet, and not just because he hooked me up with some food. Though I don't know how long I can look at him in that dreadful wig.*

Katharina buried her head in her hands and bounced her shoulders against the door. "What in the hell did I get myself into? I'm *it?* I'll be the only one? I'm not only supposed to carry this movie, I *am* the movie."

Bianca cleared her throat. "I've never heard of such a thing before, Miss Minola."

Katharina waved a hand and went to the table, sitting and letting her hands hang loosely at her sides. "It's been done. Tom Hanks was alone in that movie where he talks to a basketball."

"Oh yeah." *But it was a volleyball, you out-of-touch wench.* "You're right, Miss Minola. But he wasn't completely alone the entire picture, was he?"

"That's beside the point." She sighed. "What am I supposed to think? That this is the role of a lifetime or something?"

Yes, you cow! Bianca's stomach growled. *When the mean witch goes to her dungeon, little tummy, we'll go eat raisins and granola, okay?*

"Damn. I shouldn't have said 'role,' " Katharina said. "I am so hungry!"

It's spelled differently, you dyslexic cow! "It *is* getting warmer in here, Miss Minola." *I can finally feel my toes.*

"It's because I'm steamed, that's why," Katharina said.

Keep it up, Katha-diva, and we won't miss the humidifier. "Um, Miss Minola, I'll get your bed ready for you."

Bianca opened the door to the right of the bathroom and saw a queen-sized bed, a dresser, and a nightstand.

Katharina trailed behind and stopped in the doorway. "They expect me to sleep in here? It's half the size of my shoe closet! What about the other bedroom?"

Think fast, Bianca! "Um, this bedroom is closer to the fire and the bathroom than the other one, so it will be much warmer." *Eventually.*

Katharina bounced on the bed, sighing and yawning. "Sturdy old thing. Probably made out of petrified wood."

Bianca pulled back the covers and fluffed the pillows. "Will there be anything else, Miss Minola?"

"You have anything on you to eat? And I mean anything. Maybe in that backpack of yours. A mint. A cookie. A piece of gum. Some peanuts from the plane?"

I almost feel sorry for her. "Sorry, Miss Minola."

Katharina flung herself onto the other side of the bed. "No. There won't be anything else."

Bianca scurried from the room to the other bedroom and felt under the mattress. *Yes! A big bag of raisins!* She tiptoed to her doorway, waved at the cameras, then zipped back to her mattress. She ate whole handfuls greedily, making sure not to leave any strays on the down comforter. After eating half the bag, she slipped over to the fireplace and added another log. She pulled a chair closer, took off her socks, and let her bare feet warm near the grate.

Yeah, this is the life, she thought.

"What are they doing now?" Walt asked, returning from a quick call to his wife and kids.

"I'd say they're thawing," Fish said. "Looks like Bianca is on fire duty. Poor thing."

Walt brought a folding chair next to Fish. "I don't know. Bianca seemed to be having fun. She's easy to look at, huh?"

"Katharina is still sexier," Fish said. "A whole lot sexier."

"Ah, but Bianca is nicer," Walt said. "That makes her beauty all the more appealing."

Fish clicked from Bianca to Katharina, who had yet to move from her "flung" position. "Katharina's pissed."

"She's just exhausted."

"She slept five hours on the plane," Fish said, zooming in. "Look at how she's gripping her comforter. That woman is pissed. Her knuckles are almost white. By the way, aren't we supposed to keep her awake all night?"

"Let's give her one good night's rest." Walt squinted at the screen. "She's mumbling something . . Can you punch up the sound?"

"Volume up . . ."

"I am so hungry," Katharina mumbled, "I could eat a mule, even a mule that smells like thousand-year-old shit . . ."

Chapter 13

In her dream, Katharina Minola was reaching for a chunky chicken salad sandwich lying on a huge blue dish, Grandma Pearl humming "I Don't Feel No Ways Tired" in the kitchen. The dish, a relic from Grandma Pearl's grandma's slavery days, however, was sitting on a strangely ancient wooden table in front of a roaring fire somewhere out in the open in the woods. Katharina's hand had just grasped the sandwich when a shotgun blast shook the cabin, rattling the windows. She jumped up and ran out of her bedroom.

"What . . . the *hell* . . . was that?" she wheezed.

Bianca, groggy but sated by half a bag of juicy raisins, sat up and stretched. "It sounded like a shotgun, Miss Minola, 20 gauge, I think." *Or something like that.*

" 'It sounded like a shotgun, Miss Minola, 20 gauge, I think,' " Katharina said, mocking Bianca. "I know what a shotgun sounds like." She retreated to her bedroom. "You go look."

Bianca added two more logs to the fire, threw on her jacket, and stepped outside.

Whoa, she thought. "Wow," she whispered. *Whoa,* she thought again. "Whoa," she said aloud.

Bianca looked out into the forest primeval. Mist rose from thick green vegetation and curled around pine trees. Streaks of sunlight reached through a thin layer of fog into the ice-blue sky. She saw no paths at all and could barely see the smoke from Pietro's cabin in the distance to the west. The trees around Katharina's cabin were so thick that Bianca imagined herself to be on an island of pine, the crisp scent thrilling her nose.

I'm in an Ansel Adams picture, she thought, *only this one's in color.*

The wind whipping up and the tree branches swaying, Bianca's toes told her to go back inside. As she turned, she saw a plain wooden box on a rocking chair at the far end of the rough-planked porch. She picked up the box, saw "Katharina" stamped in black ink in one corner, and sat in the rocker, creaking back and forth and smiling.

This place is so beautiful, she thought. *And I bet Kathadiva doesn't even notice.*

"Bianca!"

"Right on cue," Bianca said. She stood, heard the sound of rushing water far to her right, and went inside, laying the box on the table.

"I didn't see anything, Miss Minola," she said. "Maybe Alessandro shot a grizzly bear."

Katharina shuffled from her bedroom to the table. "I hope he shot his mule by mistake." *And this morning, I would eat me some mule steak.* She stared at the box. "What's that?"

"I don't know, Miss Minola. It was just sitting outside on a rocker. It has your name on it."

Katharina shook her head. "Funny way to deliver a costume. You open it. It might have mule spit on it."

Bianca pried the top off the box, pulling out a plain brown dress with a single large pocket the width of the dress. She laid it flat on the table.

Katharina sighed.

Bianca pulled out a pair of flattened brown leather boots, white leggings, a brown headband, and a wicked-looking knife, its handle rough and weathered.

"It all looks authentic," Bianca said.

Katharina sat in front of her costume. "It all looks low-budget." She picked up the knife and sliced the air several times. "This is nice." She felt the edge. "Sharp, too. I might skin me a mule today." *Or the man leading said mule.*

"You know, Miss Minola," Bianca said, "it looks exactly like what a runaway slave might have actually worn."

Katharina rolled her eyes. "Of course it does, Bianca. But they had better rags on *Roots.*"

Footsteps sounded on the porch.

Katharina started to get up but sat back down. "I hope to God that's my breakfast."

After a single knock, Pietro barreled in with a steaming cast-iron pot and two wooden spoons. He waved the pot over the table until Bianca had removed Katharina's costume and laid it carefully on a chair. He set down the pot, removed the top, and stuck in the wooden spoons.

To Bianca in Italian he said, "Eat first, and eat fast. Find some buckshot. It's on the bottom. Act sick, run out, I'll come back in, take the pot, and throw out what's left. Everyone else has already had seconds, and although it's venison, you tell her it's grizzly bear." He nodded and left.

Katharina picked up the knife. "That is a rude man." She stuck the knife in the table. *I wouldn't skin him, though. Too hairy. The man has hog bristles. He might dull my knife.* She peered over the edge of the pot. "What is that . . . lumpy goo?"

"It's grizzly bear stew," Bianca said. "It smells delicious, doesn't it?" She took a spoon, dipped it, found a nice healthy lump of meat, and put it in her mouth. "Oh, this is so good."

Katharina gingerly dipped her spoon. She brought the spoon to her lips, then pushed it back to analyze it. "What's this chunk here, Bianca?"

Bianca swallowed her second spoonful and looked at Katharina's spoon. "Looks like a huge hunk of grizzly gristle." *I'll bet that's the first time anyone heard "grizzly gristle" in a movie.* "I wouldn't eat that if I were you."

Katharina curled up her lip and dumped the "gristle" back into the pot. She dipped her spoon again and came up with a small chunk of meat. "What's this?"

Bianca dug for some buckshot with her third spoonful, found some, and carefully lifted it to her lips. "Ooh, Katharina, you are so lucky. That's part of the grizzly bear's liver. It's supposed to be the best part, an Asian delicacy. And it looks so bloody and rare! I'll eat it if you don't want it."

Katharina returned her spoon to the pot.

Bianca let the buckshot roll around in her mouth before removing three little pieces of metal and dropping them one by one onto the table. "Watch out for buckshot. I'll bet he just killed it! Hmm. Nice and fresh and *rare.* The grizzly bear's flesh was probably still steaming when he put it in the pot."

Katharina gulped hard. "Wonderful." She dipped her spoon again. "Any buckshot in there?"

Bianca looked carefully. "I don't think so. Unless it

splintered. The slivers are too small to see, and I hear they can do some serious damage to your intestines, but I wouldn't worry about it."

Katharina held the spoon in the air over the pot and turned the spoon over. "I'll just get some broth, then." She skimmed the top and filled the spoon to the brim, audibly licking her lips.

Just as Katharina was bringing the spoon in contact with her lips, Bianca grabbed her stomach, belched loudly, and screamed, "Oh my God!"

Katharina dropped her spoon into the pot.

Bianca ran outside and leaned over beside a tree, retching, gagging, and smiling for the unseen cameras.

"She's fantastic," Walt said.

"A natural," Fish said.

"And sexy," Walt said.

"An outstanding regurgitationist," Fish said.

Walt blinked. "That's not even a word."

Fish shrugged. "It should be."

Pietro appeared from behind a thick stand of pine trees. He nodded once to Bianca. Bianca winked.

Pietro barged inside and snatched the pot off the table. "No good!" he yelled. "Make sick." He collected the pot and spoons and left, slamming the door behind him.

Walt pointed at the interior shot of Katharina. "Zoom in on Katharina."

Fish smiled. "Zooming . . ."

* * *

Katharina's eyes fluttered, her tongue lolling around her lips. She seemed to be muttering something.

Fish laughed. "Boosting volume . . ."

"Grizzly bear–freaking stew and bullets for breakfast?" Katharina muttered. "Lumps of grizzly gristle? Rare bloody bear liver? Buckshot slivers?" She pulled the knife from the table. "I'd kill for a bloody English muffin."

"Cue Vincenzo," Walt said. "Hey, I better start typing some of this."

Fish pointed at another computer. "All set up for you. Everything dumps into that one. Just press REWIND. You can run the video on one half and Word on the other." He pressed the squawk button twice on the transmitter. "You're on, Vinnie. You got the headset?"

"Roger," Vincenzo said.

Vincenzo knocked on the door and entered holding a headset, a so-called "point-of-view" camera with a lens in the center of a headpiece, a wire microphone on the side. He saw Katharina slumped on the table. "Ah. You are up. A beautiful, misty, foggy day to begin, yes? The light outside is fantastic, the sky so blue." He put the headset on the table. "This is what you will wear today and every day."

Katharina laughed softly. "I'm a runaway slave with a tiara on my head?"

"No. *You* are the camera, and this is—"

"Not now, not now," Katharina interrupted. "I need breakfast. Coffee. A croissant. A Pop-Tart. Hell, some damn Raisin Bran. An Egg McMuffin. Anything."

Vincenzo sniffed the air. "You did not have the grizzly bear stew? It was *delizioso.*"

"It made my assistant sick to her stomach," Katharina said. "You probably passed her."

"Oh. So sorry. Is she all right?"

A guttural, gagging sound emanated from outside the door.

"Oh. So sorry. I guess not." Vincenzo lifted the dress from the chair. "Have you tried on your costume?"

Katharina shook her head slowly. "Like I said, I need to be fed first."

Vincenzo took the rest of Katharina's costume and laid it on the table. "Ah. But this is, how you say, kismet, fate? Your character would be hungry, too, yes? She might even be starving."

Katharina nodded. "Yes, but c'mon, Sly," she moaned. "Some coffee at least."

Vincenzo rapped the table with his knuckles. "She would have no coffee. She would not have eaten maybe for days, a week. You ate yesterday, yes?"

"I need my strength, *yes?*"

Vincenzo shook his head. "Your character would be very weak, very tired. Desperate."

"I *am* desperate, Sly. A plain piece of toast?"

Vincenzo picked up the headset. "You must wear this at all times unless I say otherwise. The viewer will see what you see, hear what you hear. Very cutting-edge stuff. If you fall, the viewer falls. If you run, the viewer is running. If you swim, the viewer goes—"

"I understand the concept, Sly," Katharina said. "I'm not three years old."

"Good. I will be able to see what you see on my monitor, and we should have immediate playback capability. I will take wide shots every now and then, but mostly it is you who will determine what the audience will see, hear, and feel."

Katharina smiled an eerie grin. "And if I really just want to *see* a plate of eggs, *hear* bacon sizzling, and *feel* buttered toast sliding down my throat, will all that happen if I put on my magic crown?"

Vincenzo sat back. "Ah, but your character—"

Katharina shot out of her chair and leaned heavily on the table. "Shut the hell up about my character! This is a freaking movie, Sly, not reality. *I* eat. It's something *I* do. I am not this slave woman, and I will not leave this cabin until *I* am fed. Understand?"

Time to instill a little fear. "Ah, but the light, the fog, the mist—it is calling for you. It will be much, much colder and cloudier tomorrow. It may even snow, and when it snows around here, it snows a great deal. It snows meters, not centimeters. We *must* get these shots this morning."

"What shots? The script still hasn't arrived."

Vincenzo darted his eyes to the mantel over the fireplace. "The script will be along any minute, I assure you. Any minute now. But I already know the opening scene very well."

"You ready?" Fish asked.

"I've *been* ready, Fish," Walt said. "I've just been waiting for the best moment to send it. It's all about timing, you know."

"Um, Vincenzo just said 'any minute now,' like he expects it, um, any minute now."

Walt shook his head. "He said 'any minute.' So, I'll pick a *random* minute. And this isn't it."

Fish returned his gaze to the monitor. "You writers take things way too literally."

"I tell you what," Vincenzo said. "We will do the opening scene this morning, and then you will get your breakfast. I promise."

Katharina closed her eyes. "*What* will I be fed?"

"Alessandro has made his special porcupine and turkey gizzard salad. Very tasty and nutritious."

Katharina coughed.

Fish coughed, too. "That even sounds nasty to me, and I like sushi."

"I make joke, Katharina, I make joke!"

Katharina tried to smile. "Yeah, a joke."

"No, no. Alessandro has another stew cooking, and it is not grizzly bear this time. It is venison. Very tender. I promise. So. Please get dressed." He stood. "Alessandro's mule will take you down to the set."

"Uh-uh," Katharina said. "I am not riding that mule."

Vincenzo smiled. "But did you not ride him last night?"

"Yes, but it was dark as shit out. I can see today. Thanks, but I'll walk."

Vincenzo nodded. "As you wish. You are the star! I will go see about your assistant."

"Wait, wait a minute," Katharina said. "Did the other plane arrive yet?"

Vincenzo shook his head sadly. "Um, no. Sorry to say, but the plane that replaced the first plane had engine trouble, too. Too much weight, they said. All that luggage. Something about shoes. They got only to Las Vegas and had to land. They have to wait to get a bigger plane."

"How long?" Katharina asked.

"Oh, I don't know. There is a big poker tournament in town, they say. Not many planes available. Maybe several days. Scottie is fine, though." He went to the door. "*Ciao.*"

Katharina covered her head with her hands. "Don't say that word."

Vincenzo leaped off the porch and saw Bianca bent over and gagging beside some trees. He squatted next to her and whispered, "You were wonderful last night, Bianca."

"Thank you," Bianca whispered. "And thanks for the food."

"I'll bring you more whenever you tell me to," he said. "But about last night. You were sensational. I really mean it. I don't give out empty praise. Okay, I just did with Katharina, but . . ."

Bianca burped loudly and grimaced.

"Are you really sick, Bianca?"

She nodded. "I kind of am. I ate too many raisins last night. I may have the runs later."

Vincenzo put his lips very close to her ear and whispered, "You just told Fish and Walter that."

Bianca looked up. "I don't care." She held her stomach. "I need to find a *gabinetto freddo.*" She smiled. "That was pretty funny."

Vincenzo looked up as Pietro came into view, leading Curtis. "My cabin, Cabin 1, the first one you passed? It has a nice modern bathroom. When Katharina finally gets going, why don't you go down there until you feel better?"

"Thanks, Vincenzo," she said. "I will, if she'll let me."

Pietro turned Curtis around up at the porch.

"Katharina won't ride him again," Bianca said.

"That's not the point," Vincenzo said. "Check out Curtis's eyes."

Bianca squinted. "They're . . . blue-green. Are they contacts?"

"Nope. Pietro found him and brought him up from Virginia."

"Amazing," Bianca said. She looked briefly into Vincenzo's eyes, then back at the ground. "You really go all-out, huh?"

"Bianca!" Katharina howled.

"Oh God, how I hate that sound," Bianca said, slowly rising. "I wish I could change my name."

"I like your name," Vincenzo said.

Yeah. He likes me. "It's showtime."

Vincenzo winked. "Break a leg."

Bianca took a step and winced. "I'd rather break both of hers."

Chapter 14

"Where have you been all this time, Bianca?" Katharina whined, struggling with her leggings. "Help me get into these."

Bianca helped Katharina get dressed, grabbing her belly occasionally.

Once Katharina was fully dressed, she moved around the cabin, bending, stretching, and spinning. "What's this made out of, burlap? I'm itching all over already. The boots have holes. The right boot is too big, and the left boot is too small. On top of that, it all smells like mothballs. I like realism as much as anyone, but this is ridiculous."

"You think maybe it's an actual slave's outfit, Miss Minola?" Bianca asked.

Katharina scowled. "Right. It would have to be over one hundred and fifty years old, Bianca." She snatched the headset and handed it to Bianca. "Put on my crown."

Bianca placed the headset snugly around Katharina's headband, positioning the microphone against her right cheek. She saw a switch on the headset and slid it to the side.

* * *

"Does the headset have to be turned on every time?" Walt asked.

"Nah," Fish said. "It's always on. That's a dummy switch." He typed several commands and watched a blank monitor glow to life. "Would you look at that?"

Walt looked at the screen and blinked. "That's amazing. The picture is so clear. You can see Bianca's pores."

"All high definition all the way," Fish bragged. "Checking zoom."

Bianca's face filled the screen.

"Now we're cookin'," Fish said.

Katharina sat. "Time for makeup. You'll have to do it. The others are all stuck in Vegas."

Bianca froze. "But you're a runaway slave, Miss Minola. You wouldn't wear makeup."

"I don't care. I will not leave this *cabina* without makeup. I haven't been seen in public without makeup in . . . a long time." *Fifteen years. I didn't even wear any makeup for my first screen test.*

Bianca glanced around the room. "Um, I didn't bring any. You know I don't wear any makeup, Miss Minola."

"Well, get a kit from Sly."

Oops. We didn't think about this, did we? "Um, I already talked to Sly. He didn't bring any makeup kits because he knew you were bringing your own makeup artist. You wouldn't want me to put makeup on you, anyway. I'd probably mess you up." *And I'd enjoy every minute of it.*

Katharina rubbed her cheeks. "My face can't shine, Bianca."

"Put some dirt on it, then, Miss Minola. Isn't mud supposed to be good for your skin?"

Katharina sighed. "I'll pretend I didn't hear that."

Pietro slammed open the door and yelled, *"Andiamo!"* He left the door open behind him, Curtis blinking his blue-green eyes their way.

"Um, that means—"

"I know what it means," Katharina interrupted. "It means get the hell out." She blinked up at Pietro. "I'll come out when I'm good and ready, Fonzi. And as you can see, Fonzi, I am not good and ready, so you will just have to wait."

Pietro waited, his arms crossed, cold air filling the room.

Katharina stayed in her chair, her arms crossed, feeling the cold air flowing into the room and sneaking up her leggings. "You mind shutting the door, Fonzi?" she asked.

"Is Alessandro."

Katharina smiled. "Whatever, Fonzi."

They locked eyes.

I am more warmly dressed, Pietro thought. *She will crack first.*

I am closer to the fire, Katharina thought. *He will crack first.*

Minutes passed.

Bianca shivered. "Miss Minola?"

Katharina looked hard into Pietro's eyes. *He has the Devil's black eyes. He is evil. I will not back down.*

Pietro returned Katharina's stare. *She has . . . beautiful eyes. I like how oval, how sexy—But she is evil! I will not back down.*

"Miss Minola," Bianca pleaded, "the draft is making the fire burn faster, and we're almost out of dry wood, so maybe we should, um, go."

Shit! Katharina thought. She stood slowly. "I am now ready."

Pietro pointed to the mule. "Go. You ride."

"No." Katharina breezed by Pietro to the porch and stopped. "Well, come on, Fonzi. Don't keep me waiting." She walked down one stair step and stopped. *I knew it! That stank beast has my blue-green eyes!* She blinked at Curtis, and Curtis blinked back. *Kind of pretty, actually, but I am so pissed at the world this morning. Better let my diva reputation be my guide.* She leaned as closely as she dared and looked Curtis in the eye. "This mule has got to go."

Pietro nodded. "Yes. Go. You ride."

Katharina backed up the stairs and stood by the rocker. "I am *not* getting on that thing again. Bianca!"

Bianca stumbled through the doorway holding her stomach. "Yes, Miss Minola?"

"Tell Fonzi here that I cannot ride this mule because of those eyes."

Bianca felt a gorge rise in her throat for real and tore off the porch, falling over and vomiting behind the cabin.

"Never mind, Bianca," Katharina said, turning her attention to Pietro. "Fonzi, let me explain something to you. This mule has my eyes. I'm sure no one told you"— *though it is a lie*—"that I do not work with anyone or anything that has my eyes."

Pietro looked from Curtis's right eye to Katharina's eyes. "No. You have Mule's eyes."

Say what? "Fonzi, I am older than this mule." *I can't believe I just said that.* "What I meant to say is that this mule is *younger* than me."

Pietro scratched his head. *"Che?"*

Katharina enunciated her words and spoke loudly. "I had these eyes *first.*"

"Che?"

"Oh, for the love of ..." Katharina squared her shoulders. "No ... mule! I ... not ... ride! Mule ... must ... go!"

Pietro smiled. "Yes. Mule go. You ride."

Katharina's feet were already killing her, her assistant was barfing all over Canada, and a massive moron who couldn't understand English was trying to get her to ride a mule. *Wait a minute. What do they put on horses?* "Blinders! Mule must wear blinders!"

Pietro widened his eyes. "Mule can see." He ran a finger in front of Curtis's right eye, and Curtis's eye lazily followed his finger. "See?"

Katharina gave up and walked off the porch. "Never mind, you moron. Where do I go?"

Pietro smiled. "Go. Yes. You ride."

Katharina threw up her hands and stormed away in the direction of her retching assistant, who was stumbling ahead of her through the woods.

"Here we go, sports fans," Fish said. "And it is a beautiful day to make a film here at the friendly confines in the middle of nowhere. It almost feels like Chicago in January, I'm tellin' ya. I'm Fish, and this is my broadcast partner, Walt, and we'll be giving you the play-by-play on this glorious morning. Target is leaving Cabin 3 for the stream, and after last night's rainstorm, the stream is much deeper and faster today, isn't it, Walt?"

"You wish you could announce Cubs' games, don't you?" Walt asked.

"You know it, Walt," Fish said. "That's right, sports fans, it rained to beat the band last night. Tubs full, not buckets. Huge bullmastiffs, not dachshunds. The heavens opened up and poured Clydesdales, not ponies."

"You're beating that metaphor to death, Fish," Walt said. "Get on with it."

"The headset cam is a go and working fine. Houston, we have liftoff."

"And now you're mixing your metaphors." Walt shook his head. "You are seriously strange, Fish."

"Thank you, Walt. But it ain't easy. I have to work at it. Play ball!"

Katharina caught up to Bianca, who was still doubled over, drool dribbling from her lower lip to the ground. "Do you know where you're going, Bianca?"

I'm know I'm going to spew again, Bianca thought. "I think it's this way, Miss Minola." She nodded to the right. "Sly went that way."

"What's that sound?" Katharina asked.

Bianca looked up and smiled. "A stream. I am so thirsty. I have to rinse out my vomit breath." She stood and loped away, Katharina following, Curtis and Pietro trailing behind.

Katharina didn't look back, threading her way through scrub pines until a roaring stream stopped her cold. *This wasn't here last night!*

Bianca gulped from the stream. "This is so good, Miss Minola," she said, cupping the water in her hands and taking healthy slurps. "You have to taste it. It's delicious and so icy cold."

Katharina shook her head. "You just . . . drink any ol' water passing by?"

Bianca looked up. "It's refreshing and clean."

"It's full of fish shit and piss. I'll pass." Katharina looked up and down the stream, water tumbling over rocks, several miniwaterfalls splashing into swirling pools. "Now, where's the bridge?"

Bianca stood, wiping her chin. "There wasn't one last night, Miss Minola."

Katharina turned to frown at Pietro. "Where's the bridge, Fonzi?"

Pietro halted Curtis within inches of Katharina's back. "No bridge. *Mulo.* You ride."

No mulo, he's an idiot, he's high, Katharina thought. "I am getting tired of repeating myself, Fonzi. I am not getting on that thing ever again. *Ever.*" Katharina saw several flat rocks, just under the roiling surface, that formed a lazy line across the creek. "I can just step on those rocks. Look, Bianca. They're like stepping-stones."

"I don't know, Miss Minola," Bianca said. "That water is moving by pretty fast."

"You go first," Katharina said, giving Bianca a little shove.

Bianca, light on her feet, splashed across the stepping-stones with ease and climbed up the bank on the other side. "They were pretty mossy rocks, Miss Minola, and the current was pretty powerful. I'd take the mule. The mule went through the stream last night, right?"

It did? "I didn't hear it splashing around last night," Katharina said.

Because you were too busy complaining, wench. Bianca shook the water from her boots. "It rained hard last night. This must be the runoff."

"It rained?" Katharina asked. "No, it didn't."

"It did, Miss Minola," Bianca said. "You must have slept better than I did. Please take the mule. If you fall in . . ."

Katharina threw back her head. "If you can do it, so can I. I won't fall in, Bianca."

Oh, please do, Bianca thought. *I want a lifetime memory right now!*

Katharina took a hesitant step to the first stone, the hem of her dress sucking up water and pulling her slightly downstream. She stepped back to dry land and hitched up her dress a few inches. She took another shaky step and planted her foot. "See? Nothing to it." She took a longer step to the next stone—

And slipped.

Pietro caught her by her shoulders before she could go fully under, pulling her back to drip in front of Curtis.

Katharina looked at what was once a light brown dress. "Why didn't you tell me the rocks were slippery, Bianca?" Katharina yelled, icy water bubbling through the holes in her boots.

"I told you they were mossy, Miss Minola."

"And that obviously didn't mean shit to me, Bianca!" Katharina said.

"I'm sorry, Miss Minola. I'll be more specific from now on."

Katharina stared hard at Pietro but said nothing.

"You okay?" Pietro asked.

Katharina said nothing more.

"Mule go," Pietro said. "You ride."

Katharina ignored him and started down the hill beside the stream, her dress sloshing side to side, dodging birch trees and pine trees while skidding over lichen-covered boulders and rocks. The more she descended the hill, the more the stream became deeper, faster, and louder, the boulders in the water larger and mossier.

Bianca followed Katharina's progress from the other side, Pietro and Curtis stepping silently behind.

At the very bottom of the steep hill, the stream widened to fifty feet across and at least three feet deep.

Vincenzo appeared on the opposite bank holding a camera, a sizable monitor at his feet. "Yes! This is good, Katharina! This will make an excellent shot. A wonderful idea!" He waved her over. "I will take wide shots, too. From waist down only!"

Katharina blinked. *That man is high. I am* not *crossing here.* She looked back up the hill.

"Come, come!" Vincenzo cried. "The light is perfect! The mist is rising! The sun is slanting! It is glorious! The water is so clear and reflects the trees and the clouds! You come!"

If he starts singing "Wade in the Water," Katharina thought, *I will spontaneously combust.*

"She'll go across," Walt said.

"No, she won't," Fish said. "That water is barely above freezing."

"She'll go," Walt said. "I know she will."

Fish laughed. "Well, can she swim? The current might take her downstream. That dress is heavy-duty. It could weigh her down, and she could drown." He blinked. "That would be better, actually. The element of danger. Lots of thrashing. We have to remember the suspense factor."

"She'll make it," Walt said. "But will your headset make it?"

"It's fully waterproof. In fact, it would be better if she went under and tumbled downstream a while. We might even get a few shots of some fish looking at her. How deep is it there?"

Walt stared at Fish. "You're weird and you're warped."

"I thought I was strange."

"That, too."

Katharina turned to Pietro. "Will your mule make it across?"

Pietro shook his head quickly. "No. Mule not swim. Mule sink. Mule drown."

No great loss, Katharina thought. She looked at Vincenzo, who was letting Bianca look through the camera. "Bianca, you'll have to come back here and carry me."

"Oh no," Vincenzo said. "You are a woman alone. Come, come. The mist! The sunlight! The water! The clouds! It is perfect, Katharina!"

That man is out of his freaking mind. Katharina looked briefly at Pietro. *He could carry me across. He could probably throw me across. I bet he'd like that.*

"Katharina!" Vincenzo had the camera on his shoulder. "What a wonderful opening scene this will be! It will take the audience's breath away! Come, come!"

It will take my life away! No! No! I stay! I stay! Katharina set her jaw. *Forget this nonsense,* she thought. She walked past Pietro and Curtis and struggled up the hill and out of sight.

Pietro kissed Curtis on the nose, turned Curtis around, and began a slow ascent.

"Now what?" Bianca whispered to Vincenzo.

"We'll leave her be," Vincenzo whispered. "She's a woman alone, right? Let's leave her alone for a while."

"She doesn't have the *ability* to be alone," Bianca moaned. "She's going to—"

"Bianca!" echoed all around them.

"See, Vincenzo?" Bianca pouted. "I gotta go."

Vincenzo touched her arm. "You're definitely earning your keep, there, missy."

Bianca giggled. "Well, thank ya kindly, Tex."

Chapter 15

"She's mumbling again," Walt said.
"Up volume," Fish said.

Katharina crashed through the woods, branches and briars catching at her sopping dress and slashing her arms. "I have never done method acting. Only the deranged, the desperate, the English, and the Australians do that shit anymore! I use a damn script, and the script creates my character! *Bianca!* And when I have a damn script, which I obviously don't, but whenever I *do* have a damn script, I change it and do what I damn well please with it until I like my character. *Bianca!* Where's the damn script? Why isn't this damn path marked? Why isn't there a damn path? Are they trying to kill me the first day? *Bianca!*"

Bianca caught up, out of breath and still feeling queasy. "Yes, Miss Minola."

"Are you puked out yet?" Katharina asked.

"I think so," Bianca said. "I'm feeling much better." *Not.* "Thanks for asking."

They had almost reached their cabin. "I only asked so you don't puke inside."

Katharina waited until Bianca opened the cabin door before walking in and slamming the door in Bianca's face.

Bianca knocked.

"Who is it?" Katharina yelled.

Who else would it be, you wench? "Bianca, Miss Minola."

"Well, get your ass in here."

Bianca opened the door, stepping in. The fire sputtered fitfully in the fireplace, so Bianca added several more dry logs.

Katharina struggled with the buttons on the back of the dress. "Help me out of this shit, Bianca. Damn."

Bianca unbuttoned the dress, then went to work on Katharina's sopping boots, pulling them off and emptying drips of water on the floor as Katharina pulled down the top of the dress. She let it flop in front of her.

"Give me your coat."

Bianca draped her coat over Katharina's shoulders.

"Go get some more wood."

Bianca stepped out, saw Pietro, mouthed, "More wood, please," and stepped back inside.

"Where's the wood?" Katharina asked.

"Alessandro is getting us some."

Katharina stretched her wet toes toward the fireplace screen. "I told *you* to go get it. We don't need Fonzi's help."

"I'll go back out, then, Miss Minola." *And without my coat. Lovely.*

"Check the fax machine first."

Oh God, Katha-diva! Just because your life is out of control doesn't mean . . . Never mind. "There's nothing in the tray, Miss Minola."

"Well, is it turned on?"

"Yes." Bianca tramped to the door.

"I know what they're trying to do," Katharina said in a soft voice.

Bianca froze.

"They're trying to turn me into a slave." Katharina wiggled her toes in the air. "That's what they're trying to do. Look at how they're treating me. Look at how I'm dressed. Look where the *hell* we are. They're starving me, treating me like shit, and making me wear these nasty clothes. I ought to call the NAACP on their asses. It's an outrage."

Bianca took a deep breath and moved silently toward Katharina. "Or, it's the opportunity of a lifetime for you to create an original character from scratch."

Katharina growled.

Bianca stepped back. "I'm just, um, saying, Miss Minola. This is a, um, I'll shut up."

Katharina stared into the fire. "You're full of shit, Bianca, you know that? Don't give me your opinions about acting or making movies. You don't know shit about this business. I was making movies when you were still in diapers."

I wasn't in diapers when I was seven, Bianca thought.

"No," Katharina said, slowly shaking her head. "I wouldn't have crossed that stream if there was a tableful of roast beef and all the trimmings on the other side. I wouldn't have crossed that stream if Scottie was on the other side barking for me. It's the principle of the thing, you know? They ain't runnin' nothin' here. *I'm* in control." She sniffed the air. "What's that smell?"

Oh, I hope it's something really nasty. "I don't smell anything but pine and smoke and fresh air, Miss Minola. It smells good. Fresh. Clean. It even has a taste."

Katharina stood. "No, you tree hugger. Another smell. A dead smell. Like ass. Like something died in here." She sniffed around the fireplace and stepped back.

"Something died in there, and I think it's cooking. Get Fonzi in here *right* now."

Bianca opened the door and nodded at Pietro. "Alessandro, we need you."

"His name is Fonzi," Katharina said.

Pietro entered the cabin, a huge stack of wood in his arms. He laid down the stack and added one log to the fire.

"Tell Fonzi that something died in here, Bianca."

Oh, how childish! Not this game. "*Did* something die in here?" Bianca asked him in Italian.

Pietro looked at Bianca holding herself and shivering slightly. "Just her humanity, obviously," he said in Italian. He sniffed the air and nodded. "Might be some mice or bats cooking in the chimney," he said in Italian.

"Yuck," Bianca said.

"Yuck?" Katharina asked. "What's yuck?"

Bianca approached Katharina. "He says there may be some dead mice or some dead bats in the chimney." *No need to embellish on that!* "We kind of smoked and cooked them to death with our fire last night."

Katharina left her chair and backed toward the door. "I am *not* staying here. We need a better cabin. No. We need a real house with heat and electricity and hot water. Do they have one like that in this country? Well, ask him."

In Italian, Bianca asked, "Is there one?"

Pietro shook his head. "Tell her," he said in Italian, "that *this* is the nicest dwelling within fifty miles."

Bianca sighed. "He says this is by far the nicest one for a *hundred* miles in all directions. The, um, the other cabins don't even have inside toilets."

Katharina stepped away from Pietro. "Where does Fonzi shit, then, in the woods?"

Bianca tried to laugh. "Oh, Miss Minola, I don't think—"

"Ask him, Bianca," Katharina demanded. "Ask Fonzi if he shits in the woods. I want to know."

Bianca looked at the floor. "I can't ask him that, Miss Minola. It's rude."

"I don't care," Katharina said. "I'll bet he does. I'll bet he shits in the woods. He probably doesn't even use toilet paper. He looks like a bear, and he acts like a bear." She walked into the bathroom. "I need a bath, and I don't care if it's cold." She turned on the cold water.

Pietro shook his head and whispered, "I'm already regretting this."

Me too, Bianca thought.

Katharina looked at the brown water gushing into the tub. "Oh my God! Bianca, get Fonzi in here!"

Pietro went in and smiled. "Yes, Katharina?"

Katharina pointed at the water. "What is this, sewage?"

"Calma, calma," Pietro said. "You wait." A moment later, the water turned clear. "See!"

"Can you make it hot?" Katharina asked. "Can you do that for me?"

Pietro nodded.

Katharina blinked. "You can?"

Pietro nodded again.

"Well, don't just stand there, go make it hot."

Pietro shrugged at Bianca and left.

Katharina turned off the water. "Now we're getting somewhere. You just have to know how to talk to him, show him who's boss."

Ten minutes later, Pietro returned with a huge black cast-iron cauldron and set it under the faucet in the tub. He turned on the water.

"You have to cook it first?" Katharina asked.

"*Sì,*" Pietro said.

"Where?" Katharina asked.

Pietro pointed to the fireplace.

Bianca looked in the fireplace and saw an iron bar flush on the side of the chimney. "He'll hang it over the fire, Miss Minola. There's an iron bar there."

The cauldron full, Pietro hoisted it out of the tub and carried it to the fireplace, setting it down and pulling back the screen. He used a poker to pull the bar toward him and hung the cauldron over the fire.

"How long will that take?" Katharina asked.

Pietro shrugged and left.

Katharina stormed to the door. "I asked you a question, Fonzi!"

Pietro continued walking away without looking back.

Katharina turned to Bianca. "Did you see that? Did you see how he ignored me?"

I wish I could do that, Bianca thought. *At least he gets to leave.* "We'll just wait until it boils, Miss Minola." *At least the witch now has her cauldron.* "Double, double, toil and trouble"* . . .

Katharina turned and smiled. "Guess what *you'll* be doing every morning before you wake me?"

Bianca didn't guess. She knew. "I don't mind, Miss Minola." *It is my lot in life to suffer.*

Pietro returned seconds later with a long metal rod. He pulled back the screen and began poking the bar up the chimney, soot falling into the cauldron.

"Hey, what are you doing?" Katharina yelled. "Cut that out!"

Pietro ignored her and thrust the rod higher, more soot falling into the cauldron, along with a singed and smoking mouse—*plop!*—and finally, a bat.

Pietro snatched the dead mouse and bat from the cauldron, smiled at Katharina, and left the cabin.

Katharina sat, her lower lip trembling. "That . . . that was disgusting. He expects me to bathe in that water? Is everyone crazy around here?"

"I'll pour it out and get you some clean water, Miss Minola."

Katharina shook her head. "Don't bother. That pot is contaminated now. It probably has some rodent disease cooking in it. Get it out of here."

Bianca struggled to lift the cauldron but couldn't budge it an inch. "I can't lift it, Miss Minola."

Katharina closed her eyes. "Can't take a bath. Can't shave my legs. Can't wear makeup. Haven't eaten. Italians running around high on crack. Weak-ass assistant. I can't win."

Bianca tried again but failed, afraid if she stepped closer to get more leverage she would set herself on fire. "I can't lift it, Miss Minola. I need your help."

Katharina's eyes popped open. "I am not touching that thing. Get Fonzi to help you."

Bianca stuck her head outside. "I don't see him."

"Go find him, then!"

Bianca approached Katharina. "May I, may I please have my coat back, Miss Minola?"

Katharina stared at Bianca.

"I'll take that as a no," Bianca said, and she left the cabin.

"She's muttering again," Walt said.

"Volume up," Fish said.

* * *

"Grain must be ground to make bread," Katharina whispered. "And I'm the grain." She sighed heavily. "'By the rivers of Babylon we sat and wept.'"

"What the hell was that about?" Fish asked.

"She's quoting scripture," Walt said. "I didn't know Katharina and the Bible were on speaking terms. An apt choice, though. The Israelites were in captivity in Babylon. She's starting to feel her role."

Fish watched Katharina walk into her bedroom and take her tiger outfit off the dresser, laying it on the bed. "I don't think she's feeling her role, Walt."

Walt sighed. "She's obviously not done playing her other role."

"I think she's getting ready to walk."

Chapter 16

"Now we let her see some script," Walt said. "Can you split the screen between Katharina's face and the fax machine?"

"I can do anything," Fish said. He tapped a few keys, and the fax machine filled the left side of the big screen, and on the right Katharina putting on her tiger blouse over the brown dress.

"Sending now."

The fax machine spit out several pages and stopped.

"I sent twenty-three pages," Walt said. "There are only three in the tray."

"Must be jammed," Fish said. "Paper must be humid from the rain last night or something."

The screen containing Katharina showed her working the dress down her hips. "Bianca!"

"Damn," Fish said. "She can't even walk, what, fifteen feet to a fax machine?"

Katharina pulled the dress back up over her shoulders and her tiger blouse. "I have to do everything around here," she muttered. She left her bedroom and went to the fax machine, snatching three pages from the tray. She tugged on a page stuck in the machine and wrestled it out until it tore, a loud beep sounding.

"Oh man," Fish said. "She shouldn't have done that. She went and broke it, Walt. Someone has to take it apart now to get all the little pieces of paper out."

Walt tented his fingers and stared at Katharina's face. "Shh. A jammed fax might even work more to our advantage. Go full screen."

Katharina mumbled what she read. " 'Thousands of American slaves used the Underground Railroad to escape slavery during the mid-1800s. Many of those who escaped Virginia traveled through western Pennsylvania and western New York and to Niagara Falls, the gateway to southern Ontario. This is the story of one such slave, a woman who finds how free and freeing freedom can be.' How free and freeing freedom can be? Who wrote this shit?"

"Ouch," Fish said.
"It's a play on words. Don't you get it? 'Free and freeing freedom.' "
Fish winced. "I get it, Walt. But still . . . ouch."

Katharina sat at the table and read.

Scene 1

WOMAN runs through woods in
predawn darkness, panting, hiding,
crouching, her clothes soiled, torn, her
arms and face bleeding. She attempts
several times to cross a rushing stream
but fails. Her brown dress becomes
soaked with water. She sees a clearing on
the other side of a deep stream and
wades, swims, and flounders across it. On
the other side she slips in mud, and
crawls up the bank and across the
clearing as the sun begins to rise. She
hides under thick brush, holding her
legs and shivering—ad-lib prayers, songs,
words, etc.

"I already ruined a shot like that today," Katharina
whispered. "It wasn't my fault it rained last night."
She continued to read:

Scene 2

As clouds roll in, threatening heavy snow,
WOMAN shivers. She tries to build a fire
with her only protection, a sharp knife,
and a piece of flint she finds nearby. She
collects materials for her fire, occasional
howls from wolves heard echoing in the
distance. Ad-lib talking to fire, knife,
clouds, etc. She eventually coaxes a small
fire, playing her hands over the glow.
Ad-lib prayers, songs, words, etc.

I am not filming at night in this cold-ass place, Katharina thought. *I don't want the grizzlies to come and get me.*

Scene 3

> WOMAN combs forest for food, berries,
> leaves, and / or nuts. She eats ravenously
> in the forest, spits out sour berries, and
> returns to her fire, eating greedily, her
> eyes sharp and darting toward every
> rustling movement in the forest. Ad-lib
> throughout.

"So *this* is how they're going to feed me," Katharina whispered. "All the way over in Scene 3. Shit, I better get to work so I don't starve."

Scene 4

> WOMAN traps and kills small game
> (chipmunks, squirrels, birds). She guts
> and skins them like an expert, then
> cooks them over the fire. She eats with
> gusto. Ad-lib throughout.

Uh, no. Not gonna happen. I don't even roast marshmallows anymore.

Scene 5

> WOMAN builds shelter using sticks, logs,
> stones, mud, foliage, animal sinews,
> snow, and ice (if available). Ad-lib
> throughout. She whittles weapons and
> hums a spiritual. When weather cooper-

ates, she attempts to fish in stream using
wooden spears. Ad-lib throughout.

"Oh," Katharina said, tossing aside the pages, "they
didn't spare any expense writing *this* shit."

"Ouch again!" Fish said.
"Shh," Walt said. "It's supposed to be like a skeleton.
She's supposed to provide the muscle and the meat."
"I can't see Katharina doing chipmunk kabobs, can
you?" Fish asked.

She looked back to the instructions for Scene 1. *Well,
it's a start. I've always wanted an action flick, and I sure as hell
got one. The action doesn't start until I do. At least I get to make
up my own lines, something I usually do, anyway, but . . . I get
to make them all up.*
She looked at the door. "Bianca!" *I also get to hum
again. I can do that.* "Bianca!" *Singing a spiritual? Kinda
cliché there. Lord knows I can't really sing. I wouldn't want
the Pentecostals coming after me if I botched "Nobody Knows
the Trouble I've Seen."*
Katharina rose wearily from the chair and went to the
little window beside the door. Coming up the path were
Pietro, carrying another load of wood, and Bianca, who
looked like a dwarf next to him.
Katharina returned quickly to the table, grabbing
the pages and "reading" them again.
Bianca opened the door, Pietro following close behind. He laid down the wood quietly and quickly removed the cauldron, carrying it through the doorway
with one hand.

"Don't toss out that water near this cabin, Fonzi," Katharina said.

Pietro smiled, spilled a few drops of water on the threshold, and left.

"He did that on purpose," Katharina said.

"That cauldron was heavy, Miss Minola," Bianca said. "And he only used one hand."

All brawn, no brain—like this script. Katharina waved the partial script in the air. "This, Bianca, is the sorriest script I have ever seen. Put my boots on."

Bianca narrowed her eyes. "Put your boots on?"

"I don't stutter," Katharina said. "Put my boots on."

While Bianca struggled with Katharina's boots, Katharina removed her tiger blouse. "It's barely an outline, really, and I have no set lines. I have to make up this shit as I go along."

Bianca pulled the strings tightly. "Is that the entire script?"

"Button me up."

Bianca worked the buttons at the back of Katharina's dress.

"The rest of it wouldn't print out," Katharina said. "I had to yank out the last page."

Bianca took the tiger blouse and folded it, staring at the pages. "What do they say?"

"They don't say much. It's basically a list of what I'm to do with the headset on." She pointed to the headset, and Bianca put it on. "While I'm out, you see what's wrong with that machine. Maybe you can get the rest of the pages to print out."

I like this *Katharina,* Bianca thought. *She's on the ball.* "Yes, Miss Minola. I'll do my best."

Katharina took a deep breath and stood, smoothing out her dress. "How do I look?"

Like a new person. "You look ready, Miss Minola."

Katharina nodded. "I am." She squared her shoulders and set her chin.

Bianca heard Katharina's stomach growling.

Katharina's eyes faltered a moment, and then she left the cabin, striding out with purpose and power.

Bianca felt the goose bumps on her arms subside by themselves. *I think I've just seen the old Katharina! I wish I had my camera!*

"Target has left the building with a gurgling stomach," Fish said, "target has left the—"

"Cut it out," Walt interrupted.

"You're no fun. You're just mad your script sucks."

Walt smiled. "And you saw the result. I'm glad it sucks. Now we'll see some magic."

"You hope."

Chapter 17

Katharina walked with purpose past Pietro's cabin, and past Pietro holding an empty cauldron and Curtis chewing on a bush. She came to the part of the stream where the stepping-stones were and frowned. The water had fallen off to a trickle, each stone several inches above the water. Deciding that crossing there would be too easy, she crashed and slid down the steep hill.

"Whoa," Walt said. "That's kind of disorienting."

"Wait till she falls," Fish said. "That will mess you up completely."

Katharina wandered farther down, nearly stumbling the last few feet to her former spot in front of the widest part of the stream. She waved at Vincenzo, who hadn't seemed to have moved since earlier in the day.

"Miss Katharina!" Vincenzo yelled. "The stream, it is

lower now. It will not be so hard." He swung up his camera. "Whenever you are ready."

No problem, she thought. *No problem at all.*

She took two steps into the water, then jumped back on dry land.

Problem.

"Shit!" she yelled. *My feet are ice, oh geez, I have no toes! My ankles have locked in place!*

"Is cold," a deep voice behind her said. *"Freddo."*

Katharina nodded at Pietro as she stamped her feet. "I can handle it, Fonzi. Now you just . . . run along and play with your mule."

Pietro nodded and trudged up the hill.

"We're trying for less than an R rating here, aren't we?" Walt asked.

"I don't know," Fish said. "Did they say 'shit' back then?"

"Yes, but I have a feeling she's going to be saying more than that by the time she crosses that stream."

"She ain't crossing that stream today," Fish said, pulling out a twenty. "And I got twenty that says she won't."

"All right." Walt found a Canadian twenty in his wallet and put it on top of Fish's twenty.

"Nah, nah," Fish said. "None of that play money."

"Fish, the way the U.S. economy is going, my twenty is worth more than your twenty." He looked at the big screen. "She'll cross. It's not as deep, and the sun is coming out. Get ready to zoom."

The transmitter squawked. "Everybody ready?" Vincenzo asked.

"It's a go," Fish said.

"I'm going to cut it a few times, so be patient," Vincenzo said.

Fish smiled. "Oh man, that's cold." He turned to Walt. "We're gonna get Miss Katharina seriously wet today."

Katharina's toes tingled to life. *Maybe if I run across quickly it won't be so bad.* She hitched up her dress and crashed into the stream, lifting her legs high, splashing water up and over her head.

She also cursed like an overworked, underpaid truck driver cut off by a tree hugger driving a hybrid.

She stopped and panted on the other side, giving a thumbs-up to Vincenzo and feeling the icy cold seep into her pores.

"Why did you stop?" Vincenzo asked, letting his camera droop. "It must be a continuous shot. You are running for your life. You would not stop and rest."

I can't feel my knees! My nipples are tearing my dress! "Can't we just, you know, take it from here?"

Vincenzo shook his head. "The headset footage will jump if we cut and splice. It must be one smooth take. You understand."

Katharina blinked. "You want me to go back across and do it again."

"Yes," Vincenzo said.

She looked down at her dress. "But I'm already wet. You want me to be wet *before* I get wet?"

"It is a brown dress, no one will notice," Vincenzo said. "And if they do, who cares? It is a wet forest. You were bound to get wet before you hit the stream, yes?"

How can I convince this idiot . . . "Look. The headset shows me crossing, you pick me up on this side as I climb. It will work."

Vincenzo shook his head. "It is what I want, Miss Katharina. It is what the audience needs to see. They must see the entire movement with no intermissions. It will leave them breathless, yes?"

"I guess, but . . ."

"And when you get to the top of the bank, you must crawl through the clearing to the heavy brush on the other side and hide. I want several minutes in a row of just what you see. It will be a sensational beginning, you will see."

She looked upstream. "I'll, um, I'll just walk on this side until it's shallow enough to cross back."

"Fine," Vincenzo said.

She reached up a hand. "A little help?"

"Oh no, Miss Katharina," Vincenzo said. "I misunderstand. You cannot come up this way. The bank has no footprints on it. You must cross back the way you came, and then come over here again. We can see no footprints but your own for this entire movie."

Which makes total sense, Katharina thought. *Maybe he's not such an idiot.* "So I have to go back across."

"Please, Miss Katharina. It will be a perfect shot, I assure you."

She looked at the stream. "Doesn't anyone have a boat or a raft or something?"

Vincenzo smiled. "Just Curtis. The water is low enough now. He will not drown."

Shit. "All right. We'll do it your way."

She pulled her dress nearly up to her head and slogged back across the creek, not lifting her legs at all. *I can only imagine what this looks like.*

Fish tilted his head as Vincenzo's camera zoomed in on Katharina's butt. "Those leggings don't leave much to the imagination, do they? This will make a nice addition to the blooper reel, huh?"

"You're sick, Fish."

"Don't forget 'twisted.' "

During the second take, Katharina crossed more quickly than on the first with more splashing and shivering. She was about to attempt the bank when Vincenzo yelled, "Stop!"

Katharina froze.

"I must play it back," Vincenzo said. "I think I heard hammering."

"Hammering?" Katharina asked. "I don't hear any—" She stopped and listened to hammering sounds and their echoes. "You can edit that out, can't you?"

Vincenzo turned his head. "Oh, the hammering has stopped. Um, go back across the stream and come over again."

"You're kidding."

"No," Vincenzo said. "You are doing so well, Miss Katharina! The shot was good, but we must make it *fantastico!*"

Katharina turned and waded across again. *I ought to make* you *come across with me, Sly. Then* your *shot will be* fantastico. *I have officially lost all feeling below my booty.*

The third take went swimmingly and without interruption until Katharina attempted to crawl up the muddy bank. She clawed and tore at the soil, the slick soles of her boots giving her no traction at all. She clawed (and cursed) and slipped (and cursed) and fell back (and cursed) and even backed into the water several times to take a run at the now seriously muddy bank. She was almost to the top, with one arm over the edge, when the bank underneath her gave way and sent her tumbling to the edge of the stream.

"She's not moving," Fish said. "Will you look at the mud on her lens? That is so cool."

"Get up, Katharina," Walt whispered. "Get up!"

Katharina looked up at Vincenzo filming her, his camera less than ten feet away. She wiped mud from her face, growled fiercely, and leaped up that bank, crawling on all fours until she was up and over and lying in the clearing, wailing in pain, groaning in victory.

She turned her head to Vincenzo's camera with the slightest of smiles.

Walt walked toward the big screen. "Would you look at that smile."

"That's a smile," Fish said.

"A smile of victory," Walt said.

"And now her lips are moving," Fish said. "Up volume . . ."

"It's about motherf—king time," Katharina muttered as she got to her feet and crawled toward the brush at the back of the clearing. "I'm gonna kill the asshole who was doing that motherf—king hammering!"

Walt looked at Fish.

Fish looked back at Walt. "Any suggestions?"

"Maybe we can overdub it and turn it into a prayer of thanksgiving."

Katharina looked from side to side once she was deep in the brush. Vincenzo's camera and several cameras mounted in nearby trees showed her muddy brown dress and face blending perfectly into the brush, where she held her legs, rocked, and whispered something she thought only she could hear.

Vincenzo set his camera and monitor on a fallen log and ran to Katharina. "You were wonderful! Just wonderful!"

Katharina extricated herself from the brambles and brush, picking twigs out of her hair and flicking gobs of mud from her nose. "I must eat now, Sly. I must get warm now. I must have a bath now. I must kill whoever was hammering now."

Pietro, riding Curtis, came up the same muddy bank Katharina had fought earlier, a hammer hanging prominently from his tool belt. "You ride now," he said.

"*You!*" she yelled, and she ran at him, skidding to a halt in front of Curtis's nose. "Were you hammering just now, Fonzi?"

Pietro nodded, his eyes cast down.

"Did you know we were filming the first scene just now?"

Pietro shook his head. "I not think you cross today."

Katharina blinked. "You didn't think I would go across the stream?"

"No. You . . . *testardo*. Like Curtis."

"Are you saying I'm stubborn as a mule?"

Pietro nodded. "*Sì*. Stubborn as mule. *Testardo.*"

Katharina shot a look at Vincenzo. "I am not stubborn."

Pietro slid off Curtis, grabbed Katharina, and lifted her onto Curtis's back before she could take her next breath.

"Don't put your hands on me!" she howled. "Understand? And I do not want to ride this beast!"

Pietro smiled. "So. You are being *testardo*."

Katharina shot another look at Vincenzo. "You better do something about your cousin here, or I'll—"

"*Calma, calma,*" Pietro said, turning Curtis and leading him up the hill. "You tired. You *freddo*. Curtis *caldo*. You ride."

Katharina, surprised Curtis's body was so warm, looked back at Vincenzo. "You tell your cousin that he is *never* to touch me. *Never.*"

Vincenzo ran up beside Pietro and bopped him on the back of the head. "She was great today, wasn't she?" he yelled angrily in Italian.

"Why are you yelling?" Pietro asked softly in Italian.

"We have to make it look like an argument!" Vincenzo yelled in angrier Italian. He poked Pietro in the chest for good measure.

Pietro nodded. "You do that again," he said softly in Italian, "and I'll kick your ass from here to the border. Why does she hate to be touched so much?"

Vincenzo took a deep breath. "Because," he yelled in Italian, "you and I and all the other little people on this planet are not supposed to touch greatness! Now, I want you to apologize to Katharina!"

Pietro looked at Katharina. "I sorry."

"You got that right," Katharina said.

Vincenzo approached Curtis. "Great work today, Miss Katharina. Superb! Rest well. *Ciao.*"

Pietro led Curtis through a maze of trees to a

makeshift bridge of planks, logs, and plywood spanning a narrow and shallow part of the stream.

"Oh, *now* there's a bridge," Katharina said.

Pietro smiled. "I build for you."

Katharina stifled another criticism and looked more fully at Pietro. Even though she rode the mule, he was nearly as tall as she was. "Will it hold all of us?" she asked in a nicer voice than normal.

Pietro nodded. "It hold me and Curtis just now." He handed the lead to Katharina. "You go. I wait."

"You want me to . . . ride this thing without your help?"

Pietro nodded. "Safe." He blushed, or seemed to. "I big." He slapped Curtis on the butt, and Curtis walked easily across the bridge, Katharina holding on for dear life. Pietro crossed behind and again took the lead. "You ride well."

"It was all of ten feet," Katharina whispered under her breath. "Um, how's the turkey gizzard salad coming?"

"*Che?*"

"The stew," Katharina said slowly.

"Oh. Sorry. Bad."

"I meant the new . . . never mind." She smiled. "You are an ignorant brute, you know that?"

"*Sì.*"

Katharina almost laughed. "I can say anything I want to you, can't I?"

"*Sì.*"

"I have died and gone to hell."

Pietro smiled and said, "*Sì.*"

When they finally arrived at the cabin, Pietro lifted Katharina off Curtis and placed her on the porch.

He lifts me as if I weigh nothing at all! "Um, Bianca!"

Bianca opened the door. "Yes, Miss Minola?"

"I don't care how you do it, Bianca, but I want you to get me food and coffee, even if you have to sell your body to Fonzi here. Or to his mule. Get me some food! Now!"

Bianca looked hard at Pietro and hesitated. *No. It's too early to quit.* She sighed. "Yes, Miss Minola."

Katharina turned with a flourish at the door. "I am not to be disturbed." She slipped inside and closed the door.

Pietro led Curtis toward his cabin, Bianca following.

"Okay," Bianca said, "what do I feed her?"

"I know just the thing," Pietro said, and slipped behind a thick pine tree. "Walt, Fish?" he said to the tree.

"You're talking to a tree," Bianca whispered. "Katharina is getting to you."

"In the cabinet above the refrigerator is a box of old cereal," Pietro said. "Bring it to my fence, and Bianca will come and get it. Have some hot chocolate ready for her, okay?"

Pietro drew a map in the dirt. "It's about a half mile or so, and take your time."

"I may run my ass off on the way there," Bianca said. "Will it be enough for both of us to eat?"

"No," Pietro said. "It's some really old Kashi."

Bianca blinked.

"Cereal."

"Oh."

"And I'll make my famous hockey puck espresso." He smiled. "If she even drinks half a cup, she'll be awake for days."

"How thick is this stuff going to be?"

"She'll need to use a knife and a fork."

Bianca smiled. "Hot chocolate, here I come."

* * *

"I'll make the hot chocolate, you get the cereal," Fish said to Walt. "You're married."

"Kashi?" Walt asked, showing Fish the box. "What the hell is Kashi?"

"Cereal," Fish said.

"This is cereal?" Walt looked inside. "It looks like Kansas in there." He checked the expiration date. "These . . . weeds expired two years ago."

"Perfect," Fish said. "You think Bianca likes little marshmallows? She looks like the type."

Katharina started to remove her own boots and stopped. *I have people, I mean, I had people. Damn. I just sent my person out of here. The fire is dying, too. I should add a log. No. My person can do it when she comes back.*

She removed her headset and saw a mud smudge on the lens. She cleaned it off with her sleeve and noticed her nails caked with dirt. Two were slightly cracked, one torn, and one thumbnail had a sliver missing. *I should trim them all back. What am I saying? Bianca can do it when she comes back.*

The things I think about having to do for myself . . .

Pietro knocked and entered a split second later.

"Why knock at all if you're just going to come in anyway, Fonzi?" Katharina asked.

Pietro held out a pan and a tin cup.

Katharina smelled something heavenly. "What's that? Is that—"

"Espresso," Pietro said. He set the tin cup in front of her. "May I pour?"

Katharina nodded.

And then she waited.

And waited.

And waited some more until a single spaghetti string of espresso left the pan and yawned toward the cup.

Katharina could wait no longer. She grasped the pan and took it to the bathroom, adding some water. She wanted to swirl it around with something, and her fingers were out of the question. She jiggled the pan back and forth, the lavalike espresso slowly turning into molasses. She returned to the table and poured herself a cup, dropping the pan and drinking it all before the pan stopped ringing.

So bitter! Where's the sugar? "You have any sugar?" Katharina asked.

"No," Pietro said. "Best no sugar."

Katharina poured herself another cup anyway. "What's the point of espresso if you don't have any sugar?" She showed Pietro the goo in her cup. "See? You didn't add enough water. I thought you Italians knew how to make this shit."

Bianca then entered with the box of Kashi and two bowls and two silver spoons.

Katharina squinted at the box. "What the hell is that?"

Pietro took the box and poured two bowls, then took the bowls to the bathroom sink to run water over them. He set Katharina's in front of her. "Enjoy!"

Bianca dug into hers with gusto. "Yummy." *Oh God,* she thought. *This sucks so bad! It tastes like lint! It tastes like cat hair, not that I've ever eaten cat hair! The things I have to do!*

Katharina put a spoonful in her mouth. "This shit tastes like cardboard!" She flipped the box around. "And it went bad two years ago!" She pushed away her bowl. "Is this the best you could do, Bianca? I'd get more nourishment from eating the damn box!"

Pietro grabbed Katharina's right bicep. "Grain good. Make strong."

Katharina ripped her arm away. "I *told* you about touching me. Don't you touch me again. Tell him that if he touches me again, I'll have him arrested for assault."

"This is really bad," Bianca snarled in Italian.

Pietro nodded. "I like it," he said in Italian. "It tastes much better with milk, even as old as it is. For some reason, I don't think Kashi can go bad. I thought you'd bring some milk with you. Tell the queen here that I'm tired of her bad attitude and will handle her any way I please."

Bianca hesitated. "Um, you're not going to like what he just said, Miss Minola."

"Spit it out, Bianca!"

"Okay, here goes." Bianca glanced at Pietro. "Um, he said he would touch you as often as he wants to, anywhere he wants to, however he wants to, and whenever he wants to because you have such a bad attitude."

Katharina's mouth dropped open. "Did you tell him that I'd have him arrested?"

"Um, yeah, I did," Bianca said. "He said he can't be arrested because the police are fifty miles away and most of them are his relatives, anyway. He also says you can be arrested for cursing in Ontario, so you better watch out."

This girl was made for this role, Pietro thought. *Amazing creativity!*

Katharina stood and took a deep breath. "Screw him! And screw Canada!" She smacked the bowl onto the floor. "And screw whatever the hell that shit was!" She grabbed her headset, settled it on her head like a crown, and walked out of the cabin with her head held high.

"Should I follow you, Miss Minola?" Bianca asked. *Please say no!*

Katharina stuck her head back into the cabin. "No. I want you to sit in there and eat burnt grass. Come the hell on, Bianca!"

Pietro stooped and whispered, "The espresso is having an *immediate* effect. Be careful, Bianca."

Chapter 18

Katharina, with Bianca trailing a few steps behind, forded the stream easily using the bridge, almost leaping across in her haste to get to the next scene.

Bianca stopped in the middle of the bridge and burped. *Oh God.* "Miss Minola, I think I'm going to be sick!" *For real! Raisins, stew, and Kashi do not mix!*

"Well, don't puke in that stream, damn," Katharina said, continuing down the steep hill toward the clearing.

Bianca burped again, felt *much* better, waited until Katharina's bobbing form disappeared, and headed directly to Vincenzo's cabin.

Katharina entered the clearing and found Vincenzo wearing headphones and sitting on a log looking at a monitor. *I'm almost beginning to respect this man,* she thought. *He seems to know exactly where and when I'll need him at any given time.* She sat beside him and took off his headphones. "Roll it back," she said, putting on the headphones.

Vincenzo slid the monitor into her lap, hit a few buttons, and smiled broadly. "This is where I started filming. See the wonderful splashing?"

"I don't want to see this," Katharina said. "I want to see what I saw with the headset."

"Oh." Vincenzo looked up at the camera in the tree to his right, hoping Fish was paying attention.

"Um, Fish?" Walt said. "If what he's watching in that monitor is from his camera, how can she see what the headset recorded?"

Fish flexed his fingers, then typed in several commands, hitting a button here and there, rolling his mouse and clicking. "We broadcast her footage from here to there."

"We can do that?" Walt asked.

"We can," Fish said.

"What if she wants to freeze or rewind or fast-forward or just see one part of a scene?"

Fish frowned. "This ain't like TiVo, Walt. She can only see it start to finish, but I already edited it down to just her crossing. I'm good like that." He cued up Katharina's first dash across the stream. "Sending." He hit another button.

"What's taking so long?" Katharina asked.

"Is, um, rewinding," Vincenzo said, sweat trickling down his back. "Ah. There it is."

Katharina watched and listened in amazement to the Canadian world through her eyes and ears. She saw her hands, her feet, snatches of her dress, the spray of water all around her, her muddy hands, even the steam of her breath. The stream thundered, her curses echoed, and her filmed panting hummed continuously in her ears. The top of the bank looked so far away, then close, then far away as she tumbled. She felt the thrill of cresting that bank, resting a moment, then crawling close to the ground to the shelter of the brush. She saw her arms reaching around her legs and pulling her knees in, her right arm scratched and bleeding, the only sound a whispered "Thank You, Jesus."

I said that? she thought. *I don't remember saying that. I guess I did.*

She took off the headphones. "That was, that was intense, Sly."

"A good idea, yes?"

"Yeah. Wow." *The audience is going to be as amazed as I just was.* "But I cussed a lot, though."

Vincenzo shrugged. "We can cover your curses with thunder, more stream noise, tracking dogs, the howls of wolves—or erase it entirely. Your choice."

"Tracking dogs?" Katharina asked. "That's a little cliché, isn't it? I mean, this is the place she sets up shop, right? She has to be far across the border by now."

Vincenzo nodded. "But she does not know that. She has no map to tell her."

Good point, Katharina thought.

"And what is she running from?" Vincenzo asked. "Why is she hiding? Something is after her."

Katharina pondered his questions. "She's running because . . . she's been running for weeks, and that's all she knows to do. She's hiding because she's been hiding for weeks. She doesn't know she's safe yet. She doesn't know she's made it to freedom." She laughed softly. "She doesn't know how free and freeing freedom can be."

"Bingo," Walt said.

"You got lucky," Fish said.

"I have my moments."

* * *

Katharina stood and looked around her. "This place, all the shadows, all the places the unknown can hide, all these freaking trees! She has to feel a constant sense of paranoia, constant feelings of dread, has to feel watched, can't let her guard down, even for a second." She reached under her dress for the knife tucked all this time at the top of her leggings. "I can't believe I've been running around with this blade so close to my skin. I'm surprised I haven't cut myself. I never even thought about using it."

"You had no time to use it," Vincenzo said. "You were acting by instinct. Your mind said, 'Get away, hide, stay quiet.' "

My mind actually said, "Run, bitch, it's freaking cold!" Katharina nodded. "But now . . . Now she needs to build a fire or she'll die." She looked around the clearing, picking up several rocks.

"What are you looking for?" Vincenzo asked.

"Flint," Katharina said. "Only I don't know what flint looks like."

Vincenzo looked at the ground as well. "But what do you need the flint for?"

"The script says I have to start a fire with this knife and some flint."

Vincenzo shook his head. "Um. No. We will use a lighter. Much more efficient, the audience will never know. Just hit the knife on any rock a few times, I will swing around behind, you will start fire with lighter . . . Your character would know how to start a fire, yes?"

Katharina kept searching the ground. "She might, she might not. Kitchen slaves kept the fires going all day. They had no need to start one, get me? I mean, those kitchen fires might have been going for generations."

J. J. Murray

Vincenzo nodded.

"And not all slaves were in the kitchen." She picked up a slab of black rock and put it in the pocket of her dress. "Look at me. Am I a kitchen slave, a house slave, or a field slave?"

Vincenzo looked at his star nearly covered with mud speckles, the hem of her dress already starting to tatter. "I will say . . . field. You are strong and lean."

"I'm lean because I'm still hungry," Katharina said, "but we'll talk about that later. Right now . . . I want to start a fire."

Vincenzo looked at the clouds rolling in above, some of them dark and forbidding. "The light is okay, not great. Fire scenes always look better at night."

"But she's freezing," Katharina said. "She's just been through a stream. She's wet and cold. I doubt she'd wait for night to set in to make the fire that will save her life."

"Ah. I see your point." He again looked up. "And if we are lucky, it will begin to snow."

Katharina looked up. "Those are snow clouds?"

Vincenzo nodded. "They are predicting snow, but not much. A few, um, how you say . . ."

"Flurries?"

"Yes, flurries." He smiled. "I hope they are big flurries. That will look spectacular, and I will do this scene from here very wide." He framed the clearing with his hands. "Yes. It will be intimate. You will be a small person in a large space."

Say what? "You mean 'impersonal,' not 'intimate,' right?"

"Um . . . yes. That is what I mean. English is such a precise language, yes? Um, I will start wide to capture your isolation, then come close to capture your determination." He shrugged slightly. "What do you think?"

For all his sheer weirdness, Sly is all right. "Okay." She looked at the rocks in her hands. "I wonder which one of these rocks will spark." She reached into her pocket for the large black rock. "Maybe this one?"

"Probably not, but do not stress. Hit it a few times. If it sparks, it sparks. If it doesn't, we can add the spark later."

Katharina shook her head. "Nah. I'm going to do this right." She walked to the brush and took ten steps forward. "I'll put my fire pit here." She dropped her rocks. "I need to get some big rocks." She smiled. "I saw some at the stream."

"Now she's thinking," Walt said. "This is good. Is there any flint in these woods?"

"Hell if I know," Fish said. "But that is one serious knife. Pietro picked it out from his personal collection. You should see all the weaponry he has. The dude is Rambo."

"And Vincenzo is Sly," Walt said.

"Go figure." Fish rolled his eyes. "It must be an Italian thing."

With Vincenzo filming through some brush at the top of the bank, Katharina searched the edge of the stream for large stones, lifting them from the muck and taking them to form the circle for her fire pit. She tossed several smaller stones into another pile. Once she had her fire pit arranged, she took pieces of dead twigs and branches from the brush pile and laid them in the center. Hunched over these twigs and branches, she took her knife and picked up the first rock, striking the rock at an angle.

*   *   *

"Wrong rocks," Fish said. "They have to be."

"And wrong technique," Walt said. "She should be striking the rock against the knife."

"Really?"

"Hey, I was a Boy Scout for a few weeks," Walt said.

Fish rolled to another computer screen and typed "flint" into a search engine. " 'Flint . . . is found in limestone formations, and limestone formations . . . are usually found near water.' "

"She needs to go back to the stream."

Fish smiled. "More splashing! More mud! More skin!"

"Okay, now you're leaning toward sick."

Fish laughed. "You say the nicest things."

Katharina struck every rock in her pile several times and from different angles until she became frustrated, her hands hurting, sweat dripping onto the twigs and branches.

"Cut!" Vincenzo yelled. "Miss Katharina, really it is not necessary. We can use the lighter and continue."

Katharina kept striking rocks.

"Katharina, you will dull your knife," Vincenzo said. "We can add the spark later."

Katharina tried the large black rock again, striking it, the knife vibrating in her grip.

Pietro sneaked down the hill and came up behind her, snatching the knife from her hand.

"Hey!" she yelled.

Pietro picked her up, his hands under both armpits.

"I told you that if you *ever* touched me again—"

Pietro held a rock in front of her nose.

Katharina focused on the dark black rock, which almost looked like a lump of coal. "Is that flint?"

Pietro nodded.

"Where did you find it?"

Pietro pointed to the stream. "But not knife on rock." He tapped the rock against Katharina's knife. "Rock on knife."

Katharina reached for the flint.

Pietro held it high in the air, turned, and threw it into the stream.

"You . . . you *son of a bitch!*" she cried.

"*Sì,*" Pietro said. "You find. Sly film."

Katharina took several deep breaths, her blue-green eyes fierce. "I'm ready, Sly. You ready?"

"Ready when you are, Miss Katharina," Vincenzo said. "Whenever you are ready."

Katharina swept by Pietro to the creek, Vincenzo following and filming. She saw the large lump several feet from shore. She first tried to use a fallen branch to bring it closer, gave up, and splashed in after it, reaching down and pulling it to the surface.

"Such a clear view," Walt said.

"A perfect shot," Fish said. "Angle's right, too. No reflection except for the clouds rolling by above."

"Those are snow clouds, Fish."

"Yes!" Fish pumped his hand several times. "C'mon, snow. Just pour down on her, give her some ice-cold dandruff."

Walt blinked. "I have no words for you right now."

I have now soaked myself all the way to my titties, Katharina thought painfully. *My poor nipples are going to chafe completely off! Think warm thoughts, think warm thoughts . . .*

Katharina waded back, climbed up the bank, carried

the flint to the circle, and hunched down once again. She brought the flint to the knife with a jerk.

A spark.

She smiled, moving the knife closer to the twigs and stems. She struck the knife again with the flint.

Another spark, but no smoke, flame, or fire resulted. She tried different angles, saw lots of sparks, and even hit the twigs dead-on with sparks—still nothing.

"Cut!" Vincenzo yelled. "Everything is too wet, Katharina, and you are dripping on your wood. You will be making sparks for hours to no effect."

Pietro swept into the clearing, his hands full of moss, several slivers of birch bark, and some dry brown grass. He opened his hands under Katharina's nose.

She blinked. "All that?"

Pietro nodded. "Tinder."

Katharina reached for his hands.

Pietro pulled his hands back. "No touch. I call *polizia.*"

Katharina *almost* smiled. *There's more to this Fonzi than meets the eye,* she thought. *But I still hate his ass.* She pulled her hands back to her lap. "No touch."

Pietro put his hands out in front of her eyes this time. "Take picture."

Katharina tried to memorize what she saw. She recognized the moss and the birch bark, but she had no idea where he had found dry grass. *I ought to go get the rest of that cereal,* she thought. *I've seen that bark on trees all over the place, and the moss grows on the rocks just up the hill.* "Okay." She stood.

Pietro dropped the contents of his hands into the fire pit.

Katharina stooped and picked them up. "Here," she said, giving them to Pietro. "I have to find them." She nodded at Vincenzo. "Ready?"

"Yes," Vincenzo said, swinging the camera to his shoulder.

"And we're rolling," Fish said, watching Katharina racing through the forest collecting moss and birch bark.

"Pietro almost has her trained on the second day," Walt said. "Did you see her almost smile just then?"

"'I call *polizia*,'" Fish said. "Katharina Minola isn't trained. She can't be tamed."

"It's happening," Walt said. "I can feel it."

"Nah," Fish said. "Hell hasn't frozen over yet."

Walt smiled. "The temperature *is* dropping outside . . ."

Katharina collected the "correct" items to start her fire, ripping several small strips of birch bark off trees, scraping dry moss from rocks into her hands. She returned to her fire pit and aimed her spark at the bark.

Nothing happened.

She changed her angle and struck the flint against the knife.

More nothing happened.

"Cut!" Vincenzo yelled. "Miss Katharina, we do not have to do it this way."

Katharina kept throwing sparks onto the bark. "*I* have to do it this way. What am I doing wrong?" She looked up at Pietro. "Tell me."

Pietro squatted and picked up the bark, feeling it between his thumb and index finger. "Wet."

Katharina held out her hand. "Let me see that."

Pietro placed the bark in her hand.

Katharina rubbed the bark with her fingers. "It looks just like what you had."

Pietro shook his head. "Bark on ground dry most of time. Bark on tree stay on tree. You take." He pantomimed ripping the bark off a tree. "Make scar on tree."

"Oh." She looked at Vincenzo. "Let's try this again, shall we?"

Vincenzo nodded.

Katharina flew through the woods with her eyes to the ground, finding bits of birch bark here and there, feeling each piece for dryness before putting it in her pocket. She returned again to the clearing, made a small pile of bark and moss, and struck the flint against the knife.

The spark hit the bark, and a thin whisper of smoke rose into the air.

Yes! Katharina thought. *Smoke! I am officially a fire starter. But where's the fire?* She resisted the impulse to look for Pietro, thereby ruining the shot. She sent several more sparks onto the bark and added moss to wherever .it smoked. *What do they freaking do in the movies?*

I'm glad I didn't say that out loud, she thought. *Oh yeah!*

She flattened herself onto the ground and blew softly on the bark and soon saw a glow, then a single wisp of a flame, and then she heard a crackle. She added more moss, more bark, several twigs, a larger branch, and a real live fire grew in front of her. She slid a large branch into the mix and watched it smoke—

What the hell just happened? Where are the flames? She panicked and blew some more, but all she accomplished was a severe case of hyperventilation.

"Cut!" Vincenzo yelled.

Pietro stepped behind Katharina, crouched, and whispered, *"Poco, poco. Molto lento."*

Katharina looked at Vincenzo for the translation. "What's he saying?"

"He means a little at a time very slowly," Vincenzo said.

"Poco molto lento," my ass, Katharina thought. *I knew that. This stupid wood is just too wet.* She pulled off the offending branch, threw sparks on another piece of bark, blew gently, and had another fire crackling in less than a minute.

Then it started to rain, a fine haze spitting down on her.

She tried to shield her fire with her hands while adding more twigs and sticks, eventually breaking the wet branch into several pieces before adding one piece at a time. Eventually, she had a small blaze going despite the rain, but she worried the rain would douse it unless she did something drastic.

Katharina stood, hitched up her dress, and stood over her fire.

Fish tilted his head. "That's not something you see every day."

"She could set her dress on fire!" Walt shouted.

"Nah, it's too wet to burn," Fish said with a smile. "But what if it did? We'd get another stream scene for sure. Marilyn Monroe, eat your heart out."

The rain abating slightly, Katharina stepped back and sighed. *I built a fire and it's still burning. My dress even feels drier. Yes! Did they pump their fists back then? I better not.*

"Cut!" Pietro yelled, striding toward Katharina.

"Who's the director here?" Katharina whined. "He's in my shot, Sly. Get him out of here."

"Must . . ." Pietro said. He pantomimed taking off his clothes. "Get dry."

Say what? "That ain't in the script, Fonzi."

Pietro shook his head. "You wet. Must get dry. You die."

Katharina backed away toward the brush. "You're out of your damn mind, Fonzi. I am not taking my clothes off."

Vincenzo set his camera and monitor on the log. "Alessandro! Come!"

Pietro walked quickly toward Vincenzo, his eyes fierce.

Vincenzo yanked Pietro's arm, whispering, "We have to have a long argument. Make it good." He pushed Pietro back with two hands. "This is working!" he shouted angrily in Italian. "We've done two scenes in one day! It has to be a record for Katharina! Isn't she beautiful?"

Pietro threw up his hands, and in Italian bellowed, "Oh, she really is nice looking once you get past her horns and the pitchfork tail!"

Vincenzo dug a finger into Pietro's chest, wincing as he did so. "She doesn't have to take off her clothes today, does she?" he spat in Italian.

Pietro balled up his fists. "It's going to start raining heavily in half an hour!" he yelled in Italian. "It would be great if the rain put out her fire, yes?"

Vincenzo nodded and walked slowly to Katharina, his hands in his pockets. "I hate to say it, but Alessandro, he is right. You must take off some of your clothes."

"Wet," Pietro said. "Must dry."

"Y'all aren't serious," Katharina said. "My clothes aren't that wet."

"Your dress, Katharina," Vincenzo said. "At least pull off the dress. You still have clothes on underneath, yes?"

Katharina shook her head. "Oh, like she's just going

to disrobe in the wilderness because of a little wetness. Why can't she just sit by the fire and get dry that way?"

Vincenzo sighed. "In this weather, in this place, staying dry is most important for survival. Yes, you will shiver, but that is good. That is the body's way of keeping itself warm. Wet clothes will only make you colder, and they will dry much faster if you, I don't know, um, hang them on something."

"Branches, sticks," Pietro said.

"Near the fire, but not too close," Vincenzo said. "Your dress is irreplaceable."

"You don't have another one?" Katharina asked.

"No," Vincenzo said. "That dress is one hundred and forty years old. A rare find, yes? And so well preserved."

That explains the mothball smell, Katharina thought. *These clothes should be in a museum, not muddied up by me. An actual slave woman wore these. Amazing.*

"All right," Katharina said. "I'll take off and dry the dress, but not in front of him." She pointed at Pietro. "Or his mule, or even you." She tapped her headset. "I've got this shot, now . . . get on and get out of here."

Pietro, Vincenzo, and Curtis left, winding their way up the hill.

Katharina fashioned some longer sticks into a tripod of sorts near her fire pit, using a piece of the long grass to bind the sticks together. She pulled her dress over her head, draping it over the sticks, and then warmed herself, rubbing her hands over the flames.

Her stomach rumbled mercilessly.

That's my cue, she thought. *I am doing Scene 3 now. Time to go find some food.*

Chapter 19

Fish flashed his fingers over the keyboard, watching Katharina, who wore only her undershirt, bloomers, leggings, and boots, on monitor after monitor as she walked, finally stopping at the edge of a wilting field. "Where is she going? What is she doing?"

"So effortless," Walt said. "That's the Katharina I remember."

"Walt, what is she doing?"

Katharina stooped to pull out a weed of some kind.

"She's gone on to Scene 3!" Walt cried. "She's actually following my script!" He turned to Fish. "It's the food-gathering scene. Run me a search for edible plants in this part of Ontario."

"Why?"

"She has to eat something," Walt said, "and I don't want her eating the wrong thing and dying or getting dysentery."

"Pietro will know. He lives here, remember?" He pointed to another monitor that showed Pietro hiding behind a tree near Katharina. "He's not letting her out of his sight. And, anyway, how are we going to get the information to her? The fax machine is still jammed."

"Oh yeah."

Fish zoomed in on Katharina's hands. "I hope that shit isn't poisonous," he said. "Diarrhea is the least of our worries."

Katharina smelled the weed, which looked like just about every other piece of vegetation in the forest, and it smelled like grass. She had run by moss on rocks and lichen gouging several trees, and hoped she could eat something leafy. She pulled a single leaf from the weed and brought it to her mouth—

Pietro grabbed her wrist from behind. "No."

Katharina turned and tried to break Pietro's grip. "Why not?"

Pietro let go of her wrist and put both of his hands to his neck.

"It would kill me?" She dropped the leaf and the weed.

"No," Pietro said. "Make sick."

Katharina walked to an evergreen-looking shrub that held bright red berries. "I don't appreciate you following me, Fonzi. You keep ruining my shots. And, anyway, what if I want my character to get sick? You ever think of that?"

"Che?"

"Sick." She pantomimed gagging. "Now go away. You're still in my shot."

Pietro moved in front of her, crouching down and picking several berries, popping them into his mouth. "No. Keep you safe."

"You're a real pain in the ass, you know that?"

Pietro smiled as he chewed. "*Sì*. You try."

She plucked a tiny berry. "What is it?"

"Kinnikinnick," Pietro said. "Bearberry." He ate several more.

Katharina put a single berry in her mouth. It was bitter but palatable. She looked around and saw more of the same bushes sprouting between the rocks on the hillside.

"Okay, Mr. Pain-in-the-ass, what else can I eat?" she asked.

For the next hour, Pietro led Katharina through the forest, pointing out but not plucking or picking the various plants she could eat safely. She did the picking and the sampling, tasting dark blue and black elderberries, the pith of fireweed, wrinkled blueberries, chicory, crowberries, and lotus leaves.

Pietro cracked the shell of a walnut and handed her the pieces. "Much protein," he said. He looked up.

Katharina nodded and took a small bite. "Decent." She, too, looked up, but not at the ominous clouds. "If I could eat these pine trees, I'd be set."

Pietro reached up to a thin pine branch and snapped off the end. He peeled the bark off a thin twig and chewed the wood. "So-so. Sour. Better in spring. Sweet."

She jumped for a branch but missed. "I'm too short."

Pietro blinked.

She jumped again. "Do you mind?"

Pietro pulled down a limb but released it before she could grab on. "Vitamin C."

"No shit," Katharina said.

Pietro smiled. "Eat many berries, lots of shit." He laughed heartily and pulled the branch down again. "Joke!"

As before, he released the branch before Katharina could latch onto it. "Must go," he said.

"Why?" Katharina asked.

A thunderous, cold rain plummeted from the sky, as if a drain plug had been pulled from the clouds.

"Go!" Pietro yelled. "Get dress!"

By the time Katharina slogged through the forest to the clearing, the rain had soaked her dress completely, her fire only smoked, and smaller puddles were forming into larger puddles, ministreams running in snake-like rivulets through the clearing. She wrung out her dress as she ran for the bridge, her nipples threatening to chop down trees as she passed them by.

"She looks as if she's done for the day," Fish said. "Crossing the stream on the bridge."

Walt sighed. "I wish I could resend the entire script." He had watched and listened to Bianca cussing at the fax machine before kicking it and throwing up her hands. "We're good for a few days. She still has to get the fire going again, gather some food, and build her shelter."

"Approaching Cabin 2, Pietro on the porch drinking coffee." Fish zoomed in on Pietro. "Ah, shucks. I know he's gonna start some shit. Why does he have to do that?"

Katharina no longer felt the rain by the time she approached Pietro's cabin. In fact, she was numb from the top of her head to the tips of her big toes. Her leggings clung to her body, her nipples threatened to secede from her body through the fabric of her undershirt, and her boots made squishing sounds.

Pietro, warm and dry on his porch, held out his coffee mug. "A good day, yes?"

Katharina paused to catch her breath. *Is he toasting me? Smiling? Like he saved me or something. His cooking is terrible, his espresso is sludge, his mule—*"Shit!"*—has loose bowels.*

"*Ciao, bella,*" Pietro said. He winked and went inside his cabin.

Why isn't this my *cabin?* Katharina wondered. *It's closer to the set.*

She continued on, scraping her boot on a rock and the side of a tree. *He called me "beautiful" again. Right. Soaked to the bone, though I am right perky up front. He didn't give me attitude this time, either.*

But Pietro's grin annoyed her. *Fonzi had a shit-eating grin. He doesn't think I can do this shit on my own. I'll show him. I know what to eat now. I know how to build a fire now. I'm even going to trap some critters, build a shelter like the Taj Mahal, and I'll even do it all without any of his help.* Poco molto lento *that, Fonzi.*

Chapter 20

Bianca heard steps on the porch and dashed from her bedroom to the bathroom, shutting the door behind her as the front door banged open.

"Bianca!"

Bianca counted to ten before flushing the toilet and the wrapper from the granola bar she had just finished. Opening the bathroom door, Bianca jumped when she saw Katharina.

I shouldn't even be thinking this, but damn! Bianca thought. *I wish I had a camera! The* Enquirer *would pay top dollar to see what's left of Katharina Minola.*

"Who else did you think it'd be?" Katharina asked. "You look like you've seen a damn ghost."

"You're soaking wet," Bianca said, rushing to Katharina and taking the dress. She took it into the bathroom and wrung it out over the tub. "I'll get that fire blazing for you in a minute, Miss Minola."

"Whatever," Katharina said.

She said "whatever" like, well, "whatever" is supposed to mean, which is "I don't care." That's a good thing, isn't it?

Bianca peeked out and saw Katharina sitting in a chair, her legs crossed and resting on top of the table.

After hanging the dress from a hook attached to the mantel, Bianca stoked the fire and added more wood. "I tried to get the fax machine to work, but it's still jammed or something. It says there are twenty pages waiting to be sent."

Katharina sighed. "Don't worry about it. I won't need them."

Bianca smelled something vile. "What's that smell?"

Katharina nodded at her boots. "Mule shit. Watch your step out there."

Bianca blinked. *Is she suddenly being nice?* Bianca trembled for a split second. *This is scary.* "Um, I will, Miss Minola."

"Where's my coffee?" Katharina asked.

Bianca sighed. "It's all gone. I'm sorry, Miss Minola."

"Whatever," Katharina said again.

Twice she says that, Bianca thought. *Geez, the suspense is killing me!* "Um, how'd it go out there?" She winced and waited for Katharina's normal venom.

"It went well, actually," Katharina said. "That fire feels nice."

My God, Bianca thought, *is this the old Katharina back already?* "Thank you, Miss Minola. Um, I'm glad things are going so well. I'm still not feeling that well, so if you don't mind, I'd like to go lie down for a while." *And eat some more granola bars.*

"Where'd you go, Bianca?"

To Vincenzo's nice bathroom to relieve myself of half a pound of raisins, "bear" stew, and Kashi. Oh, and I ate some microwave popcorn. Movie-theater butter. Yum! "My stomach was still bothering me, so I came up here to relieve myself." *That was weak.* "I, um, I am feeling a little better."

"I expect you to be close to me at all times."

"I'm sorry, Miss Minola. I'll try not to let it happen again." *Oh, but it will!* Bianca thought joyfully. *Vincenzo also has ham-and-cheese Hot Pockets, too!*

Katharina drummed her boots on the table. "Well?"

"Oh. Sorry." She removed Katharina's boots, careful to avoid touching the sole soiled by mule dung. She propped up the boots against the screen, but the heat from the fire reactivated the stench. "I'll, um, I'll put these outside."

"Don't bother," Katharina said. "I'd rather have stinky dry boots than wet ones."

"Um, okay," Bianca said, and she sat in the other chair. "So, it's really going well?"

"It's going," Katharina said. "I have to build a shelter down there next. How would you do it? You used to frolic through the woods, right?"

Bianca nodded. "Yeah, but I use a tent when I go camping. I wouldn't know how to build a shelter if my life depended on it."

Katharina closed her eyes. "So you know what I'm up against, then." She snapped her eyes open. "Do we still have that pan that had the coffee in it?"

"It's in the bathroom sink soaking."

"Well, rinse it out and warm up some water." She smiled. "You're giving me a sponge bath. We don't have a sponge, do we?"

"No."

"A washcloth?"

Bianca nodded. "Two."

"Soap?"

"A little bar, um, like you get in a hotel."

Katharina chuckled. *They have thought of just about everything to make me miserable.* "Well, don't waste it. I just need you to knock off some of this dirt."

Bianca rinsed and filled the pot, pushed it into the

coals under the fireplace grate, and waited until she could hear it bubbling. She pulled it out carefully and left it on the floor to cool for a few minutes. Dipping in one of the washcloths, she brought it steaming to Katharina's face. She dabbed it on the back of her own wrist. "It's kind of hot," she said.

"I'll be fine," Katharina said.

Bianca wiped off Katharina's face, neck, shoulders, arms, and hands with one washcloth, drying them with the other. The water in the pot turned beige. "I can boil more water if you like, maybe get Alessandro to bring that cauldron back so you can take a proper bath."

"It's okay," Katharina said, starting to nod off.

"I can go get you something to eat if you like," Bianca said.

"Sure," Katharina said, her eyelids drooping.

I like this person, Bianca thought. *She has character. She even takes naps like normal people.*

Bianca took the comforter off her own bed and snuggled it around Katharina's body. She slipped into her coat and left the cabin for Vincenzo's.

"That was hot," Fish said.

"What was?" Walt asked.

"You were watching, weren't you? One hot woman giving another hot woman a bath like that? Man, you have been married too long." He pressed the squawk button. "Vincenzo, Bianca is on her way to your place to get some food. What do you have?"

"I could whip up some macaroni 'n' cheese," Vincenzo said.

Walt smiled. "Is it the kid kind, the one with funny shapes?"

"I'll check." A few moments later, Vincenzo said, "Yeah. It is."

"That'll do," Walt said. "Our girl had a good day today, didn't she?"

"Yeah," Vincenzo said. "What's she doing now?"

Fish zoomed in on Katharina's face, her eyes rapidly moving behind her eyelids. "That girl is dreaming hard. I don't know how she can sleep, though. That espresso looked 180 proof."

"I thought we were supposed to try to keep her awake, Vincenzo," Walt said. "If we had that fax machine working, we could spit out pages whenever she started to doze off."

"Maybe tomorrow," Vincenzo said. "She deserves her rest."

Bianca knocked on Vincenzo's door, and he opened it without a wig on his head.

Bianca entered. "What if I had been Katharina?"

Vincenzo showed her his walkie-talkie. "Fish told me she was sleeping."

Bianca went into the little kitchen and examined a pot. "Are those noodles?"

"For macaroni 'n' cheese," Vincenzo said.

"Yum!"

He opened a tiny refrigerator sitting on the counter. "And because you've been so good, I'll even add hot dogs."

Bianca bit her lower lip. "How good have I been?"

Vincenzo counted out three hot dogs.

Bianca took two bowls from a cupboard and two spoons from a drawer. "I'm her official taste-tester, so I'll have to eat some before I go back."

An *hour* later, the two had polished off an entire batch of macaroni 'n' cheese with hot dogs and had to make more, this time without the hot dogs.

"You have a little cheese right..." She wiped a smudge of cheese from Vincenzo's cheek.

"Thank you." He sighed. "I, um, I wish you didn't have to go. I wanted you to be able to see all the footage we got today."

"And pop some more popcorn?"

He nodded. "But . . ."

"Yeah . . ."

The walkie-talkie squawked. "Target is awake and hungry," Fish's voice said, "target is awake and hungry."

Bianca took the walkie-talkie from Vincenzo's back pocket. "Is she pissed off, awake, and hungry, or just awake and hungry?"

"Hey, Bianca, this is Fish, and Katharina is *pissed*."

Vincenzo put a top on the pot and handed a serving spoon to Bianca.

Bianca shook her head. "Only give her, oh, about one . . . fifth of the pot. Just put it in a bowl."

"It will be cold . . ." Vincenzo stopped. "Revenge is a dish . . ."

"Best served cold," Bianca said.

Vincenzo filled a bowl, covered it with foil, and put it in Bianca's hands. *"Ciao."*

As Bianca backed out of the door, she said, "Save me some popcorn, okay?"

"I will."

By the time Bianca returned to the cabin, Katharina's dinner had turned lukewarm at best. She set it in front of Katharina and handed her the spoon. Katharina immediately dug in but stopped chewing immediately. "It's cold."

"That's the way, um, people eat it around here," Bianca said.

"Did Alessandro make this for me?" Katharina asked.

"Um, no. Sly did."

"Sly is a better cook," Katharina said, and she inhaled the rest anyway, scraping every little speck of cheese from the sides of the bowl. Bianca half expected her to lick the bowl, but Katharina didn't.

"I know where to find food in the forest now," she said, "so eventually I won't need to eat anyone's cooking. Fonzi showed me this afternoon. Most of it was close to the ground, and you know what? I didn't know there was so much to eat in the woods . . ." She told Bianca about every bush, berry, and branch she could eat as Bianca stared out the little window by the door.

It had started to snow.

Huge snowflakes the size of silver dollars.

I hope it snows a foot or two tonight, Bianca thought. *A hungry and pissed-off Katharina is a Katha-diva I can understand.* She looked back at the woman babbling by the fire. *I have no idea who this nice person is.*

Chapter 21

In the morning, though there was only a scattering of snow on the ground, Katharina balked at going out.

"No," Katharina said after one glimpse of the snow from her window, and she returned to her bed.

Bianca relaxed. *Katha-diva is back.* She offered Katharina long johns to wear under her leggings.

Katharina only turned over in her bed.

Bianca offered the long johns and a pair of wool socks.

Katharina covered her head with her comforter.

Bianca offered the long johns, a pair of wool socks, and a flannel undershirt.

Katharina thought about it. . . . "No."

"I don't have much left, Miss Minola," Bianca said. "I have another pair of wool socks."

"Deal," Katharina said.

"You can't wear those old boots and two pairs of thick wool socks," Bianca said.

"Sure I can."

Katharina dressed—and put the wool socks on her hands.

"Why have you been holding out on me, Bianca?" Katharina asked.

Bianca looked for a place to hide. After a good night's rest, Katha-diva had made a brutal return to the cabin. "Have I?"

"You knew we were coming to a place like this, didn't you? Don't try to deny it."

Bianca nodded. "Yes, Miss Minola. I knew we were going someplace cold."

"Yet you let me dress as I did anyway, and I'm sure some animal has run off with my shoes. Am I right?"

"Um, and maybe your sunglasses." Bianca nodded. "They were pretty ruined, anyway."

"That is beside the point." Katharina put on the headset. "Why, Bianca? Why did you lie to me?"

Bianca looked up briefly. "I didn't consider it lying at the time. I was afraid." *Not.* "I mean, any time I make a suggestion or speak my mind or give you my opinion, you just shoot it down, anyway."

"I do no such thing."

I just spoke my mind, you wench, and you shot me down again! "It's as if I'm only entitled to *your* opinions!"

Katharina ignored her. "Bianca, I distinctly remember asking you directly if you knew where we were going, and you said, 'I don't know, Miss Minola.' You weren't making a suggestion or giving your opinion with that answer. You lied to me, Bianca. I don't like people lying to me."

"I'm sorry, Miss Minola." Bianca looked at her cold bare feet. "I'll, um, I'll just—"

"Haven't I taught you anything?" Katharina interrupted.

Where is she going with this? How schizophrenic is this woman? "I don't understand, Miss Minola."

"Bianca, look at me. I didn't get where I am without

asserting myself, without speaking up for myself. I have been hoping that by watching and learning from me, you would learn how to be more assertive, to stand up for yourself." She sighed. "It is obvious that you are a *very* slow learner."

Oh . . . my . . . God!

"We will discuss this further when I return." She started for the door.

"Aren't I going with you?" Bianca asked.

"Bianca, darling, you cannot go out there dressed like that. You'll catch pneumonia."

Katharina slammed the door behind her.

Bianca stared at the fireplace. *What the hell just happened?*

"What the hell was *that?*" Fish asked.

Walt was at a loss for words. "I have no idea. It was like watching *Wild Kingdom* or something, where one animal reestablishes dominance over another. And just last night I was betting that Katharina had mellowed a little. And now this."

"Women," Fish said. "You can't live with 'em, and you can't take 'em to a Cubs game."

"Huh?"

"Trust me," Fish said. "I took this girl to Wrigley Field, and she hated baseball, just hated it. 'It's too boring, it's too slow, there's not enough excitement.' That night was like watching *Wild Kingdom,* too."

Walt looked up at the big screen. "At least her fire skills are improving. Look."

Katharina already had a fire blazing in the fire pit.

Fish zoomed in. "Hear that crackling? She's using some really dry wood. Where'd she get that?"

* * *

Pietro closed his eyes and sighed. *What is that woman doing?* He had collected two dozen long, sturdy, dry branches during the night for Katharina to use to start her *shelter,* and here she was cracking them into three and four pieces and burning them. *She's setting fire to her "house" before she even builds it!*

After warming for several minutes, Katharina slinked off into the forest to gather food, putting most of the berries she found in the pocket of her dress. On returning to the fire, she had a feast, even loosening her boots for a while, kicking back, and taking a little nap.

"Cut!" Vincenzo cried. "Brilliant! Alessandro, bring coffee!"

Pietro brought Katharina a Styrofoam cup full of high-test coffee, Vincenzo's idea of a reward for all of Katharina's hard work so far.

Katharina popped the top and sniffed the steam. "Real coffee?"

Pietro nodded. "Four sugars."

Katharina sipped it greedily by the fire. "Now *this* is coffee."

Pietro sat across from her and stared at her through the fire. "Good fire."

"I don't need your opinion, Fonzi," Katharina said.

Pietro tossed a twig into the blaze. "Was wood for *cabina.*"

Katharina shook her head. "No, I think we have enough wood in our cabin."

Pietro pointed to the remaining dry branches. "Wood for *cabina.* Um, shelter." He outlined the shelter in the air around him. "Wood for walls, not for fire."

"Oh?" Katharina said. *Shit!* she thought. *He could have told me, couldn't he?* "I'm sure I'll manage. There's a lot of wood in these woods." *Shit! There's wood for fire and wood for shelter and never the twain shall they meet. How the hell am I supposed to know that?*

Pietro withdrew a small block of peat from his coat pocket. He had collected it from the nearby bog while Katharina had frolicked in the woods. "Is peat. Burns slow."

Katharina leaned around the fire to look. "It looks like dried mule shit."

Pietro nodded. "Too wet to burn now. Must be dry. Puts off heat, smoke. Burn long time."

"Burn long time," Katharina said in a deep voice. "Where do I get this magic heat source, Fonzi?"

"Bog," he said, pointing across the creek. "We take Curtis."

Katharina stood and wiped some dirt from the back of her dress. "I don't need your help or his. Just point me in the right direction."

He pointed to the knife lying on the ground. "Bring knife."

"Peat?" Fish asked. "What the hell is peat?"

Walt had a description from the Internet on the screen. "I'll skip how nature makes it. Just know it's dead, compacted foliage a few steps from becoming coal. Canada is one of the world's leading producers of peat, and in parts of Ireland that's all they have to make electricity. However, it has to be dry to work."

"More snow in the forecast tonight," Fish said. "For peat's sake!"

Walt moaned.

"I thought it was a good pun," Fish said.

"Just don't re-*peat* it," Walt said.

"Your pun was worse," Fish said.

Walt smiled. "That's why they pay me the big bucks."

Katharina cut a thick welcome mat–sized piece of peat from the bog using her knife, even though Pietro had recommended smaller blocks the size of her hand. When she found that peat held together much like a rug, she started dragging it back to the clearing, saying, "Bigger is better."

By the time she got her rug of peat to the clearing, however, it had disintegrated into a piece of turf only two fingers thick.

She tried to spark it, but it would not light, much less smoke.

"Must be dry," Pietro said.

Katharina waved her knife in the air. "Now how am I supposed to do that?"

Pietro shrugged. "Make oven."

"Oh, sure," Katharina said. "I'll just whip me up a stove using my knife and a few of these magic berries."

Pietro sighed. "Big, flat rocks. Put near fire. Floor. Walls. Roof." He framed it with his hands. "Oven."

"Oh. Like a brick oven."

Pietro nodded.

"So one day I can make pizza for you, Fonzi?"

This woman, this woman . . . "Can cook bread, fish, meat."

"Oh." *Great! I feel like a moron, but if I just had a script that spelled this shit out, I wouldn't be sitting here getting schooled by a mule, um, leader.* "Do the rocks have to be dry, too?"

Strangling her would be too nice of a way to kill her, Pietro thought. "Just flat. Same size. Make box or rectangle."

Katharina looked at the piece of peat she had cut. "About the size of this?"

Pietro nodded. "Dry better if smaller."

"All right, Fonzi," Katharina said. "You're the expert on shit that smells like shit."

Katharina spent the rest of the morning wrestling large, flat rocks into position near her fire pit, and by the time she was through, she had a makeshift oven with two flat rocks on top, one of which she could move with ease. She nodded and smiled at her handiwork. "Ta-da!"

"Cut!" Vincenzo yelled. "You would not say 'ta-da.' "

Katharina grabbed her knife. "I know that," she said. "I was just feeling the moment. Lighten up." She started cutting up the peat into smaller squares, stacking them inside the oven. "Don't I have to keep this fire going all night?"

Pietro nodded. "But I will do it."

"Good idea, Miss Katharina," Vincenzo said. "And in the morning, you will have peat to burn. Then you can begin your shelter."

Katharina smiled a dreamy smile at Vincenzo. *Time to pay back Alessandro for not telling me shit.* "Sly, there's a *lot* of room left in my oven. Maybe your cousin could, oh, cut me some more peat, you know, fill it up for me."

Pietro's eyes narrowed to little dots. *Don't give in, Vincenzo. If you give in a little now, she'll—*

"Ah, but Miss Katharina, won't you feel a greater sense of exhilaration knowing that you did it all by yourself?"

And that's why he's the CEO, Pietro thought, *and I'm just the woodsman.*

Katharina held up her hands, turning them so Vincenzo could see her nails. "Do you see what this shit is doing to my nails, Sly? Do you know how much this shit smells?" She waved her fingers under his nose. "I have done enough shit today, okay? Fonzi likes playing in shit, so let him do it. He'll be out here all night keeping the fire going anyway, right? This will break up some of his monotony."

Vincenzo caught the look in his brother's eye and understood it perfectly. Katharina was slowly but surely turning diva, and he couldn't let that happen. But he knew a concession here could pay dividends later. "You have worked extremely hard today, Miss Katharina. It is the least we can do for you."

Katharina smiled at Pietro, batting her eyes. "Who knows, Fonzi? Maybe one day I won't be able to tell you from your *mulo. Ciao, bella.*"

After Katharina sashayed and danced away up the hill to the bridge, Pietro confronted Vincenzo. "This is only the third day, Vincenzo. Yes, she worked her tail off for two days, but this . . . this is dangerous. We can't let her get her way at *any* time."

"I know, Pietro, I know," Vincenzo said. "But it's partially your fault."

"My fault? How is it my fault?"

"You're helping her too much," Vincenzo said. "You're not allowing her to solve her character's problems by herself. We *want* her to fail. We *want* her to make mistakes. That's the beauty of this picture, even the inherent humor of it. We're trying to make her an everywoman, and you're turning her into a superwoman. The audience will have trouble believing in her if she never makes a mistake."

Pietro sat on the log. "I don't mean to be doing that. I just hate to hear all her cursing and whining."

Vincenzo sat. "Is that all?" He patted Pietro on the leg. "It's okay. You can tell me."

"Tell you what?"

Vincenzo sighed. "You're smitten with her."

"I am not! That . . . person impersonating a person is *not* the person for me."

"Wow," Fish said. "Pietro is someone who mangles the English language almost as much as you do, Walt."

"Pietro likes her," Walt said. "She's hard not to like. She has a dream body, a sharp mind, and a killer tongue. What man wouldn't want to try to tame her?"

"Me," Fish said. "I know my limitations."

Walt stared at the confusion on Pietro's face. "Let's just hope Pietro doesn't know any of his limitations."

Vincenzo stood. "Can you try not to help her as much?"

"I'll try," Pietro said. "But what will I be doing all night thanks to you?"

"It's only one night," Vincenzo said. "At least you'll be warm."

Pietro stood. "Bring me some coffee before you go to bed, okay?"

"I will." He smiled. "Cheer up. You might actually get a compliment from her before all this is said and done."

"The only thing I want to hear coming out of that woman's mouth is the word 'good-bye.' "

Bianca jumped from the pot she was stirring when Katharina blew into the cabin and slammed the door behind her.

"What is it and who made it?" she demanded.

"It's oatmeal with cinnamon, and I made it, Miss Minola," Bianca said. "It's instant. Just add water."

"Where'd you get it?"

"Pietro brought it by just after you left. He gave us enough so we can have breakfast, too."

Katharina sat, removing the headset. "I am going to cure that man from trying to help me." She rolled her shoulders. "My shoulders are killing me."

Bianca grimaced for the camera. "You want me to rub them, Miss Minola?"

"No rush," Katharina said. "You can massage me while I'm eating."

Bianca set a bowl in front of Katharina. "There's more if you want it."

"Let's see. Macaroni 'n' cheese yesterday, oatmeal today. Are you trying to relive your childhood?" Katharina rolled her shoulders and grunted.

I do not want to touch this woman, Bianca thought. *I don't want her evil sticking to me.* She reached out her hands and squeezed Katharina's shoulders gently.

"Put some muscle into it, woman," Katharina said. "I can take it."

"Don't do it, Bianca," Fish said. "She *can't* take it. She just wants another reason to scold you."

"She can't hear you, Fish," Walt said.

"It's a habit," Fish said. "I do the same thing when I'm watching my soaps."

Bianca bore down and ground the heels of her hands into Katharina's shoulders, and Katharina didn't cry out in pain. "Um, weren't macaroni 'n' cheese and oatmeal part of your childhood, Miss Minola?"

"I was a kid once, Bianca," Katharina said as she began eating, each spoonful bigger than the last.

"What was your childhood like, Miss Minola?"

"Some things I do not talk about. That's one of them." Katharina scraped the bowl and took one last bite. "Serve me some more."

Bianca plopped another blob into Katharina's bowl. "How is it?"

"Lumpy and thick as paste. Add more water next time, and definitely add some sugar."

"Oh, but it's better for you this way, Miss Minola."

"I don't need you to tell me what I need, Bianca," Katharina said, finally slowing down and actually chewing.

Bianca took a chance. "But you said earlier that I should have told you what to wear. Didn't you need me to tell you then?"

"I need you to be honest with me."

And to know my place, right? "Yes, Miss Minola."

Katharina finished her second bowl. "Bianca, you had better learn how to cook."

"I can cook."

"No, you can't. This is from a mix, right?"

Bianca nodded.

"You can't possibly get and keep a man by 'cooking' that way. A man needs more than just what comes out of a box. He needs to know that you put some time and effort into the meal, that you cared enough to go through the trouble of making it perfect."

Of all the hypocritical things I've ever heard! "I've never seen you cook, Miss Minola."

Katharina sighed. "Believe me, I can cook, thanks to my Grandma Pearl. I'm at a place in my life where I don't have to cook anymore, but if the need ever arose,

I could cook my man a real meal." Katharina squinted at Bianca. "You are interested in men, aren't you?"

Can't cook, and now I'm a lesbian? "Yes."

"You wear men's clothing. You like the outdoors. You wear flannel undershirts and boxers, for Christ's sake. You don't wear makeup, you like wearing hiking boots. I just thought . . ."

Bianca's face felt hot. "I have a boyfriend, Miss Minola."

"First I've heard of it."

Me too. I can't tell her his name is Vincenzo, since, well, Vincenzo doesn't know he's my boyfriend yet. "I do. His name is Louie, and he lives in L.A."

"Good ol' L.A. Louie, right." Katharina blinked. "When's the last time you saw Louie?"

He filmed your sorry ass today, wench! "It's been . . . almost two months. Since I started working for you."

"And now you're blaming me for keeping you from your man?"

This could work. "You have me on call twenty-four hours a day, Miss Minola. What choice do I have?"

"You call him at least."

"When you give me a few minutes of 'free time' I do."

Katharina frowned. "I don't think I like your tone."

Rant and rave now? No. It's too soon. "I'm sorry, Miss Minola. I've been cooped up in here all day with no one to talk to. I read the novel I brought twice out of sheer boredom."

Katharina widened her eyes. "Oh, cry me a river. I built a fire in the snow and cut peat all day. You had it easy."

"Will you be needing my clothes again tomorrow, Miss Minola?"

"Bianca, I'm going to need them until we're done with this thing."

Lovely. "So I'm just supposed to sit around this cabin in my jeans and go barefoot in my boots?"

"You have a coat, hat, and mittens. I don't have those luxuries. Suck it up."

After Katharina had finally snored herself to sleep, Bianca stood in front of the bathroom mirror. She whispered, "I've about had it, everybody. I have to get her to try to fire me. Tell Vincenzo I'm sorry I couldn't last any longer." She stepped away, then turned back. "And tell Vincenzo to save some of that movie-theater butter popcorn for me because that's my favorite."

Chapter 22

Bianca's attempts to get fired started before she went to sleep that night. She didn't clean the pot of oatmeal or let it soak in the sink, leaving it to harden on the table. *That will be one crusty mess in the morning.* She didn't set her travel alarm clock so she could wake Katharina on time. *Oh no! She'll miss all that natural morning light! At least her face won't shine.* She didn't stoke the fire or add any more logs, letting it die on its own as she snuggled under her covers with a granola bar. She wasn't worried that Katharina would freeze solid because, she thought, *evil never dies, and she's wearing my draws!*

Katharina shivered herself awake and looked around. The room was much brighter than it was the previous days when she woke up. "Bianca!"

She heard no reply.

"Bianca, you let me oversleep, and I've lost all that good morning light!" *I can see my breath? What the hell?* "Why is it so cold?"

She draped her comforter around her and opened her door, feeling at most another degree of warmth in the larger room outside. "Bianca!" *Has she left for the shoot already? Did she even try to wake me?* She opened Bianca's door and saw a lump under the covers. "Bianca!"

"What?" Bianca asked without moving.

No one says "what" to me! "I've been yelling for you, Bianca. Why haven't you answered me?"

"I was asleep," Bianca said.

"You let me oversleep. You let the fire go out. You haven't fixed my breakfast!"

Bianca pulled her covers more tightly around her head. "Make it yourself," she mumbled.

"What did you say?"

Bianca sat up. "What time is it?"

"How the hell should I know?"

Bianca blinked and yawned. "I was having this horrible dream about a witch. Is it time to get up already?"

What has gotten into this girl? "Yes, and I'm late, and I'm hungry."

Bianca ran her tongue over her teeth. "Man, I have a rug on my choppers. I need to brush my teeth." She left the bed, sidestepped Katharina, and went into the bathroom, closing the door.

Katharina scowled at the pot on the table. "Why didn't you clean this pot?"

Bianca smiled for the camera in the bathroom. "This is fun," she whispered. "No, Miss Minola. I don't smoke pot."

Katharina put her nose in the crack of the bathroom door. "I didn't ask you that. This pot is useless!"

Bianca gargled and spat. "Oh, I know pot is useless, Miss Minola. I never use drugs. I've seen all those commercials. 'This is your brain. This is your brain on drugs.' "

The girl is on drugs! Katharina thought.

Bianca opened the door. "Good morning, Miss

Minola. How did you sleep?" She looked past Katharina to the fireplace. "And why is the fire out?"

"Because *you* let it go out!" Katharina shrieked. "It's not *ever* supposed to go out!"

"Oh, sorry," Bianca said with a little smile. "I was awful tired after yesterday. You ever feel real tired after you didn't do anything all day?" *Just like your life back in L.A., Miss Katha-diva.* "That's the way I felt. I mean, all I did was read my novel twice and make some oatmeal. That shouldn't have worn me out, but it did. You ever have any days like that?"

Katharina wanted to shake the living shit out of her. "Just . . . help me get dressed, Bianca."

"Sure."

Bianca skipped several buttons on the dress and tied one boot tighter than the other.

"What is your function, Bianca? I feel a draft at my neck, and you have to retie both boots." *Is she sick or what? She's acting higher this morning than those damn Italians have all week!* Katharina slapped on her headset. "You're coming with me this morning, Bianca. Get dressed."

Bianca crossed her arms over her heart. "But I'll freeze."

"You'll just have to keep moving, then."

Although Katharina exhorted Bianca to "keep up or else," Bianca lagged far behind, and by the time Katharina reached the clearing, Bianca had disappeared for good inside Vincenzo's cabin to get a hot breakfast ("Fudge Pop-Tarts!") and a steaming mug of hot chocolate.

"Why didn't Katharina fire her already?" Fish asked. "That girl was begging to get smacked and sacked."

"This is going to sound crazy," Walt said, "but I think Katharina needs her."

Fish wrinkled his lips and shook his head. "Yeah. That does sound crazy."

Despite a roaring fire and an "oven" of dried peat to greet her, Katharina looked unusually frazzled when she arrived to work on her shelter.

"Are you feeling okay today, Miss Katharina?" Vincenzo asked, readying his camera.

"Bianca didn't set her alarm or something." She looked behind her. "That little . . . She's run off again."

"It is no matter," Vincenzo said. "It is just you and me today, anyway. Alessandro had to take his *mulo* to the vet. A spastic colon."

In truth, Pietro was in the forest on the *other* side of his house cutting branches off fallen trees to transport later for Katharina's use, and he needed Curtis's help to drag it over. His goal was to space these massive, thick branches around the grid in the hopes that Katharina would use them for the walls of her shelter.

"So, we begin," Vincenzo said.

Katharina's first attempts even at digging into the soil were a dismal failure. No matter how much she stabbed and lifted her knife like a little trowel, she could break through only the top layer. She spent hours excavating a rough rectangle around her fire pit about four meters wide by three meters deep (thirteen feet by ten feet). Then she tried to plant a dozen sharpened stakes into the groove she had dug, only to have them fall over like dominoes again and again.

"Why won't they stay up?" Katharina muttered.

"Cut!" Vincenzo yelled. "You must dig deeper."

"You got a shovel?" Katharina asked, her face streaked with dirt.

"*She* would not have a—"

Katharina heaved a long sigh. "Okay, okay. I'll dig deeper. You have anything I can eat in your cabin? I'll even settle for some oatmeal. You have any more of that good coffee?"

Vincenzo tried to look as sad as a puppy dog. "I am so sorry, Miss Katharina. We ran out of coffee, and Alessandro gave Bianca the last of the oatmeal last night. It is already at your cabin, yes? Alessandro is supposed to bring some more home with him this evening."

"Great." *Sure, they'll pay so a mule can get his colon checked, but a decent cup of coffee? No. I should have asked them to pay me only $4.9 million so I could get some damn coffee and some decent freaking meals!*

"So, you will dig again?" Vincenzo asked. "I will get closer to absorb all your intensity."

Oh, Katharina thought, *I'll dig. I'm so pissed the Chinese better watch where they step.*

Her knife dull, the subsoil filled with rocks deposited by the Ice Age ten thousand years ago, her stomach singing bass, Katharina floundered around her future foundation for another two hours. She cried when she struck an unseen rock. She moaned when she couldn't pry up a particularly stubborn stone. She broke two more nails. She cut her finger on the edge of a rock. She earned a sliver in her right palm from an ill-fated jab of a stake into the earth.

Vincenzo, the cameras in the trees, and Katharina's headset recorded it all in living color and breathtaking sound.

*   *   *

"I have a lot of editing to do, Walt," Fish said. "Why does she curse so damn much?"

"She has no lines," Walt said. "She's ad-libbing. Those are real feelings she's expressing."

"And that is one pitiful start to a shelter," Fish said. "We'll be here for months at this rate." He glanced at several other monitors and saw snow cascading down. In moments, all but the big screen showed a torrent of snow, and then—

The snow made a *sound* as it landed on Katharina's face, sizzled as it hit her fire, and rapidly swathed her foundation line into whiteness.

"Miss Katharina," Vincenzo said, "I cannot see you, and I am three feet from you. I am afraid what the snow will do to my camera and your headset. We are done for the day."

This is madness, sheer madness, Katharina thought. She stood, brushing flakes of snow from her shoulders and seeing more flakes take their place.

"We will try again tomorrow." *Under a foot or more of snow! What a movie this is turning out to be!* Vincenzo hurried away.

Katharina was alone in the clearing, her fire hissing and smoking, her face completely blank.

"There's a poster shot," Fish said. "One brown blur of a person standing in an ocean of snow. You can't even see her headset." He widened his shot. "No snow machine or indoor set could give us something this awesome. I hope she doesn't stand there until she's completely covered."

"Go back to your cabin, Katharina," Walt said. "Go get warm."

Fish switched to the headset cam as Katharina slowly made her way up the hill to the bridge. "These are some nice shots, too. How can she even see where she's going?"

As she slipped and slid, Katharina tilted her head forward to keep the snow out of her eyes. Hers were the only footsteps in the snow, and it was easy for her to imagine her character trudging a similar path, feeling so isolated and alone, her every positive step thwarted by the brutality and unpredictability of unforgiving nature. *She's finally free and feeling safe when Nature with a capital N kicks her in the ass. If I didn't know there was a cabin somewhere straight ahead, I'd feel like giving up and dying, letting the snow bury me until the spring thaw . . . or until a grizzly bear made me part of him forever.*

Katharina walked much faster now through the waterfall of snowflakes, reaching out to trees to steady her shaking legs, using branches to propel her forward. She passed Alessandro's cabin, dark and forbidding, no sign of man or mule. Snow a fist thick sat on the windowsills, a dusting on the porch itself. She fought the urge to rest under the cover of his porch and pressed on, the snowflakes abating the deeper she went into the thick forest. She looked up and saw only a trickle of flakes, the rest caught high in the treetops.

I should have set up shop here, she thought. *Those trees could be my roof, and I wouldn't need much of a shelter.*

She stopped. "Hmm," she whispered, "but when it rained . . ." She smiled. *Maybe my character will have a winter home and a summer home.*

She continued until she saw the outline of her cabin, a ribbon of smoke fighting against the falling snow. She stamped off most of the snow from her boots, wiped off her shoulders and sleeves, and entered the cabin—

And found Bianca curled up in front of the fire eating a steaming bowl of oatmeal while reading a book, her comforter wrapped around her.

"You're back so early," Bianca said with a smile. She looked out the little window. "Oh, look at the snow! It's so beautiful."

Katharina began to peel off her clothes. "Where did you go, Bianca? I told you to stay by me all day."

"I think I'm really sick, Miss Minola." She coughed for good measure. "I was so cold, I coughed up something blue, and I think I have a fever."

Katharina nodded at the oatmeal. "And that's to help the fever?"

"I was hungry, too."

Why did I ever hire this woman? "Is there any left?"

Bianca showed Katharina the empty pot. "Sorry. I can make you some more."

Draping her dress on the fireplace screen, Katharina took a deep breath. Then she yanked Bianca's comforter from her body, wrapped it around herself, and sat in the other chair. "Go get me some dinner. Now."

Bianca stood, her legs a little shaky. "But it's snowing like crazy, Miss Minola. I might get lost."

"I don't care," Katharina said slowly. "I need some meat. I need some protein. I'm turning into a bag of bones. Even your skinny little clothes are hanging on me now."

"But I'm . . . but I'm not feeling well, Miss Minola."

Katharina froze Bianca with a stare. "I don't care if

you are an hour from your deathbed, Bianca. Get off your ass and do your damn job. Now."

"Yes, Miss Minola. Right away, Miss Minola."

"What does Bianca have to do to get her ass fired?" Fish asked. "I would have fired her ass just for eating all the oatmeal."

Walt closed his eyes. "Maybe, just maybe now, Katharina didn't fire all those other assistants." He opened his eyes and nodded. "Maybe they all quit, and she just *said* she fired them to protect her reputation. While Bianca has shown remarkable patience and humility, Katharina has shown . . . more."

Neither spoke for several moments. The screen showed Bianca dressing, throwing on her coat, and leaving the cabin.

"Okay, smart guy," Fish said, "so what does this mean?"

"Fish, I think Bianca has to *quit*. As venomous as Katharina is, she doesn't seem to have the heart to fire her."

"Uh-oh," Fish said. "Look at Katharina."

Katharina had stood and was folding Bianca's comforter as she walked into Bianca's room.

"You see something shiny, Walt?"

Walt nodded.

"Zooming."

The picture grew until a silver granola wrapper jutting out from the mattress filled the screen. "Bianca did that on purpose," Fish said.

"Yep," Walt said.

They watched Katharina snatch up the wrapper, stare at it, and shake her head. Then Katharina flipped Bianca's mattress off the bed.

"That's a *shitload* of granola," Fish said. "And raisins! I could go for some raisins."

"The wench!" Katharina howled on the screen.

"Oh, it's on now," Fish said, laughing. "Call Vincenzo. I think Miss Baptista is about to lose her head."

Walt hit the squawk button. "Vincenzo? Bianca's on her way to you to get some dinner, preferably meat. And, um, Katharina found Bianca's stash."

"It was bound to happen sooner or later," Vincenzo said. "I'll tell her when she gets here."

Fish leaned under the table and flipped one of the two backup switches. In a few moments, a fish-eye–lens view of Vincenzo's cabin filled one of the screens.

Walt's mouth dropped open. "That's not a backup."

"Nope," Fish said, adjusting the picture quality with a few keystrokes. "This is what happens when I have too much time on my hands."

"What's the other one for, Fish?"

Fish shook his head. "Oh no. I ain't telling." He "swapped" Katharina's angry face showing on the big screen with Vincenzo's wide body on the smaller monitor.

"There's only one other cabin, Fish."

"Look at that," Fish said. "Vincenzo's gaining weight. Fish-eye lenses are like that. They make everyone look"—he glanced at Walt—"um, fat."

"It's Pietro's cabin, isn't it?"

Fish adjusted the volume until he could hear Vincenzo breathing. "Look. It was partially Pietro's idea from the start, all right?"

"*Both* cameras?"

"Okay, not both. He and I were just being careful. I mean, what if Katharina refused to go back to Cabin 3 and demanded the 'nicest' one? Vincenzo's is a palace compared to the other two, right?"

"That still doesn't explain the one at Pietro's."

Fish rubbed his hands through his thinning hair. "You can't tell a soul, okay?"

"I won't."

"*Vincenzo* wanted a camera in Pietro's cabin, two, actually, just in case there were some sparks between Katharina and his brother."

Walt closed his eyes. "The other one is over his bed."

Fish nodded.

"And that switch turns both cameras on."

"Yeah. Now you know all my secrets."

Walt shook his head. "Do I?"

Fish sighed. "Okay, okay. I was the one who drank the last Coke. It wasn't Pietro."

"Is that all, Fish?"

He crossed his heart. "I swear it is."

Walt stared harder. "Fish?"

"Okay, okay, damn." He motioned Walt to follow him to a dark computer monitor. "Now don't think I'm a freak, okay?" He turned on the monitor.

At first, Walt didn't understand what he was seeing. "It's a . . . *No.* You're auctioning off Katharina's tiger stilettos?"

"They weren't hard to find, I mean, all I had to do was rewind the tape and run out to the spot while you were sleeping. I thought about going for the sunglasses, but the risk was too great. But the amazing thing was, I wasn't getting much interest until I added the phrase 'slightly soiled.' And then . . . Look where it's at now."

"Unbelievable," Walt said. "There's actually someone out there who is willing to pay you two thousand dollars for a muddy, ruined pair of Katharina's shoes?"

" 'Slightly soiled,' " Fish said. "I can only imagine the fetish this person has, but who am I to judge?"

Walt laughed softly. "Fish, I take back some of the

things I've said about you. There's actually someone out there who is sicker than you." A movement on the big screen caught his eye. "Bianca made it to Vincenzo's."

"Volume up . . ."

"You're about to be fired," Vincenzo said, taking her coat and setting it on a plush sofa next to a woodstove.

"How do you know?"

"Fish called to tell me that Katharina found your stash."

Bianca continued to the little kitchen. "Oh. How?"

Vincenzo smiled. "You tell me."

Bianca stared at the ceiling, her eyes dancing. "Oh no. I must have left a shiny silver wrapper sticking out from the mattress. Oh, darn, I should have been more careful. What do you have to eat?"

"Is that all I'm good for?" Vincenzo asked, opening the small refrigerator and taking out a box of ham-and-cheese Hot Pockets.

"Well . . . yes." Bianca opened the wrappers and placed two Hot Pockets into the microwave. "But this time, I'll cook for you."

"Oh, thank you." Vincenzo felt so alive whenever she was around that he couldn't keep his feet still. "You'd make a good diva."

"Please don't curse me like that. I'm normal, remember?"

"Yes, you are."

Bianca waited for the bell to ring and took out the Hot Pockets, handing one to Vincenzo. "You can have the bigger one."

"They're both the same size." He nodded to the round and modern kitchen table. "Shall we?"

"Oh yes."

He sat and looked into her gray-blue eyes. "So, how do you want to play it?"

Bianca took a careful bite, steam rising from the corner of the Hot Pocket. "It really depends on how she plays it, right?"

Vincenzo squawked his walkie-talkie. "What's Katharina doing now?"

"Acting as if nothing has happened," Walt said. "Now she's moved to the chair in front of the fire and is drumming her nails on the table."

"Did she eat anything?" Vincenzo asked.

"No . . . Fish says it's because Katharina doesn't like granola."

Bianca shook her head. "She is practically *starving* in there. She must have some reason." She grabbed Vincenzo's forearm across the table. "For more ammunition, maybe? Am I insured against granola bar damage? Now I'm scared."

Vincenzo put his hand on top of hers. "You can't show fear when you go back. She's probably going to try to catch you in a lie."

Bianca took a bigger bite. "Maybe if I bring her something really good to eat, she'll forgive me. And *then* I'll quit." She slowly released her hand that was under Vincenzo's hand.

"Uh, Walt, have Fish zoom in on Katharina's face and tell me what you see."

"Very scary," Walt said. "Her jaw is set. Wait. Fish just turned up the volume. What's that? Fish says we're hearing her teeth grind."

"Yikes," Bianca said. "I'm about to walk into the proverbial buzz saw."

"Talk to you in a few, Walt," Vincenzo said, and he set the walkie-talkie on the table. "I think you are definitely about to be fired, Bianca. Try to quit before she can do it, okay?"

Bianca nodded and finished her Hot Pocket.

"Are you ready?"

Bianca set her own jaw. "I think so."

"Nervous?"

Ow. She relaxed her jaw. "I'm relieved, actually. I finally get to say the lines I've been rehearsing in my head since I started working for her." She looked at her hands. "Will you be watching, Vincenzo?"

Vincenzo waved at a widescreen monitor on a little TV stand. "Sure. I, um, I've been watching you the last couple nights."

"You have?" Bianca whispered.

Vincenzo nodded. *God, that is a sexy whisper.* "Um, yeah."

"Have you been watching me sleep?" she whispered again.

Vincenzo's heart beat a little faster. "Um, I usually say good night to you."

Bianca's eyes softened. "That's sweet. Do you have any ideas for me, *direttore?*"

Vincenzo nodded. "Okay, um, well . . . We're going for passion here, okay?"

Finally, Bianca thought. *It took him this long to flirt back.* "We are?"

Vincenzo stood. "Yes. We, um, we are. Lots of passion. We want her to explode. We want her to go off. We want her to lose it completely."

Bianca felt warmer all the way down to her toes. "Reckless abandon, huh?"

"What the hell are they talking about?" Fish asked.

"I think some major flirtation is going on here," Walt

said. " 'Passion. Explode, go off, lose it.' Maybe it isn't flirtation at all. Maybe it's seduction . . .''

Vincenzo's hands started to sweat. "Um, yeah. Complete, total, reckless, howling-at-the-moon abandon."

"Oh, come on now!" Fish cried. "He's old enough to be her cool uncle, the one who lets her drive the Jag."

"I think it's sweet," Walt said.

"He's robbing the cradle."

Walt sighed. "She's a consenting adult, Fish."

"She's just a kid."

Walt nodded. "So is he. At heart. He has young eyes like his father and his grandfather. You have to have young eyes in this business. That's what she sees when she looks at him."

Bianca's toes squirmed uncontrollably in her boots. *He's not flirting anymore. He's pawing at me with his words, undressing me with his phrasing, licking me with his sexy brown eyes.* "How loud should I be?"

Vincenzo was afraid to wring his hands for fear they would drip onto the floor. *She's tempting me with her pouting lips, drawing me into her web with her gray-blue eyes, luring me to my heavenly destruction with her cute little dimples.* "How loud do you want to be?"

Oh, so now he's playing it cool and turning it back on me? I'll show him. "I want it to echo off the mountains."

So do I! "I want that, too, Bianca. Um, I'll, um, save you some movie-theater butter popcorn."

"You will? Why?"

"I mean, after you quit, you have to go somewhere."

*He knows where I'm going, and I know where I'm going,
but I have to make sure.* "I thought you said I could go to
Pietro's and hang out with Walt and Fish after I quit."

"I knew she liked me," Fish said. "Too bad you're
married."
"Hanging out is not getting busy."
Fish laughed. "It can be. It's your night to monitor
Katharina's snoring, anyway."

"That was before, Bianca." Vincenzo looked outside
at the torrent of snow. "Will you look at that snow!"
Bianca locked her eyes with Vincenzo. "So pretty."
"Yes, so pretty."

"Ha!" Walt cried. "She blushed!"
Fish typed a few commands and zoomed in. "No, no.
It was the glow thrown from the fireplace onto her
face."

Vincenzo turned away. "So you would rather go hang
out with them than . . . Yeah. Maybe you should."

"Yes!" Fish cried. "If that's what the boss said, that's
what you're gonna do."

"Do they have popcorn?" Bianca asked.
"I'm sure they do," Vincenzo said sadly.

"Popcorn like yours? Popcorn that gets real big when it gets hot?"

Fish blinked.

Walt blinked.

"Okay, she blushed before because now *he's* blushing," Fish said. "Damn. Passed over for some damn popcorn."

Walt patted Fish on the back. "Guess it's still just you and me, pal."

"Oh, I can't wait."

Vincenzo felt a stirring in just about every part of his loins. "Um, yeah. My popcorn is very, um, puffy. It, um, it gets real big. Bianca, after you quit, I would like you to come back here. It's a much shorter walk, you might even be able to follow your own footsteps, it's snowing heavily, you're not wearing any socks or long underwear—"

"How do you know . . . ? Oh, right. You know about that whole scene." She moistened her lips. "So you know about my . . ."

"Boxers?"

He knows! "Well, you would know better than Katharina why I wear them. They're so comfortable and they keep things ventilated down there."

Vincenzo could make no reply.

Bianca stood on her tiptoes and kissed his cheek. "I may have to shorten my tirade a little."

"Play it for all it's worth, Bianca," Vincenzo said.

"I'll do what I have to do."

*   *   *

"He's so wooden," Fish said. "He ain't smooth at all."

"That's how most men are when they're being seduced by wood nymphs."

"Wood nymphs?"

Walt rolled his eyes. "I read a lot of Greek mythology."

Bianca kissed Vincenzo's other cheek. "Leave the light *off*, okay? I just want to see the glow of the fire."

"Okay."

"I'll just have to adjust the contrast a little," Fish said. "No sweat."

"We're not going to watch!"

Fish stretched his arms over his head. "You know, I think I've gotten my second wind. I'll mind the monitors tonight. You go talk dirty to your wife."

"I don't talk—hey! Do you have a camera in my room?"

Fish laughed so loudly that he nearly fell out of his chair. "No, Walt, I don't. I was just messing with you, and now I know it's true. You still do that?"

"I'm away from home a lot, so . . . yeah."

"Walt, I hardly knew ye."

Walt sighed. "She's out with friends tonight, anyway, so . . . We'll both mind the monitors."

Fish nodded. "I knew you couldn't walk away from this."

"*Ciao,*" Bianca said, slipping into her coat.

"*Ciao, bella.*"

Bianca was halfway out the door when she walked right back in. "I'm supposed to bring her dinner."

Vincenzo shrugged. "How about a Hot Pocket?"

"Or *half* of one. Yeah. One with little ragged bite marks in it."

Vincenzo shuddered. "How about a frozen one?"

"That's cold." She kissed him lightly on the lips this time. "You're pretty smart."

Vincenzo took another Hot Pocket from the minifridge and handed it to Bianca. "Make sure you drop it on the table in front of her. I want to hear the echo down here."

"But it might thaw out by the time I get there," she said. "My hands are so sweaty now." She grabbed his. "So are yours."

Nice, soft, strong hands . . . "Um. Yeah." *I'm fourteen again!* "You better go."

Bianca bit her lower lip and looked up, but didn't let go of Vincenzo's hand. "Yeah. *Ciao.* Again."

Vincenzo looked down at their hands. "*Ciao, bella.* Again."

"They are so cute," Walt said.

"Nauseating," Fish said.

Chapter 23

Bianca had but one thought as she raced through the deepening snow: *I hope he doesn't mind my funk later because I haven't had a bath in four days!*

After missing the bridge, finding it, and getting lost for a few tense minutes, Bianca first found Pietro's cabin by a glow in his window. After reorienting herself, she aimed through the snow and stumbled into Katharina's cabin, busting in and slamming the door behind her.

Katharina jerked her head to the door. "What took you so long?"

Bianca dropped the Hot Pocket onto the table.

It *thumped* loudly *twice*.

"What the hell is that?" Katharina asked.

"It's called a Hot Pocket," Bianca said, removing her coat. "It's what average, ordinary, normal, skinny people like me eat. But you wouldn't know anything about it since you haven't been grocery shopping in probably fifteen years. Normal people sometimes even use coupons so they can get more for their money at the grocery store."

Katharina blinked several times.

"Really. You know, coupons? You cut them out?" Bianca warmed herself in front of the fire. "Anyway, I'm so sorry, Miss Minola. I know it's not what you wanted, but it was all I could find on such short notice way up here in the middle of the middle of nowhere. I'll just fry it up in the pot. Oh my! Look at the gunk in there. All that crusty oatmeal might not come out, but that's okay. Hot Pockets are sealed in plastic."

Bianca nearly stumbled on her way to the bathroom carrying the pot. She made a face in the mirror and rinsed out the pot for less than five seconds. "I am shaking so bad," she whispered. "I can't believe the things I'm babbling. Did you hear the *thunk?* It was so loud that it scared *me.*"

Bianca raced to the fireplace and hung the pot over the fire, dropped the Hot Pocket inside—plastic, cardboard sleeve, and all—and sat in the other chair. "It shouldn't take too long, Miss Minola."

Katharina continued blinking. *The child is on drugs. But I can't let that keep me from what I have to say.* "Are you gaining weight, Bianca?"

So that's *how she's going to play it.* Bianca examined her butt. "Maybe. It must be the air up here. I did eat a lot of that stew, that cereal, and that oatmeal. I guess it's all just sticking to me."

"Uh-huh." Katharina breathed evenly. "I thought you barfed your guts out the other day."

"Oh yes, big chunks, too," Bianca said. "Some of it went back down, though. I hate when that happens. Up it comes and then—nope! Back to the cauldron. Be careful when you're out picking berries, okay?"

What has this child been smoking? Katharina thought. *And why didn't she bring any for me?*

"Is there anything I can do for you, Miss Minola?"

Katharina almost forgot her rage. When she felt for

the wrapper hiding under her leg, her rage returned. She tossed the shiny wrapper onto the table. "You can explain this."

"Granola? Where did you get granola? I'd *kill* for some granola right now."

Walt sighed. "She's fantastic."
Fish sighed. "She's also in deep trouble."

Katharina stood. "Would you? Would you really *kill* for some granola?"

Bianca smiled. "I might."

"What about some raisins? Would you kill for raisins, too?"

Bianca didn't bat an eye. "Only if they're fresh and juicy and sealed in a plastic bag so the grizzly bears can't get at them."

Where has this assertive child been hiding? Katharina thought. *I like this Bianca. She has spunk and personality! She has fire! She's not mousy—she's the cat! But, I still have to reprimand her. I am, after all, her employer.* "You've been holding back on me for more than just clothes, Bianca."

"And you're the biggest bitch who ever lived, Katha-diva Bologna."

"Yes, sports fans!" Fish said in his announcer's voice. "We have a catfight brewing here tonight! Oh, and it's gonna get rough. In this corner, the challenger, Bianca-dunk. In this corner, the champ-een, Katha-diva Bologna. Zooming in on the combatants!"

Walt said nothing.

* * *

She isn't telling me anything that I don't already know, Katharina thought. *Though it kind of hurts to hear it coming from the person who gave me her* draws. "So I'm a bitch."

"You have no equal, Katha-diva."

Katharina began to circle toward Bianca. "Uh-huh. That is true." She tapped the table with her four remaining good nails. "Your Hot Pocket is burning, Bianca."

Bianca eased to her feet and edged toward the fireplace. "No, thanks. I already had a *few*. That's *your* Hot Pocket burning." She sniffed the air. "And melting. It must be the plastic. And if you're lucky, another mouse or a bat will fall into the pot to spice it up even more, give it a wild, gamy flavor."

Katharina smiled. "Uh-huh. I see. Um, what are you trying to tell me here, Bianca?"

"I'm not trying to tell you anything, Miss Bologna. I think I'm stating my views very well."

Such a sweet, innocent, stupid *child.* "You know I have a knife, right?"

Bianca smiled. *Thank you for this opening!* "That knife is as dull as your life by now."

"Whoa!" Fish said. "Nice cut!"

"That had to hurt," Walt said.

Katharina stopped circling. "You think *my* life is dull?"

"I don't think it," Bianca said. "I *know* it."

Katharina put both hands on the table. She had almost had enough. "You know something?"

"I know lots of things, but you've never listened to me. Which something are you referring to?"

Oh my, oh my, oh my. Doesn't she know "You know something?" is a rhetorical question? "You were nothing when I hired you, and—"

"I quit."

Katharina froze. "What?"

Bianca smiled, her dimples shining out. "I quit." She went to her bedroom, threw off the mattress, took one granola bar, ripped it open, and started eating. "You can have the rest of these granola bars, Miss Bologna. I'm full." She walked by Katharina. "You can also have all my *draws*. I can't even *believe* you asked to wear them. Wait until that hits *Entertainment Tonight*. 'Muddy Diva Wears Assistant's Dirty Draws.'"

The Hot Pocket finally sizzled.

"I'd flip that Hot Pocket if I were you, Katha-diva," Bianca said. "They're good crunchy but taste like ass when they're scorched."

What the hell just happened here? Katharina thought. *I wasn't going to fire her! Scold her, yes. But fire her? Why would I do that? What did I say to make her quit?*

"Miss Minola?" Bianca asked sweetly. "Is there something wrong?"

I said, "You were nothing when I hired you," and she said, "I quit." I was going to say, "You were nothing when I hired you, but look how much you've grown in seven weeks. Look how much more confident you are in just the last few days." I was about to give her a damn compliment! She had finally got tired of my shit and was shooting the shit right back at me! I respect that. I respect her. In fact, I respected all of my assistants who finally quit. I know they were stronger for it.

"You don't understand, Bianca," Katharina said. "I . . . I wasn't—"

"Can't find your line, Katha-diva?" Bianca interrupted. "Can't think or speak without a script? Can't *be* yourself without your clothes, your shoes, your hairstylist, your makeup *painter,* your dresser, and your dog? I'm sure they don't miss you, especially Scottie."

What . . . what? "Where's Scottie?"

Bianca giggled. "Way down in Costa Rica with your clothes and your thongs and thongs."

"Yes, catfight fans," Fish said, "the cat, or in this case, the *dog* comes out of the bag during the catfight. What do you think about that, Walt?"

Walt jotted down a few notes to himself.

"Uh, Walt, we're on the air."

"The dynamics here are so intense. You see the look on Katharina's face? That's real pain. This is all a real shock to her."

"Quit analyzing and enjoy. We should have popped some popcorn."

"So . . . my stuff . . ." *I need to get a grip.* "You sent all my luggage and my dog to Costa Rica."

"Yep."

"Why?"

Bianca squared her shoulders and narrowed her eyes. "Payback's a bitch, bitch."

The child thinks she's in some movie or something. "All this was part of some . . . plan? This is all some petty payback?"

"It was kind of easy, too." *Time for me to lie!* "I simply told the others that you were rewarding them with a vacation to Costa Rica. They didn't believe me until I showed them the plane tickets, which I bought with my *own* money. I only sent them there for the weekend, and they're all back in L.A., Scottie, too. That old lady you saw on their plane? She was my grandmother. Did you even know I had a grandmother? Of course you didn't. You aren't into other people's lives unless you're getting paid to *be* them."

Katharina felt suddenly smaller and claustrophobic. "This is *all* just for revenge? So there's not even a contract?"

Bianca shook her head. "Of course there's a contract, silly. Surprise, surprise, but that's legit. Though I don't know why they want to waste their money on your tired ass. When you sent me to Lucentio Pictures with your letter, I tried to talk them out of it, but those people are crazier than you are. Yes, you are really filming a movie for five million dollars. By the way, you're in Ontario, Canada, a few miles from the Quebec border. You're not in the Arctic Circle. Thought you should know."

Katharina gripped the top of her chair. "But Bianca, all of this . . . for a little revenge?"

Bianca looked at the ceiling, then stared hard at Katharina. "Yeah. That about sums it up. When I write my memoirs of this moment, I will say, 'I sent her shit'—and most of it *is* shit, by the way. You are so out of touch with today's fashion—'I sent her shit to Costa Rica with her farting dog, who, by the way, has more humanity in him than she ever will. At least he warmed up to me and appreciated what I did for him.' "

Katharina sat. "I didn't hire you so I could . . . warm up to you, Bianca," she said softly. "You had a job to do, and frankly, until the last two days, you were doing a *wonderful* job. You've been indispensable to me. I don't know if I could have survived without you."

Oh shit! She wasn't going to fire me! Now what? Shit! I want some damn popcorn! I want Vincenzo's hands on me! What do I do? What does Katharina do when she's faced with a problem? Oh yes. She ignores it. "You know, Katha-diva, *darling*, I understand that I was the only person to apply for this job. Why was that, do you think?"

What does this have to do with anything? "There were other applicants." *Weren't there?* "I don't remember exactly how many."

"I showed up at nine o'clock sharp, waited alone for an hour, and then you hired me on the spot. How can you forget that?"

What the . . . what the hell is happening here? "Bianca, I don't want you to quit on me, okay? Not now. Not ever. I'll . . . I'll double your pay. Please, Bianca. Please listen to me."

I feel like shit on a Popsicle stick. "Why? Why should I listen to you? You never listen to me."

Katharina's eyes dropped to the table. "I'm . . . I'm not used to . . ."

"And all those interviews you did a long time ago, all that shit you said? *Darling*, the world stopped listening to you before you opened your mouth."

Katharina felt the beginnings of tears. "I'm listening now, aren't I?"

Don't look at her eyes, Bianca. They're getting shiny. "You treat me like shit. You treat me like I'm some little kid, Katharina." *Damn. I used her real name.*

"I haven't . . ." Katharina nodded. "Okay, I have. I mean, Bianca, until tonight, I thought you were a mousy little girl with no self-esteem. I've been trying to give you a reason to be more assertive. I've been waiting for you to back-talk me, to sass me." She smiled. "And here you are so . . . powerful. You're amazing. Really."

I can't keep doing this, but I have to! "Cut! You still understand 'cut,' don't you? You are completely out of touch with reality, *darling*. You think the rest of your porta-posse doesn't sass you behind your back? I'll bet they're laughing it up right now and looking for other jobs. You should hear what they say about you."

But I pay them better than I pay her! "What? What are they saying?"

"I'm not a mousy little backstabber, Katharina. You'll have to wait for the book."

Katharina closed her eyes, willing the tears to stay within her eyelids.

"But you know," Bianca continued, "if you really think about it, though I doubt you will, I've been the only person in your life since you hired me." *And that's the truth!* "Oh sure, your makeup painter and hair 'fluffer' came around to prune and primp you, but . . . I was your only friend, and I use that term loosely. I've been a foot or two away from you for most of your waking moments for fifty days. I'm the only person at the other end of the intercom. You could say that I've been your closest friend."

"But I . . ." *She's right. She's been my only friend.* "But I didn't hire you to be my *friend,* Bianca."

"You might as well have," Bianca said. "That's the only way you'll have any friends." *Damn. That made even me shiver.*

Ouch, my heart hurts! "I have friends, Bianca."

"Name them."

Katharina blinked. "You wouldn't know any of them."

"Okay, name the last friend that either you visited or visited you."

Katharina tried to remember. "Well, um, last Christmas, I had several—"

"That was like nine months ago," Bianca interrupted. "Okay, who's the last friend to call you?"

Katharina fought her tears, blinking rapidly. *My grandma.* "I don't remember."

"Okay, who's the last friend *you* called? And remember, I paid all your bills and got all those phone statements, so I know."

I haven't called anyone, either, Katharina thought. *My life* has *been dull.*

"Face it, *darling*," Bianca said, "the only phone ringing is the one inside your head." *And that silly brush! Yes.* "Or the one you 'use' in your room of mirrors. I know what you do with your brush."

Has she been spying on me? "How do you know this?"

Bianca laughed once loudly. "You forget to turn off the intercom every single time, *darling*. Gotta watch the help close, huh? Especially the Latina help. They're the sneaky ones. Isn't that so?"

"I never said—"

"Didn't it shock you when I started speaking Italian on the plane?" Bianca interrupted. "You didn't know that about me. I can also speak fluent Spanish. Didn't it dawn on you that maybe I was more than just an assistant? I graduated magna cum laude from UCLA, bitch. I'm trilingual. I am a freaking saint, you know that? I put up with more shit from you in seven weeks than most people put up with in a lifetime. You are the meanest, cruelest *monster* of a person I have ever met. I don't know why I didn't quit sooner. I would rather flip burgers or sell shoes at the mall than work for you. I'd rather get out some cardboard and a squirt bottle than work for you. You know why? Because you . . . ain't . . . shit."

These walls, these fucking walls . . . "Please get out," Katharina whispered.

"You're gonna kick me out during a blizzard? That will play very nicely on *Entertainment Tonight*, too. Kathadiva Bologna has fired yet another assistant, sending her out to her most certain death during a Canadian blizzard. The body has yet to be found, and most likely grizzly bears have devoured her. 'It wasn't *my* fault,' Katha-diva said. 'She had a bad attitude. She deserved to die.' "

"Please," Katharina whispered, "get out."

But I'm not through with my last scene in this movie! "I need to get what little stuff I have first. I will be taking one of my pairs of socks back. I assume they're in your room. I'll get them. No. Don't move. I wouldn't want you to tire yourself since *so* many of your friends will be over later for the big pity party."

Bianca practically dashed into Katharina's room, found the socks, and put them on. *Damn. That was so harsh. I feel like shit!* She wiped away several tears, took a deep breath, and returned to Katharina. "Will there be anything else, Miss Minola? Anything at all? A crustless sandwich, perhaps? Your lingerie folded? Should I shoot Scope down your gargling dog's mouth?"

Katharina put her head on the table. "Please . . . Just leave."

Bianca couldn't stop her tears now, storming to the door to escape. She grabbed the doorknob and stopped. Without looking at Katharina, she said, "A few years ago, I watched *My Honey Love* in the only film class I took at UCLA. It was one of the best movies I had ever seen. I really mean that. You were amazing. I couldn't take my eyes off you." The tears poured from her eyes. "I thought, wow, I have the opportunity of a lifetime working for that amazing person. And I have been waiting seven *excruciating* weeks for that amazing person to appear. Where'd she go, Katharina? I hope you find her quick, or one day, there won't be anyone left to walk out your door."

* * *

Fish zoomed in on Katharina, who had put her hands over her head. He looked at Walt. "You okay, Walt?"

Tears slid down Walt's nose. "That was heartbreaking." He stood and left the room, walking up the stairs to his room.

"Too much talking for my tastes," Fish whispered, watching Bianca on screen after screen as she flew through the snow. "Not enough shit flying through the air. I mean, she had all those granola bars, that knife, that pan. Fire! She could have at least waved a stick on fire. She could have done some serious damage." He shook his head and pushed back from the computer, closing his eyes. "Yeah, Walt was right. That *was* heartbreaking." He gazed up at Katharina. "C'mon, girl. Raise your head. The sun will come out tomorrow."

Chapter 24

Walt returned to Pietro's great room and sat on a couch. He saw Katharina clawing at her hair, her head still on the table. "I think we broke her, Fish."

"She'll be all right," Fish said.

"I don't know."

Fish swapped the shot of Katharina for the fish-eye view of Vincenzo's cabin. "Let's see what Bianca has to say."

Walt stood. "I'd rather not." He started for the stairs but stopped when he heard Bianca crying. She sobbed for several minutes in Vincenzo's arms. Walt returned to his seat.

"I was so horrible," she bawled eventually. "I was the only bitch in that cabin. I said the cruelest things, the harshest, the meanest things, and I didn't even mean half of them. I just couldn't stop myself. I have to go back now and apologize."

Vincenzo felt Bianca's heart beating rapidly through his chest. *And this . . . dream of a woman is a normal girl?*

"You did what we asked you to do, Bianca, and there will be plenty of time to apologize to her when this is all over."

She left his embrace and flopped onto the sofa. "She'll never speak to me again. I'd never speak to anyone again who said those things to me. You saw her face. It had the look of absolute . . . loss. I feel so shitty, so empty."

Vincenzo sat close to her, rubbing her back. "You actually feel pretty good."

Bianca looked up and smiled. "So do you." She kissed him forcefully, passionately.

"Well, I suppose it was bound to happen," Fish said. "The first real kiss of this picture, and it isn't Katharina doing the kissing. The lighting is perfect. This is romance, huh, Walt? This is—"

Walt bolted upright. "What is she doing?"

"Daa-em, she has very fast hands," Fish said. "What color were his pants?"

Walt blinked rapidly. "I don't remember, but—"

"Where'd her clothes go?" Fish cried. "Look at those tattoos. I didn't know she had tattoos on her back. They're like little—"

Neither Walt nor Fish spoke for a full minute.

"Um," Fish whispered, "Houston, we have liftoff."

Walt stood and approached the big screen. "That poor cabin!"

"It's, um, it's well built. Solid Canadian wood. They might get splinters, though." Fish winced. "Ooh. That's gonna bruise."

"Where are they going?"

Fish clicked a few keys, the scene shifting to Vincenzo's room. "His room. Going to infrared . . ."

Walt sat again, mesmerized by the scene on the screen. "They aren't saying much."

Fish's eyes glazed over. "Must have something to do with all that kissing and sighing and body slamming." He zoomed in. "Nice legs. She could run triathlons."

Walt looked away. "Um, that's a pretty sturdy bed."

Fish tried to look away but couldn't. "Yeah. They don't make beds like that anymore. That's real craftsmanship. What do you think it's made out of, oak?"

"Probably."

Fish tilted his head sideways. "What are they doing . . . ?"

"Ah-oooooooh!" Vincenzo howled.

Fish leaned back and heard the echo outside.

"Um, Walt, he's howling."

Walt nodded.

"Ah-oooooooh!" Bianca howled.

Fish heard the echo again.

"Um, Walt?"

Walt nodded. "I heard it, I heard it."

Fish tilted his head the other way. "Nice rhythm. They got a little calypso beat going."

"This is, um, this is . . ." Walt stopped. "I feel like a voyeur."

More howls echoed through the night outside.

"Did they . . . ? No." Fish looked out the picture window. "Um, Walt?"

"Yes, Fish?"

"I think they've awakened the *real* wolves."

Walt jumped up. "I'm going to call my wife now."

"Yeah," Fish said. "You do that."

Chapter 25

Except for an occasional visit to the bathroom, Katharina didn't move from her bed for three full days.

She didn't answer the door when Vincenzo knocked and came in to check on her. She didn't speak when Vincenzo tried to cajole her out into the cold each morning. Pietro kept her fire going, even cracking her door open wider so more of the heat could get inside her bedroom. Katharina rose only four times to drink one glass of water and four times to use the bathroom. She ate no granola, no raisins, and left the stews Pietro brought for her untouched on the table.

Vincenzo, Bianca, and Pietro sat in Vincenzo's cabin using the walkie-talkie and discussing the situation with Fish and Walt.

"How's she doing this morning, Fish?" Bianca asked.

"Same as yesterday," Fish said. "Eyes open, looking outside, not eating, barely sleeping. We have to do something."

"She'll come around," Walt said. "Let's give her another day at least."

"We are ahead of schedule," Vincenzo said. "And at least she has the sense to keep drinking water. And we wouldn't be filming as much anyway in this snow. We'll give her two more days, and if necessary, I'll go in with the stew and . . ."

Pietro shook his head. "You'll what? Force her to eat? That would be an interesting scene. No. I say we wait her out for as long as it takes. She's in there having a pity party, and the only way for her to break out of it is to do it on her own. We're not talking about a child here. She's supposedly a grown woman."

"Well, what about her health?" Bianca asked. "She has to have lost at least ten pounds or more already. I say we get her some real food, like a Philly steak and cheese and some home fries, or some of my chunky chicken salad sandwiches. She likes those for some reason."

"Or a pizza," Fish said. "All the meats. Lots of cheese."

Pietro sighed. "Look, she's an adult. She knows her own needs. When she gets hungry enough, she'll eat. We're not dealing with a two-year-old here. And didn't we want the diva to disappear? The diva is gone. So until then, I say we wait, keep her warm, and offer her food. That's all we can do, and that's all we *should* do. She is under contract for a lot of money, and she has to earn that money, right?"

"This ain't right," Fish said. "None of this is anymore. Send Bianca back in there. Have Bianca say she lost her damn mind, and 'What was I thinking, you're the best actress who ever lived.'"

"I have to agree with Fish," Walt said. "She's a broken woman. Bianca *has* to go back."

"I really want to go back, Vincenzo," Bianca said. "Just look at her. She needs me."

"I can't believe what I'm hearing!" Pietro yelled. "Are you all forgetting who is in that room? That is one of the most headstrong, stubborn, and capable women on this planet. She was, at one time, one of the most powerful people in Hollywood. You all assume that she has no coping skills. As much as I dislike her, I believe in her ability to shrug all this off and get back to work. She is a survivor. She made that rotten movie, and she didn't crumble, right? This is minor in comparison to that. She's lived without assistants before. She went on then, right? No. We leave her alone until she decides to get it in gear."

Vincenzo hated to admit it, but Pietro was right. "Seventy-two hours," he said. "If she hasn't snapped out of this in seventy-two hours, we may have to have another intervention. Be thinking of how we should do that, okay?"

"*Another* intervention?" Pietro scowled on his way to the door. "We haven't even finished the first one yet."

Pietro and Curtis plowed through the snow to his cabin. He tied two bundles of split wood to Curtis's back and continued on to Katharina's cabin. He knocked, heard no reply, and entered. He stoked the fire and had it blazing in no time with the new wood. He picked up a pot of venison stew—uneaten again—and carried it to the door. He fought the urge to speak, but he couldn't help himself. He went to Katharina's door. "I bring food later. You eat."

He received no response.

"I make chicken soup."

He heard only the crackling of the wood in the fireplace.

"I come back soon."

After Pietro left, Katharina turned away from the window, staring at the crack in her door and listening for the cabin door to shut, then closed her eyes. She had no tears left to shed, no desire to warm up properly in front of the fire, no inclination to even open her door wider so the heat could flow in.

I never really wanted to do any of this in the first place, Katharina thought. *Never in a million years.*

I just wanted to get out of Roanoke, to see the world, to have an adventure or two before I finished college, found a regular job, and maybe settled down and got married. That's all. I just wanted something exciting to happen to me, one major rush to look back on and remember for the rest of my life. One last chance for Grandma Pearl to be proud of me before . . . before she died.

The summer after graduating high school, I answered a call for extras for a blockbuster movie filming in northern Virginia. I showed up, and so did half of northern Virginia, it seemed. It was like the day-after-Christmas sales at Walmart, a stampede of people crowding each other, pushing, shoving, being rude, trying to be first. All those people jockeying for position, and most of them carried portfolios containing glossy pictures and résumés.

I just showed up. Here I am. Take me or not.

I left most of the little application blank, walked in front of some people writing on clipboards, and smiled.

"You've never done any theater?"

"No."

"Not even in high school?"

"No."

"Commercials?"

"No."

"Modeling?"

"No."

I thought it was over.

And then I got a callback and an itty-bitty contract.

That movie turned out to be track practice. I ran from unseen monsters, I ran from blasts of death rays, I scurried for cover around barns, I looked up in anguish at the skies, I cried, I screamed, I sweated, I trembled.

Hmm. Kind of like I'm doing now. Curtis is kind of a monster. I guess the death rays are the snow showers now.

Luckily (or unluckily) I didn't get stepped on, zapped, or pulverized. I was a survivor, making it into the last scenes of that movie. The whole process was kind of fun, too, though the hurrying up and waiting became tedious.

When the movie came out, I watched for myself, and there I was, running for my life, pure fear and real sweat on my face. My friends . . . who I don't even know anymore . . . Yeah, Bianca was right about that. Those friends who I don't know anymore thought I was fantastic, great, believable, a star.

I shrugged it off and was in community college when I got another call. "It's a small role, a bit part," the casting agent said. I took it. I was the smart older sister to a precocious little brat. It went so well they even added a few more scenes and lines for me.

I thought that was it.

But the calls kept coming, so I hired Cecil. The first thing he told me: "Get yourself a new name. Dena Hinson isn't knocking anyone's socks off."

I didn't have to think about it for very long. Grandma Pearl suggested "Katharina" since Katharine Hepburn won four Oscars and was nominated twelve times. I chose "Minola" because it sounded exotic, European, and said "not American"—since so many foreign women were winning awards and getting the choice roles in those days.

And Cecil, as greedy as he was, came through. He found me supporting roles, mostly. I was the best friend, the gal-pal, one of the girls, the guy-pal and confidante, the dedicated fill-in-the-blank. I never had a major role and was kind of a foil to the main character. I was a helper, and I was actually content. The money was great, the hours decent, I got to travel, and I could even afford not to work at all for months at a time so I could spend time with Grandma Pearl.

Then Lucentio Pictures plucked me out of that happy rut,

said, "You da woman," and gave me the role of a lifetime—the devoted single mother who finds love and fulfillment despite a slew of obstacles. At first, I was still Dena from Tenth Street, so agreeable, so kind, so malleable. I did everything they told me to do the exact way they told me to do it.

One day, though, I just couldn't say the line as written. I fussed at the writer, Walter Yearling, a few times. "She wouldn't say it that way. She'd say it this way." Walter, always the most patient man, agreed, and the lines were changed in my favor. Paul Stewart, the director, worked me to death and pissed me off often with take after take and suggestion after suggestion, and I pissed him off take after take with suggestions of my own.

And it all paid off. I was proud of my work in that movie. I could look at that movie and say, "There's a black woman who isn't a stereotype. She's real. She's nobody's doormat, punching bag, sex object, comic relief, or femme fatale. She's an African-American Everywoman."

I didn't even think I'd get nominated for best actress, but when I did, my life took off so fast I had little time to think or to even breathe. Talk shows, interviews, photographers, endorsements for this and that, money like rain, suggestions from Cecil to hire this, buy that, invest in this.

Cecil told me to have a huge Oscar party and get Vogue to pay for it. I figured, Vogue, that's a major magazine, they can afford a big one. They said no. I should have asked Ebony or Essence or at least hired a decent Southern-style caterer that made edible, home-style food. That party sucked so bad. No one came.

No. Walter Yearling came. Yeah. He even stayed and helped me clean up after I fired the caterer and threw some burgers and hot dogs on the grill. He wrote My Honey Love just for me, he said. Just for me. I thought: older guy, unmarried, trying to get some attention from a young starlet, maybe trying to get some from a young starlet.

But it wasn't like that. He wanted to be my friend. "After you win the Oscar," he said, "I'll have another script for you."

Only Walter and Antonio Lucentio thought I had a chance to win.

Sitting there at the Academy Awards on TV in front of a billion or so viewers, I heard my name the first time as a nominee. When the lights hit me, I did a little wave and a shy smile. I looked so relaxed, but my heart was banging hard against my ribs. When I heard my name a second *time, I shook. "Katharina Minola quivered," they said the next day. "She was shocked and overwhelmed."*

I didn't even have a speech ready. I never expected to win. I was almost crying by the time I took the Oscar and stood shaking in front of the microphone and a billion people. "I cannot believe this," I babbled. "Are you sure?" I saw people standing, heard the cheers, felt the warmth of the lights, felt this tingling rumble up my body.

"I have so many people to thank . . ."

And then I blanked.

Completely.

I couldn't remember the director's name, or Walter, or my costars, no one. I simply held up that chunk of metal . . . and cried.

The next day the phrase "overwhelmed by emotion" appeared in twenty-seven different newspapers and news reports. I called everyone *connected with the picture the next day to thank them personally, apologizing especially to Walter, who took it, as always, in stride. "You were just being human, Katharina," he said. "I wouldn't expect anything less of you."*

And then the offers flooded in, but out of respect and for launching me, I stayed with Lucentio Pictures for three more projects. They were wonderful films with messages, depth, feeling, and emotion. But I thought I was in a rut playing the long-suffering, sassy, savvy sweetheart who gets her man in the end. I didn't think Lucentio Pictures was giving me a chance to show my range.

So I did the dumbest *thing probably anyone on earth has*

ever done, and jumped for the money and the title role in Miss
Thang. *That role turned me into a caricature, a cartoon character that has given me a reputation that I just cannot shake.
Oh sure, I lived the part for ten months since Cecil and that
studio (which shall remain forever nameless and hopefully will
file Chapter 7 soon) thought it would be great publicity if I
lived the role until the premiere.*

*And then . . . It's like I got stuck, my development arrested,
the things coming out of my mouth beyond bizarre; the more I
talked, the more ridiculous I became. I still cringe at some of my
appearances on late-night TV, wondering who was that freak
wearing fake tiger-skin sunglasses at night and inside a building. Didn't she have any home training? Even Grandma
Pearl had her limits: "I raised you to be the show, baby girl, not
the sideshow."*

They had planned to do Miss Thang 2, *but when the re-
views came out . . .*

*I turned off my phones, my TVs, stopped the magazines, the
newspapers—I hid. At least I tried to. I took vacations to exotic
destinations, and somehow the paparazzi always found me,
taking unflattering pictures of me in bikinis and wet T-shirts.
You can't hide from fame or infamy, gaffes or glory anymore,
and I was stupid enough to think I could.*

*And then I got mad, and when I'm angry, my heart turns
to stone. I took out my frustrations on the rest of the world. I became the angry (though well-dressed) bitch. Bianca nailed that
one right on the head.*

I have wasted so much time and talent hating.

*Cecil (when I wasn't firing and rehiring him) suggested I
play an evil bitch on a daytime soap opera. It had its appeal.
Because of who I had become, I wouldn't have had to do much
acting. I asked him what else.*

*He said, "There is nothing else, Katharina. You've become
a, um, a specialty act."*

"What?"

"You're a diva," Cecil said.' "When diva roles come up, I put in your name, and truly, Katharina, there is nothing else."

I asked, "C'mon, really, Cecil, what else? There have to be other roles out there for me."

"There is nothing else," he repeated.

"Well, what if I read for parts that don't specifically say 'black woman' in the script? Why not a judge, or a lawyer, or a doctor, or a mayor? Or the boss? Why can't I read for the part of someone's boss?"

Cecil actually laughed at me. "You know those roles exist only for white people."

"Those roles do exist, Cecil, and they should exist for everyone, regardless of color. Whatever happened to hiring the best person for the job and forget the race or gender of the actor? Hollywood is the most freaking backward, most close-minded, most uncreative—"

"You want the part or not?" Cecil interrupted.

Evil soap opera bitch. That was the last time I fired Cecil.

That was also the last time I saw most of my money.

From running for my life in front of a blue screen to running from my life here in the middle of a Canadian wilderness. And where am I?

Hiding again.

And who am I?

A runaway slave from Virginia. I know I'm capable of playing this role. I mean, I've been in this role . . . for most of my life. I've been a slave to the dictates of Hollywood, a slave to what the media says I'm supposed to be, a slave to what the United States expects me to be . . . a slave to where the money is.

Katharina turned and looked into the snowy gray day outside her window.

Who I am is out there somewhere.

And tomorrow, I hope I find her.

Chapter 26

Fish, nearly nodding off, noticed movement on the big screen a little after sunrise. "Katharina has left the building."

"All *right*," Walt said, leaving the couch for the command center. "Good for her."

"Headset is a go, tree cams are on, and . . ." Fish cleared his throat. "She's, um, she's walking the wrong way. She's not going to the clearing, Walt. She's walking . . ." He looked at Walt. "She's coming *this* way."

The transmitter squawked. "Fish, are you seeing this?" Vincenzo asked.

"Yep." The next camera to pick up her progress went dark. Fish sighed. "There must be a camera out."

"Where'd she go?" Bianca asked.

Fish zoomed in from a camera farther away. "I got her. There's just a dead spot in the grid because of that malfunctioning camera. Cold might have killed it."

"So she's still in the grid," Vincenzo said.

"Barely," Fish said.

"Maybe she's just out stretching her legs," Walt suggested. "Or getting some nice shots of all the snow with her headset. Or . . ."

"Trying to escape," Fish said. "She's only two hundred yards away from Pietro's fence line, and closing. She's going to see this house, Vincenzo. She's going to make a house call."

"I guess if she comes to the house . . ." Vincenzo's voice trailed off.

"One fifty and closing," Fish said. "Finish your sentence, Vincenzo."

"But Bianca," Vincenzo said, "that wouldn't . . ." The rest was garbled.

"Young lovers and their spats," Walt said.

"One ten and closing," Fish said.

"Fish," Bianca's voice said, "if she comes to the house, don't let her in."

"Gee," Fish said, "I wouldn't have thought of that."

"I mean, look how she's dressed," Bianca said. "Would any homeowner open the door to let something looking like that come in?"

"I would, shit," Fish said. "If I lived alone on the prairie and a hot woman stumbled up to my door, I'd give her a bath my damn self. Seventy-five yards and closing, and she ain't slowing down."

"Does she know you, Fish? Would she recognize you?" Walt asked. "She'd probably recognize me."

Fish growled. "Listen, y'all. It doesn't matter if she recognizes me or not. She'll know something's up the second I open the door. Oh my, there's a black man opening the door way up here in northern Ontario, where so many black people love to live in all this cold, ice, and snow. Oh, what's that over his fireplace? A whole bunch of monitors and a huge TV. Oh look—there's *my* room back at Cabin 3."

"She's within fifty yards of the fence now, Vincenzo," Walt said, "maybe eighty yards from our door. What about Pietro? Could he get here in time?"

"And do what, Walt?" Fish asked. "Tell her this house is poisonous, don't touch?"

"Pietro's too busy making his stew, anyway," Vincenzo said. "He swears he can get her to eat tonight."

"That might not be necessary," Fish said. "Walt and I might be cooking for her in a few minutes."

"Why is that shot so wide?" Bianca asked.

"I only put a few cameras on Pietro's fence line because I didn't think she'd ever come this direction," Fish said. "This is our last line of defense."

"She's slowing down," Walt said. "Look! She's hiding."

"She stopped." Fish adjusted the closest camera, zooming in on Katharina's face peering out from around some tall grass. "She has to see the house. Why would she just . . . stop?"

Katharina crouched behind a clump of tall grass topped with snow. *Civilization? Here?* She saw three huge windows framing a two-story room jutting out from the rest of a completely brown and beige stone house with countless small windows and skylights. *I hope Bianca made it over there that night,* she thought. *She has to have made it somewhere safe. Sly or Alessandro have to know she's gone for good. They would have said something to me otherwise.*

Damn! What a massive house! Big SUV, smoke coming from the chimney, electricity, hot water. I'll bet they even have showers, cereal from this *century, hot chocolate. I would kill for hot chocolate right now. I could just go over there, ask to use*

*the phone, maybe get warmed up by their fire, eat a chicken
salad sandwich with or without the crust . . .*

"She's . . . she's crying," Bianca said in a small voice.
"Vincenzo, let *me* go to her."

"No," Vincenzo said. "We're still good. As long as she
stays on that side of the fence, we're okay."

Katharina wiped her eyes. *The things I used to take for
granted are now luxuries to me. I hope I never take those things
for granted again.* She smiled at the clouds. *Look at me
now, Grandma Pearl. Just look at your baby now. I'm the show.*

She turned her body to look at what she thought
someone looking through the picture window would
see. *Excellent view of those hills. Pretty. Cold as shit, but
pretty.* She looked back to *her* mountains and forest. *Just
as pretty, and just as cold as shit. But . . .*

She stood, not looking at the house, a woman alone
on a snow-swept prairie. *Five million and more humilia-
tion, or back to my sorry life . . .*

"That is an amazing view," Vincenzo said. "Imagine
an audience drinking *that* in."

Walt grabbed Fish's arm. "She's turning. She's turning around. She's going back. She's actually running,
too!"

Fish sat back and rubbed his eyes. "That was too
close. You think she recognized the Suburban?"

"No way to tell," Vincenzo said. "It was dark, she had
been blindfolded. I hope she didn't. Let me know when
she's back inside her cabin."

"Um, wait up," Bianca said. "She's really hauling. She's almost *to* her cabin. She's going inside . . . and coming out with . . . a granola bar."

"She's eating!" Walt cried. "She's going to work!"

"I'm on my way," Vincenzo said.

Fish shook his head. "She's going to get her shelter going *today?* On only a granola bar? And after what she's been through? Damn, I wish she had a sister."

Pietro stepped out of his cabin just in time to see Katharina approaching. "Good morning," he said.

Katharina nodded and stopped, munching on a granola bar. "How's your mule?"

"Better," Pietro said. "I have soup and stew ready."

Katharina held up the granola bar. "I'm good. Can you save it for my dinner?"

Pietro smiled. "Yes. Better if cooking all day."

"Good," Katharina said. "Good. I'm sure I'll be hungry." She finished her granola bar and crumpled the wrapper. "I, uh, I better not take the wrapper down there."

Pietro held out his hand. Katharina put the wrapper in his hand.

"I will bring coffee," Pietro said.

Katharina started to walk away. "Only if it's not that sludge you tried to feed me."

"Maxwell House," Pietro said. " 'Good to the last drop.' "

Katharina waved.

She's back, Pietro thought.

And in a small space not too far off the beaten track inside his heart, he realized he had missed her.

And it made him laugh.

Chapter 27

Pietro, Curtis, and Vincenzo watched Katharina at work. She fashioned a broom of sorts out of a leafy branch from a pine tree and swept the snow off the clearing down to the dirt. After several tries with the flint and knife, she started a small fire using birch bark, twigs, and several blocks of peat. Then, she tore the bottom off the hem of her dress and tied together a bundle of small, wet sticks to form a log, setting this bundle on top of the peat.

She's learning, Pietro thought. *Dry wood is life.*

She used the flint in an attempt to sharpen her blade, then tore another strip from her dress, tying the blade to a long, straight branch. The first time that she plunged this makeshift digging tool onto her old foundation outline the knife broke free. She tied it on again to the same result.

Notch the branch, Pietro thought in his mind. *Wedge the knife inside.*

She tried tying the knife on several different ways, removed more strips of cloth from her dress, and eventually shook her head and tried digging just with the knife as before. Her blade pinged into rocks, bounced off hidden stones, and had little if any effect.

You've dug down far enough, Pietro thought. *Use the rocks you're prying up as your foundation. Get more rocks from the stream. You have to know houses built with stone foundations last longer! Think, Katharina, think!*

Whenever Vincenzo said "Cut," Pietro took her coffee, which she sipped and handed back without comment.

Then she'd start digging again, wrapping more strips of her dress around her hands to cover her blisters.

Katharina had a lot of blisters.

"She keeps tearing away her dress like that," Fish said with a smile, "we'll get an R rating for sure."

She'd do this until dusk, earning a bowl of soup or stew for her efforts.

She did this every day for the next *four* weeks.

She said *nothing* as she worked hard at getting nowhere.

She'd occasionally prop up long branches for walls, only to have them clatter to the ground. She built all day and slept all night, rationing her granola bars and raisins, eating only half-bowls of the soup or stew Pietro made for her. She now collected her own wood for her cabin fires and tended them herself, and sometimes slept in front of the fire. After Pietro left a small box of detergent on her porch, she washed her clothes and Bianca's "draws" in the tub.

* * *

Fish, surprisingly, did not zoom in on these revealing shots.

Katharina gave herself cloth baths, using just enough soap to get a lather going. She took one hot bath a week, making many trips with a pot of hot water to fill the tub.

Fish, with Walt looking over his shoulder, did not film these baths.

Fish was not a happy director of photography.

Vincenzo rarely yelled "Cut" anymore.

Fish rarely said anything witty or risqué. Walt went days without speaking, instead sitting in front of a computer screen and typing.

Bianca could only watch and wonder—and rest all day for the howling and body-slamming to come during the night.

Pietro, though, just couldn't help himself. All this relative normalcy was boring to him. And at the rate Katharina was *not* building her shelter, her contract would run out before her first wall stayed put.

I have to piss her off, he realized. *She only makes great leaps when she's angry at someone.*

He first tried whistling "London Bridge" whenever he was around her.

That didn't even earn a scowl, and one time, Katharina whistled along with him.

He left a box full of dominoes in her cabin late one night.

As far as he knew, the dominoes had not even been touched.

He used a stick to "draw" a typical nineteenth-century hut in the snowdrift just outside her cabin, complete with stone foundation, gate, and roof.

Katharina used the snow in the snowdrift to throw snowballs at Curtis.

One morning, Pietro left a small hatchet on her porch for her to step over on her way to the clearing.

The fireworks finally began a few minutes later.

"Yo, Fonzi!" Katharina yelled as she stood in front of Pietro's cabin. She slashed the air with the hatchet, the box of dominoes under her other arm.

Despite the frigid temperatures, Pietro stepped outside barefoot and wearing only a pair of jeans and a tight T-shirt.

"Is this your hatchet?" she asked.

Pietro played dumb. "No."

"Liar." She tossed the dominoes box onto the porch, the wooden box shattering into a hundred pieces.

Pietro noticed that each of the dominoes had been cut in half, most likely by the hatchet Katharina was holding.

She waved the hatchet in the air. "Nice balance, and very sharp. I suppose you want me to use this in some way to build a proper shelter."

"I do," Pietro said.

"So you and your cousin don't have to sit out in the cold and watch my shelter come falling down, falling down?"

"Like the London Bridge." Pietro smiled. "No. I worry about you."

"Ah." She faced Pietro's door and cocked the hatchet behind her. "I'd step aside there, Fonzi. I'm not sure where this is going."

Pietro didn't move. "You use. To help."

"Don't need it," Katharina said.

"Is getting colder." He stuck his hands into his pockets.

"I'm aware of that, probably more than you are."

Pietro looked down the steep hill. "If you go to stream, you will find large—"

Katharina let the hatchet fly, barely missing Pietro's right shoulder as it plowed cleanly into his front door. "I don't need your help."

Pietro tried to show no surprise. "But your hands, Katharina."

Katharina held them up in front of her. They were cut up, cracked, and blistered. "I'll survive." She stepped away. "Oh, and I won't be drinking coffee anymore, so don't bother bringing me any."

Pietro looked from the hatchet to the person cutting a swath through the snow. *The diva is gone, but who is this person?*

And why can't I get her out of my head?

Chapter 28

For the next five days, Katharina woke up whispering, "Today is the day."

For the next five nights, Katharina went to sleep whispering, "Maybe tomorrow."

Walt printed out a little slip of paper with the words TODAY IS THE DAY. He taped it to the top of his computer monitor.

Fish noticed and printed out MAYBE TOMORROW and taped it over Walt's little sign.

Walt wouldn't speak to Fish for four days.

Pietro spent his days gathering more long, polelike branches from high on the mountains behind his home and having Curtis haul them to a pile in front of his cabin. Katharina walked past these "poles" each day without, it seemed, even glancing at them.

He then stayed up past midnight one night hauling

the entire stack by hand to make a pile on the other side of the bridge.

Again, Katharina ignored them as she passed by.

I know what he's trying to do, Katharina thought as she looked at the poles that would be *perfect* wood for her walls. *But I'm not going to give him the satisfaction. I will get this shelter up today if it kills me. I just need to dig down more, dig down deep.* She looked at her nonexistent fingernails, smelled her stank and sweaty body, felt the dull edge of her knife, and heard her stomach rumble.

She was ready.

She sharpened her blade on the flint and began digging and scraping in the dirt. An hour passed. She set down her knife and went to a small pile of her own mostly straight poles, each sharpened at one end. Using a large, flat rock, she used both hands to hammer ten poles into the ground, leaving a little space between them. When she had them all standing for more than a minute without wobbling too badly, she smiled.

Until she looked at the rest of the foundation line and realized she would need more than *two hundred* poles to finish her walls. *There are some just up the hill . . . Shoot! And what about the cracks, the gaps between the poles? I can't have the winter winds whistling through my crib! I need to seal them somehow, and it's so cold that mud is now out of the question.*

She looked around her.

I could use snow.

I have plenty of that.

Katharina packed snow in the gaps between the poles, blowing on her hands often. In less than an hour, she had a workable wall that kept the wind at bay.

She smiled.

And then the wind picked up, ruffling what was left

of her dress at times up to her neck. The poles swayed and leaned. The first pole fell, and like dominoes, the rest of the poles followed suit. As if on cue, thunder rolled and echoed across the sky, and snow flooded the clearing. Katharina dropped to her knees and wailed, "Why have you forsaken me?"

She dropped her head, and she wept.

"Cut!" Vincenzo cried, running to Katharina. "That was wonderful."

Katharina's body shook.

"It was inspiring!" Vincenzo shouted. "The indefatigable spirit of humanity reborn!"

Katharina still wept.

"Why don't you take the rest of the day off? We can pick up again tomorrow. Let Alessandro take you home."

Katharina looked up. "No." She wiped her face.

"He has some good ideas for your shelter," Vincenzo said. "He wants to tell you—"

Katharina stood. "I *don't* want or need his help, Sly."

"It is supposed to be Arctic cold tomorrow," Vincenzo said. "Very bad wind chills. Perhaps we can try again in a few days."

Katharina shook her head and trudged up the hill to the bridge. She looked at Pietro's pile of poles, estimating the pile to contain more than three hundred straight sticks.

Pietro left Curtis in the clearing and walked a few steps behind Katharina, smiling. "You look, um, beautiful today."

At least his English is improving. "Shut up, Fonzi. I don't want to hear it today."

Pietro took two long strides and was beside her. "Is *complimento*. You are *bellezza*, beauty."

Katharina crossed the bridge in front of him. "Look,

you're not fooling me. You're just saying that so you can gloat. So I didn't get the shelter built today. So I haven't gotten it built in a month. So what? You don't have to rub it in with your sarcasm."

"*Che?*"

Katharina wheeled on him at the other end of the bridge. "*Che? Che?* Learn some damn English, Fonzi."

Pietro pulled out a well-thumbed Italian-English phrase book. "I try. I use book. So I can talk better. To you."

Katharina caught her breath. *He's trying so hard . . . to help me.* "Just . . . just leave me alone. You understood that, didn't you?"

Pietro acted as if he were reading from the book. "Your, um, hair . . ."

Katharina stopped and marched up to him. "What about my hair?"

Pietro flipped a few pages and held up one finger. "Is, um, *naturale,* natural. Is *bella,* beautiful."

The man is blind! Katharina thought. *It's in knots, flying out, puffing in all the wrong directions. He looks sincere, but . . .* "Is nappy, is dirty, is gross, is ruined. I should just cut it all off."

Pietro waved his hands. "No, is . . . *libero.* Is free. Like the wind. Goes where it wants to go. Like you. You go where you want to go."

Katharina's heart hurt. "I'm not . . ." *I'm not free, am I? I can't be!* "Just leave me alone!"

Pietro watched her storm off, imagining his hands rubbing her nice, toned legs, his tongue licking her tight, trim stomach. *Where did* that *image suddenly come from? I've obviously been alone in the woods for too long.* "Um, I make *manzo stufato* for you. Is especial stew."

Katharina threw up her hands this time. "More stew?" She turned to face him. "Is that all you can cook?"

"Oh no. For here, the stew. I am chef. Stew is good. No buckshot."

Katharina almost smiled. "Porcupine balls, bear liver, wolves' nuts, or chipmunk scrotum?"

Pietro mumbled "wolves' nuts" under his breath as he flipped through the pages.

Katharina turned away and smiled. "What kind of stew is it, Fonzi?"

"Oh. *Manzo*. Beef." He sniffed the air. "You can smell. Is cooking. You smell?"

Yes, I smell, and the stew does smell good. "It's real beef?"

Pietro nodded. "Yes. Beef. Potatoes. Carrots. Onions. I get from store."

Katharina blinked. "You went to a store?"

"Yes," Pietro said. "I travel all night. You not eat for days. I take SUV. Go to Rouyn-Noranda. Wait till open. Buy beef, *verdura*. Come back. Cook for you. You eat." He hesitantly reached out his hand and touched her arm.

Katharina looked at his massive hand. *I don't have the strength to stop him anymore.*

"You are thin, Katharina. You need strength."

Katharina slowly shook her head. "No," she whispered.

"*Per favore*, Katharina. Please."

She turned her back on him. "No," she whispered again. *A vow to myself is a vow I cannot break.*

"Please, Katharina. I only think of you."

Katharina's eyes misted. "No." *I want to thank him for his extremely nice gesture, but I can't!* "No."

She left him behind her and passed his cabin, smelling the heavenly stew. She could almost taste it in the air.

"I will save it for you, Katharina," she heard Pietro say. "I will keep it warm for you."

Katharina burst into tears. "Whatever, Fonzi."

She ran the rest of the way to her cabin, falling on her bed and weeping. *I should have had one bowl! What's one bowl going to hurt besides my pride? He drove, what, a couple hours both ways for me? And it took some preparation time, too. All that cutting, chopping, dicing . . . He looks as if he hasn't slept in years, but how do you tell with Italians and their dark, mysterious faces?* "I will save some for you," he said. "I will keep it warm for you."

Her tears subsided, her sobs abated, and in five minutes, she was sound asleep and snoring.

Chapter 29

Katharina woke a few hours later in darkness to the howls of wolves and a pungent aroma drifting in from the other room. She wrapped herself in her comforter and saw a bowl, a soup spoon, a serving spoon, a napkin . . . and a long-stemmed red rose in a clear glass vase on the table. A silver pot of stew simmered over a glowing amber and red fire.

She knew Pietro had come in weeks before to keep her fire going, she knew he showed more than normal care for her, and she knew he was only thinking of her. She also knew Pietro was a moron, a nice moron, but a moron nonetheless. She had had admirers before, most of them insane, of course, but none of them ever made such a fuss over feeding her and keeping her warm.

She dipped the serving spoon into the stew, blew on the spoon, and tasted it. *Damn, that's good. I have missed salt!* She tasted oregano, she tasted garlic, she tasted something like cilantro. *Gourmet stew. What a concept.* She dipped again and came up with noodles and ground beef, celery and carrots, a piece of a potato. She sniffed the rose and found it fresh, its petals almost purple. She noted that the napkin was linen, not paper, the bowl nice china, not plastic. Even the spoons had nice little filigrees on their handles.

If he were only . . . What? Less hairy? An American? Employed in a real job? Less arrogant? More intelligent? The man drives a nice SUV yet owns a mule?

She shook her head. She couldn't let this go on. *If it breaks his heart, so be it. I can't let him treat me like this . . . because I cannot return his many favors with any of my own.*

She gathered the pot, bowl, spoons, and linen napkin. She decided to keep the rose for the scent, not the sentiment, tightened her boot strings, picked a twig from her hair, and left the cabin to the higher-pitched sounds of the wolves.

"Bianca and Vincenzo are at it again," Fish said.

"He'll be hoarse in the morning," Walt said.

"Not if he wolfs her down," Fish said.

"Ha." Walt noticed Katharina's door was open. "Katharina's leaving her cabin."

Fish tinkered with some of the controls. "It's really dark tonight."

"Go infrared, then," Walt suggested.

"I knew I'd infect you sooner or later."

Katharina stopped in front of Pietro's cabin. She dinged the serving spoon against the pot. "Yo, Fonzi!"

Pietro came out onto the porch wearing a fluffy blue bathrobe and moccasins. "You like?"

Katharina stepped closer. *Geez! Look at his hairy legs! Why does the man ever wear pants!* "I know you understand a lot of what I say, so I'll just say it and get on. I don't need your help. I have *never* needed your help. I will *never* need your help. Understand?" She set the pot, bowl, spoons, and napkin on the porch. "I know you admire me, and I'm touched. But after this movie is over, I'm going back to California, and you're going back to wherever it is you're from. Understand?"

Pietro's eyes dropped. "I will not help. But where is the rose?"

"I'm keeping it so my cabin doesn't smell so funky."

Pietro nodded. "I understand. Let me know when it dies. I will get you another."

Oh, that's so sweet, but . . . "What is up with you? Don't you understand what I'm saying? You're just a handyman, a jack-of-all-trades. You're not the director, you're not the producer, you're not even an extra. Yet you try daily to tell me how to do my job."

Pietro frowned. "I don't tell you. I show you. There is difference."

Okay, so he's not a complete moron. "Well . . . stop showing me, then. It's getting on my nerves."

Pietro bowed his head. "*Mi dispiace.* I am sorry."

Why does he have to have such kind eyes? I have to end his infatuation with me now! "And you know what else? You are one of the meanest, most stubborn, rudest, most arrogant people I have ever met. And you act like you know me all the time. You don't know me! You don't know the first thing about me."

"No. I do not know you well. I know I am good cook. I know you are hungry." He stretched out his hand. "I not touch you without your permission anymore. It is in me to touch. *Italiano,* yes?"

Katharina didn't take his hand, instead pulling her hands close to her body. "Haven't you been listening? I don't need you or your food, capeesh?"

Pietro smiled. "Is *capisco,* not 'caw-peesh.' "

Katharina growled. "Oh, and now you're correcting my *Italiano?* You'll be correcting my English, too, huh?"

"I never do that." He stepped closer. "You are the actress. I am the help." He picked up the stew, the bowl, the spoons, and the napkin.

The aroma drifted to Katharina instantly. *I should have had a few more bites.* "Um, you're right."

Pietro nodded. "So, I am help. I make food. You eat." *He got me. How did I let him get me like that?*

"I can bring to you or . . ." He extended his hand again.

Katharina looked at her tracks leading up the hill and far away to her cabin. "I can walk on my own."

Pietro stepped aside, and Katharina entered his cabin.

Fish flipped the other "backup" switch, pointing at the big screen, showing Katharina sitting at Pietro's table. "I only have two fish-eyes in there, Walt, but as you saw from Vincenzo's cabin, they'll be enough."

"How'd you put those cameras in there without Pietro finding out?"

"I am magic."

Walt looked up at the big screen and sighed. "Now *that's* romantic. Nice fire. A few candles around. Is that the tub? He was about to take a bath!"

"Priceless," Fish said.

"I couldn't write this stuff," Walt said.

Pietro started immediately to serve Katharina, but she grabbed his wrist and took the serving spoon. She served herself a bowl, nodded once to the "help," and inhaled a bowl of stew in less than a minute. Pietro tried to serve her more, but Katharina's eyes stopped him.

He turned the serving spoon around, Katharina took it, nodded again, filled her bowl, and savored her stew this time.

"How much English do you understand, Alessandro?"

Walt threw his head back and yelled, "She finally said his name correctly!"

Fish shrugged. "I kind of liked Fonzi."

Pietro eyed the other chair. "May I sit?"

Katharina nodded. "If you must."

He sat and slid into his chair, his naked knees brushing Katharina's ragged leggings. *"Capisco un po'.* I understand a little. You must talk *lentamente,* slow."

His knees are touching mine, and he doesn't notice? Maybe because his legs are so hairy? Eww. The nerve! "Why is your cabin so warm, Alessandro?"

Pietro looked at the fireplace. "I build fire right."

Katharina noticed a bathtub steaming in a much bigger bathroom than hers. "Um, and I don't?" *He has hot water, too. Why does he—Oh yeah, he uses the cauldron.*

"You make good fire, Katharina," Pietro said. "But it burns too fast. Must have foundation."

Katharina noticed the fire's nice, even flame, the logs stacked like Lincoln Logs, and the bathrobe he was wearing. *I must be blind!* "Were you about to take a bath?"

Pietro nodded. "Yes. Water too hot still. You smell something?"

Katharina felt his knees leave hers. "No. Just this stew."

Pietro stood. "Something . . . *Aglio.* Garlic."

Katharina sniffed the stew. "Like I said, the stew. You put garlic in it."

Pietro nodded. "But not this much . . ." He circled the table once, returning to Katharina. "It is you."

Katharina dropped her spoon. "I beg your pardon!"

Pietro jumped back. "I am sorry. But it is you, Katharina. *Aglio*. Garlic. Very strong."

I can't believe this shit! "I've been a little busy making a movie, and y'all have only given me one little square of soap. What do you expect me to smell like?"

He pointed to the tub. "You go. Is ready. You need."

Fish leaned forward as he zoomed in on Katharina's face. "Please take a bath, Katharina. If not for him, do it for me."

"Shrews smell like garlic so their predators let them go," Walt whispered.

"What?" Fish asked.

"Um, nothing."

Katharina searched all around the nice, cozy cabin for the right words to say, but the water kept calling her name. "You want me to take a bath just like that?"

Pietro smiled. "Water *caldo*. Ready. Hot. Good for hands."

Katharina turned away from him. "No," she said softly. *That wasn't very convincing. I better try again.* "No," she said evenly.

"I have soap, shampoo, the cream," Pietro said.

"The cream?"

Pietro moved so he could look Katharina in the eye. "For legs."

"Lotion?"

"Um, no." He pantomimed shaving his legs. "For legs."

Katharina's mouth dropped onto the table, rolled around for several moments, then snapped back up into her head. "My legs are not . . ." She felt between the bloomers and Bianca's socks. *Jesus, I'm as hairy as he is. I could set them with curlers. When's the last time I . . . It's a damn forest down there!*

"*Per favore.* You need bath, Katharina."

If he had any more nerve he'd be two *people!*

"I will close door. Door has lock. Only you in there. No keyhole. No window. All alone. Water stay hot for hour. I go outside and wait."

God, he makes it sound so good. "I do not . . . look at my lips, Fonzi. I do *not* want a bath. Okay?"

Pietro sighed. "Okay. Then I will take."

Pietro shrugged out of his robe and walked into the bathroom, kicking off his moccasins before he stepped into the tub, turned, and settled into the water, steam rising all around him. "Ahh," he said. "*Perfetto!*"

Katharina's jaw was getting tired from dropping, and this time it decided to stay on the table. *He just . . . that was . . . He . . . Damn, he just . . .*

Pietro soaped his hairy chest to a lather and began to sing a soft Italian love song.

And now he's . . . She finally closed her mouth. *Damn, he has a fine booty.*

Fish couldn't speak.

Walt couldn't stop speaking. "You saw her face, didn't you? When he dropped that robe, she just . . . Wow! Her eyes said, 'Wow!' She *has* to go in, Fish, she just *has* to!"

Fish nodded.

"You're agreeing with me, Fish?"

Fish nodded again. "She smells like garlic."

Chapter 30

Katharina saw her hands push back from the table. She felt her legs push her out of her seat. She caught a whiff of garlic, and she wasn't near the stew. She heard a hairy man singing something sexy from a bathtub. She watched herself walk across the cabin floor all the way to the tub. She smiled when she looked down and thought of some of the poles she had tried to plant earlier in the day.

"Get up," she heard herself say.

"No," Pietro said.

Katharina snapped out of her daydream. "What?"

"I say no," Pietro said, rinsing the soap from his chest.

Katharina stepped to the other end of the tub and pulled out a silver chain. "I'll do it."

Pietro smiled and began soaping his legs. "You won't."

"Watch me."

Pietro paused and watched.

Katharina dropped the chain. "Get up!"

"I am not done," Pietro said. "When I am done."

Katharina gripped the tub with both hands. "Then . . . move to this end."

"No."

"Okay." Katharina stepped into the tub fully clothed and sat at the other end of the tub, leaning her head to the side to avoid the faucet. *Hot water! How I've missed hot water!* "Are you done with the soap yet?"

"No." Pietro stood and soaped his back, legs, booty, and penis. He sat, the soap foaming to the surface. "Now I am done." He rinsed off the soap and handed it to Katharina.

He just . . . And I just sat here and watched him do it. What am I, hypnotized? She began scrubbing her face and her clothes rapidly, the soap stinging the cuts on her hands.

"You need *assistente*, Katharina?"

My turn to say it! "No."

Pietro reached under the water and grabbed one of Katharina's feet.

"No!" she yelled, jerking it away.

"I rub your feet."

"No."

Pietro reached under the water again and grabbed one of Katharina's feet again, this time holding her by the ankle. "I rub your feet."

She tried to jerk away again. "No!"

Pietro removed the wool sock and massaged her foot with his free hand.

Oh shit, that feels so good! She used her other foot to push Pietro's hand away. "Cut it out!"

Pietro slid closer. "Give me feet."

"No."

* * *

"She looks like a deer in headlights," Fish said.

"Like a scared little rabbit."

"Like one of them big-eyed gecko-looking things," Fish said.

"What?"

"Her skin has to be scaly as hell, right?"

Pietro slid even closer, Katharina's legs resting on his shins, his feet pressing against her thighs. He removed the other wool sock and threw it against the wall. "I rub feet."

"Okay, okay," Katharina said. "You rub feet."

Katharina had to hold on to the sides of the tub for ten minutes while her feet soared with the angels, flew through marshmallow skies, and landed in a land of cotton.

I almost came for real just now! "Are you done? I have a lot of work to do."

"No." He took the shampoo and lathered his hair.

Katharina pointed at his chest. "Do your chest while you're at it."

Pietro lathered up his chest. He pushed back and dunked his head. When he emerged, he blinked away some water, wiped his eyes, and stood.

I'm thinking of a statue, Katharina thought. *I think it was in Rome, only the one in Rome was much smaller, especially . . . there.*

Pietro stepped out of the tub and took a small towel from a towel rack, drying his hair.

"You, you, you can leave now, Alessandro." *And take that club with you!*

Pietro dried his chest thoroughly before wrapping the towel around his waist.

"Um, close the door on your way out."

"No," Pietro said. "You will get cold."

"Don't watch."

Pietro shrugged. "I would not watch. Is only bath."

As Pietro left, Katharina got an eyeful of Pietro's butt cheeks peeking through the towel.

She smiled and looked at the ceiling.

"This is beyond classic," Fish said.

"The most," Walt said.

"I can zoom in a little, but it will become more skewed . . ."

Walt laughed. "Zoom away. It can't get any more skewed than it already is."

Katharina removed her clothes as she soaped them, draping them over the edge of the tub. She kept her back to the door at all times and took off her leggings last before slipping fully into the water.

Walt tried to get the image of Katharina's booty out of his mind. "That's some seriously, um, soapy water."

Fish was struggling with the vision, too. "I wish I could get a better focus, but she's splashing so much . . ."

Walt and Fish stared at each other.

"The worst thing is," Fish said, "that we can't tell a *single* person on earth what we've just seen. You can't tell your wife."

Walt shook his head rapidly.

"And I don't have a wife or girlfriend to tell." Fish shook his head. "And from this moment on, I will compare every booty I see to what I just saw, and I will cry, Walt. I will cry my damn eyes out."

"Alessandro!" Katharina yelled.

Pietro didn't move from his chair.

"Alessandro," Katharina said more softly.

Pietro still didn't move.

Geez! "Yo, Fonzi!"

Pietro, still in his towel, went to the door. "Yes?"

"Alessandro, could you wring out my clothes and put them near the fire to dry? I would appreciate it very much."

Pietro walked in, collected her clothes, even the socks he'd thrown against the wall, and left the bathroom without looking even once at Katharina. "I will bring you something warm to wear."

"Take your time, Alessandro." *He didn't even look at me!* Katharina looked at the beige water. *Geez, he probably couldn't even see me.* "Alessandro!"

"Yes?" Pietro called from the other room.

"May I borrow a razor?"

Pietro finished stretching and hanging Katharina's clothes near the fire, then went into the bathroom, finding a fresh razor under the sink. He handed it to her without looking at her.

Okay, then. Don't *look.* She snatched the plastic razor. "Where is the cream?"

Pietro rolled his eyes and took a can of shaving cream from behind the mirror. He looked at Katharina this time. "Here is the cream."

Katharina stood, lifting one leg to the edge of the tub.

* * *

"Um, Fish?" Walt asked in a tiny voice.

"Yes, Walt?" Fish barely said.

"That's some full-frontal nudity there, um, Fish."

"Yeah, it is," Fish said. "I am deep in hell right now."

Pietro turned to leave.

"Wait," Katharina said. She squirted some shaving cream into her hands and handed the can to Pietro. "*Grazie*, Alessandro."

"She's speaking Italian, Fish."

"Don't talk to me," Fish said.

Pietro put the can back behind his mirror, looked once at Katharina, felt a stirring, and hurried out of the room.

Katharina smiled.

Thank heavens for little towels on big men, she thought.

Chapter 31

Pietro carefully restretched Katharina's clothes over chair backs, the table, and on hooks above the mantel. He had to adjust his towel several times while trying to remove the image of Katharina standing up in the bathtub from his mind.

He was failing, and the towel was complaining against the strain. He thought about running out and diving into a snowbank, and just the thought eased the pressure on the towel. He tried to sit on the bearskin on top of his bed but jumped up immediately.

Geez, he thought. *She's a few feet away looking very sexy and wet, I'm in here wearing a small towel, I am semierect, it's snowing again, the fire is hot.*

Time out. Take deep breaths. Calma, calma.

Nothing is going to happen.

I will get fully dressed. Yes. That's best. I will give her some sweats to wear. We will have a little chat while we eat some more stew. I will make her some coffee. Her clothes will dry, and then she will leave.

Nothing is going to happen.

He looked at the bearskin on his bed.

She'd really look good with that draped over her shoulders, though. Just knowing there was nothing but her sexy body underneath—

Calma, calma. *Take deep breaths.*

She isn't even close to the kind of woman I've been with, not even close to the woman I need. She's bossy, arrogant, narcissistic, crude, rude, and—

She had the nicest little—

Take deep breaths.

And the way her—

Calma, calma.

He went to his wardrobe, opening and taking out a pair of sweats. *She could camp out in these.* He pushed aside some clothing, lifted a stack of shirts, and shook his head at his boxers.

I don't have a thing for her to wear.

He looked at the bearskin again.

She wouldn't wear that, would she?

He set his jaw. *If Alessandro tells her to wear a bearskin, she will wear the bearskin. She cannot deny Alessandro, the fearless shrew tamer.* "You wear this," *Alessandro will say, and Katharina will wear it.* "Take this off," *Alessandro will say, and she will take it . . . off.*

I need a much bigger towel.

Wait.

I only have this one clean towel in this cabin. He smiled. *I'll just hand her this one.* "Why is it so freaking wet?" *she'll ask. Or, she'll say,* "I don't need your towel, I don't want your towel, I will never need your towel."

He looked again at the bearskin.

Get a grip on yourself, man! She isn't the one for you. She could never be. She's been a pain in your ass since—

Oh, but her ass was just . . . so . . . nice!

It's only an act. She is, after all, an actress.

But I met her up here. *Up* here *is where the others said good-bye.*

Katharina hates *this place!*

She's surviving now.

Because of you and your help!

No. I haven't done a thing for her in weeks. It's been all her.

You put her on the right path. You gave her the direction.

She has those eyes . . .

Yeah . . .

And those thighs . . .

Oh yeah . . .

And she's tough.

No more body parts?

The towel's too small.

Oh.

I like her toughness. She's strong. She has her own mind and she uses it. She says what she means and means what she says. There's no deception with her. She's honest.

And hateful.

Hatefully honest.

He looked at the bathroom door. *I should just go in there and show her who the man is, show her what I'm made of, make her* beg *me to stop—*

He sat on the bed and breathed deeply, the sounds of splashing water echoing around him.

Calma, calma.

Chapter 32

Hello? Are you one of my fingernails, too? Hi. I'm your owner. I haven't seen you since September. How have you been?

Katharina didn't want to leave the tub—*ever.* Though the water was now an oddly beige-brown color, it surrounded her with warmth and softened her rough hands. She sniffed her skin and didn't smell garlic anymore. Her legs were smooth again, though the razor had died a grisly death. Her hair was still in knots, but it was a collection of clean knots. *That's what matters. I feel and smell clean again.*

And there was a man in the other room, too.

A man. She sighed. *I haven't known too many real men. The actors I worked with were great, but they had to act like real men. Alessandro.* She sighed just thinking his name. *It's not an act for Alessandro. Yeah, he's bossy, arrogant, narcissistic, crude, rude—*

And he's only wearing an itty-bitty towel! She giggled.

Oh, I'm sure he got dressed. "Is only bath." *He's probably wearing a damn sweater, boots, and jeans. He looks good like that, though, rugged, strong. Nicely proportioned upper body, sturdy, tight butt . . .*

The hair on his chest can go.

She shuddered.

Can a person spontaneously combust if enough static electricity is generated by chest hair? Would there be enough friction to start a fire?

"Oops," she whispered, dropping the soap in front of her. "I've dropped the soap again. Now where did that slide off to . . oh . . . yeah . . . there it *is*."

She closed her eyes and imagined him beside her, caressing her shoulders, massaging her neck, laying a whole big stack of wood right inside her—

Poco, poco. Molto . . . something.

He's not eye candy, though there's certainly a lot of him. He's so dark for being so white. All that hair. So serious. Yet today, when he smiled and said, "I learn for you," my heart fluttered.

A little.

He says he has a girlfriend a thousand times prettier than me.

Poco, poco.

I bet she's an Amazon woman with really big teeth, toes all the same size, and arms that hang to her knees.

She slid under the water one more time, wiping her eyes and shivering slightly.

This water is getting cold.

She stood.

I need a hot man.

She sighed.

No. I just need a man.

A real one.

Chapter 33

"Alessandro!"

Pietro went only to the edge of the door this time, afraid to peek inside the bathroom. "Yes?"

"The water is getting cold. Didn't you promise me something warm to wear?"

Without another thought, Pietro took the bearskin from the bed, brought it to her, held it out, and turned away as she stepped out of the tub.

Katharina wrapped the bearskin around her shoulders. *"Grazie."* So warm. And now I'm as hairy as he is! And he's still in that itty-bitty towel!

She followed him to the fire, sat in her chair, and put her feet up on the table. *Yeah, I'm giving him a free shot of my stuff. But why isn't he looking?*

Oh yeah. He's still wearing that itty-bitty towel.

"Why is she doing this to me, Walt?" Fish whined. "Why, Walt, why?"

"You know, I remember a scene like this somewhere before."

"How can you be so analytical at a time like this?"
Fish huffed.

"It keeps me calm, Fish," Walt said. "Otherwise I'd be
as befuddled and bothered as you are."

Pietro touched several of Katharina's undergar-
ments, feeling them with his fingers and thumb.

What is he doing? "Why are you touching my draws?"
Katharina asked.

"To see if dry."

Oh. I thought he was getting kinky. "Are they?"

"Your panties are wet."

Katharina got up and touched her underwear.
"They're just moist."

"I'm not even going to say another damn thing," Fish
said.

"What damn thing could you say?" Walt asked.

Katharina sat again and put up her feet, opening the
bearskin even further. "How long before they're dry?"

Pietro shrugged and paced in front of the fireplace.
"They may not dry for a long time, Katharina."

"Oh. Um, what should we do until they dry? Should
we . . . talk?"

Pietro stopped pacing but did not turn away from
the mantel. "I am no good talking." He turned slowly,
took a quick breath, and drank in her body.

Yes! Katharina thought. *He's going to drop that towel
and take me right here! He's going to lay the wood to me, and
I'm going to scratch all his chest hair off!* "Then . . . don't
talk, Alessandro."

Pietro dropped the towel . . .

Yesssssssss!

And then he stepped around the table, went to his wardrobe, put on a pair of red long johns with a flap in the back, and buttoned them up the front.

Nooooooo! Shit! Did I say that with too much attitude? I probably did. Damn! I've hurt his feelings, and now he's wearing Santa's draws!

Pietro disappeared into another room and came out with a steaming mug of coffee. He stirred it slowly before placing the mug in front of her.

Katharina smiled. "Thank you, Alessandro."

"We have a breakthrough!" Walt yelled. "Call Vincenzo now!"

"Because she said thank you? She said *grazie* earlier."

Walt could barely contain his joy. "But this time she said it in English. She never says that phrase. Never."

Fish scowled. "Let's give it a little more time. And why didn't he just . . . take her a few minutes ago?"

"Can't you see?" Walt asked. "He's testing her. He's making sure that he's tamed her."

Katharina sipped her coffee, sweetened just right. She set down her mug and stood, letting the bearskin fall low to her back. She felt her panties again, her nipples feeling the warmth of the fire. "My panties are still wet."

Pietro nodded.

* * *

"He just . . . nods?" Fish shouted. "A woman says, 'My panties are still wet,' and he just nods? He's not human!"

Walt smiled. "He's playing hard to get."

"I could say something here," Fish said, "but I won't."

Pietro suddenly sprinted across the room to the door, opened it, ran outside, and left the door wide open to the wind.

Katharina shivered and pulled up the bearskin, draping it around her shoulders and covering her chest. "Hey, shut that . . ." She sighed, wrapped the bearskin more tightly around her, stood, and shut the door herself.

Pietro returned with an armload of wood, adding several long branches to the fire.

"So, tell me about your girlfriend," Katharina said. "What's her name?"

Pietro rested his back against the mantel. "You say you do not want me to talk."

Yep. I did it again. I hurt someone's feelings. "That's not what I meant, Alessandro. I like hearing you talk."

Pietro frowned. "Then what did you mean?"

His eyes are right scary when he frowns. "Well, the way you were standing there and looking at me, I thought you were about to . . ."

"To what?"

Katharina's lips fluttered. "To . . ." *To lay the wood, to drop that ax, to split me open.* "To make love to me."

Pietro's frown turned ever so slowly into a smile. "Is this what you thought?"

"It's what I *thought.*" She looked away. "I . . . I don't think it anymore." *For an actress, I am a terrible liar.*

Pietro nodded thoughtfully, taking a step closer to her. "But I have girlfriend. Want to know her name?"

Katharina saw his shadow hovering over her. "No, no. Not really."

"Her name is Dena."

"Holy shit!" Fish yelled.

"What's Pietro doing?" Walt cried. "He can't give it away now!"

"Maybe he's not giving it away. Maybe he chose that name at random."

Walt shook his head. "Oh yes. Dena is a random name to use when *Dena* is in the room!"

Katharina shook at the mention of her name. "That's my . . . Where is she?"

Pietro pointed at Katharina.

"Okay, you're right," Fish said. "That wasn't random. I think Pietro's having a crisis of conscience here. You better call Vincenzo."

"Wait," Walt said. "Something's about to happen. I don't want to miss this."

Katharina glanced at Pietro and saw his eyes shining. "Oh, I'm not your girlfriend, um, Alessandro. I mean, I'm grateful for all you've done for me, but . . . You know my real name?"

Pietro nodded. He reached over Katharina's head and turned her chair to face him. Then he stood in

front of her and unbuttoned his long johns. "I know,"
Pietro said, and he pushed his long johns to the floor.

D-damn, Katharina thought.

Pietro knelt and parted the bearskin. "I not talk for a
while."

Katharina couldn't speak. She caressed Pietro's hair
and thought only, *Grazie, grazie, grazie* . . .

Walt tilted his head. "Um, perhaps we shouldn't . . ."

"Damn," Fish said. "I feel so inadequate. Should we
call Vincenzo?"

"And tell him . . . Geez, look at her face! It's shining!" Walt caught his breath. "And tell Vincenzo what? I
mean, Pietro, I mean, *Alessandro* could have known her
real name, right? He's just staying in character."

"As the Italian Stallion," Fish said. "Damn."

Katharina cried out in ecstasy, in pure joy, as waves of
pleasure rippled up from Pietro's tongue to her neck.
Her body vibrated, buzzed, trembled, and as Pietro carried her to his bed, she felt weightless as a feather . . .

"I can't see this, Walt," Fish said, turning off the
backup camera. "This would ruin me for life."

"Me too," Walt said.

"Let's leave this one up to the audience's imagination." Fish turned off all the cameras. "I think Katharina has just been tamed."

"And it only took five weeks. Amazing."

Fish stood and stretched. "I've had some champagne
chilling in the fridge since we got here just for this occasion. Want some?"

Walt nodded. "Shouldn't we tell Vincenzo what's going on?"

Fish laughed. "We're not out of the woods yet."

Walt rolled his eyes.

"And we still don't have a movie. Let's just . . . see what happens. I mean, Vincenzo hasn't told Pietro that he has Bianca tied up at his place, right?"

"So you want to keep all this a secret," Walt said. "Fine with me." He walked to the picture window and looked out into the night. "I just hope to God the old Katharina's back."

Fish joined Walt at the window. "I just hope all four of them don't start howling at once. I'm going to have enough trouble getting to sleep tonight as it is."

Chapter 34

Oh God, fur is surrounding me, under me, on top of me, an oak tree inside me—

Katharina held on for dear life.

She is silk, so soft, so hot, such passion, so glad she has no nails or my chest hair would be gone—

Pietro held on for dear life, too.

"Turn me over," she sighed, and he did.

Ow.

"Turn me back," she sighed, and he did.

Less ow, but . . .

"Let me ride you."

Ah, that's better . . . poco, poco . . . Have to hold on to his . . . mane. . . . He doesn't seem to mind. Damn, just one of his hands covers my entire booty. . . . No . . . No . . . don't sit up!

"Are you okay, Katharina?"

My stomach! He's bumping my stomach from inside!

"Yes, Alessandro."

Push him back down. That's better. Good. So out of practice, so sweaty. Oh God, riding his mulo . . .

"Um, let's try from the side. . . ."

I can't get enough of her, and there's not enough of her, so thin! Vise grips for legs, though. Very strong booty muscles, so tight, so . . .

"Let's try standing up," she whispered.

I am floating in air. He picks me up like I'm not there, settles me down . . . whoo . . . poco, poco . . . Oh God . . . I can't help bending back. . . .

She's bending back, and she's horizontal and—

I am coming and my entire body is cramping and he's not letting go and—OW! Thank God!

They fell to the bed, wide-eyed and staring into the darkness.

"Katharina?"

"Yes?"

"Are you there?"

"Barely."

"Me too."

He searched for her hand, found it, and squeezed. "I have never . . . had such . . . a time before," he whispered. "Have you?"

Chapter 35

"It was nice," Katharina whispered. *I don't want to say it was frickin' awesome, dude! But it was!*

"Just . . . nice?" Pietro crooned.

Katharina crawled on top of him, keeping his penis far away from her stuff. "It was heaven, all right? It was unbelievable." She kissed his warm lips. "You know it was. Thank you, Alessandro."

"For what, Katharina?"

She grabbed his penis. "For this good wood."

"Is that all?"

Is that all? It was more than plenty. "And for everything else. I've been meaning to thank you for all your help with the other wood, the plants, the hatchet, the shelter designs, the food . . . I should be thanking you for everything."

Pietro sniffed a small laugh. "You have not been thinking of thanking me."

"Yes, I have."

"Be honest, Katharina."

Katharina propped her elbows on Pietro's chest. "I am. I couldn't have survived without you."

Pietro smiled in the darkness. *And now for a little revealing conversation.* "You could have. Easily."

"No, I couldn't have."

Pietro let his voice change subtly from "Italiano" to Californian. "You didn't need any help, Katharina. When's the last time anyone called you 'Dena,' anyway?"

Why is Alessandro's voice changing? "Your voice. What's . . . happening?"

Pietro rolled her over and tapped her breastbone lightly. "You have a lot of heart under there, lady. It's just been hiding for fifteen years."

What . . . is . . . happening? "You can speak . . ."

Pietro kissed her nose. "I can speak American. I was born in L.A."

Katharina squirmed out from under Pietro, backing all the way to the headboard. "Please don't tell me you're just an actor."

Pietro pulled her legs back, the rest of her body following. "No. I'm not an actor." He kissed her neck.

"I'm confused." *And kiss me a little lower . . . there. Nice.* "You're really a handyman, then?"

Pietro brushed each of Katharina's breasts with his nose. "Yes and no." His tongue made circles down her stomach.

"Well, whatever you are, you are extremely rude. You heard and understood everything I've said and acted like you didn't!" *Oh shit. He's back at my happy place again!*

Pietro laughed and continued tasting her.

"It's not funny!" *Oh, damn, there I go again! Shit. I have to have the most sensitive stuff on earth!*

Pietro trailed his tongue up her body, stopping at her neck. "You have quite a sting with that tongue of yours. And yet, here I am. Here *we* are. No worse for wear. You seemed to like wearing me."

I love *wearing him.* "That's beside the point. Who are you?"

Pietro put his face close to hers. "You don't recognize me? I'm not surprised. We met for only about an hour fifteen years ago. *My Honey Love.* The cab scene."

Katharina stared. *The guy who kept staring at me in the rearview mirror?* "You were much skinnier then."

He rolled onto his back. "Yeah, I was. But you didn't know or care who I was back then."

"Who are you?"

"I am Pietro Lucentio, son of Antonio Lucentio, brother to Vincenzo Lucentio. And you are on my estate."

Katharina's mind went completely blank.

Pietro ran his knuckles down her arm. "I like this quiet side of you, Katharina."

"That huge house I saw over there," Katharina whispered.

"Yeah, that's mine. I built it myself. Built all these cabins, too."

She rolled toward him and bounced her fist off his chest. "Why'd you build cabins without electricity, hot water, or central heat?"

He covered her fist with his hand. "Cabins are supposed to be rustic. No frills. Raw. Just enough of the necessities of life." He kissed her palm. "I wish I could kiss these cuts and calluses away."

Katharina settled her head on Pietro's shoulder. "I . . . I don't know what to say. I can't think of . . ." She sat up. "What's . . . what's going on? I mean, what's *really* going on here, Alessandro? I mean, Pietro, I mean, whatever your name is."

"Is Pietro." Pietro pulled her back to him, massaging

the back of her neck. "My brother Vincenzo got it in his head to put us together since we're both allergic to marriage and relationships. I've been engaged six times."

Is this just a five-million-dollar hookup? Oh God! It can't be! "Why have you been engaged so often?"

"What woman would want to live up here?"

Though the house is nice . . . "I see your point."

Pietro sighed and hugged her to him. "Yet here we are."

Katharina's mind spun, flip-flopped, and ran into a brick wall. "So I'm not making a movie at all?"

"Oh no. You're making a movie all right. In fact, you're probably making two."

"What?"

Pietro sighed. "Now don't get mad. We've been filming you one way or another since you got here."

Katharina's mind did a somersault, bounced off a mountain, and tumbled down a hill. "What?"

"I don't think there are any hidden cameras in here, but in your cabin . . ." He winced. "They're just about everywhere."

Katharina tried to jump up, but Pietro held her down.

"No," Katharina said slowly. "No, they aren't! Sly is the only one filming unless I'm wearing that headset."

He pulled her on top of him, holding her face in his hands. "Sly is my brother Vincenzo in a *very* bad wig."

Oh . . . shit. I am being out-acted here. They said they were cousins! They argued so convincingly! Pietro let his brother smack the shit out of him!

"Vincenzo is helping to film the main movie, yes. The other film is being monitored by John Fisher over at my house. I have no idea what they're going to do with it, but right now, I don't care. I'm sure you have a few questions."

That's all I have! "Who sent those shitty script pages?"

"Walter Yearling. He's at the house, too."

Oh, Walter! How could you do this to me? "So Walter sent those simple ideas . . . This is all beginning to fit." *No, it isn't. I just sometimes say things that make me feel saner when I'm losing my freaking mind!*

Pietro pushed her back just enough. "We fit together, yes?"

He's inside me again . . . I can't think. "Yes, we do, and nicely, but . . . just . . . don't move, okay? I'm a little sore."

"You're just a little small down there."

Katharina smiled. "It's been a long time. No thrusts." *It's so hard to think with all this wood inside me.* "So this has all been a . . . a joke? Was Bianca in on it?"

"You don't pay someone five million dollars for a joke. Bianca was in on it, and most of what she told you, especially about Costa Rica, was the truth. She's been shacked up with Vincenzo since she quit."

Katharina tightened her booty. "Don't thrust. Hold it right there." *That's . . . filling.* "Bianca, that child has a future in the movies. She blew me away. And so did you!"

"What did you really think of me?"

Katharina bore down all the way and held herself against him. *I will pay dearly for this tomorrow.* "I hated you! You had an answer and solution for everything, and you were always around, and you were always touching me."

Pietro gripped her booty. "Like now."

"Lower," Katharina said. "Get under my cheeks."

His hands slid lower and squeezed. "There?"

"Oh yes!" Katharina cried. "But they went to all this trouble for what?"

Pietro sat up, and Katharina wrapped her legs tightly around his back. Katharina's entire body went rigid. "What's wrong?" Pietro asked.

"It's just that . . . you are very deep inside my pancreas right now."

Pietro dropped his hips. "I'm sorry."

Katharina shook her head, sweat flying in the air. "No. It's okay. I have to get used to this. I have to get used to making love to you. Y'all went to a lot of trouble over little ol' me. Why?"

"They wanted 'my honey love' back. I think she's back. I like your back. It bends in so many interesting ways."

Katharina plunged down, then up quickly. "They wanted . . . I'm still confused."

"They've been calling it an intervention. My brother thinks you are the greatest actress of all time, and up until recently, I disagreed. I thought you were an absolute bitch."

Say what you mean, Pietro.

"I mean," Pietro continued, "you put the prima in donna, the stuck in up, the ego in maniac."

Katharina eased down and came up slower this time. "I understand what a bitch is, Pietro. I've been looking at her in the mirror for fifteen years now. Go on. And if you want to thrust up—*poco, poco*—you can."

Pietro thrust up gently. "The bitch is gone, Katharina. You are really an amazing actress, Kate. Can I call you Kate?"

"No."

"Too plain?"

Katharina slid down as Pietro thrust up. "My last boyfriend—" *Who was my last real and not media-inflicted boyfriend? It had to be when I was in the tenth grade. Geez. Twenty years ago?*

"Wasn't Ward Booker your last boyfriend?"

Katharina rose to the top of his shaft and rested. "Ward Booker and David Stanley were boyfriends."

Pietro blinked.

"Both of them called me Kate, and that has led to fifteen years of dropping the soap . . ." *Going down . . .*

Pietro smiled. "Is that what you were doing in there?" *All stop. Wiggle.* "The soap didn't seem to mind." *I'm close again? I am such a ho!* "Pietro, I'm going to hold my breath and probably make the ugliest face you've ever seen. I don't want you to be scared. I want you to thrust up with all your might, okay?"

Pietro nodded, thrust as powerfully as he could, and watched Katharina have the most intense orgasm.

That is a scary face! he thought. *I'll just have to remember to close my eyes.*

She fell, panting, and sucked on his neck until her spasms subsided. "Thank you, thank you."

He pulled the bearskin over her and felt her heartbeat banging into his chest. "Watching you work out there is just . . . breathtaking," he said softly. "You've been giving me goose bumps on top of my goose bumps. After that rough start, I believe that you are, indeed, an escaped slave trying to make it on her own in nineteenth-century Canada. You've taken me back in time, Katharina. It's magic. You're magical. Vincenzo thought, and as it turns out, rightly, that you needed to be put through the wringer for a while until you turned on that old magic."

"I can't build that shelter for shit, though," Katharina said. "It keeps falling down. I've tried digging down, but . . ."

"She would have had trouble, too. It's believable. Building any structure in this weather and in this place with just a knife and some sticks would have been next

tò impossible. And yet you're so close to actually doing it."

"If I just had some better tools," Katharina said.

"Let me be your tool," Pietro whispered.

Katharina smiled. "I do like your tool." She kissed
him on the cheek. "And in, oh, a year, I'll be recovered
enough to play with it again."

"I have an idea," Pietro said, and he whispered it in
Katharina's ear.

"But then I won't be alone, Pietro. We'll have to
change the title."

Pietro whispered his idea in more detail for several
minutes.

"Yeah, I guess so, and it makes a lot of sense. When
do we start?"

Pietro let his hands roam Katharina's soft back. "Tomorrow. But you can't let on that you know about all
the cameras. Just stay your moody, bitchy self."

"Thanks a lot." Katharina giggled. "We're going to
flip the script on them, huh?"

"Yes," Pietro said, digging his fingers into her lower
back. "And there's really no script for this, either, right?
Despite all your directions."

"You take directions well, Mr. Non-Actor," Katharina
said. She slipped off Pietro and lay on her back, tugging
his hand. "And I want to take all of you right now."

Pietro rolled over. "Are you sure?"

She guided him inside her. "Yes. But you better hold
my hands. If you value your back, do *not* let go of my
hands."

He covered her hands with his and begin to thrust,
Katharina's hips rising to meet his. "I'm not hurting
you, am I?"

Katharina's eyes filled with tears, several escaping.
"Not at all, Pietro."

He kissed a stream of tears. "Why are you crying?"

"I'm happy, Pietro. I haven't been happy in a long, long time."

He looked into her blue-green eyes. "Neither have I, Katharina. Neither have I." He thrust deeply and held it. "You know, if you, um, ever feel like it, you can call me Fonzi, or Alessandro . . ."

Katharina laughed and broke free from his hands, raking his back with the nubs of her nails. " 'Freak me, Fonzi' is too funny. 'Pork me, Pietro' is just wrong. How about . . . 'Andiamo, Alessandro'?"

"Go. You ride."

Katharina deepened her voice. "Your panties are wet."

Pietro raised his voice. "They're just moist."

Katharina gripped Pietro's booty. "My voice isn't that high."

Pietro thrust as deeply as he could. "It's about to be . . ."

Chapter 36

Vincenzo woke to find Bianca still snuggled up to his chest. He loved the smell of her hair, the sound of her voice, the passion of her whispers, the strength of her legs, the way she howled . . .

The walkie-talkie on his nightstand squawked.

What is it now? Vincenzo thought.

He reached over Bianca, amazed that she could sleep through the movement and the noise.

"Yes, Fish?"

"This is Walt. Fish said to call you at eight."

It's eight o'clock already? "Where's Fish?"

"Asleep. He told me to tell you that one of the cameras near the clearing is iced over. He wants you or Pietro to, um, fix it, de-ice it, thaw it out, make it work, do what you gotta do."

Vincenzo scratched some crust from his eyes. "I'll do it. Where is it?"

"From the log you usually sit on, it's on the tree to your immediate right about six feet up."

"Got it. Is Katharina up yet?"

"No movement at all. Probably sleeping like a baby after all her hard work yesterday."

"Let me know when she wakes up." He returned the walkie-talkie to the nightstand.

He looked at *his* baby, Bianca, all balled up and reaching for him. Four weeks of bliss, four weeks of utter, total happiness. He had had trouble concentrating on Katharina and the movie, often taking "bathroom" breaks just to get a hug, a kiss, a little more, sometimes a lot more from Bianca. He was probably the most sleep-deprived person on the set, but he had never been as happy.

Bianca looked up and squinted. "What's up?"

"Walt. One of the cameras is out of commission. He needs me to fix it."

"Want some oatmeal?" she whispered with a yawn.

We're so domestic already! "Sure."

"'K." She kissed his cheek, hugged him, and squeezed his butt. "Morning." She rolled out of bed naked and padded across the cabin. "Don't forget your wig." She turned and went into the bathroom, closing the door behind her.

I can get used to seeing that every morning for the rest of my life.

Vincenzo got up, plopped the wig on his head, and pulled a knit cap over the mess. He threw on his coat and boots, took the walkie-talkie, and left the cabin, trudging through several inches of new snow to the tree that directly faced the clearing and Katharina's fire pit. He located a circle of snow on the tree trunk and brushed it aside, revealing the tiniest of camera lenses. He squawked the walkie-talkie: "Walt?"

"Yes."

"What's it look like?"

"A little fuzzy. Can you shine it up?"

He used the meat of his fist to shine it. "Better?"

"Step away."

Vincenzo stepped away.

"Yep. I can see the whole clearing now. Checking zoom. Zoom okay. Panning . . . What's that?"

Vincenzo whirled around in a circle. "What's what?"

"Behind the thick brush, stuck in a tree."

Vincenzo looked and saw a hatchet, its blade embedded deep into a tree four feet off the ground. "Pietro must have left it there. His idea of a bad joke on Katharina." He heard a splash. "Who's in the stream?"

"Jesus, it's Katharina!" Walt shouted. "How'd she get by me?"

Vincenzo tucked the walkie-talkie into his pocket and sat on the log. *I look unprepared. I don't have my camera or my monitor. I'm quite helpless.*

Katharina entered the clearing in costume, her headset on.

Vincenzo tried to look natural.

Katharina began making her fire. Seemingly distracted, she saw the glint of something behind her. Standing, she stared, then ducked down, looking side to side. She crouched and moved into the thick brush, looked around once more, then reached through the brush to take the hatchet. She checked the hatchet's sharpness and put her thumb in her mouth. She looked out past the stream to the woods, slipping her knife out from under her dress. She then continued to build her fire, looking into the woods and muttering.

I wish I knew what she was saying! Vincenzo thought.

Katharina rushed to a stack of short sticks and began sharpening their ends, still muttering, still searching the trees.

* * *

"I take a little nap for a few hours," Fish said, "and all hell breaks loose. Did Vincenzo change the script?"

"Nobody did as far as I know," Walt said. "She found the hatchet and now this."

Fish watched Katharina for a few moments. "Looks pretty good. Natural. That new snow is glistening."

"But what's she muttering?" Walt asked. "I figured out the zoom, but I couldn't increase the volume."

Fish hit the correct keys. "Volume up . . ."

Katharina's lips moved at rapid speed, saying, "Now I lay me down to sleep, I pray the Lord my soul to keep . . . You don't want none a me . . . and if I die before I wake I pray the Lord my soul to take . . ."

Vincenzo's walkie-talkie suddenly squawked, and Katharina yelled, "What the hell, Sly?" She stalked to him, waving her knife and the hatchet.

Vincenzo pulled the walkie-talkie from his pocket. "I so sorry, Miss Katharina. Is walkie-talkie. I use it to, um, to get weather reports. The weather changes so *rapido* up here. We must be careful for your safety."

Katharina sighed. "Well, keep it off or on vibrate during the shot, okay? Where's, um, where's your camera? Where's the monitor?"

Vincenzo tried to smile. "Oh. I, um, it's back at my cabin. I did not think you would come out so early this morning with so much snow. I just come to plan, um, to map out my, um, angles." *That was extremely weak.*

Katharina widened her eyes, raised her eyebrows, and dropped her jaw. "So you *missed* all that? That was pretty damn good, if I say so myself. That was a fantastic idea to include a hatchet there. Now I'm not alone. Isn't that freaky? I mean, *she's* not alone anymore. There's someone else out there." Katharina patted Vincenzo on the shoulder. "Good idea. It *was* your idea, wasn't it?"

Vincenzo didn't know what to say. "Um, yes. It was my idea. I had been thinking, um . . ." *No, I hadn't! I haven't been thinking of anyone but Bianca!*

"Yes?" Katharina asked.

"I, um, I had been thinking that it is, um, conceivable that our woman would eventually run into others, perhaps, uh, other runaway slaves."

Katharina sliced the air with the hatchet. "Or just the folks who live here, right?"

Vincenzo nodded.

"I knew it wasn't your cousin's idea. He is a moron. Where's he been, anyway? I haven't seen him around today."

Yes, where is that hatchet man who is making me lie to Katharina? "Um, I have no idea."

Katharina sighed as if in relief. "Well, I'm so glad he's not around. He ruins my concentration most of the time." She swished the hatchet through the air. "And with this I should be able to put up the shelter quicker. Excellent thinking, Sly. You must have gotten some more pages of the script, right?"

Yeah, today is certainly sucking pretty badly. "Um, yes." He pointed at the tree on the right. "And since I put in a camera there last night, I got all that footage." *Liar!* "It is automatic. In case I oversleep and you start early." *Oh, right. She'll believe that one.*

Katharina smiled and nodded. "Yeah? You put a camera in that tree? Wow. What will they think of next. Very

cool. Another good idea, Sly." She blinked a few times.
"I want to see this morning's footage, Sly."

Vincenzo stared into her headset. "You . . . want to
see the footage."

"Yes," Katharina said with a tinge of attitude. "Yes. I
would like to see the footage of what I did this morning.
What you got from that tree camera and what you got
from my headset. And I'd like to see it now."

Fish's fingers flew over the keyboard. "Why didn't
you wake me up earlier, Walt?"

"I didn't think *this* would happen." He looked at Vincenzo's lips mouthing "Hurry!"

Fish hit a couple wrong keys and had to start over.
"We can't do that right away, Vincenzo! The camera on
that tree gets sent here. The servers automatically save
it, but that takes time. Only after that can I broadcast it
to the monitor, but it's completely raw. The headset
works the same way, and I have to edit it to the right
spot. We'll see her from the second she puts it on, her
walk to the clearing . . . She'll know something is up.
Shit."

Walt was on the verge of hyperventilating. "Vincenzo
said he uses the walkie-talkie for the weather report.
What was he thinking?"

Fish stilled his fingers. "Okay. We can do this. All we
have to do is . . ." He breathed heavily. "Um . . . No, we
can't. All the footage is here, but it will take some time
to sort it all out, save it, cut it to what she wants to see,
and then send it."

"How long?" Walt asked.

"Damn, at least thirty minutes. I'm good, but I'm not
a magician. If we can't stall her for thirty minutes, she'll

just have to do the entire scene over in front of Vincenzo's camera."

"But we don't have any way to tell him all that."

Fish tapped the transmitter. "Give him a weather report."

"What?"

"You're the writer. Give the man his weather report."

Walt pressed the squawk button, took a deep breath, and said, "This is a weather report from the Canadian National Weather Service for northeastern Ontario . . ."

Walt? "Ah, another weather report." He held the walkie-talkie in the air.

"A storm front has *stalled* over northeastern Ontario. We will update again in *thirty minutes*. A storm front has *stalled* over northeastern Ontario. We will update again in *thirty minutes* . . ."

Katharina frowned. "What a creepy computer voice."

"Yeah." *Stall Katharina Minola for thirty minutes? Is he insane? That won't work!* He switched to another channel on the walkie-talkie. "I will see if I can get another channel for weather." He pressed the squawk button.

"I guess one squawk and the way his head is shaking means no," Fish said. "Say something else!"

Walt's eyes darted around the house. "Um, the recent snowstorms have knocked out transmissions to the reporting stations in Fishersville. The monitor at . . . *Cabina une,* Quebec, is also out of commission. To repeat an earlier report, a storm front has *stalled* over northeastern Ontario. We will update again in *twenty-nine minutes*. A storm front has *stalled* over northeastern

Ontario. We will update in *twenty-nine minutes*. More later as this news develops . . ."

"Wow," Katharina said, trying not to laugh, "that sounds like a pretty big storm. Where are Fishersville and *Cabina une?*"

Vincenzo wanted to have a second take on his entire day so far. "Not too far from here, actually, um, over in Quebec. Seems like a storm is brewing." *Twenty-nine minutes? They have to be high.* "Is a beautiful day, yes?"

"Yes," Katharina said firmly, "and I'd like to capture more of this beauty, but I can't until I see that footage. Why don't you go get your monitor?"

"He can't get that monitor yet!" Fish cried. He worked feverishly to move Katharina's headset footage to his computer he could begin the edit. "No! I need at least twenty-seven more minutes!" Fish looked at the first footage and swallowed.

"Give him the raw feed," Walt suggested, "and he can fast-forward or something."

"She put the damn thing on *before* she went to the bathroom." He fast-forwarded. "Geez. She was in there at least ten minutes. I can't send this until I edit it."

Vincenzo nodded to Katharina. "I am going to my cabin to get my camera and my monitor."

He's so wooden! Katharina thought. "I can't wait to see this scene from both points of view."

Neither can I. "Um, why don't you, um, rehearse what you plan on doing for the rest of the scene."

Katharina smiled and faced the large tree to her left. "Time for some target practice." She pointed where she *knew* the camera was. "Is that thing rolling? I might do pretty well the first time and nail it."

Vincenzo had trouble breathing. "I will hurry."

Vincenzo hyperventilated as he collected his camera gear while Bianca ate some cereal at the table, a black and red flannel shirt her only clothing.

"Let me guess," Bianca said. "Katha-diva came down early."

"Yeah," Vincenzo said, "and she found a hatchet, which I know Pietro planted, and then she did a dazzling scene, which we have over at Pietro's house but don't have"—he tapped the camera—"in here. And now she wants to see the scene from her headset *and* the tree camera on this monitor."

Bianca looked at the monitor in his hands. "You weren't there to get any of it, and Fish can't send it for some reason."

"He *can* send it, but not for twenty-five minutes or so. I'm sure he has to edit it first. I can't stall her that long."

"Lock yourself in the bathroom," Bianca suggested. "Tell her you had diarrhea."

Vincenzo relaxed. "She wouldn't believe that."

"She believed me." She tipped the bowl to her lips and drank the milk. "Drop it, then."

"Drop what?"

"The monitor." She dropped her bowl. It bounced and flipped off the table. "Oops? So sorry, it broke, my mistake, I will get another."

That has possibilities, but . . . "That would work, but this is a twenty-five-grand monitor, Bianca."

Bianca shrugged. "Take it out of her pay . . ." She

frowned. "Wait a minute. You said Pietro put the hatchet in the scene. Why would he do that?"

"To mock Katharina. To speed things up. I don't know. He either wants to torture Katharina some more or just get this picture over and done with so he can go back to his lonely and barren existence. Remember, Bianca, with you quitting, Pietro has to deal with her the most now, and I'm sure he's not very happy about it. She did say she hadn't seen him today, and I bet he's up in the woods having a good laugh at my expense."

Bianca picked up her bowl and put it in the sink, running water into it. "I don't know, talk her out of the whole idea. Tell her there shouldn't be anyone else in the woods. Tell her we can't call it *A Woman Alone* if we include this scene. Tell her the audience will see through it. No, tell her it will be *Miss Thang* all over again. Scare her out of it."

And now Bianca is high. "Scare Katharina Minola?"

Bianca yawned. "Well, do something. Take her for a walk, get lost in the woods, barf near a tree."

Vincenzo sighed. "But the scene was brilliant, Bianca. You had to be there. She was . . . She is dazzling now. And the idea of another person in the woods is compelling, even mysterious. The audience will be saying, 'Uh-oh, there goes the neighborhood.' "

Bianca dove onto the couch. "But it is contrived and forced, Vincenzo. Audiences aren't dumb. Like someone is just going to give a weapon to a runaway slave. It doesn't make any sense."

"I know it doesn't, and that's what's so compelling. Who would do that? Who is it? And what does this person want? Why would this person leave it there and not use it on her? How long has this person been watching?" *Whoa. Maybe . . .* "Is it a man, and is he . . . ?" *Can't be. Pietro hates her with a passion.*

"Is he what?" Bianca asked.

"I was going to say, 'Is he in love with her?' "

Bianca laughed. "Right. And this hatchet is his way of showing his love for her. That's pretty twisted."

Yeah. That is a strange love gift. Didn't van Gogh once give an ear? Hmm.

"And who is *he* going to be? Pietro?"

Vincenzo shuddered. "Pietro? It can't be Pietro. They hate each other." He grabbed his gear.

"Then who? You?"

Vincenzo backed toward the door. "Not me, no. I don't know, Bianca. Maybe . . . Fish? No. That's extremely creepy. Walt? He's a bit old, but he's always had a thing for her. Maybe he's loving her from afar. Maybe this is all *Walt's* doing! Walt told Pietro to plant the hatchet so Walt could get in the movie. Every writer thinks he can act. It makes perfect sense!"

Bianca shook her head. "No."

"A May-December thing in the middle of December might work!"

Bianca blinked at her man. "You're under a lot of stress, aren't you?"

Vincenzo nodded.

"It can't be Walt, and you know it. It has to be Pietro or no one." She sighed. "We can still make it no one. Maybe she never knows who helps her. Maybe she gets 'gifts' throughout the movie from an unnamed, unseen person . . ." *I just got chills!* "Or maybe it's the ghost of someone, the ghost of an earlier runaway slave who's doing this for her, an unseen being that walks these woods."

Vincenzo blinked. *She has to be kidding. We are not making* Poltergeist II: A Woman Not Quite Alone. He fumbled for the door. "I gotta go. We'll talk about it later."

Bianca rolled over and stared at the ceiling. "What are you going to tell Katharina about her precious footage?"

Vincenzo pressed the squawk button. "Fish, do we have another monitor?"

"If you stall her for twenty more minutes, I can do this thing," Fish said.

Vincenzo shook his head. "You know that's impossible. You have another monitor, right?"

"Oh man, you know I do, but if you're going to do what I think you're going to do . . ."

Vincenzo snapped off the walkie-talkie, winced, and dropped the monitor. It didn't exactly shatter, but the glass cracked and several dials bent. "I hope this works."

Bianca laughed. "I hope it *doesn't* work."

"Oh yeah," Vincenzo said. "Right."

Vincenzo lumbered back to his log where Katharina waited. He put on his best hangdog look and shook his head slowly. "Miss Katharina, I am so clumsy. I dropped the monitor and it is broken."

Katharina acted shocked. "You lost my scene?"

"No, no. I watched it in my cabin, to make sure it is there, and then I trip. It is there, and it is amazing. We will load onto a computer. You don't have to do it again."

Fish zoomed in on the broken monitor. "Vincenzo should take it out of *Bianca's* paycheck."

"You do have another monitor, don't you?" Walt asked.

"Yeah, but how do I get it to Vincenzo? Pietro has vanished." He looked at all the monitors, even at the ones in Pietro's cabin. "Geez, we have a lot of cameras out. The snow must have melted and iced over the lenses."

Pietro sat with his back against a pine tree, the camera lens facing him covered with a well-thrown snowball. It was just one of many cameras he had sabotaged earlier that morning. He looked down the hill at his brother making a complete ass of himself with Katharina and smiled. It was good to be back in the moviemaking business again, and for the first time, he actually understood it. It was total, utter madness. It wasn't supposed to make sense, and despite the insanity in the making and the marketing, it was a good business. The world obviously needed its insanity and enjoyed paying for it. *Escape,* he thought. *This is how you help people escape their troubles for two hours.*

Pietro hoped he wouldn't laugh too loudly during the next scene.

Katharina pointed at Vincenzo's camera. "That still works, right?"

He turned it on. "Of course."

"Okay. Start filming, and don't laugh."

"I am filming," Vincenzo said. *And why would I laugh? There's nothing funny about any of this!*

"I have to show whoever's in the woods that this woods woman knows how to use a hatchet."

She returned to the fire, picked up the hatchet, stepped into the clearing, and faced the tree to Vincenzo's right, taking careful aim at the little camera hiding in the bark.

* * *

Vincenzo's walkie-talkie squawked immediately.

Katharina let the hatchet droop. "What now?"

"Sorry. Another weather report." Vincenzo turned away to listen with the walkie-talkie's speaker hard against his ear.

"You can't let her throw that hatchet at one of our cameras," Fish said. "You have to have her throw it at the tree on your left."

Vincenzo pocketed the walkie-talkie. "The weather is okay. It is, um, supposed to warm up. Um, Katharina, the light in this direction is bad." He pointed to his right. "Throw at this tree over here." He pointed to his left.

"But I've been looking in the woods to *my* left, your right. That's where I 'heard' the noise. That's where I think *he* or whoever is. I have to throw it in that direction."

"A good point." *And we'll probably lose another piece of equipment. It's been that kind of day.*

The walkie-talkie squawked.

"Oh, another report. Excuse me." Vincenzo walked farther away from Katharina this time, leaning his back against a tree. "How high is the camera?" he whispered.

"Oh geez, here it comes!" Fish yelled.

Vincenzo looked around the tree in time to see a hatchet tumbling end over end to the tree on his right, sticking firmly five feet up the tree.

"That was close," Fish said. "And very cool. Have her do it again."

"You're kidding!" Vincenzo whispered.

"She'll never hit it, Vincenzo," Fish said. "She'd have to throw it too high for her to retrieve it. And if she does hit it, what a shot! The audience will jump out of their seats!"

* * *

Vincenzo shook and winced a lot as he filmed Katharina throwing the hatchet for a half hour. Since the walkie-talkie stayed silent, he felt confident that the camera was still intact.

Katharina rubbed her shoulder. "I'm pretty tired, Sly. It's not like I throw a hatchet every day."

Vincenzo smiled, glad this ordeal was over. "You throw it well."

Katharina stretched and rubbed her shoulder again. "I'm gonna call it a day, okay?"

That's the best news I've heard all day! Vincenzo thought. "Sure. You take a rest, Miss Katharina."

And then, he thought, *I can go quietly crazy with Bianca.*

Pietro packed another snowball, slipped behind a cameraless tree, and covered another lens with an accurate throw. *Two more to go, and then I can get to Katharina's back window unseen, climb in her back window, throw out some granola bars for Curtis to munch on, and give Katharina a backrub.* He hoped she'd let him sleep a little. Tomorrow was a big day. Tomorrow he would return to the silver screen.

In a starring role with the woman of his dreams.

Who was one of the main reasons I left the States fifteen years ago to create this rugged paradise . . . so we could be together.

He packed another snowball. *Life is strangely wonderful.*

Chapter 37

"Where the hell is Pietro?" Vincenzo yelled into the walkie-talkie. "He can't just disappear! This is where he lives! He has to be somewhere!"

Bianca rubbed Vincenzo's shoulders, wishing her man would just relax and give her some good loving to forget all his problems.

"He's not on any of the monitors, Vincenzo," Fish said, "and believe me, I've been looking."

"Find Curtis," Vincenzo said. "Pietro wouldn't just let a mule wander around. Find Curtis, and you'll find Pietro."

"Curtis isn't on any of the monitors, either," Fish said.

"How can you hide a half-ton mule?" Vincenzo cried.

Bianca froze. "I am not eating the stew tonight."

Vincenzo wanted to pull out his hair—and then pull on Bianca's hair for a while. "I thought you said you had thirty acres covered, Fish."

"I do," Fish said, "but, *A*, Pietro owns one *hundred* acres, and *B*, we've got cameras out of commission all over the place now."

Fish clicked over to see Bianca massaging Vincenzo. "*Both* our directors are asleep. Look at her triceps. Where were these women when I was growing up?"

"It's something in the air up here, I tell you."

Fish dialed down the volume entirely, left his command center, and stood in front of Walt. He handed him a piece of paper. "I had some time on my hands last night and wrote a song."

Walt read it to himself, eventually bopping his head back and forth. "This has a familiar rhythm."

"It's to the tune of 'The Devil Went Down to Georgia.' Want to hear it?"

Walt smiled. "Don't tell me you sing country."

Fish returned to his monitor, clicked his mouse, and Charlie Daniels Band music began playing. After the violin solo, Fish started to chant:

"The diva flew into Canada lookin' for a role to
    heal,
she had lost her mind, she had a nice behind,
she had signed a five-mil deal.
She saw an Italian woodsman chopping wood
    and the boy was hot,
so the diva jumped up on her tiger-striped broom
    and said,
'Fonzi, let me tell you what.
I guess you didn't know it but I'm a sucker for
    some stew,
and I'll bet an Oscar of gold against your mule
    cuz I know I'm hotter than you.'
The boy said, 'My name's Alessandro, and gosh I
    like to grin,
I'm gonna take that bet, gonna make you wet,
    you know I'm gonna win.'

Alessandro, you sharpen up your ax and don't
    you drop your guard,
cuz hell's broke loose in Canada and the diva
    makes life hard.
And if you win her heart you get a shiny band of
    gold,
but if you lose the diva gets your mule . . ."

Walt laughed more than clapped, nodding and snick-
ering. "That's . . . that's really good, Fish."

Fish bowed. "Thank you, thank you. I'll be here all
week."

"You and I should collaborate on something sometime," Walt said. "Maybe something to run by Quentin
Tarantino."

"Yeah?" Fish asked. "It's because I'm warped, right?"

Walt nodded. "You're warped and witty, a wonderful
combination for the cinema these days." He pointed at
Fish's song. "We have to use that somewhere, like on
the DVD."

"A music video," Fish said. "We can do that." He
looked at four sleeping people on the screens. "We may
have a few hours." He went to his computer, clicking
the keys. The monitors for the cabins winked out one
by one until they were all blank. "I'm giving us a day off,
anyway. Let's make a video, Walt."

"Who are we going to get to sing this?" Walt asked.

"Hey, man. I *can* sing. I sang in the choir and everything."

"Did they put you *way* in the back and away from the
microphones?"

Pietro pulled the bearskin up to Katharina's neck
and left the bed. He looked into his wardrobe for any-

thing ancient-looking and came up with some ripped jeans, a solid-red flannel shirt, and a well-worn, frayed leather jacket with buttons instead of a zipper. He chose his grungiest boots over his moccasins and got dressed. His hair was too short to be an Indian's, and his skin was too white for him to be anything but a Caucasian. Maybe he was just a Canadian drifter, an immigrant, just like the woman.

All I have to do is move quickly and be a shadow tomorrow. Let the rest of them figure out what to do with me and my mysterious character after that.

He looked back at Katharina, so sound asleep and almost purring. *Yeah. She's the one. The others didn't move me, make my heart hurt, piss me off, or make my mind ache. She's the one. The others were only dates on a calendar. This woman . . . this woman is the calendar. Fifteen years ago she cast a spell on me through the rearview mirror of a cab.*

Love is indeed a powerful spell.

And I hope this spell never breaks.

Katharina stirred and sat up. "How long have I been asleep?"

Pietro posed for her. "A few hours. How do I look?"

Katharina grabbed her knees. "Who are you supposed to be? Paul Bunyan?"

Pietro spun around and shook his booty. "Not sure. An aimless drifter, perhaps."

"Drift over here."

Pietro drifted.

She grabbed his coat and popped the top button. "A red shirt?"

"Very Canadian. Like the Mounties."

Katharina raised her eyebrows. "You will be Mountieing me shortly." She sighed. "This shirt is too bright and brazen. You're supposed to be hiding from me, playing the bashful man-meat who is trying *not* to be seen. Find something dark."

Pietro smiled and caressed her cheeks with both of his hands.

"Something dark to *wear,*" Katharina said.

Pietro smiled and caressed Katharina's shoulders. "I will wear you . . . out."

She removed his hands from her shoulders. "A dark shirt." She pointed at a blue flannel shirt hanging in his wardrobe. "Put that one on."

He changed shirts. "Better?"

Katharina shrugged and looked him up and down. "Those boots are as old as mine."

"They were my grandpa's."

"They'll do." She licked her lips. "I *might* do you."

"I am flattered."

She stared at the coarse growth on his face. "The beard looks right, too."

Pietro felt his face. "I haven't shaved today."

"Just one day? Man! Don't shave in the morning, either. I want to be attacked by a grizzly man." She stood on the bed, the bearskin leaving her body entirely. "That coat, though. Why not just wear the bearskin? I foresee a bearskin scene in my shelter later."

He caressed her sides and lingered on her hips. "I like your bare skin."

"Your paws are too big for my body," she said. *Along with that other thing.*

He pulled her to him. "And when you're looking into the woods, you can think I'm a grizzly bear instead of a man."

Katharina unbuttoned his coat and threw it to the floor. "I am going to have so much trouble tomorrow."

"Why?"

"I will be thinking some extremely nasty thoughts."

She unbuttoned his shirt and tossed it behind her. "And I will not be able to frown." She grazed his chest with her fingers. "So, what is my shy forest lover going to bring me tomorrow?"

Pietro kissed her ear. "Some dried meat, like beef jerky."

She let her hands drift to the crotch of his pants. "Is it beef?"

He rose immediately to the occasion. "No. Dried bear and venison."

She felt for his zipper. "Oh. So I'm getting some dried meat from my shy forest lover. How romantic. And what else?" She zipped it down and reached inside. "Ooh. Beef." *USDA Prime beef.*

Pietro took several short breaths. "A fish of some kind. Probably a trout."

Katharina licked her lips slowly. "You nasty man."

Pietro put his hands on hers. "No, really. I'll bring you a fish. You know how to clean it and cook it?"

Katharina removed his pants entirely and peeled down his underwear. "I only know how to eat it."

Oh shit! "Well, first, you start at its, um, anus, and with the knife, you . . ." *Oh, that feels good!* "Katharina, are you listening?"

Katharina paused in her labors, stretching her jaw. *This was not a good idea.* "Something about a fish's anus. Not very romantic conversation when I'm working on you down here."

Pietro talked fast. "All you really have to do is start your cut there and rip it up for the headset cam."

Katharina flicked her tongue. "Sounds gross."

He looked down, anticipating her tongue. "It is."

Katharina slid her hand down his shaft. "Perfect." She kissed the tip. "How do I cook it?"

Pietro could hardly stand. "Just, um, just gut it and set it on your oven." *Her lips are so soft!*

Katharina looked up. "I wish you could wear the headset while I do this."

"Why?"

She stroked him slowly. "I don't know. So maybe if I'm not around, you could watch it, relive it . . ." *So I don't have to do it again. Damn, he's wide.*

"I . . . I don't want you not to be around."

Katharina pulled him toward the bed. "Speak English."

Pietro lifted her legs over his shoulders. "You make me very happy, Miss Katharina."

"Thank you." She guided him inside her. *Wide is very good.* "You make me *very* happy, too."

Pietro began to thrust. "And tomorrow, we are going to piss off a lot of people."

Katharina squeezed his booty. "I know. Isn't it great?"

After several takes, with Walt acting as cameraman, Fish gave up. "I can't sing a lick, can I?"

"But that's what makes it so funny," Walt said. "You *think* you can sing. It will be a hoot."

Fish flipped both backup switches, saw furious, X-rated action in both bedrooms, and snapped them off. "It's like going on the Internet. I have *got* to get a girlfriend."

"A couple of couples," Walt said, "and neither couple knows the other couple is, um, coupling."

"Do you stay up late thinking up stuff like that?" Fish asked.

"Yeah."

"I just think of the coupling part."

Walt sighed. "You know, it would be next to impossible to sell any of this to another studio."

"It would? How do you figure? This is fantastic stuff!"

Walt nodded. "It's *too* fantastic. It's practically unbelievable. A diva disguised as a runaway slave transforms into one and falls in love with a former extra actor disguised as a handyman who hates, and then gets handy with, the former diva."

"I . . . *won't* ask you to repeat that."

"Add a diva's assistant turned amazing actress who becomes a fake director's howling love interest. Add a batch of secrets and the Greek chorus—that's us—commenting on the action, and you have the ultimate myth. I couldn't make up any of this stuff in a million years."

Fish shook his head. "We're not the chorus, Walt. We're the gods." Fish stared at the backup switches. "Makes me feel powerful, you know, being able to zoom into and out of their lives whenever I feel like it. I'm God zooming in on His creation from every possible angle."

"You won't be watching them tonight, right?"

Fish laughed softly. "Of course not. I'm giving them their privacy."

"And they have a right to that privacy, Fish. I've known Pietro and Vincenzo for close to twenty years, and for the first time, they're both content, happy, and alive. What those four people are sharing shouldn't be sullied by our intrusion."

Fish nodded. "So, when are we gonna tell 'em what's really going on when the lights go out?" He looked outside. "Or during the day when the cabin doors are closed? Don't they ever get tired?"

"We're not going to tell anyone anything. We're going to act as if nothing is going on other than the making of a movie."

Fish grabbed his song lyrics. "I'd like to try this again, only this time, you're going to use a tripod. The last take bounced all over the place. Anyone watching would get motion sickness."

"Don't make me laugh, then!"

"You weren't laughing, Walt. You were cringing. I could tell. No cringing this time."

"Only if you just mouth the words . . ."

Chapter 38

The next morning, Fish powered up his command center and watched all of the monitors come to life. *It must be warmer today,* he thought. *Either that or . . . Naw. Pietro wouldn't have done that.*

Hmm. He might have done that. It's something I would do if I wanted some privacy.

He shook off his doubts and turned on the backups. He saw two forms under the covers in Katharina's bedroom, and two oversexed maniacs going at it again in Vincenzo's bedroom. He heard a creak on the stairs and quickly shut off the backups.

"All cameras are up and running, Walt," he said, spinning in his chair. "No action."

"Really?" Walt said. "No action of *any* kind?"

Fish knew he was busted. "Okay, already. Katharina and Pietro are spooning under the covers, and Vincenzo and Bianca are forking like wolves in heat. I think they're trying to make little wolf puppies."

Something Fish said nagged at Walt, but he couldn't figure out what. "Say all that again."

"Katharina and Pietro are spooning, and Vincenzo and Bianca are forking."

"No, you said something else. Show me Katharina and Pietro."

Fish flipped his backup. "See, they're spooning under the covers."

Walt snapped his fingers. "*That's* what you said. They're *under* the covers. They're rarely under the covers, Fish. They're usually on top of the—"

"Jesus!" Fish screamed, interrupting Walt. "Did you see the size of that bear?"

Something bearlike flashed from tree to tree near the clearing.

"Oh my God!" Walt cried. "Katharina's in the clearing!" He pointed a trembling hand at the big screen. "The bear is coming for her!"

Fish started laughing, muttering, "Oh, he got us good, so good."

"Have you lost your mind?" Walt cried. "We have to save her!"

Fish typed a few commands until the "bear" appeared on the big screen. "We've been had, Walt."

Walt turned and saw Pietro facing a tree camera, the bearskin draped over his shoulders.

Pietro winked and put his finger to his lips. "It's showtime, fellas," Pietro whispered. "I hope you're ready. Oh, and you might want to wake Vincenzo. He's just going to *love* this."

Katharina again tried to build her shelter by pounding a few poles with her rock, but she gave up and began wailing. She placed her headset in the direction of the woods to her right and ran crying into the woods, sitting against a tree with her back to the camera, her body shaking with sobs.

Fish switched over to the feed from the headset. "That's a good idea, Katharina! Zooming in for a close-up of her crying."

"What's going on, Fish?"

"The movie has just taken a decided turn for the better, as they say," Fish said. "Watch Pietro, the Italian Indian."

Pietro sneaked from tree to tree until he was within a few feet of the clearing. He dashed to the headset, put it on, and ran to the creek, bringing several large, flat rocks up to the clearing. He hastily laid them down, one on top of the other. He made several trips in silence, the only sound the rushing of the stream.

"He's building her a foundation," Walt said.

After Pietro had several levels built on one side of her fire pit, he set strings of dried meat and a fish on top of her oven.

"Wake Vincenzo now," Fish said.

"Wait," Walt said. "I don't want the director to ruin this shot."

* * *

Pietro "saw" Katharina turn, dropped the headset pointed in his direction, and scampered off into the woods.

Katharina returned, put on the headset, and stared down at the meat and the fish. She looked around the clearing, whispering, "Lord Jesus, if this ain't manna from Heaven." She "noticed" the stack of stones. She "saw" glimpses of Pietro leaping from tree to tree. She tore off a strip of the meat and tasted it. She withdrew her knife, grabbed the fish, and gutted it from its anus to its gills.

"Holy shit!" Fish cried.

"This is fantastic!" Walt cried. "I'm going to be sick, but this is fantastic!" He pressed the squawk button on the transmitter. "Vincenzo, you have to see what's happening!"

Ten seconds passed before Vincenzo answered. "I'm kind of busy right now."

Walt nodded at Fish, and Fish flipped one of the backups, revealing Vincenzo and Bianca making wolf puppies near their back window, Vincenzo holding the walkie-talkie with his neck.

"I'm sure you are, Vincenzo," Walt said, "but you have to come out to the clearing. Pietro is dressed as a native and is helping Katharina build her shelter. She just gutted a fish, and it was awesome!"

"What?"

Fish mouthed, "Let me."

Walt nodded.

"Vincenzo, this is Fish. You didn't know about this? This isn't something you and Pietro cooked up without telling any of us?" He grinned when he saw Vincenzo stop thrusting. "They're just rehearsing now, I think.

You have to get out there and get some wide shots and close-ups of both of them in action."

"He's right, Vinnie," Walt said. "This is golden. You know second takes are crap. This is spontaneous."

Bianca reached behind her, but Vincenzo was backing away. "You've got it covered, right?" Vincenzo asked.

"Well, yeah," Fish said, "but we can't get the same close-ups as you can. Get out there, man!"

Bianca tackled Vincenzo, pinning him to the bed.

"I'll be there in . . ." Vincenzo said. "An hour. I'm busy."

"Please don't take this the wrong way, Vincenzo," Walt said, "but you must give Bianca a rest and get your ass over there and start filming." He clicked off the transmitter.

Fish blinked. "You just practically told him . . ."

"He'll know soon enough," Walt said. "What's Katharina doing?"

"Defending herself, by the looks of that pointed stick, the knife, and that hatchet."

Katharina's headset moved side to side as Pietro flitted from tree to tree.

"Don't you come any closer or I'll gig you, I swear!" Katharina yelled. "I'm warnin' you."

Pietro raced in with a dead squirrel, dumped it, and ran away.

Katharina blinked. She was genuinely confused. *This wasn't in our little script. What am I supposed to do with this rodent?* "Lord, more manna from Heaven," she said. She looked into the woods, hoping to see Pietro. "I'm a Christian woman, y'hear?" she yelled. "I don't truck with no heathens!" She kept looking until she saw Pietro pantomiming the gutting of a squirrel.

Katharina smiled. "Jes' like a man. He kill it, I cook it." Katharina looked at the squirrel. *Lord,* she thought, *please don't let me barf all over myself when I do this!* She flipped the squirrel on its back, took her knife, stabbed it just in front of its bushy tail, and sliced the squirrel up to its neck.

"I'm going to be sick . . ." Walt ran to the bathroom.

Fish clapped. "Now *this* is good cinema! Look at all the pretty colors! Yes!"

Katharina's headset gave excruciating close-ups of the gutting and skinning of the squirrel. When Vincenzo finally showed up and started filming, she was chopping off the squirrel's tail.

Vincenzo felt light-headed.

Katharina sharpened a small branch, located the squirrel's anus, and rammed it home, placing the skinned, gutted, and now-spitted squirrel on top of her oven.

Vincenzo faltered, swayed, and stumbled back to the log.

"Cut!" Katharina yelled.

Vincenzo doubled over, trying not to faint, as Katharina did a forward roll in front of him and began to make a snow angel.

Chapter 39

Pietro crashed out of the woods growling, pulled Katharina to her feet, kissed her passionately, and stepped back. "You were great!"

"No, *you* were," Katharina said. "Where'd you get the squirrel?"

"I found it dead in a snowdrift," he said, laughing. "You should have seen the look on your face!"

"I did it right, didn't I?"

Pietro nodded.

They both turned to Vincenzo, grinning and making faces.

"What . . . what . . . ?" was all Vincenzo could say.

"Yo, Vinnie," Katharina said, "how's it goin', big guy?"

Vincenzo's mouth opened, but no sound came out.

"Where's Bianca, Vinnie?" Katharina left Pietro and waved her bloody knife under Vincenzo's nose. "I have a few things I want to throw at her, see if they stick." She turned to Pietro. "Get me my hatchet."

Pietro nodded rapidly. "Yes, Miss Katharina. I get for

you." He collected the hatchet from near the fire pit and handed it to Katharina. "Is sharp."

Vincenzo found his voice. "She . . . knows?"

Pietro nodded.

"And you're still here, Katharina?" Vincenzo asked.

Katharina giggled. "Where else would I be?" She waved the hatchet, the reflection shooting streaks of light into the forest.

Vincenzo shrunk back. "And you're not, um, you're not angry?"

Katharina slammed the hatchet into the log next to Vincenzo. "Hell, no. I'm baaaa-ck. Now, where is that hussy of yours?"

Vincenzo pointed weakly toward his cabin. "Don't, um, don't hurt her."

Katharina ripped the hatchet from the log. "Now why would I ever do that, darling?"

Katharina ran to Vincenzo's cabin, Pietro close behind her, and pounded on the door. "Open up, in the name of the law!"

Bianca came to the door wearing only a T-shirt and a smile—a smile that turned into a scream when she saw Katharina with the hatchet and the knife. "Holy shit!" Bianca screamed as she slammed the door and locked it.

"Backstabbing whore!" Katharina yelled. She waited for the echo. "That was cool, wasn't it, Pietro?"

"It was," Pietro said, keeping his distance from the hatchet and the knife.

Katharina laughed. "I've never gotten to say a line like that. That was liberating. Can I say it again?"

Pietro nodded. "It's your picture."

"Yeah, it is. Backstabbing whore!" She knocked nicely on the door this time. "Bianca, *darling*, we have some business to discuss."

"Katharina, I can explain," Bianca said, her voice quavering, her body pressed heavily into the door.

Katharina planted her knife into the door. "I'll huff, and I'll puff, and I'll chop your house down! I am the big, bad wolf, Bianca. Oh, wait. You're the howler." She laughed. "Open the door, Bianca. I won't hurt you. Much."

Bianca opened the door a crack. "Will you put down the hatchet?"

Katharina smiled. "I'd rather bury the hatchet, Bianca." She turned and threw the hatchet into a tree thirty feet away, narrowly missing a stumbling Vincenzo. She turned back to a shut door. "Bianca, open the door. I am completely unarmed now, and I have no nails to speak of."

Bianca opened the door, pulling down the bottom of her T-shirt.

"Nice outfit," Katharina said. "I may want to borrow it sometime. But don't stretch it so much. It's much sexier if you don't."

Bianca's teeth chattered. "I c-c-can explain."

"You don't need to explain anything," Katharina said. She stepped in and hugged Bianca, leaving a blood stain on her T-shirt. "Thank you, Bianca. Thank you. You helped me more than you'll ever know."

"You're, um, you're welcome, Miss Minola. And what's that smell?"

Katharina stepped back. "Let's see. Bear jerky, fish guts, squirrel guts, a little of Pietro. Oh, and please call me Katharina from now on."

Bianca stepped back into the cabin. "So you're not mad at me?"

Katharina threw her head back. "Oh, I'm still mad, you little hussy. And I'd never rehire you. Backstabbing whore!"

The echo was just as thrilling the third time to Katharina.

Bianca jumped back *twice.*

Katharina looked from Vincenzo, keeping his distance, to Bianca. "But from the looks of things, Vinnie has given you a new job, anyway, so . . . Of course, I'm sure you've given him a few jobs, too." She stared at Vincenzo. "Well, get back in there. Bianca looks cold. And fat."

"I do?" Bianca cried. "Really?"

Katharina shook her head. "I make joke." She looked more closely at Bianca. "But not much of one. I doubt your clothes that I'm wearing will even fit you anymore, you porker."

Vincenzo approached his porch. "Katharina, did Pietro explain *why* we did all this?"

"Yes, he did, and though it was a pretty weak plan, it somehow worked." Katharina looked around the ceiling of the porch. "Where's the camera out here?"

"Oh shit!" Fish said, ducking in his seat.

"Why are you ducking?" Walt asked.

"Habit," Fish said. "They say she used to throw things at the camera back in the bad old days."

Vincenzo tried to smile. "There isn't a camera out here. Only your cabin has them."

Katharina's eyes popped.

"I mean . . ." Vincenzo looked for a place to hide. "But you knew that already, right?"

Katharina stormed toward him until he tripped and fell into the snow. "If I didn't know before, I'd know now. You're terrible at keeping secrets, Vincenzo." She stepped over to Pietro and laid her head on his chest. "This man right here is the best-kept secret of all."

Pietro grinned at Vincenzo. "Miss me, brother?"

Vincenzo stood on shaky legs. "Where have you been?"

Pietro held Katharina close. "Here and there, throwing snowballs at cameras, hiding mules."

Katharina looked at the ceiling of the porch. "Where is it, Pietro?"

Pietro kissed her forehead. "I'll bet it's somewhere inside."

"Oh shit," Fish said.

"Oh shit," Walt said.

"Why are you saying, 'Oh shit'? If anyone in this room has a right to say, 'Oh shit,' it's me, Walt. I put the camera in there."

"And I knew about it and said nothing," Walt said. "I'm your accomplice."

Katharina swept into Vincenzo's cabin. "Where's the bedroom, Bianca?"

Bianca's eyes looked to the right.

"Thanks, buddy," Katharina said, and she entered Vincenzo's bedroom. "Now, where would I put a camera to capture all the action, hmm?" She turned to the far wall facing the bed, took two steps, and pointed. "Is that one in the middle of that knot of wood in the paneling?"

Pietro nodded.

Katharina smiled for the camera. "Okay, now, Fish and Walt, listen up."

Bianca shrieked and locked herself in the bathroom.

"That was a real good shriek, wasn't it?" Katharina said. "Bianca could do slasher flicks. Anyway, Fish, I'm just now realizing that you have been filming Pietro and me, too. He has little knots of wood all over his walls, and I'll bet you've seen every square inch of me. I don't think we care as much, I mean, we are, after all, actors who love to perform."

"We go, you ride," Pietro said.

"Ooh, you say the nicest things," Katharina said. "Now, Walter, darling, I know I've 'written' most of this script, and that fax machine hasn't worked since day one, anyway, so yesterday and today Pietro and I have given you the start of something. Think you could maybe give us an ending? You know I'll veto everything you write, anyway, but at least try to earn your keep. Oh, and the sexier the ending, the better. Lots of skin. Lots of bare skin on the bearskin, got it?"

"She is truly not of this earth," Walt said.

"And I *still* wish she had a sister," Fish said.

"And, Fish? We'll need another headset rigged up for Pietro." She raised her eyebrows to Pietro. "I want to see what really goes on down there." She turned to Vincenzo. "We won't need Sly anymore. You've been wearing that wig backward the whole time, anyway."

Vincenzo grabbed his head and spun his wig around. "I wondered why it felt so weird."

"Take it off, please," Katharina said. "And don't leave this cabin, okay?"

Vincenzo blinked. "But you're going to need some wide shots—"

"As if!" Katharina interrupted. "Like you've been

doing any directing for the last five weeks, Mr. *Direttore.*
We're going to headset cam this bitch till it drops, okay?
And if we need any—how'd you say it? . . . 'wide intimate shots'—we'll pull you off Bianca for a few minutes. No. She seems to be a wild woman. We'll pull
Bianca off *you* for a few minutes." She knocked on the
bathroom door. "Bianca, darling, are you okay?"

"No!" Bianca cried.

"Why?" Katharina asked.

"They filmed me howling!"

Katharina laughed. "And there are some real wolves
in the hills who are real jealous about that."

Pietro offered his arm, Katharina took it, and the two
of them walked out of Vincenzo's cabin and into the
glorious sunlight. Halfway through the clearing, Katharina dropped Pietro's arm. "Race you."

"You're on."

"Wait a minute," Katharina said, and she approached
the tree cam. "Fish, I want you to shut down every camera in Pietro's cabin right now. Oh hell, shut it all down.
Free day for everybody. But I'm warning you, Fish. If I
see any of what we've already done or what we're about
to do on the Internet, I will sue you back to using a little
Brownie camera to take pictures for the tourists in Ti-
juana. Got me?"

Fish started hitting off switches. "Shutting down."

"Yes," Walt said, still wide-eyed. "Quickly. *Rapido.*"

"Go write that ending that she's going to change,
anyway."

"Yes," Walt said. "Quickly."

"Rapido," Fish said.

* * *

Katharina and Pietro raced up the snowy hill, crossed the rickety bridge, and reached Pietro's porch at the same time.

"We tied," Katharina said, her breath steaming the air. "Ooh," she cooed, "I haven't tried that yet. Got any rope, cowboy?"

"Just some bear jerky, ma'am."

"No," Katharina said, and she opened the door. "Let's build a big fire, get naked, and sweat all over each other."

"Sì."

The fire blazing, their bodies blazing, Katharina and Pietro paused to drip on each other. "Do you think the cameras are still on?" she asked.

"I don't know. It's kind of a turn-on, isn't it? Having cameras record your every move, groan, cry, and gyration?"

"Mine? What about yours?"

Pietro smiled. "I was talking about mine."

Katharina plunged down again, grinding against him. "Tell me nasty things in Italian."

"How nasty?"

She bit his earlobe. "The nastiest . . ."

Pietro closed his eyes. *"Figa deliziosa! Capezzoli dolce! L'immersione bagnata! Un bel culo! Dea di sesso!"*

Katharina arched her back. "You had me at *figa deliziosa . . .*"

Chapter 40

Vincenzo and Bianca wanted Pietro's character to be Italian and speak Italian. "He could be an immigrant, right?" they asked. "He's come over from Italy to start a new life as a homesteader in Canada, and the woman just happens to be trespassing on his land."

Katharina vetoed that idea. "Yeah, um, an Italian immigrant living in the woods on the Ontario-Quebec border in the mid-nineteenth century . . . No."

Walter and Fish wanted Pietro's character to be an Algonquin warrior shunned by his tribe and shorn of his hair for fraternizing with the white man. "The only way we can lengthen his hair is to use that blond wig or use some of Curtis's hair," they said. "Pietro has to be an Indian because of all his forest skills."

Katharina vetoed that idea as well. "Indians, in general now, could not or did not grow facial hair."

Katharina and Pietro's idea was to make Pietro's character mute. "Let the audience decide what he is," Katharina said. "Just keep him quiet so I can have all the best lines."

"The only language they really have to understand," Pietro said, "is the language of love."

Pietro's muteness worked on so many different levels. Vincenzo's close-ups revealed his brother's many faces, his smiles, his scowls, his squints, the tenderness his eyes portrayed. Pietro's body language was essentially shy and hesitant around Katharina's character but bold and adventurous in the woods.

Pietro became "UNIDENTIFIED MUTE MAN" or "UMM" in the script, and Katharina soon added "CURTIS, THE MULE" in a few scenes.

The shelter she and Pietro built was sturdy, stout, and waterproof. They stacked stone three feet high all the way around except for a little gate facing the clearing. They used Curtis to bring down the pile of poles from the bridge. They strung the poles together using plant fibers to form the rest of the walls and the roof. They used daub—a mixture of clay, lime, and dried grass—to fill all the cracks. Except for a hole in the ceiling for the smoke to escape and a small window facing the clearing, the shelter was completely enclosed, warm, and dry in just two days' work.

Once Pietro had sewn a deerskin-and-squirrel coat for Katharina, her ratty dress became a bag to collect berries and plants. She wore her new coat with the fur inside, where, she said, "fur ought to be."

Walt "wrote" the script using the raw footage Fish had pieced together so far and found only a few lines of actual dialogue. Katharina rewrote it so much that Walt put Katharina's name on it. In the end, there were only around one hundred total spoken lines in the script, all whispered, prayed, or shouted by Katharina.

Katharina enjoyed getting back at Pietro for fooling her so well with his innocent-Italian-moron act. She wrote a morning bathing scene for him. It was so cold a thin sheen of ice had formed overnight on the edges of the stream. He had to crack through it, immerse himself, "bathe," and get out, all under the watchful, shy eyes of THE WOMAN.

Katharina decided that the *seventh* take would do.

Pietro enjoyed the warm-up process *very* much.

UNIDENTIFIED MUTE MAN taught THE WOMAN how to hunt and trap. Unfortunately, they trapped only a shabby-looking raccoon (extremely happy to be set free) and shot an arrow at only one moose, Katharina's arrow falling a safe fifty feet short of the huge animal. The moose, all fifteen hundred bull moose pounds of him, snorted and charged.

"More cinema magic!" Fish shouted. "Run through the forest, run!"

Katharina and Pietro escaped with only minor injuries, making it to the shelter as the moose crashed around the forest after them. Luckily, Vincenzo decoyed the moose away from the shelter before any real damage could be done.

Vincenzo escaped with minor injuries, too.

The moose held up production for a solid hour, sniffing around the clearing and "talking" to Curtis, who barely blinked his blue-green eyes, before the moose drank from the stream, snorted loudly, and ambled off through the snow.

The climax of the movie involved a tasteful love scene under a bearskin. It was, indeed, brutally cold that day, and when Katharina slid under the bearskin and said, "Jes' to keep warm, Mr. Man, no shenanigans," she meant it—for about a minute. Pietro and Katharina somehow stayed completely under that bearskin the entire time, Vincenzo's camera capturing the sheer rapture on their faces. After a final shot of her hand finding his hand outside the bearskin, Katharina donned her headset one last time to look out their little window at the snow drifting down. Vincenzo, directed by Bianca, backed away from the shelter to the log and sat.

Fish "picked up" the scene with two of the lower cameras, handing it off to a camera he had placed high over the clearing. This bird's-eye view closed the movie—the shelter down below, the smoke rising up through the falling snowflakes to the sun cracking and streaking gloriously through the clouds.

Filming finished early a week before Thanksgiving, which was cause for celebration and long, hot baths and showers at Pietro's house. While Fish worked swiftly around the clock assembling a raw first cut of all one thousand hours of the "real" movie, Pietro and Katharina took the Suburban to Rouyn-Noranda to get some real food, returning ten hours later with a whole ham, a side of beef, two turkeys, four chickens, and lots of *verdure.*

Katharina, of course, had sampled Pietro's "meat" several times on their journey, hence the reason a five-hour round-trip excursion lasted ten hours.

They celebrated buffet style and sat around Pietro's great room, a roaring fire in the fireplace, a blizzard howling just outside the windows.

"So, how are my shoes, clothes, and Scottie doing in Costa Rica, Bianca?" Katharina asked.

"Notice the order," Bianca said. "Shoes, clothing, dog."

"A girl has to have her priorities in order," Katharina said.

"Well, they're doing just fine, darling," Bianca said. "They all have tans, even Scottie and your thongs and your thongs. Oh, I *do* hope they put some sunscreen on little Scottie. Those Scottish breeds sunburn so easily."

Katharina had found out quite a bit concerning the intervention, but she still had a few gaps to fill. "You didn't fold any of my lingerie, did you?"

"Nope. Balled them all up. Squished them in. Wrinkled them to death." Bianca winked. "You really like boxers now, don't you?"

Katharina nodded. "I like the ventilation. Keeps me fresh."

The men said nothing because they really had no intelligent things to add. Their thoughts, of course, ranged from the practical (Walt) to the romantic (Pietro and Vincenzo) to the downright erotic (Fish).

Katharina smiled. "I understand you were getting paid a nice chunk of change for this little charade, Bianca. What'd they give you?"

Bianca munched on a chicken wing. "One seventy."

Katharina choked on a piece of turkey. "I didn't get paid that much for *My Honey Love*, Vincenzo!"

Vincenzo, who hadn't been able to sit comfortably since the moose attack, turned from the window. "Um, that was a long time ago, Katharina. You know, inflation?"

"Yeah," Katharina said, "inflation of your penis and your ego! You're old enough to be—"

"The love of my life," Bianca interrupted.

There was a general "Aww" from those present.

"So," Katharina said, squeezing and releasing Pietro's hand, "you like 'em young and fat, huh, Vincenzo?"

Vincenzo blushed. "It's not like that, I mean, it is like that *now*, but it wasn't—"

Bianca jumped up from the couch and stalked toward Vincenzo. "One, I am not fat. And two, it *was* like that, oh yes, it was. I saw you looking at me in your office with lust in your heart." She turned to Katharina.

"He undressed me with his eyes at least five times in his office. I was getting chilly. His right eye was getting fresh with my legs, while his left eye blinked against my booty. His tongue was on the floor following me around the entire time. He even made me lie down in a very suggestive pose on his casting couch, Katharina."

"Do tell," Katharina said.

Vincenzo blushed again. "Hey, that's not—"

Bianca silenced him with a kiss. "Thankfully, Penelope came in before he could deflower me. Innocence is such a burden."

"You poor, poor dear," Walt said. "Such a merciless business."

Vincenzo looked into Bianca's eyes. "You know it didn't happen that way."

Bianca winked. "It still can . . . when we get back to L.A. Give Penelope the day off, and we'll see if that couch really works."

There was a general "Whoo" from those present.

"Maybe we'll even be able to see Catalina Island while we do it," Bianca whispered. "And if it's smoggy, we'll have to look for Catalina a long, long time."

Vincenzo added a quiet "Whoo" of his own.

Fish raised his hands in the air. "People, I think I have something. It's raw as hell and jumps around a little, but it looks damn good. Get the popcorn, Walt, and dim the lights, Bianca. It's showtime!"

After only one simple black-and-white title shot—A WOMAN ALONE—and one other shot—STARRING KATHA-DIVA BOLOGNA—the movie began with Katharina running through the stream.

"My nipples were so hard," Katharina whispered to Pietro.

"Why do you think we did that scene three times?" Pietro whispered back.

As the film, and Katharina's character, progressed and regressed, the audience made numerous comments.

"Just listen to that sound quality," Fish said.

"Nice nails," Bianca said.

"Nice hair," Katharina said. "Why didn't somebody tell me about all this pine sap up here?"

"Oh, I love your boots, *darling*," Bianca said. "Wher*ever* did you get them?"

"You need a bath," Pietro said.

"Oh no, don't eat that!" Walt shouted.

The entire group whistled "London Bridge"—twenty-four times.

"Oh, don't put the stick in there . . . ouch!" Fish cried.

"I didn't know a squirrel looked like that on the inside," Bianca said.

"That moose is in love with Curtis," Katharina said. "Look at those eyes. How couldn't a moose fall for a mule who had those eyes?"

When Pietro finally entered the clearing and stayed, despite Katharina's character waving a knife in his face, the audience cheered.

"Hey!" Katharina cried. "Why didn't you cheer for *me* earlier when I was running through the stream?"

"If the unidentified mute man didn't show up," Vincenzo said, "we would have been filming through Christmas and maybe even New Year's Day, and we would all have gotten frostbite, lost toes, fingers, noses, and other appendages."

Katharina pouted. "I would have finished that shelter on my own."

Popcorn rained down on Katharina so hard that she had to pull Pietro on top of her for protection.

Fish stopped the feed before the climactic scene.

"Now, I know we all want to get less than an R rating for this thing, but I have to warn you. This ending is, um, kind of *hard* to watch."

Pietro squirmed in his seat.

"What's wrong?" Katharina whispered.

"Just watch," Pietro whispered.

The feed resumed, and the love scene began. Katharina said her line, moved closer to Pietro, and then—

"Geez, he's got a boner," Vincenzo said. "Pietro, please. It was 20 below that day."

Pietro sighed. "She has the warmest hands."

Katharina put her mouth to his ear. "You moved that entire bearskin. You aren't holding back on me, are you?"

"I won't hold back on you later tonight," Pietro whispered.

They then watched the blooper reel. Katharina's shelter fell and rose and fell—twenty-four times. Katharina fell in the mud—fifteen times. Katharina fussed at Curtis—too often to count. Pietro brought, at various times, a rubber chicken, a raccoon hat, a Hot Pocket, a granola bar, and a pot of stew for Katharina's character to "cook" on her stone stove. Katharina ate berries and made faces, spitting something offensive from her mouth into the camera lens. Katharina cursed often. Katharina and Pietro threw mud at Vincenzo's camera. The last "blooper" was yet another of Pietro's pranks. He acted as if he chopped off his foot with the hatchet, a stream of red ketchup bloodying the snow. The shot of Bianca nearly fainting earned a standing ovation.

"We got you good," Katharina said.

"I still have nightmares," Bianca said.

The screen went blank. "Don't get up, Katharina," Fish said. "I want you and Pietro to see what Walt, Bianca, Vincenzo, and I finished while you two were out, um, shopping for food and having sex among the *verdure*. Before I show it to you, Katharina, you have to promise not to get mad."

"I'm going to get mad," Katharina said.

"It was all in fun," Walt said. "You'll like it."

"Bianca, will I like it?" Katharina asked.

Bianca shook her head. "No. You're not still carrying that knife around, are you?"

The blank screen went black until the MGM lion morphed into a tiger before morphing into Katharina's *Miss Thang* character. A title—THE TIGER GOES TO CANADA—rippled onto the screen.

"I got your tiger, Fish," Katharina said. "I know that was your idea."

The next shot was of Walt in front of Pietro's fire sitting in a plush lounge chair and wearing Pietro's blue robe while chomping on a pipe. "Katharina Minola, Oscar-winning actress," Walt said.

A shot of Katharina and Pietro from the cab scene in *My Honey Love.*

"Razzie-winning actress," Walt continued.

A shot from *Miss Thang* with Katharina's heavily lipsticked mouth wide-open.

"Diva," Walt said.

A shot of Katharina in her tiger outfit snoring on the plane.

"Lover of mud," Walt said.

A shot of Katharina flopping in the mud at the stream.

"What you will witness is beyond belief, ladies and gentlemen," Walt said. "You will see a tiger-diva turn into a tiger lily before your very eyes. How did this happen? How *could* this happen? Let's find out, shall we?"

The scene shifted to Walt standing in front of Cabin 3 wearing a yellow wig, Katharina's tiger stilettos and sunglasses, and a bearskin. "Inside these rough-cut walls, Katharina Minola experienced agonizing, excruciating, unbearable heartache and deprivation."

A shot of Katharina in the cabin on the first night: "Where is the humidifier? I have very dry skin. Oh, right. There's no electricity. Where are the flowers? Oh, right. They'd already be dead in this freezer of a cabin. Where is the all-black furniture? Oh, right. We're in the Dark Ages up here where everything is made of sticks, stones, and branches. Where are the blackout drapes? Oh, right. There's no need. It's black as *bleep* outside. But where . . . is my *bleep* . . . dinner? How hard could *that* be to have ready for me?"

Food scenes followed with Katharina eating (and not eating) stew, Kashi, oatmeal, macaroni 'n' cheese, and the infamous frozen Hot Pocket.

Walt appeared again, this time wearing what was left of Katharina's dress as a bandana, her boots on his hands. "And then, friends, she hit rock bottom when her longtime assistant, Bianca Baptista, quit during a blizzard."

Bianca's horrible speech: "I put up with more *bleep* from you in seven weeks than most people put up with in a lifetime. You are the meanest, cruelest *monster* of a person I have ever met. I don't know why I didn't quit sooner. I would rather flip burgers or sell shoes at the mall than work for you. I'd rather get out some cardboard and a squirt bottle than work for you. You know why? Because you . . . ain't . . . *bleep*."

Katharina gripped Pietro's hand tightly. "That was the old me," she whispered.

"I know," Pietro whispered. "Though I was pretty fond of the old you, too."

The next scene had the camera bursting through Vincenzo's cabin door and finding Bianca eating raisins and a granola bar while Vincenzo painted her toenails. "Yeah, I was Katha-diva Bologna's last assistant," Bianca said while chewing gum loudly. "Yeah, I quit on her *bleep*. She pissed me off. Be careful, Vinnie. Don't get it on my skin. *Bleep*. That's when Katharina went insane." Bianca paused, and the camera zoomed in on her face. "If you ask me, Katha-diva Bologna was insane from the very beginning. Where is my *bleep* dinner, Vinnie! *Bleep!* I ask you to get one thing right, and you *bleep* it up!"

Katharina stood up and waved her arms in front of the screen, tears of laughter streaming down her face. "Okay, okay. That's enough. Funny, but I've seen quite enough. Is the rest of this mock-umentary like that?"

Fish nodded. "It actually gets worse. You have to see my song."

"No, you don't," Walt said.

"Forget you, Walt." Fish found the segment and shot it to the screen, "The Diva Flew Into Canada" flying in letter by letter. "Walt filmed this, so if the camera jumps around, it isn't my fault."

As Fish's voice whined its way through the song, the camera bounced from pictures of Katharina to pictures of Pietro to a broom and to Curtis's tail, which somehow kept time with the music.

When the song ended, Katharina clapped once. "That was horrible." She rolled her eyes. "But I liked it." She turned on the lights. "Now, Fish, tell me the rest of the extras on the DVD are not going to be like that."

Fish smiled. "We had a lot of fun, Katharina. Most of the extras are like that."

"You had fun at my expense," Katharina said. "It's okay. I deserved it. I ought to do a disclaimer, too, you know, something halfway serious."

Nodding heads all around.

"But," Katharina said, "what will you do with the *rest*

of the footage? And you know the footage I'm talking about."

Fish frowned and looked at the floor. "Pietro and Vincenzo already have it all."

Katharina smiled at Pietro. "*You* have it?"

Pietro nodded. "We will be watching it later."

Bianca jolted and shouted, "Vinnie, tell me you haven't already watched us in action!"

"Well . . ." Vincenzo said. "Yeah. I have."

"Was I . . . ?" Bianca moved closer to Vincenzo. "Was I good or what?"

Vincenzo winced. "Fish, *you* better explain."

Bianca turned to Fish. "*You* watched us?"

"Um, Bianca," Fish said, not meeting her eyes, "um, the fish-eye lenses and even the infrared didn't pick up much, I mean, *enough*. How can I say this without you hurting me?" He shook his head. "I can't. Bianca, neither of you are that, um, endowed. Um, we might have had to use a body double for you, Bianca."

"I have nice breasts!" Bianca howled. "I have a killer ass!" She stormed toward Fish. "You watched it all, right?"

Fish backed away. "I couldn't see much. Really, Bianca."

Bianca stamped her feet. "Cut it out!"

"No, I meant . . ." Fish pinned himself to the picture window. "You guys were up under that quilt for most of it."

"Until the scene at the window," Walt said, edging toward the stairs. "You remember. The howling scene."

Bianca froze.

Vincenzo froze.

"Very seventies," Walt said.

"And I thought the hills were just crawling with wolves," Katharina said. "Damn, Bianca, show some damn restraint!"

Bianca faked several tears and sobs, falling into Vincenzo's shaking arms. "They said they couldn't see my tits, Vinnie."

Pietro kissed Katharina's ear. "Who's the diva now, hmm?" He stood. "Okay, okay. Enough. What about the real movie? Do we think it has a chance?"

Fish returned to his command center. "If y'all will leave me alone, I'll have it fine-tuned and ready to go in a couple of weeks."

"That fast?" Katharina asked. "You're kidding."

"I'm not kidding," Fish said. "We won't have a soundtrack to lay down, just the sounds of nature. The sound quality was outstanding, and except for some cussing, which I can mute, we're good there, too. But mainly, people, we did something very odd, very rare here. We shot a movie *in order*. *Totally* unheard of. *Never* happens. It's an editor's dream." He smiled. "And if the real wolf sounds we recorded don't work, I can always use Vincenzo's and Bianca's."

Bianca and Vincenzo locked Fish outside for only a few minutes. Feeling returned to his fingers a half hour later as he compared the real wolves to the two making wolf puppies upstairs at that very moment . . .

"They're very nice, Bianca," Vincenzo said, cupping Bianca's breasts. "Look. They're perfectly proportional."

"My left one's bigger."

Vincenzo looked more closely. "Really? Let me see . . . I can't tell."

Bianca reached under the covers and felt around. "Your left one's bigger, too. We were made for each other."

"I, um, had a little accident a long time ago involving a zipper."

Bianca pouted. "Did Vinnie have a little boo-boo?"

Vincenzo nodded. "Yes. And it hurt very much."

Bianca disappeared under the covers. "Then let me kiss it and make it all better . . ."

Meanwhile, across the hall, Katharina and Pietro, fully clothed like an old couple and lying on top of the covers, shared a bag of popcorn while watching themselves in action on the TV in Pietro's master bedroom.

"*That's* gotta hurt," Pietro said.

"Nope."

Pietro winced. "That *had* to hurt."

"Nope," Katharina said. "And stop hogging the popcorn."

Pietro listened to Katharina moaning. "You are a fantastic actress, Katharina."

"Nope," Katharina said. "That was real. You made me do that . . . and . . ." She watched a few seconds more. "*I* made you do that. You can't fake that."

Pietro turned off the DVD player. "Katharina, we, um, we did it an awful lot these last few weeks."

"You're not tired, are you?"

Pietro sighed. "No, not at all. That's not where this is going. I mean, we did it a *lot* over, oh, about a month's time. You know?"

Katharina threw a piece of popcorn at him. "Speak plainly, Unidentified Mute Man."

Pietro fiddled with his hands. "I mean, if you get pregnant . . ."

Katharina turned to him, lying on her side. "You know, I think I already am. I have the strangest desire to sprinkle paprika and hot fudge on this popcorn right now."

Pietro's heart thudded. "You really think you're . . ."

"If you didn't live in the middle of Iceland, we could find out," Katharina said. "I wanted to get a pregnancy test while we were over in Quebec, but I didn't want to spoil my first escape from this place in eight weeks. But yeah, I think we made us a love child, Pietro. And next year about, oh, September, we could be filming the sequel up here. We'll call it *A Family Alone.* I already have some ideas rolling around my head. My baby will get top billing, of course."

Pietro slid beside her and rubbed her stomach. "Of course."

Katharina lifted up her shirt, Pietro's hands squeezing her skin. "And Fish can make her a cute little headset with big diamonds on it."

Pietro unzipped the top of her jeans. "Or Fish could make *him* a manly headset with little bear cubs on it." He slipped the tips of his fingers below the elastic of her boxers. "Katharina, I . . . I really . . ." He looked her in the eye. "I *really* . . ."

Katharina pushed his hand lower, willing him not to say it. "Yeah. I *really* . . . too." She smiled. "Who writes this shit?" She looked down at his hand. "Well, get me warmed up."

Pietro's finger found the spot.

Katharina pulled her shirt over her head. "Let's make *sure* we made us a baby." She pushed off her pants and boxers while Pietro kissed her stomach. "We have to get her out of me and under contract as soon as possible. I have bills to pay."

Pietro looked up. "The popcorn will get cold."

She pulled the popcorn bag close to her and took a handful. "I'll be all right. I mean, it's only fair." She pushed his head down with her free hand. "If you get to eat, so do I." She turned on the DVD player.

"Save me some."

"Work fast, then."

Chapter 41

Fish and Walt returned to L.A., Fish to work with another editor to finish the movie, Walt to make love to his wife for three weeks straight. Walt's wife, Melissa, didn't know what had come over her husband of twelve years, but she wasn't complaining. Their two young sons wondered why their mommy and daddy were playing hide 'n' go seek so often, but that didn't bother them because Daddy was finally home.

The two couples, one of them *officially* expecting a child, decided it was time for some sun and flew to Costa Rica. Katharina donated all her old clothes and shoes to charity, noting that few Costa Ricans would ever want to wear most of her shoes. She parted with her porta-posse, "firing" (and therefore freeing) them in a simple ceremony.

"I'm doing my own hair from now on," she said to her hairstylist. "You're fired."

The hairstylist shed a few tears and kissed Katharina's hand.

"I'm doing my own makeup from now on," she said to her makeup artist. "You're fired."

The makeup artist fell to her knees and raised her hands to the sky.

"I'm dressing myself from now on, too," she said to her dresser. "You're fired."

The dresser *really* cried. It was only the second job she had ever had, and she didn't want to go back to Jack in the Box.

"Don't worry," Katharina said to her former employees. "I will give you all glowing recommendations. I'm sure there are plenty of other divas to serve out there."

The porta-posse was not amused by this comment. Her dresser stopped crying and decided Jack in the Box would be a safer job.

Lucentio Pictures sent out a low-key press release two weeks before Christmas:

> Katharina Minola, named best actress for *My Honey Love,* has finished filming *A Woman Alone* in the wilds of Ontario, Canada, her first picture in four years.

> A survival tale, *A Woman Alone* is the story of a runaway American slave who finds ultimate freedom—and the man of her dreams—while battling the brutality of nature.

> Shot with state-of-the-art headset cameras, *A Woman Alone* was directed by Vincenzo Lucentio and Bianca Baptista, and also stars Pietro Lucentio and Curtis the Mule. Miss Minola wrote the screenplay, her first.

> Miss Minola, who was paid five million dollars for her work, and Pietro Lucentio

are expecting their first child. The couple
is currently resting in Costa Rica with
Miss Minola's dog, Scottie.

Incredibly, no major paper or entertainment news
television shows picked up on this historic event.

"No one ever reads the entire press release," Vincenzo said while sipping a beer on the beach, Bianca
beside him sunbathing topless. "Oh well."

By the time someone at *Entertainment Tonight* had
broken the story, however, the weary (but tan) band of
four had already left Costa Rica for L.A.

ET interviewed various current divas for their reac-
tion to the enormous sum paid to a "former" star. "No
way!" several said, all of them wearing sunglasses inside
because they had no home training. "Why?" asked another while holding her lapdog that was small enough
to be caught in a mousetrap. "In American money or
Canadian money?" asked the most cerebral of the lot. "I
am firing my agent this very instant!" another cried,
and the camera recorded her, indeed, firing her agent
on the spot. The last diva, the oldest of the group,
flicked some cigarette ash at the camera and said,
dreamily, "They must have felt sorry for her." She adjusted her hospital band and accepted some pills from
her rehab recovery nurse. "You know, this is only my
third trip here. They're giving me a discount this time.
I'm like a frequent flyer, you know?"

Fish found a company who put together a slick fifteen-
second trailer, the only real advertising Lucentio Pictures did for the movie. It showed Katharina racing
through the stream, clawing at mud, a hatchet slicing
into a tree, and Pietro flitting through the woods in his
bearskin disguise. The screen went black, Katharina's
voice chanting, "Now I lay me down to sleep . . ." The

last thing anyone watching would have noticed, providing he or she didn't flip through the channels, use the bathroom, or get something to eat, was:

A WOMAN ALONE
Katharina Minola
Christmas Day
(This film is not yet rated.)

When Katharina saw the trailer for the first time, she clicked off the TV and pulled Pietro's head from her lap. "Why hasn't my movie been rated yet?"

Pietro caught his breath. "Vincenzo says we're trying for PG-13, but the fish and the squirrel, my ass in the stream, the little bit of leg you show at the end, and my extra, um, wood under the bearskin are causing problems."

"Gimme your wood, Mr. Man," Katharina whispered. "I want to set it on fire."

A Woman Alone opened in very limited engagements at small independent theaters and art houses around the country on Christmas Day. The reviewers raved, rooted, and just about screamed: "Watch this one!" Even the Roger Leonard Dicks of the world were in agreement: "Katharina Minola sizzles and shines . . . her best work *ever.*" "The cinematography will leave you breathless and give your heart palpitations." . . . "Newcomer Pietro Lucentio is the beefcake Hollywood has been yearning for." . . . "*This* is why we go to the movies!" . . . "Adventure, action, suspense, danger, romance—can it get any better than this?"

*   *   *

Because of some erroneous reporting and some excellent lies from Penelope, the paparazzi descended on
Costa Rica *and* Rouyn-Noranda, only to find sand and
snow, respectively. After *A Woman Alone* had played for
two weeks in limited markets, Lucentio Pictures distributed it around the globe, and foreign audiences raved
even more, since it was a movie they could watch and
enjoy instead of read.

Pietro and Katharina (sans makeup) went everywhere
together completely unnoticed. They shopped at Babies
"R" Us. They spent time at a Home Depot matching
paint to Petra's crib. They walked the beach together
and looked at sunsets. They hiked Yosemite with Bianca
and Vincenzo. They ate at Jack in the Box, where Katharina asked for some paprika to sprinkle on her fries.
Bianca freaked out because they had no paprika. They
went to Knott's Berry Farm just to walk around. They even
went to the post office, where they stood in line to buy
stamps.

When the Academy Award nominations came out, *A
Woman Alone* was a popular choice, one of five films
nominated for best picture, with seven nominations
overall. Fish was nominated for best sound editing and
for best cinematography—an unprecedented achieve-
ment. Bianca was somehow nominated for best costume design, and Vincenzo was nominated for best
director. Katharina, as she had hoped, was nominated
for best actress—and, amazingly, she was also nominated for best original screenplay.

Katharina laughed Pietro completely out of her
when she heard the news. "Fish is going to be so happy!
Two nominations for shit he basically just sat and
watched! How'd Bianca get a nomination?"

"She's sleeping with the director," Pietro said.

"Oh yeah. Vincenzo as best director? No way! And I

get *two* nominations, one basically for crossing out the shit that Walt wrote? This is insane!"

Pietro laughed himself back inside Katharina. "That's what I love about this business."

What was more insane were the odds posted in Las Vegas for the Academy Award winners, especially for best director. Vincenzo was the favorite to win because, as one insider said, "Anyone who can direct Katharina Minola for two months, *not* quit, *not* go insane, and *not* go into hiding, *and* put out an outstanding movie deserves to win this award unanimously."

After some lengthy discussion involving Katharina riding Curtis up the red carpet prior to the Academy Award ceremony at the Kodak Theatre, and after several days spent looking for the right dress "to maximize the fact that I'm almost showing," Katharina decided instead to walk the red carpet with Pietro, Vincenzo, Bianca, Fish and his date (a tanned and toned Latina bodybuilder he met on the beach), and Walt and his wife, Melissa. Instead of the usual stretch limousine, Vincenzo hired the driver of a stretch Cadillac Escalade with spinners, lots of chrome, and a sound system that rattled the sidewalk. They emerged from their "ride," as Fish called it, en masse, walking together up the red carpet—waving, smiling, blowing kisses, and generally ignoring every reporter who rudely shoved a microphone their way. Melissa seemed to be having the time of her life, especially when one reporter mistook her for Katharina.

There was an eerie and striking resemblance between Katharina Minola and Melissa Yearling.

Katharina gave Walt an extra kiss on the cheek for the compliment.

Once inside the theater, Katharina slipped off her shoes, wiggling her toes. No one seemed to notice, the focus of attention directed to the stage. After the awards for best art direction (which "God would have won for our movie," Katharina said) and best makeup (which "no one would have won for our movie," Katharina said), the best sound editing nominations were read.

Fish smiled at the camera as he heard his name.

He didn't win, nor did Bianca for costume design.

"It's okay," Bianca whispered. "I mean, all I did was let you borrow my *draws*." She smiled. "Which reminds me, Katharina. Where is that *Entertainment Tonight* reporter? I have an exclusive story for her."

Fish, who didn't expect to win any awards, leaped from his seat when he heard his name as the winner for best cinematography. He kissed his date on the cheek, slapped hands down the row, and ran up to take his award.

"Wow!" he said with a smile. "I'd like to thank that entire row down there for making this possible for me. Without them, I wouldn't have had anything to play with. Trust me. They gave me miles of mayhem. I really don't have a speech, but I do have a song."

Katharina led the others in standing and shouting, "No!"

Fish smiled. "I was just kidding. Lighten up, Katharina. Thank you! Thank you all!"

The very next award, after an interminable commercial break, was for best screenplay. Katharina was the only woman, the only person of color, and the only person under fifty among the nominees.

She won.

She turned her head slowly to Pietro as applause filled the theater. "They're shitting me, right?"

Pietro helped her to her feet.

"Go with me?" she whispered.

Pietro nodded.

Katharina let Pietro lead her to the stage, where she took her award and laughed out loud at it. She stood on tiptoes to whisper in Pietro's ear: "Oscar doesn't have a penis."

Pietro blushed.

"Let me first say thank you to my boyfriend, Pietro," Katharina said as the applause ended. She gave him a long, soulful, deep kiss. "You know, I don't thank him enough." She gave him a longer, more soulful, deeper kiss. She "placed" him a few feet away. "Down, boy. Stay."

Some laughter rippled through the crowd.

"When I won my first one of these fifteen years ago, I stood up here and blanked. Really. It happens. Everyone in this room knows what I mean. You're excited, you're amped, and then . . . poof. I didn't have a single thought in my head except 'Damn, I won!' In my excitement, I forgot to thank the people who helped me win that first award, and I'd like to fix all that tonight. I'd like to thank my director, Paul Stewart, for putting up with me; my costars, Jermaine Martin, Toni Collins, and C. J. Jones—also for putting up with me; and, most of all, I'd like to thank Walter Yearling for writing a script just for me." She smiled at Walter and Melissa. "Thank you, Walter. And thanks also for helping me clean up from the party none of y'all attended."

"And now," Katharina continued, "to this award. I really don't deserve it. Really. I mean, it practically wrote itself. I would think it, and there it would be on the page. You wouldn't believe the rewrites. The fax machine was broken from day one . . . I won't bore you with all that. Tonight I would like to thank Walter Yearling again for his support and John 'Fish' Fisher for bringing this script to life. Vincenzo Lucentio for his incredible direction. Bianca Baptista for her incredible costumes—and the granola bars. But mostly, I'd like to thank Pietro Lucentio, my costar, and my man. You know, I don't think I'll ever be able to thank him enough. But I'm gonna try."

Katharina set another record that evening for the longest kiss onstage at an Academy Award ceremony. If the music hadn't swelled to a crescendo, she might have still been sucking Pietro's face until well after midnight.

Chapter 42

Once offstage, Katharina ran past reporters, Academy officials, and other people who wanted to interview her, dragging Pietro behind her. "We're getting out of here," she said, zipping down a hallway to an exit.

"We're not going to wait to hear who wins the other awards?"

Katharina flipped out her cell phone. "No." She called the Escalade driver. "We're around back. Come get us." She closed her phone. "I won't win, anyway."

"You might."

She nuzzled her head into Pietro's neck. "For the first time in my life, I don't have to win. It doesn't really matter. I'm just Dena from Tenth Street from now on. I have another trophy, and if they really knew how I 'wrote' the script, they'd take it back. I have a good man, and we're having a baby. Vincenzo, Fish, and Bianca can go up for me if I win." She shrugged. "Bianca stole the show anyway, didn't she?"

Their "limo" showed up, bass thumping. A few photographers snapped shots as Katharina and Pietro

got in and the Escalade sped out of sight down Hollywood Boulevard.

"Where are we going, Katharina?" Pietro asked.

"The beach," Katharina said, looking down at her
bare feet. "Pietro, you let me go up on that stage without my shoes."

"Yep."

Katharina laughed and rested her head on his shoulder. "I may never wear shoes again." She looked at her
man. "We make a nice screen couple."

Pietro kissed her cheek. "Yeah, we do. Rambo and
the Diva."

"No. A big hairy teddy bear and the *former* diva."

The Escalade cruised down Santa Monica Boulevard
for several miles.

"Did I tame you?" Pietro asked.

Katharina thought a few moments. "A little."

"Just a little?" Pietro asked.

"A lot, Pietro, all right? You tamed my heart." Katharina looked out the window and yelled, "Stop here!"

The Escalade screeched to a halt.

Katharina opened the door and jumped out. "But
you have yet to tame my mind!"

The sand felt wonderful to Katharina as she ran toward the surf. *I will never buy another pair of shoes like those
again. Those things strangle my feet. Paying a thousand dollars for shoes that give you pain is just plain stupid! Like
Bianca, I will go through life as barefoot as possible. Though
now I'm barefoot and pregnant in a five-thousand-dollar
dress. Oh, the ironies of my life.*

Pietro caught up to Katharina, turned her around,
and held her. "You know I really . . . I really love you,
Katharina. I want to marry you."

Katharina did a happy dance in her head. *Ah, the
magic word, and, yes, this is the right time to hear it. But I*

have to make him work for it. She pushed Pietro back. "I'll see you hanged first."

Pietro, at first hurt, smiled when he saw that Katharina's eyes were full of light. "You *will* be my wife, Kate."

Katharina turned her back on Pietro. "I told you not to call me Kate."

Pietro walked around and faced her. "You will be my wife, Katharina."

Katharina looked at Pietro's fabulous suit. "Look how you're dressed. I couldn't possibly marry a man dressed as nicely as you are. I need a rugged man, a mountain man, a big, hairy, tree-hugging man who owns a mule with a spastic colon."

Pietro was speechless.

Katharina reached under her dress and took out several pages stapled together. "I'm sorry you had to see me do that." She handed the pages to Pietro. "Just follow the script. Start at the beginning."

Pietro scanned what looked, indeed, like a script. "What is this?"

Katharina smiled. "It's a script. I don't blame you for not knowing it was a script. I doubt you've actually ever seen one. Oh. I go first." She walked to the edge of the water and did a dramatic turn.

"You wrote a script for *my* proposal?" Pietro asked.

Katharina wriggled her feet deeper into the wet sand. "I scripted our romance, didn't I?"

"I had a lot to do with it, Katharina."

"So you say." She flashed her eyes. "Humor me."

Pietro looked up at the stars. "How did you know I was going to propose to you tonight?"

Katharina looked up at the stars, too. "It was written in the stars."

"No. Seriously."

Katharina picked up a foot and flung sand into the

crashing waves. "You went ring shopping with Vincenzo—you know, the man who can't keep a secret? He blabbed to Bianca, and Bianca said that she wanted one, too. Bianca came running to me all teary and crying like a diva. . . . It was a pretty ugly business."

"Oh."

Katharina cleared her throat. "Okay. I haven't memorized lines in a while, so bear with me."

Pietro laughed. "You haven't *had* any lines to memorize in a while."

"True." She cleared her throat again. " 'I must, forsooth, be forced / To give my hand opposed against my heart / Unto a mad-brain rudesby full of spleen.' " . . . She raised her eyebrows.

"I'm not full of spleen! And what's a 'rudesby'?"

Katharina shrugged. "I haven't the foggiest. And stick to the script."

"Sorry."

Katharina dropped her arms. "And now you've made me forget my lines."

Pietro found the place on the script. "I told you . . ."

"Right. 'I told you, I, he was a frantic fool, / Hiding his bitter jests in blunt behaviour: / And, to be noted for a merry man, / He'll woo a thousand, 'point the day of marriage, / Make feasts, invite friends, and proclaim the banns; / Yet never means to wed where he hath' wood."

"It says 'woo'd' here, Katharina."

Katharina smiled. "I meant to say 'wood.' I like your wood, Mr. Woodsman."

"*Grazie.*"

Katharina growled. "Now, stop interrupting your proposal. Um . . . Give me the line."

"Now must . . ."

Katharina put her hands over her heart. " 'Now must

the world point at poor' Katharina, / And say, 'Lo, there is mad' Pietro's 'wife, / If it would please him come and marry her!' " She nodded at Pietro.

Pietro read his part. "Oh." He knelt in front of her, soaking his pants, spreading his arms wide. "But you are my honey love," he said woodenly.

Katharina shook her head. "That was terrible, absolutely dreadful. Put some feeling into it. You're proposing to a goddess, remember?"

Pietro reached for Katharina this time and softly said, "But you are my honey love, Katharina."

"Whoo," Katharina said. "Much, much better. You hit my heart. We might make you into a real actor yet."

"But your next line is—"

"I just wanted you to know that," Katharina interrupted. She stepped away and did a half turn, her hands on her hips. " 'My honey love'? Please. Is that the best that you can do? Makes a jazzy title for a movie, though, huh?"

"It does."

She placed the back of her hand on her forehead. "But oh, alas, you love me only for my body. I am so fat!"

Pietro tried not to laugh. "I love your mind, Kate, 'For 'tis the mind that makes the body rich . . .' "

Katharina winked. "You read well. I didn't write in purple ink this time."

"I can see that."

"What's my next line?"

Pietro found the place. "But I cannot . . ."

"Oh." She shot her chin toward the ocean. "But I cannot marry you, Pietro. You are 'one half lunatic; / A mad-cap ruffian' . . . You are dressed in far too many clothes."

Pietro smiled. "To me you will be married, not unto my clothes."

Katharina turned to Pietro. "I feel like skinny-dipping."

Pietro searched the script. "That's not in the script."

Katharina reached behind her and unzipped her dress. "Well, I just do."

Pietro stood. "In your condition?"

Katharina shrugged out of the dress and let it fall to the sand. She unfastened her bra and threw it to the waves. "So little Petra wants to go for a swim." She yanked down her boxers.

Pietro looked at the five-thousand-dollar dress collecting seawater. "But your dress!"

Katharina jumped up and down on it. "This little ol' thing? Humph. I only put it on when I don't care how I look." She turned and ran into the waves.

Pietro hurriedly removed his suit. "What if a photographer comes by?" he yelled.

Katharina danced in the waves. "I don't care about that anymore. Bring the ring."

Pietro, naked, had to run back to his suit, get the ring, and wade out into the cold surf. "It's cold," he said as a wave splashed over him.

"Not as cold as the stream at your place, right?"

He nodded.

Katharina held out her ring finger, and Pietro slid the ring on. "Nice."

Pietro took her in his arms, smiling at his future bride, lost in her blue-green eyes. "Kiss me, Kate."

They kissed for a long time, the surf crashing around them, the stars twinkling above, their legs going numb from the cold.

Katharina shivered and smiled. "Now *that* line was in the script."

Chapter 43

FOR IMMEDIATE RELEASE

Lucentio Pictures' *A Family Alone* has begun filming in Ontario, Canada.

The sequel to the Academy Award–nominated *A Woman Alone*, the film will be codirected by Academy Award–winner Vincenzo Lucentio (best director, *A Woman Alone*) and Academy Award–nominated Bianca Baptista (costume design, *A Woman Alone*).

Starring in this action-adventure will be *three*-time Academy Award–winner Katharina Minola (best actress, *My Honey Love*; best original screenplay, *A Woman Alone*; best actress, *A Woman Alone*), her husband, Pietro Lucentio, and introducing Petra Pearl Minola-Lucentio in her first major role.

Please turn the page for an exciting sneak peek of
J.J. Murray's newest novel
YOU GIVE GOOD LOVE
coming in October 2013!

October 13

Only 72 more shopping days until Christmas . . .

1

Hope Warren was depressed because she had nothing else to be.

And her feet hurt.

Her feet were depressed, too.

"*Mes pieds font mal,*" she whispered in French, an appropriate language as any for a depressed woman to speak. Hope had owned her depression since one cold, blustery Christmas Eve when her heart broke and refused to mend itself. Depression was simply an expected guest Hope never expected to leave.

Standing in front of a Xerox Docutech High Speed Printer nine to six Monday through Friday and ten to five Saturdays didn't help Hope's *pieds*. Neither did the anti-fatigue safety mat that allegedly gave her feet some comfort. Hope looked down at the size seven indentations on the mat, indentations she had earned from working for Thrifty Digital Printing on Flatbush Avenue in Brooklyn, New York, for fifty hours a week, her feet and thoughts screaming.

For eight of the last ten years.

She focused on the digital numbers, dials, and buttons and listened to Mr. Healy, a hoody-wearing, long-haired Irishman who usually came in at 5:30 PM to get his ridiculous greeting cards printed in black and white on sixty-five pound stock coated on both sides.

Dylan Healy, the President of Odd Duck Limited Greeting Cards, usually needed his lame duck cards as soon as possible. "Have to hit the PO bright and early every Saturday morning," he said just about every time, only "early" came out as "*air*-lee," which seemed to make Dylan Healy more Irish than the Irish-American he was.

As a result, Hope rarely left at six, and Thrifty didn't pay her any overtime, an unpleasant fact that left her PO'ed at the man who had to "hit the PO bright and *air*-lee."

I get the privilege of reading Mr. Healy's cards later, Hope thought, *all one hundred of the same freaking front and inside copy. If his cards were at least mildly amusing it might not be so bad, but his ideas are brutal. One of his cards read, "You had me at . . . " on the cover and "Jell-O" on the inside with a huge mound of Jell-O in a bowl. You had me at Jell-O. What? Another card had "I will always . . . " on the cover and "shove you" inside with a feminine stick figure hand pushing a long-haired stick figure man over a ledge. Brutal! He wastes his money using heavy stock paper and coating. He could get by with lighter stock and no coating at all.*

At least he has the name of his company right. Odd Duck. Check out his beak! Are those bleach spots on his jeans? No. Those are multicolored paint splotches. Long black hair over his ears, dark brown eyes, rounded shoulders, a little over 180 centimeters, excuse me, a little over six feet tall, and definitely overly outgoing in a typical Irish-American, smiling, in-your-face way. Because we only have three major clients, however, Mr. Healy is paying a good chunk of my paycheck, so I have to tolerate him, his cards, and his accent.

"And how much does it cost to fold them again?" Mr. Healy asked.

The same cost per card as it was yesterday and the day before that and the day before that, Hope thought. *The man is only here to flirt with Kiki Clarke, who I have secretly nicknamed "Rafiki." I like Jamaicans and all "Island" people, but she is too Jamaican, if that's possible. She's too colorful! All the time! She sighs audibly as if her job is so freaking hard. All she has to do is stand there, greet customers, and smile. Instead she giggles, looks cute in her multicolored scarves, tops, and* banduu *that hold back a mountain of braided hair, and struts around in her tight jeans, singing and dancing to music only she can hear, and ringing up sales while bobbing her head back and forth like an old school Rastafarian. She jiggles through her shifts with too many teeth, too wide eyes, too long dangling earrings, and too many jingling bangles, baubles, and bracelets. The* vooman *may have more curves than a mountain road, but a speck of dust may be smarter than she is. Kiki hasn't been here long, so maybe there's more to her than meets the eye—but all she* does *is meet the eye!*

Every time I look up from this machine, it seems there's an entirely new staff here, and once again, my latest manager, Justin Tuggle, has left early to pick up "an important order" that I'll never run through a machine. Justin is almost a circle sprouting stick legs in his purple belly shirt, unkempt dusty brown hair flying over bushy blond eyebrows, a boy's face quivering on a man's middle-aged, round body, a thin voice quavering over lips lost in the flab somewhere under his nose.

Hope looked down through her thick glasses at her old Kenetrek hiking boots. *These boots have outlasted six managers.*

Bad managers.

Good boots.

Hope tuned out Mr. Healy and worked herself into a deeper, darker level of depression. She had every right to be depressed, and not only because of her stationary,

monotonous, mind-numbing job as background dancer
for a singing Jamaican *ragga*.

American television, movies, magazines, her old-
fashioned Bahamian parents, her Trini grandparents,
and her older sister, Faith, had told Hope that she
would never be beautiful. Long, brown, Medusa-like
dreadlocks framed a dark black face highlighted by a
small, flat nose, somewhat smooth skin, severe cheek-
bones that held up her glasses, dark brown eyes a little
too wide-set and huge behind those glasses, plump
brown lips pinched perpetually into a straight line, and
a long tight jaw and chin. The perfect teeth behind her
lips rarely emerged unless she was eating, and she worried that years of grinding her back teeth at Thrifty
would cause permanent damage to her jawbone. She
considered herself linear instead of flat as a board,
though her sister once told her, "Hope, you are so flat a
man will get splinters giving you a hug." Aside from a
nice set of abs, a flat stomach, and long legs, Hope Warren had none of the curves she was supposed to have as
an African-Bahamian-Canadian woman transplanted to
Brooklyn, and she wore a plain blue work smock over
baggy jeans to hide her flatness and her hardness, her
heavy locks bunched with a simple white hemp string.

I will never be an American booty queen, Hope thought.
*My derrière is not completely flat. It has some roundness, and
I am not nor will ever be a Rastafarian.*

Hope's faculty advisor at the University of Alberta in
Edmonton had told her she would never be hired anywhere in the world with only a BFA (Bachelor of Fine
Arts) and a minor in French. "Get your master's in art
and design, learn to speak French fluently, and doors
will open anywhere you go in the art world."

So, she did.

No doors opened in Edmonton, Calgary, or Vancouver. Toronto and Montreal were wasted trips.

Against her parents' wishes, themselves emigrants from the Bahamas whose parents emigrated to the Bahamas from Trinidad, Hope left Canada, escaping to New York, the supposed arts capital of the States, and she still couldn't find work in her field no matter how much French she spewed. She didn't want to be the assistant to the assistant curator at a minor museum, and she was too truthful to work for very long in any of the hundreds of galleries in and around New York City. "Those paintings and sculptures are brutal" or "*Ces peintures et sculptures sont brutaux,*" she would have to say eventually, and she would be out of a job. All she did artistically now was doodle on the backs of rejected and wrinkled copies and occasionally try to make sense of the modern art at the Brooklyn Museum.

Most of the art there looked *brutaux* to her, too.

Her Brooklyn-born almost fiancé, Odell Wilson, had told her eight years ago that she would never marry, and so far he had been right. "Who would marry your plain, hard, underemployed ass anyway?" he had said in parting. "You only needed me for a green card anyway."

Odell wanted me for more than my ability to speak French, didn't he? Hope thought. *And I only wanted Odell because . . . Hmm. It wasn't the sex. It wasn't that good. I had much more fun after he left.*

When Odell had said goodbye that fateful Christmas Eve, Hope hadn't reminded him that he had once hinted at getting married and having children, that he had craved her "long, hard, muscular body," and that he loved the feel of her "solid muscles and sharp bones." She didn't remind him that he thought she was an exotic "foreigner" since she was from the rolling prairies of Canada by way of the Bahamas and Trinidad and spoke sexy French.

Instead of running back to Alberta's turquoise lakes and prairies blazing with yellows and purples, I went through the five-year hassle of becoming a naturalized U.S. citizen. Instead of returning to a province that has half the population and over five hundred times the area of New York City, I became a citizen of Brooklyn. Instead of dodging bison, moose, bull elk, mule deer, and bighorn sheep, I dodge pedestrians, taxis, motorcycles, street vendors, and buses. Now that I'm only a plain, ordinary black American woman, no man will look twice at me, even if I drop in a French phrase every now and then, tell him that I'm originally a West Indian Island girl, and shake my dreadlocks at him. A real man, American or otherwise, should know what to do with all this hair.

Hope sighed and looked up, her bunched locks swaying across her back. *Kiki gives Mr. Healy the same information every day. Is Mr. Healy brain dead or what? Kiki and Mr. Healy would make the perfect couple. They could even make a tape of their daily conversations and play the tapes instead of talking to each other for the rest of their lives. Just press play.*

"As you know, Mr. Healy," Kiki was saying, "it takes time to fold your cards using our Baum—"

"Your what?" Mr. Healy interrupted with a smile. "Your *bomb?*"

Get me out of here! Hope moaned in her mind. *This conversation never changes! Four straight weeks of "Your bomb?" I'm about to go inhale some toner! I may paper-cut myself to death! If this machine had moving parts I could easily access, I'd stick in a dreadlock and let the machine suck me through!*

"Our Baum Eighteen Twenty-Two, Mr. Healy," Kiki said. "It is a right angle folder, and we guarantee—"

"Does it also do left angles?" Mr. Healy interrupted.

I'm sure Mr. Healy has scribbled this idea down for his next brutal card, Hope thought. *He'll probably misspell it on pur-*

pose in an attempt to provide depth to his greetings. On the cover it will say, "I'm looking for the right angel," and inside it will say, "But I'll settle for the left." Or "the leftover angel." Or "the fallen angel." Something brutally obvious like that. Some irony is just too foolish to point out, you know.

Though Hope rarely ended every other sentence with "Eh?" like a normal Canadian, she substituted "you know" to make her feel more like an American.

Hope ground her teeth, reached into her pocket, and felt a thin five-dollar bill and some change, and she became even more depressed.

Hope's checkbook and bank account told her she would never own a car, a big home, a designer wardrobe, or even a kitchen appliance from this millennium. Her retirement account, however, was off-limits, no matter how bad life got. One day Hope planned to retire to her own beach house somewhere, and so far, she had pinched and saved $48,000.

In another, oh, thirty years, I'll be able to afford the down payment for a tiny beach house looking out on the ocean somewhere. I'll be sixty, and I probably won't be able to walk over or even see the dunes or the shoreline clearly, but I'll finally have that blessed piece of peace and quiet.

Hope's smoking electric stove told her she'd never be able to cook as well as her sister did. Her sister Faith was an only child until Hope came along, and Faith played that role to the vicious hilt, even if her soufflés sometimes resembled diarrhea.

"You will never take my place as the queen of *this* family, Hope," Faith had told her. "I *own* Mudda and Fadda. They *never* wanted you. You only got the leftover *specks* of their DNA. You are a loose collection of ugly. You will *always* be the switched-at-birth mistake child."

Hope wouldn't have been surprised to find out that she had been switched at birth. Faith had curves in all the right places, curves that had the Canadian boys and now her husband, Winston Holt the "guru of natural gas" at TransCanada Corporation, eating out of her glands. Faith and "Winny" lived in a penthouse in the prestigious Carlisle condominium tower in downtown Edmonton, spent a mint on *Carrara* marble floors and washroom tile, spent a bank vault on Tuscan and French window dressings, and posed for pictures wherever they went.

Posers, Hope thought. *That's all they are. At least they don't have to worry how they'll pay their rent this month or any month of any year for that matter.*

She checked the clock. *Another hour of this monotony, and I'm still alive. Why? I'd kill for a good American drive-by right now.* She closed her eyes. *No one does drive-bys on copy shops, not even in the movies. No one even tries to rob this place.*

Hope opened her eyes and squinted at Mr. Healy flirting with Kiki. *She is gay, Mr. Healy. Can't you tell? Didn't her "another friend of ELLEN'S" button give you a clue? Can't you see the "I was gay before it got trendy" bumper sticker on her rainbow-colored backpack? Don't waste your breath. You should see Kiki's Hungarian lumberjack girlfriend, Angie, who could probably cut down a spruce tree one-handed with a nail file.*

"So I can pick these up tomorrow?" Mr. Healy asked.

Kiki shot a glance at Hope. "I am sure our production staff will once again make your order their top priority, Mr. Healy."

I am *the production staff,* Hope thought. *You shouldn't try to glorify me, you know. I doubt you even know that I have an MFA. Call me the copy girl. I know you're thinking it. You're the funny cashier girl, Mr. Yarmouth is the invisible owner, Justin is the non-managing manager, and I'm the hardworking copy girl. Know your place in the Thrifty Digital Printing pecking order.*

"Hope, do you have time to run these tonight?" Kiki asked.

Hope nodded. *Sure. I have plenty of time. I have no life, no boyfriend, no lumberjack girlfriend, and no hope, apparently, of a drive-by shooting at this copy shop this evening. I already have to lock up and turn out the lights again. What's an extra half hour of unpaid monotony anyway?*

"Great," Mr. Healy said, smiling at Hope. "Half up front, right?"

"Right, Mr. Healy," Kiki said, taking his money.

He usually pays in cash, Hope thought. *Whom is he trying to impress on Flatbush Avenue? He probably can't afford a bank account, and from the looks of his greeting cards, maybe he isn't smart enough to fill out the bank account application.*

"Um, Kiki," Mr. Healy said, "you wouldn't want to maybe get something to eat when you get off, would you? I've always wanted to go to The Islands over on Washington Avenue, and—"

"I have a date," Kiki interrupted.

With an eight-foot-tall Hungarian woman named Angyalka, which means, ironically, "little angel," Hope thought. *Where's the symmetry in that? Five-foot nothing Jamaican Kiki and Angie, who Kiki calls "On-Gee," the Sasquatch goulash woman. Ellen's friends are getting taller and wider. At least Kiki and "On-Gee" have something, though I'm not sure what, especially since Kiki never says, "I have a girlfriend" to stop Mr. Healy's advances.*

I used to be someone's girlfriend, Hope thought. *I had short hair and an apetitie then. Why did I ever put up with Odell saying I was the whitest black woman on earth? I'm not. Just because I don't use American slang and I carry myself with dignity at all times does not make me white. My Trinidadian-Bahamian-Canadian family raised me this way.* Hope sighed again. *I shouldn't miss him still, but I do. I wasn't in* love with him, and he broke my heart. Maybe I miss the idea of having a boyfriend.

"Oh," Mr. Healy was saying. "Well, um, Kiki, anytime you're free, we can . . . um, go somewhere to eat, okay?"

You can't, Hope thought. *You're not tall enough or feminine enough, and you don't have the right plumbing. I shouldn't be thinking about plumbing. My plumbing hasn't been flowing since the Winter Olympics. It was during the luge.* Hope rolled her eyes. *Odell lasted about as long as that event, too. They need to make that luge track longer.*

Kiki handed Mr. Healy his change. "Have a nice evening, Mr. Healy."

As Mr. Healy strode out to Flatbush Avenue, a blast of cold October wind fluttered paper all around Hope as she drifted away from her machine and snatched up Mr. Healy's latest hand-drawn card. The outside of the card read: "The best laid plans of mice and men . . . " Hope paused, took a breath, held it, and opened the card to read: "aren't really all that different, are they?" She almost smiled at a simple drawing of a stick figure man with long hair and a somewhat rodent-shaped mouse sharing a slice of cheese pizza.

Better, Hope thought. *The drawings are still brutal, but . . . better. That Microsoft Paint program sure makes people think they have talent. I'll bet Mr. Healy got the inspiration for this card by looking at his computer mouse. I know I can doodle better than that with my eyes closed, and all I really have to do is take off my glasses.*

The clock ticked past six.

Hope ran Mr. Healy's card through the Docutech then shot the copies through the Baum. She looked at the clock.

6:38 PM.

"*Permettez-nous de faire la promenade à* Brooklyn," she whispered, turning out the lights and locking the door behind her. "Let's go for a walk in Brooklyn."